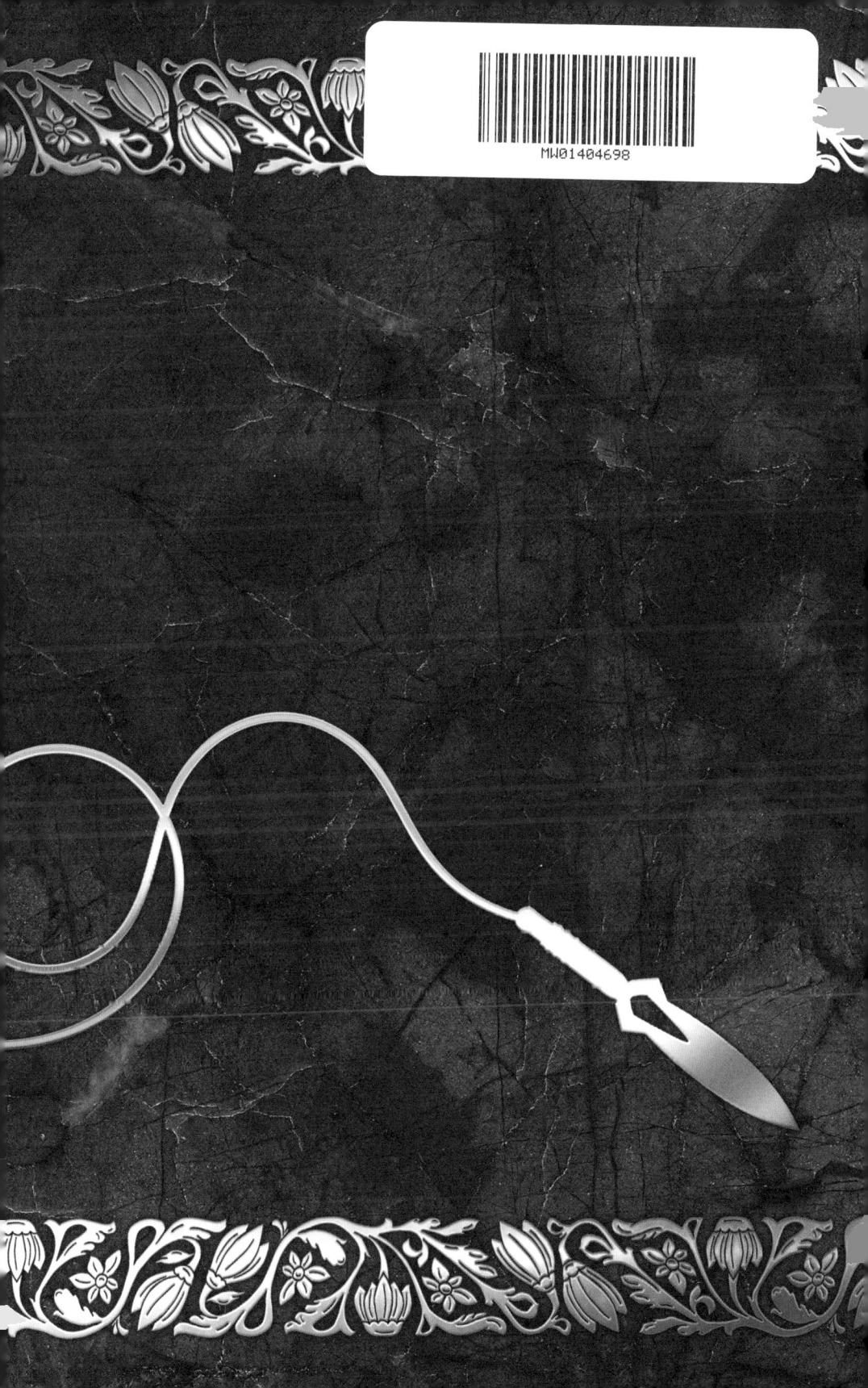

WHAT FURY BRINGS

— PRAISE FOR TRICIA LEVENSELLER —

THE DARKNESS WITHIN US
A #1 *New York Times* and *USA Today* bestseller

"A delicious fantasy full of tension, treachery, and highly addictive romance."

—Stephanie Garber, #1 *New York Times* bestselling author of *Caraval*

"*The Darkness Within Us* features a clever and deadly heroine who is just as much a beauty as a beast. Fans of Alessandra are sure to fall just as hard for Chrysantha."

—Kathryn Purdie, #1 *New York Times* bestselling author of *Bone Crier's Moon* and *The Forest Grimm*

"Chrysantha's and Eryx's wickedly charming personalities clash in the most pleasing and seductive ways . . . Banter and sexual tension abound in this enjoyable enemies-to-lovers fantasy."

—*Kirkus Reviews*

THE SHADOWS BETWEEN US
A *New York Times* and *USA Today* bestseller

"Dark, mesmerizing, and completely addictive. With a gripping mystery and layered characters, it's a glittering tale of love and the pursuit of power."

—Kerri Maniscalco, #1 *New York Times* and *USA Today* bestselling author of *Stalking Jack the Ripper*

"A decadent and wickedly addictive fantasy, full of schemes and court intrigue, and delightful descriptions of food, which I am always a fan of."

—Kendare Blake, #1 *New York Times* bestselling author of the Three Dark Crowns series

"A viciously satisfying romance featuring two well-matched opponents."

—*Booklist*

WHAT FURY BRINGS

TRICIA LEVENSELLER

FEIWEL
NEW YORK

A FEIWEL BOOK
An imprint of Macmillan Publishing Group, LLC
120 Broadway, New York, NY 10271 • us.macmillan.com

Text copyright © 2025 by Tricia Levenseller. Map artwork © Sveta Dorosheva. All rights reserved.

Our books may be purchased in bulk for promotional, educational, or business use. Please contact your local bookseller or the Macmillan Corporate and Premium Sales Department at (800) 221-7945 ext. 5442 or by email at MacmillanSpecialMarkets@macmillan.com.

Library of Congress Control Number: 2024948760

First edition, 2025
Book design by Meg Sayre
FEIWEL logo designed by Rich Deas
Printed in China

ISBN 978-1-250-37937-5 (trade hardcover)
10　9　8　7　6　5　4　3　2　1

ISBN 978-1-250-42472-3 (special edition hardcover)
10　9　8　7　6　5　4　3　2　1

FOR ROSY,

BECAUSE YOU'RE THE ONLY ONE I KNOW FOR CERTAIN
WHO WON'T BE OFFENDED BY THIS BOOK.
IT'S PAYING FOR YOUR KIBBLE.

— AUTHOR'S NOTE —

Thank you so much for picking up my first romantasy for adults! However, if you're under the age of eighteen or my father, then this story is not for you. Please come back later! Unless you're my father, in which case, this book is still not for you.

What Fury Brings contains scenes of graphic sexual content, graphic language, and graphic violence. If you're wondering what graphic violence means, let me share that there is a penis guillotine in the novel that is used on rapists.

The society I've created is a reflection of our own but reversed. What this means is that all the atrocities committed against women over the course of history have actually been committed against men. Men cannot hold property. Any money they receive belongs to their wives. Men can be married off as soon as they're old enough to perform. Men are the weaker sex. Men should be seen and not heard. Men should smile and flex whenever a woman looks at them. Only men can be punished for infidelity.

Please note that this is not what I think the world would look like if women were in charge. Far from it. Rather, this book is flipping the tables to show a new lens through which to view our own history.

This book is called *What Fury Brings*, and it is all about my fury. Every time a man cut me off when I was speaking on a panel at a convention, every time I found out a male author with my same sales numbers was receiving higher advances than me, every time someone made me feel small for having a vagina instead of a penis, every time someone told me my only calling in life should be that of a wife and mother, every time anything at all sexist or misogynistic happened in our world—I worked on *this book*.

It is my fury mixed with my love of the romance genre. It is harsh and it is sexy and it has a happily ever after.

If you, like me, are angry, I think you might like this book. If you're just here for the romance, I still think you'll like this book. I'm incredibly proud of it. That said, please be aware of the following trigger warnings:

- Mentions of sexual assault, but no scenes depicting it
- Physical and emotional abuse by a parent and a spouse
- Dubious consent
- Kidnapping/bondage, sometimes sexual
- The auctioning and selling of men
- Sex workers
- Mentions of grooming and underage sexual partners
- Animal deaths, including warhorses (shown inexplicitly on page) and a dog (that died in the past and is only referenced)
- War themes and military violence
- The aforementioned penis guillotine

If you do choose to continue, then happy reading.
All my best,

— AMARRAN TERMINOLOGY —

AMISE	asexual
DIFFERRE	heterosexual
SIREM	lesbian
SIRO	gay
TURÉ	bisexual
MADAE	trans men
MADEREO	nonbinary and gender fluid
MADORNS	trans women
LUET	wrestling technique
SEUL	title given to someone chosen to be the only partner of a royal or noble
VYRA	toxin that paralyzes and causes physical arousal

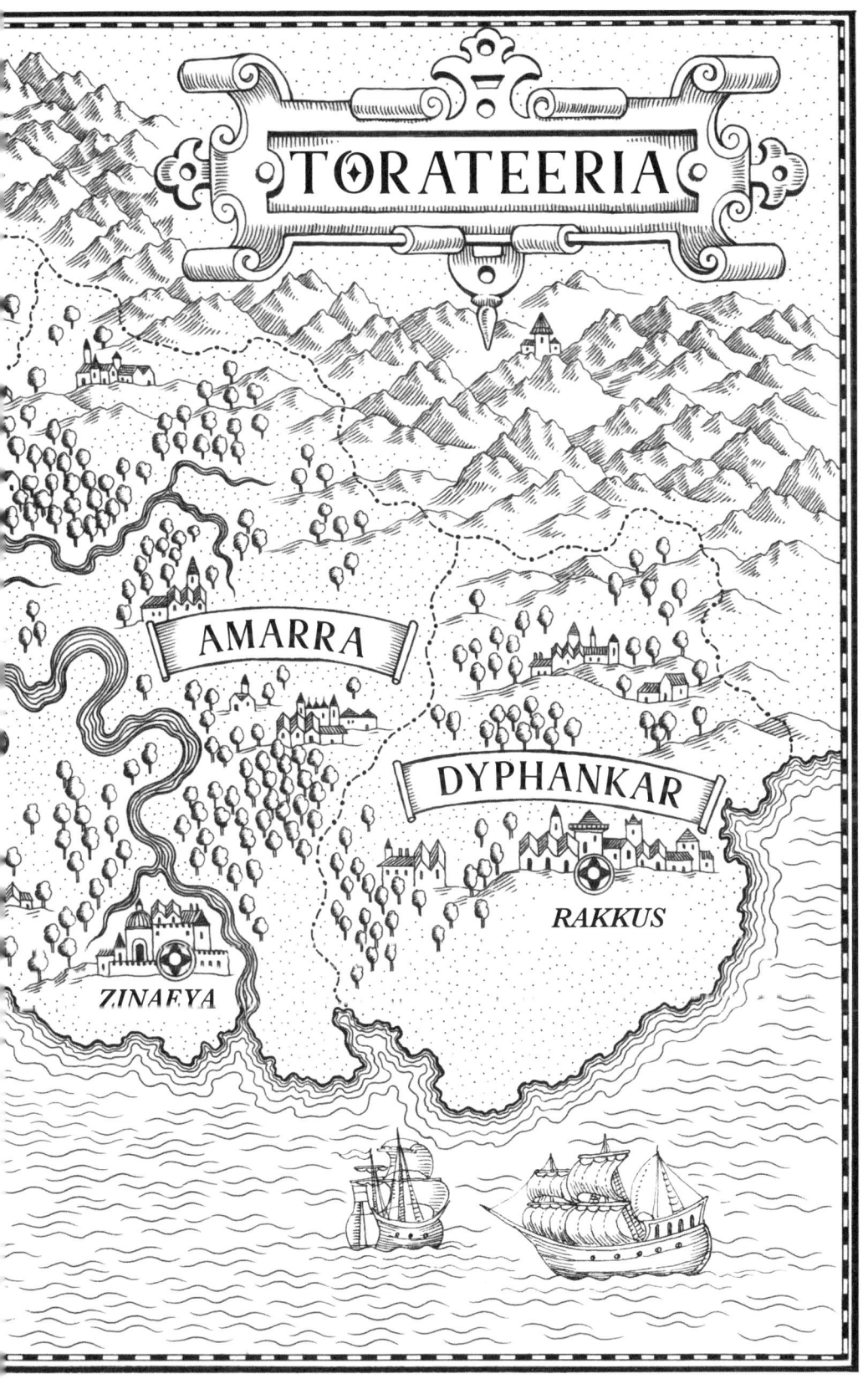

1

Given the extreme size of the king's sword, Olerra felt certain the man was compensating for something.

This was the fourth time General Olerra Corasene had met King Atalius's troops in half as many years. Always, the man would hide behind his fighters, shouting orders from the back, the coward.

Today he dared to appear on the front lines, massive sword cleaving the air like an ax. The king himself was equally massive—by far the largest man she'd ever laid eyes on—yet that didn't necessitate the size of the greatsword. Just who was he showing off for?

Furthermore, Atalius wore a tabard over his breastplate that bore a single black crown on a bloodred background: the royal crest of Brutus.

He might as well have painted a sign on himself.

I'm the king. Attack me!

It was hard for Olerra not to laugh at the thought of a king on the throne. Men were unfit to rule. They were easy to provoke, and they always thought with their cocks instead of their heads, which was why they were better suited to the bedroom.

Olerra was distracted from her assessment by three new Brutes, who all charged her at once. They tried to swipe at the legs of the horse she rode, but Olerra used her left hand and calf to direct the horse in a perfect sidestep, avoiding two of them. Simultaneously, she plunged her sword point into the third man's helmet, sliding right into the gap meant for his eyes. As she tugged her sword free, red streaked across her thigh and the white coat of the equine beneath her. The gelding was unnamed, as most warhorses were, though it helped little when they fell during the heat of battle.

Olerra was determined to ensure they both made it.

No sooner had the first soldier fallen than Olerra spun her horse around. In an incredibly fast arc that Enadra would have been proud of, Olerra brought her sword down precisely in the middle of the second Brute's helmet, cleaving both it and his skull in two. Her momentum stopped somewhere in the vicinity of the dead man's nose, and Olerra had to place her foot on his chest to wrench her sword free.

The third man fled.

Olerra returned her attention to the king—hoping he was finally in position—just in time to see him fell one of her soldiers.

Countless battles into her career, and Olerra still felt a sharp sting whenever she lost a brave fighter. She was too far to help. She had to maintain this position atop the small hill, where she could see both the front lines and the rear of the Brutish forces.

Come on. Just a few more yards. She needed the king and his troops to clear the forest.

Atalius was quick to engage another Amarran. He ducked under her strike and cut her legs out from under her, leaving her crawling in the dirt. When he faced his next opponent, he broke through her guard in two moves before driving his sword through her heart.

He never stopped. He never slowed.

Anger burned through Olerra. Atalius had to be nearing sixty years of age, yet he fought like a lion.

Everywhere else on the battlefield, men were succumbing to the superior strength of her soldiers. One woman locked swords with a Brute, only to quickly overpower him and shove his own blade into his neck. Another rode her horse alongside a Brutish rider and kicked him clean off his steed. A third Amarran picked a man off the ground and threw him into another.

Yet the king held his own. A well-timed strike from one of her soldiers broke through Atalius's defenses and imbedded into his left arm. Atalius growled, pulled the spear from his flesh, and severed the woman's head from her shoulders.

Olerra despaired at the loss of another soldier, but Atalius was finally where she wanted him, where her fighters on the front had lured him. She bent to retrieve the gonfalon from where she'd stuck it in the dirt before the start of the battle, hoisting it high and waving it back and forth. Her hidden forces in the woods joined the battle, flanking Atalius's soldiers from behind.

Now she could finally face the king.

Olerra dug her heels into her horse's sides, urging him down the hill. She struck downward against the foot soldiers who came between her and her target. Her sword sliced the gaps between helmet and breastplate, her horse jumped over fallen bodies, and the wails of the injured lowered to a dull roar as Olerra honed in on her target.

The Brutes at Atalius's back had turned to meet Olerra's reinforcements, but despite the shouts of pain and fear, the king pressed on. Rage fueled him past the point of common sense. Made him blind to the reinforcements joining the fray. Another woman fell to his blade.

"*Faster!*" Olerra urged the gelding.

"Who's next, eh?" the king shouted. He spun in a circle, having picked up a fallen spear in his free hand, keeping everyone at bay. His helmet had been knocked off in his latest scuffle. "I see your goddess doesn't have enough power to protect you all!"

Without slowing her horse, Olerra slid sideways in the saddle to scoop a rock as big as her fist from the ground.

"To me!" Atalius shouted to his retreating soldiers. "Give them no quarter. They—"

Olerra threw, hitting her mark, which was the king's rather large head. Atalius fell in a heap of bent armor and unjustified male ego.

"Let his troops scurry back to their homes," she said, addressing the soldiers nearest her. "Bring the king to my tent. I think it's time he and I had a chat."

The general's word was law, and her soldiers chased their enemy back across the border. Meanwhile, Olerra helped carry her wounded to the healers and gave a swift death to any Brutes left injured on the battlefield. She placed her dead in carts so they could be returned to their families. She surveyed the damage to the outskirts of the city, assigning soldiers and townspeople to help with cleanup and repair any damage. She paid off families who lost livestock and businesses that lost income during the hour-long battle.

She was in the running to be queen one day. Olerra would do right by her people. Make them see that *she* should be the one to sit on the throne.

Not her insufferable cousin.

When all was as it should be, Olerra returned to her tent, one last chore before her.

Atalius was strapped to a chair, bound and gagged. His wounds had been tended to, he'd been cleaned, given fresh clothing, and offered a hot meal. Not that he deserved it. Olerra, still filthy with dried blood and dirt, grabbed a chair from the war table, flipped it around, and straddled the seat with her arms resting along the back. She flicked her wrist at the king, and one of her captains stepped forward to remove Atalius's gag.

He coughed once it was gone but said nothing.

For two years they had fought over this border city. Shamire was rich in resources, with golden fields of wheat and the Fren River running through it. The neighboring kingdoms of Kalundir and Ephenna often brought their merchants here to exchange goods. It was a boon to whomever held the city.

Queen Lemya, Olerra's aunt, had won the city decades ago from the Brutes, and it was Olerra's job to maintain that control. When Vorika, the head of Olerra's spy network, had told her of Atalius's plans to attack, Olerra had rallied her forces to meet him with the might of Amarra.

The king and general were finally meeting face-to-face, yet the man had nothing to say.

Oh, she would get him to speak.

"Normally you take the coward's way, Atalius," she said, meeting his gaze head-on, "fleeing before we can be properly introduced. I didn't know you had it in you to stay and suffer the consequences of defeat. Did you grow tired of running?"

When that didn't get a rise out of him, she tried a different approach.

"My name is Olerra Corasene, queen potential of Amarra, and I have beaten you four times now in your attempts to reclaim Shamire. I think it's time you admitted you can't take it back."

Atalius clenched his teeth, trying to prevent himself from speaking.

"Nothing to say? Perhaps this topic will interest you. Your fate. What should I do with you?" She tapped her chin thoughtfully. "I could simply kill you, but I worry one of your many sons will take your place and declare a foolhardy campaign against my country to seek revenge. As much as I love our little border spats, I don't think either of us wants a full-scale war. You especially. I hear you've already got your hands full with the Ephennans on your southern border. Do you really want your forces divided to take on a second country?"

It took a moment, but the bound man finally said, "I do not wish for war between us."

At least he wasn't a complete idiot.

"I could ransom you," Olerra mused, "but we really don't need the money. Shamire provides a steady income on top of all our other assets.

Perhaps I should demand it anyway. Bankrupt your country so it'll take you longer to attack again."

Atalius didn't look away as she thought aloud about his future.

"Or perhaps a trade," she said. "One of your sons for your life."

The king glared at her with such heat she might have thought it capable of melting his bonds.

"He'd be well treated, for the most part," she continued. "A prisoner to stop a war from happening. Besides, you have plenty of sons. Isn't that the whole thing with you Brutes? Your god blessed you with virility? More children than you could possibly know what to do with?"

Rumors also suggested that the god Brutus blessed the men born in his country with large cocks, but wasn't it just like men to claim such a thing? Besides, that greatsword was evidence to the contrary.

Regardless, it was a pathetic gift in comparison to what Amarra gifted the daughters of her country: the ability to physically overpower men. It was a miracle that Atalius had lasted as long on the battlefield as he had.

"No," the king spat.

"Your god didn't bless you with too many sons?"

"You cannot have a trade," he clarified.

Did I really find his weakness so easily?

"Can't I? Are you saying you'd rather die than give me one of your sons? Are you willing to bet your kingdom's future on that? I sure hope your heir is prepared to take your place, then. I hear he's amassing quite the reputation as a general in your skirmishes with the Ephennans. What was his name? Stantos?"

The change was almost instant. One moment the king's face was pale white, the next, purple. Was it the way she'd intentionally said the crown prince's name wrong? Or was it the fact that his son was gaining more popularity than he was?

"Is that why you showed your face on the front today, waving that massive sword around?" she asked. "To remind your people that you've still got fight in you? Is your heir getting a little too popular for your liking?"

"His. Name. Is. Sanos." The words were clipped, and the prince's name came out like a curse.

His heir is definitely a sore spot, then. Good to know.

"Ahh. How is Sanos coming along? Does he have a mind for politics to match that battle prowess? Have you taught him the ways of my people so he'll be prepared to deal with me in the future?"

"You're not queen yet," Atalius spat, "and I hear your cousin has garnered more favor than you."

The words stung, as they were meant to. Olerra hated that he knew exactly where to poke to cause the most pain.

Olerra may have had the army on her side, but her cousin, Glenaerys, had the money. Glen had much of the nobility in her pocket already, and since it was a majority vote by the nobility that would grant one of them the title of crown princess (an outdated term since Amarran Queens didn't wear crowns anymore), Olerra was in a precarious position.

She needed to make a strong political move to bring more of them to her side, and Atalius was giving her an idea.

She said nothing of his jibe. "Which son can I have? Do I get to pick? Perhaps the youngest, Ikanos? He hasn't had quite as much time to be influenced by you and your heathen ways."

The king didn't say a word.

"No? Then perhaps the spare? I hear Andrastus is a very pretty man. A poet, yes? He would make a beautiful addition to my harem, don't you think?" Atalius didn't need to know that she didn't actually have a harem or any intention of starting one. "How much is your life worth to you,

Atalius? Maybe I'm not asking for enough. Perhaps I should demand two sons in exchange for you. Maybe three? Who do you—"

"Stop!"

Olerra grinned at the victory.

"Just stop," Atalius said. "You've made your point. I'm at your mercy, but do not bring my sons into this."

"And what will you give up for that, Atalius? Your pride? Would you beg? Let's hear it. Beg me not to take your sons and turn them into whores."

A vein stood out in the king's neck. He looked as though he were struggling against his bonds, but they were too tight to give him even an inch of movement. "I will see you dead for this," he said, his voice lowering to something Olerra could barely hear.

"How are you to accomplish that from your chair?"

He screamed his fury into the tent.

When he finished, Olerra said, "Before I make my decision, there is one more thing I wish to know. Why didn't any of your sons join you on the battlefield today? They can't all be fighting the Ephennans."

No answer. The mostly one-sided conversation was somehow becoming even more entertaining.

"Have you not battle-trained them all?" she prodded. "Are they cowards?"

Nothing.

"Do you know what I think, Atalius? I think that, deep down, you knew you would lose, and you didn't want them here to see your defeat."

His eyes met hers, and Olerra knew she'd struck the mark. "Oh, Atalius. At the end of the day, you're just a man. Insecure yet overconfident. Hotheaded while tied to a chair. Condescending when you've been so hopelessly beaten. A series of contradictions that will never work in your favor. You should have retreated the moment you spotted my reinforcements. Perhaps you wouldn't have taken a rock to the head. How is that pounding headache?"

She knew he wouldn't answer, so she stood when she was done. Olerra turned her back to him, which she knew was a grave insult in his country. One never turned away from a king. She smiled as she spoke low to her watching captains.

"Blindfold him. Let him think you're going to kill him, then return him to his kingdom. Leave him somewhere to be found by his sons. Let them see his defeat." After a pause, she added, "And take back everything we lent him."

"Yes, General," they said in unison.

Atalius had unintentionally given her his weakness. He cared for his sons very much, and Olerra was forming a plan that would not only strengthen her standing as queen potential with the nobles but also get back at Atalius for the battle that cost her twenty-four good soldiers.

The first step was to let him go. The fun part would come later.

"Farewell, Atalius," she called over her shoulder. "I hope to never see you again."

Then Olerra left to find a hot bath.

2

Sanos rode hard for home, eager for a respite after months away on the battlefield. The campaign was grueling work. He spent his days slaying Ephennans and his nights strategizing for more battles with more Ephennans. He caught sleep when he could, but it was becoming rarer and rarer.

Thank the gods for his upcoming birthday. It was one of the few times he was permitted to visit home, get a full night's rest, and see his family. Though his mother and sister wrote to him weekly, he was eager to see with his own two eyes that they were well.

He never knew what his father would do while he was away.

Thankfully, the king had been engaged in plans to reclaim Shamire from the Amarrans of late. Brutus needed the extra income the city would provide in their campaign against the Ephennans.

Knowing his father's temper, Sanos hoped the king had good news for him upon his arrival.

As his horse drew near the castle gates, Sanos had to weave through an unexpected crowd of soldiers and nobility. They seemed to configure around a central point, and the prince decided to see what caught everyone's interest.

"Sanos!"

The prince turned his head and found all four of his younger brothers grouped together. When he reached them, Canus, third-born, practically wrestled him off the horse, and all his brothers joined in on an enormous hug, nearly squeezing the life out of him.

"All right. All right." Sanos smacked their backs in return. "Let me go before I put you all on your asses right here in front of this crowd."

They stepped back, and he asked, "*Why* is there a crowd?"

An unnerving grin took over Canus's face. He pointed up ahead, and Sanos followed the line of his brother's finger.

He blinked twice to ensure his eyes weren't failing him.

The king was strapped to a wooden post in the middle of the road, and he was as naked as the day he was born. Ropes spread his arms and legs wide, ensuring nothing would be hidden from the crowd's eye.

Atalius appeared to be unconscious, though Sanos had to ask, "Did anyone check if he's breathing?"

"I got close," Ikanos, the youngest of the Ladicus brothers, said. "No such luck. He's alive."

"And no one has bothered to get him down?"

"Do *you* want to be the one to wake him?" Andrastus asked.

Sanos most certainly did not, but this couldn't continue. More and more courtiers were pouring out of the castle to see if the rumor was true. The crowd was growing in size, and the fallout would only get worse.

Sanos sighed. Sometimes he hated being the oldest.

He handed off his horse to the nearest guard with instructions to stable him. The soldier frowned, clearly put out to miss the excitement, but he did as he was told.

"Welcome home, Prince," he said as he left. "It's good to see you well."

At his words, more surrounding guards turned and spotted his arrival. Some of them had the decency to look guilty for making a spectacle of the king.

"You," Sanos said, firming his tone. "Go fetch a robe for the king.

You lot there, go untie him. And the rest of you, start clearing out this crowd. Now."

His orders were quick to be followed, but not before he received more greetings and well-wishes regarding his return. He was proud to be so well-liked by his fellow soldiers. He was prouder still that people listened when he spoke.

"Spoilsport," Canus said.

"You should all go," Sanos said, "before he—"

"Get me the fuck down!"

Sanos turned. The king was very much awake now. His face was turning bright purple as he discovered his state of undress and the too-slowly receding crowd.

Canus had to turn around to hide his laughter.

"Don't," Sanos cautioned. "He will beat you within an inch of your life."

"Worth it. I'm going to remember that look on his face for the rest of my life."

It was a spectacular look. The king of Brutus was a proud, ruthless man, and to see him brought so low was, in a word, *everything*.

"I could kiss whoever did this," Canus said.

"That would be the Amarrans," Sanos replied. "Father went to fight them for Shamire once again. We've been exchanging battle briefs."

"He must have been captured this time."

"Along with his clothes," Sanos couldn't help but say, and Canus lost it again.

Andrastus, Trantos, and Ikanos looked horrified at the two of them and took a step away, likely because they didn't want the king to think they were in on the joke.

When Atalius's eyes swung to them, Sanos was quick to remove all signs of mirth from his face. He was the battle-hardened firstborn son.

Stoic and lethal—his father wanted him to be just like him. But there was an unforeseen danger that came from instilling that level of brutality and ambition within the prince.

Sanos knew his father feared that he had designs on taking the throne early.

He didn't, yet there was nothing that could assuage his father's paranoia.

The king's arms were unbound now, and two men held him against the post so he didn't topple off-balance while the others were working on his legs. This kind of humiliation was worse than losing the battle against the Amarrans in the first place, Sanos knew. Whoever ordered it was calculating and conniving, and Sanos wanted to congratulate them personally for it.

Canus was right. It was worth another beating to see this.

Sanos let none of this show as his father continued to watch him. Since the Amarran general was not here, Sanos would be the one he took his rage out on. He always was.

It was going to be a very bad day.

The robe arrived at the same time the king fell from the post, collapsing in a heap of limbs, sore from being up there for however many hours. The soldier hovered near his liege, unsure what to do except hold open the robe and wait.

Atalius leaped to his feet, snatched the robe, and backhanded the soldier who'd offered it.

"You dare to look upon your king's nakedness?" he seethed.

The soldier went to his knees and said nothing.

The king strode forward, now robed, magically managing a superior gait. When he got to Sanos and Canus, he said, "Come," to his oldest son.

Canus gave him a look of sympathy as Sanos followed a step behind the only man in the country who outranked him. The only man who could raise a hand to him. The only man who could best him with the sword. The only man whose opinion mattered. The one who held his future entirely in his hands.

"Report," the king said as they walked.

"I have taken the cities of Eritus and Blathe," Sanos said. "We're pushing more into Ephenna and claiming its territory as our own. The campaign is going very well. The men are in good spirits and health." *Though more food rations would be welcome.*

Sanos did not need to ask how the fight against the Amarrans went.

They arrived at the king's chambers, and Sanos was made to wait as his father bathed and dressed. After two weeks on the road, Sanos wished he could bathe himself, but he knew better than to leave when his father had ordered him to stay.

The prince sent for food, and the king downed sausages and eggs as he eyed his son. Sanos remained stoic, waiting for the king to bring up what he really wanted to talk about.

The silence was agonizing. He might prefer shouting. At least then he would have some idea of what was on the king's mind.

"I met the Amarran general," his father finally said. "She's a dishonorable wretch. Didn't face me sword-to-sword. No, she threw a rock at my head while I took on a dozen of her best soldiers."

That was indeed unsporting, but effective, if it resulted in his father's capture. Of course, he couldn't blame anyone for not wanting to cross blades with his father. Atalius was a beast of a man, bigger than any other Sanos had met. Only Canus grew close in size, but none were the king's equal with the sword.

A rock to the head was perhaps the only way to best him.

"Despicable. Unsporting." Sanos kept his response brief.

"She also had some interesting things to say about you. Rumors of you growing more popular than I. Rumors that there are those who wish to see you on the throne before your time."

Shit.

This was what the king was building toward. More accusations of treason.

"Do I need to remind you what will happen should I meet an early demise?" the king asked.

"No, Your Majesty."

"Your mother and sister have no value to me. I already have five sons and no use for a daughter. Should *anything* at all happen to me, I have assassins in place to deal with them. It will not be quick. You will be made to wait years before finding their broken bodies."

Sanos swallowed but kept the fury from his face. He forced himself not to look away.

Gods, but he hated his father.

If Sanos wanted the throne early, it wasn't because of any ambitions he had but because he wanted to rid the world of his father's evil. He wanted his family safe.

Sanos had to learn the hard way that his father was a master at finding weaknesses and causing the most pain possible. When he was ten, his mother declared that they didn't spend nearly enough time together and took the prince on an outing into the city, just the two of them and a handful of guards. They sampled candies and purchased toys. At the end of the day, Sanos was allowed to select a pup from a local breeder.

But when he returned home, the king was furious. He said the queen had no right to take Sanos away from his tutors. To go into town without his say-so. The king wrested the pup from Sanos's fingers and snapped her neck before he could even begin to protest.

When he was fourteen, Sanos had a best friend: Vanus, the son of a count. The boys practiced the sword together in their free time. They shared their hopes and dreams. Sanos wanted out of the city. He wished to see the world. Vanus didn't want to be a count. He wanted to be a singer. Sanos encouraged Vanus to follow his dreams, and Vanus said that Sanos would make a better king than Atalius. He should take the throne early and see the world.

To this day, Sanos still had no idea how Atalius found out about the treasonous words, said mostly in jest.

Vanus lost his head, and Atalius had made Sanos swing the ax, else the king would put the prince's little sister, Emorra, on the chopping block.

Sanos learned that no one could show him any sort of favor or love. The king wanted him isolated so he had few allies should he make designs on the throne. Atalius wanted his son to rely on him and no one else. It was Sanos's good behavior alone that kept his family alive and intact.

The ax was always there in his mind's eye, waiting to drop.

So the prince fought the king's battles and did his utmost not to garner any special favor at all.

And now some Amarran general was spewing idiotic things into the king's ear. Things that could result in unspeakable horrors happening to his family.

He wanted to wring her neck almost as much as he wished he could kill his father.

Sanos said, "People will amuse themselves with rumors, but that doesn't make them true. I am devoted to serving the crown of Brutus. I am devoted to you, Father. Any victories I achieve are only because of your training. I win battles for your glory."

Talking to his father was like balancing on a rope. One wrong word and he'd suffer a one-hundred-foot drop.

The king washed down his meal with a heavy drink of wine. "You mocked me today. With your brother."

"No, Your Majesty."

"And what else did Canus find so amusing, then?"

"I told him a joke."

"A joke, is it? Let's hear it. Make me laugh."

Sanos's mind went completely blank. His brothers had told him all kinds of lewd jokes over the years, but when it counted most, when the skin of his body depended on it, he couldn't recall a single one.

"I don't remember it," he said at last.

"How unfortunate."

Sanos waited on his father as he strode through the castle. He listened in on a meeting with the advisers, as his father updated them on the situation with the Amarrans. He waited while his father visited his mother, doing gods knew what while he stood outside her chambers. He followed as his father selected a new warhorse for himself, since he'd lost his last one in the battle. The day was agonizing as Sanos was made to wait for his punishment, following and serving his king.

When Canus was sent for, Sanos knew it was time, and he could finally relax. He didn't have to guess when the ax would drop. It was here.

They were led to a room deep under the palace. Near the dungeons. The walls were padded to muffle the screams of their enemies. And of the princes.

"I know you both think I'm hard on you," Atalius said as he drew off his outer garment, leaving him in shirtsleeves and leggings and boots. "But to be a Brute is to be a hardened warrior, impervious to pain. Able to withstand torture without giving up a single scrap of information. It's been far too long since you've both undergone a training session. Today is a good day for it."

It was amazing how often these sessions corresponded with the king's foul moods.

Sanos tried to find something pleasant to think about instead of the pain that awaited him. His birthday was in two weeks. He looked forward to going out with his brothers. They always visited a brothel at the end of the night, and Sanos thought of the promise of pleasure rather than pain as the king ordered them both to strip and face the wall.

Canus was angry. His face showed everything, the loathing and fury. Sanos maintained an air of indifference.

"I take no pleasure in this," the king continued.

A lie.

"My father was also hard on me. Someday, you will look back and realize that I only wanted to make you stronger. When you are indifferent to pain, you will become a true Brute. You will thank me for this."

"Did you thank your father?" Canus asked brazenly.

Sanos wished he'd shut up.

"I did. On his deathbed."

The cane was a long stick, smooth from time and use. It was important not to break their skin. To make wounds they would heal from without scarring. They couldn't have lashes on their backs like servants. Sanos didn't know why. Perhaps it was his father's ego. He wanted perfect sons, beaten into submission to their king, yet rulers and conquerors to the rest of the world.

They weren't restrained. They didn't need to be. If they laid a hand on their father, it was treason. So they could do nothing but withstand the torture.

Slap.

Canus was struck first, and Sanos flinched. It was worse when it wasn't his turn. He anticipated pain but didn't receive it. Felt the tiniest bit of relief. Then the cane would land on him, and the pain would be worse when it followed that burst of relief. His father alternated. Sometimes hitting Canus three times in a row before switching back to Sanos. He didn't know when it would land. He didn't know when it would end. He didn't know anything.

Slap.

Slap.

Slap.

Time could only be measured by counting the strikes. Twenty-five. Fifty. Seventy-five.

On and on it went. The king even forgot the farce of "withstanding torture." Atalius didn't bother to ask them a single question. He didn't promise the pain would stop if they gave up their country's secrets. Today, the king was too far gone.

When Atalius finally decided he was done, he told them to get dressed.

"It's time for sword training."

They were both so sore they could barely stand. But the way of the Brute was to fight even when wounded. There was no choice but to follow the king to the training yard.

Sanos weathered the beating better than his brother. Perhaps because he was more used to it. As crown prince, he was trained the hardest, preparing to be king one day.

They practiced with real swords, the king taking on both him and Canus at the same time. On a good day, they could probably beat him together, but the king had set them up for failure by leaving them hardly able to move.

Yet something came over Canus once a sword was placed into his hand. He charged their father with all the rage of a boy who'd been beaten into a man far too soon. At almost twenty-three, Canus wasn't quite at his physical peak. He hadn't been sent to fight in any battles, likely because the king didn't want them banding together against him. Canus had no real battle experience, but he had all the best tutors, just like Sanos.

The move was precise, cutting straight for their father's head.

Atalius ducked and swiped, cutting a hole in Canus's shirt. Sanos charged from behind, rallying his strength. His father took his legs out from under him, too fast for Sanos to even track it in his delirium of pain.

He fell to the ground on his already-blistered back.

And screamed.

"Get up," the king demanded.

They both charged again and lost.

"Get up," the king said a second time.

It continued until there was nothing but pain and his father's voice.

Sanos didn't know how long he'd been unconscious when he woke in his rooms to a cold pinch.

"Shh," his mother said. She put another salve-soaked cloth on his aching back, covering every injury one at a time. Ferida was beautiful, with white-gold hair and smooth features that made her look doll-like. She was small. So small compared to all her grown sons. Too small to have been paired with the likes of his father.

When the queen was done, she stood, taking the bowl away to the adjoining bathing chamber. She walked a little funny.

"He hurt you," Sanos said.

"I'm fine," she said.

"Canus—"

"Emorra is with him."

"Good," Sanos managed.

He seemed to sink farther into the bedding beneath him.

"Your reign can't come soon enough," she said.

"He's too fit and healthy. It'll be years and years yet."

"He's too battle hungry. One of these days, his pride will get him. And if it doesn't, perhaps we should help it along."

The words sang to his soul, but Sanos didn't have the heart to tell his mother that they could never help it along. He didn't want her to worry over the threat his father had made to them. Or worse, hear her say she wasn't afraid of death if it meant it would save her sons and country from Atalius.

So instead, Sanos said, "One day," to give her hope.

"One day," she agreed.

3

Olerra's first order of business upon returning to Zinaeya, capital city of Amarra, was reporting to her aunt. She marched through the palace with a small retinue of soldiers, their steps loud on the red obsidian tiles. Olerra was still unused to the constant company, but precautions needed to be taken because her cousin kept trying to have her killed.

They were intercepted on the way, but not by anyone dangerous.

"Olerra!"

"Ydra!"

Her sister-chosen grabbed her by the shoulder and put her forehead to hers. "Thank the goddess you're unharmed. Why wasn't I sent for upon your return? Are you headed to a battle brief?"

The two separated, and Olerra explained, "I have to put something in motion quickly. The queen is expecting me."

"Anything I should know about?" As Olerra's second-in-command, Ydra was usually at all the important meetings. This was something a little different, though.

Olerra leaned forward so as not to be overheard. "I'm going to ask for permission to kidnap a Brutish prince for my own."

Ydra covered her mouth with her hands in delight. She had to work very hard to keep her voice low amid the excitement.

"Now? After all this time?"

"It's mostly political. I need to overshadow Glen."

Ydra nodded thoughtfully. "Yes, go see the queen, and I will start making preparations. Oh, we'll need to go to the Pleasure Market! And then the Hunters Market. Can't wait!"

Her friend squeezed her hand before taking off down the corridor.

Olerra couldn't help but smile as she continued walking. She, too, was excited by the prospect of having a man in her life, but she knew it would also be a lot of work. Especially if that man was a Brute.

When she reached her aunt's chambers, the guards on either side of the room nodded to her in greeting before opening the doors wide. Each woman was clad in steel armor that shone with just the slightest tint of scarlet. Their spearpoints were made of red obsidian, a unique variety found only in their country. Spikes protruded from their helmets, positioned above their foreheads. The queen's guard had a fondness for bashing in the skulls of their enemies.

"Wait here," Olerra said to her guard.

The queen stood near the fireplace, sipping a glass of wine, her wife, Toria, at her side with her arm slung around her back.

"How did we fare?" the queen asked. Lemya was a tall woman, broad of shoulders, with black hair cropped short to her scalp. She wore no crown, as Amarran queens did not need one to know their worth. She wore a pleated dress that came down to mid-thigh and belted at the waist. Olerra wore a similar outfit. Warrior women liked their ease of movement, and the hot climate in Amarra necessitated shorter garments.

"Very well, Auntie. We lost far less than the enemy, who turned tail and ran. Atalius was captured and questioned, then returned to his home."

"Alive?" Lemya clarified.

"Yes, I thought it best not to start a war with his death."

Lemya smiled and turned to her wife. "See? She already has the cunning of a queen. Tell me, Olerra, that you at least took a finger or something to shame him?"

"Oh, I took something." Olerra deposited the clothing she was carrying onto the floor, including the tabard that bore the king's crest.

Her aunties looked at the clothing before bursting into laughter.

"Where did you leave him?" Toria asked as she wiped tears from her eyes.

"Right outside the castle gates."

The queen composed herself. "This is why you're my favorite niece."

Olerra beamed. "I have more ideas for shaming him. Could we speak in private for a moment?"

Lemya nodded, turning to her wife. "Why don't you relax in the bath and wait for me?"

Toria kissed her cheek before retreating toward the adjacent bathing chamber, not the least bit put out to be excluded from the conversation. She knew it must be something political, rather than personal, to be asked to leave.

In fact, it was both.

As soon as the door closed, Olerra proclaimed, "I need a husband."

Lemya blinked once before processing the words. "*Arguable*, but go on."

"I've come to learn that Atalius cares for his sons more than anything, save his pride. I've decided to kidnap one and claim him as mine. Doing so will punish the king of Brutus further while also strengthening my claim to the throne of Amarra."

"I'm impressed." Lemya's tone didn't quite match her words.

"You have reservations?"

"Concerns."

"Glenaerys has secured much of the nobility in her favor," Olerra explained. "I must take the next step in proving myself the perfect candidate by kidnapping and marrying a man."

In Amarra, the art of husband hunting was as old as the Goddess's Gift. It wasn't mandatory, but many families prided themselves on keeping their bloodlines noble. That was nearly impossible to do without looking outside of Amarra, for most of the noblemen in the country were dead.

Olerra thought it was ridiculous that so many cared, considering that women with harems couldn't prove that their children were sired by their husband. It didn't matter, though. Any child born to a noblewoman was raised by her husband and, therefore, noble.

Olerra couldn't care less about the purity of her future daughters' blood. No, kidnapping a husband was a necessity for an entirely different reason.

"I'd hate to see you wedded before you're ready," the queen said. "Your mother was dear to me, Goddess bless her soul. I don't know that she would have wanted this for you."

"The throne or marriage?" Olerra asked.

"To marry at so young an age. You're only twenty-one. What if your tastes should change in the next ten years?"

It was certainly a risk, but once Olerra had the throne, she could ship her husband away to the farthest reaches of the world if she wanted to—which was indeed her plan. She couldn't risk him learning her secret.

"Husbands come and go, but Amarra is eternal," Olerra said.

The queen nodded, accepting this answer, as Olerra knew she would. "I wish your mother were still with us. Gods, but I miss her."

"I do, too."

Sometimes when she closed her eyes, Olerra could hear her laugh or smell a hint of her perfume. But her face was gone. She could not remember its shape or features, having only been four years old when she was orphaned.

Ivanisa was killed by Olerra's sire. Her mother had kept him for five years before he managed to get the better of her. It was not a quick or painless death.

And it was utterly unexpected.

Because of the magic granted to them by the goddess Amarra, Amarran women could physically overpower any man they came across. For a man to kill a woman, he'd have to have surprise or skill on his side. Olerra's sire, the third son of some earl from Dyphankar, should have had neither.

No one had witnessed the murder. Her sire had been found trying to flee the country. He was killed while the guards had attempted to apprehend him.

To die by one's husband was rare, but it happened. Just never before to the royal family.

That's why Olerra had more to prove than most. Because she was her mother's daughter, and her mother had died to a man. She had to show the women of her kingdom she wouldn't be beaten so easily. That they could trust the Corasene line.

And she had to prove it by breaking a man of her own.

Olerra would take the Amarran throne by any means necessary. The queen alone could not bequeath her kingdom. The love of the people went a long way, but it was the loyalty of the nobility that Olerra truly had to secure—a tricky feat when her cousin spent more time with them, overseeing both political maneuverings and even dipping into the spy network. Not only could Glenaerys foster the proper relationships to win over the nobility, she likely had the means to bribe them into doing her will, if needed.

A general's salary paid well, but it was nothing compared to the wealth of Glen's mother. That's why Olerra's grandmother had wed her son to her.

There was no pride in inheriting wealth. It was no more than an accident of birth. Olerra earned her station by being the best: the best fighter, the best battle strategist, the best teacher. She had a deep respect and love for her troops. Owning the trust of Amarra's fighting force went a long way. That would sway many of the nobility to vote in her favor.

Yet managing a husband would sway those who were hesitant about Olerra because of what had happened to her mother.

"You have declared yourself differre. Does this still stand true?" the queen asked.

Olerra blinked at the change in topic. She wished she could claim to be sirem and like women as her aunt did. Olerra had tried to be physical with women before, but there was no denying that her attractions lay elsewhere.

With men.

"It does."

"Most differres of your age and standing already have a kept man or have started their harems—"

At the look Olerra gave her, Lemya added, "Not that there's anything wrong with not wanting to keep a man." She grimaced at the thought. "The people of Amarra are welcome to whatever their tastes may be. As far as I've seen, you've never courted a man or even paid particular attention to one. Are you sure you're not amise?"

Olerra certainly was not indifferent to nor repulsed by sex. She'd been repressing her sexual drive all her life—but she couldn't very well admit to her aunt her greatest shame.

"I am not amise, Auntie. I have only been biding my time for personal reasons. Now, may I have your blessing in this task?"

Lemya raised a brow at her tone but let it slide. "All right. I only wanted to be sure this is truly what you want. Which son of Atalius will you take?"

"Prince Andrastus," Olerra answered.

"The king has five sons. Why Andrastus?"

There were many reasons why Andrastus. "He's said to be a timid and loyal thing, which makes him the perfect candidate for housebreaking. He's the second-born prince, so I'm less likely to start a war by taking him." Though she knew to expect some repercussions from Atalius once he found out. "He's also rumored to be very pretty."

"King Atalius may still come for his son. He is a proud man. Stupid, but proud," the queen observed.

"We will be wed as soon as he's on Amarran soil. The marriage will be consummated immediately so he will be soiled goods. No other woman of noble birth will have him, and he can be of no further use to his father."

"No noblewoman in Amarra would want him after that, but you forget that other kingdoms' ways are not our own."

Ah yes. Other kingdoms and their backward ideals. In Amarra, a differre man was only as valuable as the seed he could give a woman. Once that seed had resulted in a child, it could be of no further value to a separate woman. Mothers with children born of the same father? Ludicrous. It wasn't done. Sure, men could be shared for the purposes of pleasure. They were bought by the dozens from the common classes to fill harems. But when it came to marriage, fidelity was demanded of men.

But Olerra had heard tales of kingdoms that encouraged men to put their seed in as many women as possible. It was a sign of prowess, even. As if a man should be proud of what his cock could do. Losing his spend wasn't difficult. Pleasing a woman in bed was. Which should he be prouder of?

Olerra knew her aunt wasn't truly arguing with her. She was simply poking holes in Olerra's plan to see if she was strong enough to handle the onslaught.

Olerra said, "It is important that Atalius suffers the consequences for coming after our land. He hates Amarrans and would rather die than see one of his sons wedded to one. We have the might to withstand him should he make hasty advances, and he won't know for some time that it's me who has taken his son, despite the threats I made when I spoke with him. Why come back and kidnap a son when I could have traded the king for one? And once we're married, there's hardly anything Atalius can do about it."

Lemya nodded. "Very well. You have my blessing in this. If it's what you truly want."

"It is."

"Who will you take with you on your prince heist?"

"Just Ydra."

"Are you certain? Even the lowliest of noblewomen are permitted a retinue of three guards."

"The fewer the better. I will prove myself."

Lemya pulled Olerra into her warm embrace before kissing the top of her head. "You have nothing to prove to me, niece. I love you no matter what. You know that, right?"

"I do."

"You must do this only if you wish to rule. If you don't—"

"I do wish it."

"Very well." Lemya was silent for a moment. "You needn't marry the Brute right away. The five hundredth anniversary of the Goddess's Gift is approaching. What better way to celebrate than with a royal wedding?"

"I hadn't thought of that."

"That'll give you three months to break him once he's on our soil."

"Child's play," Olerra said.

"Let me know what resources you need and they're yours. Otherwise, happy hunting."

Olerra cracked her knuckles as she left the queen's quarters. It was the only thing she could do to get her attention off the sensation of her sinking stomach.

There was a reason she'd put off courting men for so long. A reason why she was still a virgin.

It wasn't that she didn't want a man. She'd felt a yearning for a man for the first time when she was thirteen. That yearning only grew stronger the older she became, but she'd resisted her impulses because it was the only way to keep her secret.

All women in Amarra could use the magic of the goddess to keep men in line.

All of them except Olerra.

As eager as Olerra was to see Ydra again, she needed to visit her cousin first. Politics weren't as natural to her as they were to Glenaerys, but Olerra knew when a good brag was in order.

Olerra made the trek to Glen's wing of the palace. Glen had many estates throughout Amarra, but she spent most of her time here, working and gaining the support of the courtiers.

When Olerra arrived, she walked into a private auction, happening right in the middle of the main greeting chamber.

There were two ways in which noble Amarrans found their men: They stole them from neighboring kingdoms or bought them from the common classes of their own people. While Olerra was determined to do the former like her mother before her, Glen employed the latter tactic.

While kidnapping men was a centuries-long tradition that many families participated in, it had become more common in the past ten years. A decade ago, the noblemen of Amarra, led by the queen's brother (Glenaerys's father), staged a coup against the matriarchy and lost. As punishment, they forfeited their lives and those of their eldest sons. Now the only males of noble birth were children.

Which meant that noblewomen had to steal noble husbands from other kingdoms. Men could be bought for harems, but the royals, like Olerra, needed to be able to claim their daughters had noble blood for succession.

Her cousin, Glenaerys, older by three months, didn't have a husband despite also being differre. Her harem was thirty strong already, but they were all commoners. Pretty commoners, but peasants all the same. Glen didn't have Olerra's brawn, which was why Olerra suspected she had yet to hunt down a husband of her own. The Goddess's Gift may have given her an edge, but fighting didn't come naturally to Glen the way it did to Olerra—not that that stopped her from being too rough with her men.

There were five groups of people standing in the chamber. The first was a woman and sire standing behind a young man who must have just turned eighteen and didn't have terribly much going for him. He was lean, clearly underfed, though maybe that could be helped over time with generous meals. Glen stepped up to him.

"Stick out your tongue," she instructed.

He did so.

"Is that as far as it goes?" she inquired.

The mother gave her son an encouraging motion with her hands. *Go on*, it said. The boy extended his tongue farther.

"I assure you no woman has bedded my Armandis," the mother explained. "I hear you prefer virgins."

"Hmm" was all Glen said.

She stepped up to the next group. The man in front was more handsome than the first. Glen inspected his hands carefully.

"He keeps his nails well-trimmed," the mother of this one said. "You won't find a cleaner man around than Issan."

"I have servants who prepare my men for pleasure activities," Glen said haughtily. "He won't need to worry about his own upkeep. Flex for me now."

Issan bent his elbow, showing off an impressive bicep.

"Hmm," Glen said again, and moved on.

The men grew more and more handsome down the line. When she reached the last pairing, a sire and his son, she had to look down rather than up to inspect her potential purchase. The boy couldn't be older than fourteen.

The sire waited to be addressed before speaking, as was their custom.

"His age?" Glen asked.

"Thirteen, Princess."

"And he can perform?"

"Of course. I would not be here otherwise, I swear it. Caught him with his own hand just yesterday."

The boy took a step back under Glen's assessing gaze. His hair was blond, his skin fair, his face rounded and smooth. He would make a very pretty man someday. "It is not often I see lone sires selling their sons."

"I lost my wife some years ago. I have no woman to look after me. I'm desperate for the money."

The boy turned his head and glared at his sire. Had he been bigger, Olerra thought he'd hit him.

"If you drank less, you wouldn't need the money!" the boy spat.

The sire raised his hand to land a blow, and the boy flinched, as though this were something he'd come to expect on a regular basis.

Glen grabbed the man's wrist before the blow could land. "I'll give you five ederos," she said.

The sire swallowed. "Yes, Princess. That is most generous."

Glen turned to a servant behind her to gesture for her to pay the man. When she spotted Olerra, she grinned.

Only Glenaerys Corasene could manage to make a smile look like a threat.

The cousins looked nothing alike, despite sharing blood. Glen's curls were the color of golden sand, and her eyes were as bright as the cerulean sky. Glenaerys was small where Olerra was large. Olerra had the dark hair and hazel eyes of the royal family, while Glenaerys took more after her mother. Olerra was general over the queen's armies and oversaw the day-to-day running of the troops while Glenaerys was a strategist who mingled with the spymaster and treasurer.

"Didn't see you there, cousin," Glen said. "What do you think of my latest purchase?" She waved her hand in front of the boy.

"He's a bit younger than your usual go-to," Olerra said, disgusted by the whole thing.

"I've started buying them young so they can be properly trained. On his eighteenth birthday, he'll be bedded for the first time and properly inducted into the harem."

Sure he would. Olerra didn't believe for a second that her cousin would wait until he was older. Glenaerys got off on the power play.

Olerra wished she could steal the boy away and cart him off to Ydra's estate for safety, but the only way to free that boy was for Olerra to become queen. She needed the power to make new laws. To save them all.

"Why are you here?" Glen asked. "It's been years since you've paid me a social visit."

"I just wanted to tell you the good news."

Glen inspected her nails, as though she couldn't care less about the conversation. "And what news is that?"

"I've just received Auntie's approval. I'm going to kidnap myself a husband."

Glen went very still. "Fabulous."

"It is, isn't it? You'll no doubt try to sabotage the endeavor in some way, so I thought I'd let you know that I have people watching the roads to Kalundir. And Auntie will be keeping an eye on you."

"Excellent."

Olerra rather thought so. She was about to garner so much favor. And she'd just given her cousin a false destination. While Glenaerys was expecting Olerra to head west, she'd in fact be going north.

Glen pursed her lips and turned away. She barked, "Come," to the young boy and stalked off.

Olerra relished the win all the way to Ydra's.

4

Sanos felt all the tension leave his body as he started on his second ale.

His back had healed over the past fortnight, and he'd enjoyed stolen moments with his mother and sister. Both seemed to be doing well. Emorra had taken an interest in engineering. She was building all kinds of miniature bridges, buildings, and the like. She'd rattled off numbers and words like *suspension* and *architectonic*. He had no idea what books she was reading or how she managed any of it, but that was the way she was.

Now his birthday had arrived, and Sanos could finally loosen up. He was out with his brothers, and his father didn't know where they were. They weren't being watched. Sanos knew, because he kept looking over the tavern for spies.

Here he couldn't do anything to stoke his father's paranoia.

No, instead he had good company, tolerable drink, and the promise of pleasure at the end of the night.

The Ladicus brothers were only at their second tavern, yet Andrastus was already slurring his words. He never could hold his drink.

"Saaaaaaanos. Youuuuuu're olderrrrrrrr tooooooday. You looooook ollllllllld."

"Thank you, Andrastus," he said.

Canus shoved Andrastus over and took the seat next to Sanos. "I was just chatting up a couple of very nice girls over at that table. Perhaps you'd like to join me?"

Sanos took another drink. "No nice girls. Only whores."

"Right, because sex is only fun if you pay for it."

"You know that's not why."

Yes, Canus knew. He was more observant than the others, but that didn't stop him from trying to get Sanos to have a little fun.

"He wants you isolated," Canus tried. "Don't let him win."

"I can't risk him not winning."

"Sanos—"

"I said no." His tone left no room for argument.

"Fine."

Canus left him to go sit with the girls. Trantos bounded up to take his place.

"Are you scaring everyone away?"

"I have that effect on people."

"You don't scare me."

Sanos snorted. Trantos, fourth-born, was only twenty years of age. He was old enough to be considered a man yet acted young enough to still be considered a child.

"What do you get up to these days?" Sanos asked him.

"Whatever I like."

"That's not an answer."

"It's the only one you'll get."

Sanos rolled his eyes. He knew what the rest of his brothers did with their time. Andrastus was constantly at the cathedral, studying ancient poetry and writings with the priests dedicated to serving the god Brutus. Canus was involved with smithies because he wanted to be as close to war as he could get. Ikanos was still being tutored, too young to pick up any sort of business or hobby. But Trantos? He hadn't shown any particular interest in anything.

Or so Sanos had thought. He wondered if Trantos was being sneaky on purpose.

"Whatever it is, it had better not be something that will get you into trouble."

"Will you relax? Try worrying about only yourself for a change. Else you'll go gray early." Trantos clapped him on the back and left to help Andrastus find a seat before he toppled over.

Apparently Sanos *was* scaring everyone away. Ikanos was in a corner scribbling away on a piece of parchment. And Sanos turned his head in time to watch Canus get slapped across the face by one of the young women.

Sanos nearly spat out his ale as he laughed.

"I think it's time we headed for the next tavern," Canus said.

He was already over their argument, for he took the seat beside Sanos once they reached the next establishment. Ikanos began to recite poetry for all the patrons to hear, since Andrastus was too drunk to do it. Sanos and Canus made a game of it to pass the time, taking a sip of their ale every time their youngest brother made a rhyme with the word *flower*.

"My, this ale is sour."

The lighting was low, the laughter loud, the drink tasting better by the minute.

"Brother Sanos, why dost thou look dour?"

His other brothers laughed at the rhymes. Ikanos chugged another ale as the pub cheered for more verses. Sanos wasn't drunk enough for this, yet he wanted to be sober enough to properly enjoy the last stop of the evening.

"Tonight I hope my cock shall tower."

Ikanos grew fouler the longer this went on.

"Where's the nearest pretty maid? Might I plow her?"

For gods' sakes.

"I'm leaving," Sanos declared.

"Ooooooone lassssssst taaaaaaaaavern," Andrastus begged.

They ushered him along to yet another establishment, and it was here that Canus approached him with the rope.

Shit, he'd forgotten.

"No," Sanos said firmly. He was feared by many with his deep voice and authoritative stance, but his brothers didn't bat an eye.

"Sanos, it's tradition. You must!"

He tried to make a run for it. Four-on-one hardly made for a fair fight, even when one of them could barely stand. One-on-one he could take any of them, but he didn't stand a chance when they ganged up on him.

Ikanos swung near his face and missed, but Canus got him in the gut, and he went down like a bird with an arrow through its eye. They stripped off his shirt and tied him to a load-bearing post in the establishment. His bonds were tight, too tight to wriggle free. So he gave each of the men a stare that promised death once he was free.

"How many years is it now?" Trantos asked.

"Twenty-six, I think," said Canus.

"Tweeeeeeeenty-seveeeeeeen, I thought," said Andrastus.

"Twenty-five," Sanos said. "None of you are funny."

The higher the number, the more painful this would be. Sanos didn't know how the tradition started, but for some reason, it was customary to pluck the hairs off a man's chest to match the number of years he'd aged. Fucking Brutes and their fucking traditions.

His brothers took turns, ripping patches of hair off his chest, counting aloud so the whole tavern could join in the fun. Sanos bore it with a straight face and hardened eyes, not crying out once and flinching only minimally.

"Sixteeeeeeeeeen!" called out Andrastus on his turn.

Sanos closed his eyes as a fresh sting erupted on his chest. Birthdays were something he always looked forward to. He was so eager to be home that he managed to forget this part of the night. He should take more care to remember in the future. Drinks. Pain. Women. That was the way of the Brute.

Did they all have to look like they were enjoying this so much?

"Twenty-five!" Canus proclaimed, and then finally released him.

Sanos reached out to strangle the first one he could get his hands on.

"Time for the brothel," Ikanos wisely said.

It was the only thing that could have halted his revenge.

Sanos hid his eagerness well, but the truth was that he was touch-starved. Even miles and miles away, Sanos couldn't risk his father learning of him getting attached to any woman. All he needed was one more person for his father to hold over him, or worse, take away from him. And it didn't feel right to go to the brothels of the cities they conquered.

So Sanos waited for his birthday every year.

Blanchette's was a special brothel that catered to noble clientele. It was also entirely fashioned in the style of the Amarrans, Brutus's rivals to the south. The whores wore pants or short skirts instead of tight dresses, and their tunics were made of sheer silk. The women all wore their hair in a variety of braids, as the Amarrans did. They wore bows over their shoulders or an empty quiver. Some wore sheaths around their waists or thighs and nothing else.

The Amarran wretches thought themselves so superior to every other kingdom in Torateeria, but at Blanchette's they were reduced to nothing more than common whores. As was their place. Or so his father said. Sanos had never met any Amarrans, but the rumors were vicious. Amarra was a territory ruled by women. They kept their men in chains. Drank their blood. Performed sexual acts in public. The women themselves were unnaturally strong, and they used that strength to treat men like dogs.

The madam greeted them warmly, but Sanos was already looking over the women in the room. He wasn't very discerning when it came to height or size or features. He liked *women*. Whatever women he could get away with having.

While the younger princes took their time selecting partners for the night, Sanos was of half a mind to grab the closest woman and take her upstairs. But then, out of the corner of his eye, he saw Madam Blanchette approach his next youngest brother, who was still swaying on his feet.

"Prince Andrastus," the woman said with a curtsy. "I have a new girl who I think will be perfectly suited to your tastes. In fact, if I may speak so boldly, she requested *you*."

That caught Sanos's interest. Andrastus was a sap. He liked poetry and going to the opera. He probably preferred his women on top.

"New girl?" Sanos repeated. "One who asked for Andrastus? Why?"

Madam Blanchette didn't bat an eye at his tone. "She's heard the rumors about the prince's handsomeness. She wants to see for herself."

Andrastus was the pretty one. Canus, the big one. Trantos was the troublemaker. Ikanos was the baby. And Sanos . . . what was Sanos? The absent crown prince.

Maybe it was all the ale, but something primal came out in Sanos. Some need to take and prove himself. It was the way of the Brute, his father would say.

And he'd gone without sex too long.

Ikanos laughed and elbowed Canus, who already had his tongue sliding up the exposed breast of a whore. "Sanos doesn't like that a girl fancies Andrastus over him."

Canus palmed the breast as he turned and gave Sanos a wide smile. "He'll get over it in about ten minutes. Hurry and take your pick, big brother."

Sanos ignored them. To the madam, he said, "Andrastus needs help taking off his pants to piss all the ale out of his system. He will be no good tonight. I'll keep the new girl company instead."

He'd show her she made the wrong choice.

Madam Blanchette froze in place. The pause was short-lived, but Sanos still caught it. Nobody liked to say no to him. He wondered if the madam would dare.

"I mean no offense, Prince, but that is not how things are done here. My girl requested Andrastus, and if he'll agree, she'll have no other."

It shouldn't matter. Just earlier he was thinking about how any woman would do for tonight.

But why had this one *requested* his brother?

Sanos's gold was just as good as Andrastus's. Yet this woman *wanted* his brother.

Sanos had never been wanted before. He hadn't realized it was something he should want until he was suddenly presented with the hard truth of the lack of it.

His three youngest brothers took their girls upstairs. Sanos frowned at Andrastus, who was now leaning against the wall.

"She's in room twelve, Highness," the madam said to his brother.

With a sigh, Sanos pulled his brother's arm over his shoulders to help him take the stairs. Sanos would at least catch a glimpse of the new woman. Maybe next year . . .

Amarra's tits, the thought was so damned depressing. A whole year before he would get this again. A night without worries. Another's touch.

The pleasant buzzing in his head couldn't make up for the sudden melancholy that came over him.

Cut that out, he chastised himself. *You keep your family safe. There is no better way to live.*

When they reached the top step, Andrastus nearly slipped from his grasp. It was only Sanos's quick reflexes that saved him from the journey back down.

Sanos shuffled him off in the direction of room twelve, but before they could reach it, Andrastus was suddenly deadweight. His brother landed on the floor with a *thump* that was masked by the sounds of all the bed play coming from the other rooms.

Sanos dragged his brother by the arms over to the side of the hallway, where no one would step on him. Then he took the time to turn Andrastus onto his side in case the ale came back up. Sanos ought to go downstairs and select his choice for the evening. He shouldn't be wasting precious seconds standing over his brother.

Gods, he *hated* being the oldest.

His head swerved in the direction of room twelve without his permission.

Who was this woman who had the audacity to show a preference in princes?

Sanos looked over his shoulder once, then back to the door. The hallway was still empty.

And his curiosity got the better of him.

He stepped inside room twelve and found a lone woman standing by the window. Her back was to him.

"Are you the new girl?" he asked.

She turned, and he was surprised to find that so much of her was covered up. She didn't dress like the other Amarran-looking whores. Maybe that was her gimmick. Her face was shadowed under a hood so he couldn't guess a thing about her appearance, save that she was a large woman.

His mouth watered. A large woman meant large breasts.

He shook his head to focus. He wouldn't pounce on her without first speaking to her. He wasn't an animal.

She gave him a slow perusal from head to toe, and his blood heated.

"Are you the prince?" she asked. Her voice was deep and sultry. He liked that.

"I'm the best prince," he answered, shutting the door behind him so they could be alone. He thought perhaps he could see a flash of teeth beneath her hood.

"I know you are. That's why I chose you."

Disappointment came over him as he remembered she wanted Andrastus, but she was moving toward him, and he found himself rooted to the spot.

"You are the fairest, the cleverest, the most romantic of princes," she said.

She stood before him now and placed her hands on his shoulders. With one finger, he drew back her hood.

Her hair was a dark chestnut. The strands had a natural shimmer to them even with the low candlelight in the room. She wore it in a single braid that curved over one shoulder. Two strands, one on each side of her head, were too short to fit into the plait. She wore no makeup or paint, which was unusual, but he rather liked the idea of not getting it in his mouth when he kissed her. Her skin was white but tanned from spending lots of time in the sun. Darker than most he saw in Brutus. Her eyes were hazel, and her lips were so plump he couldn't wait to taste them.

"You're beautiful," he whispered, reaching out to fiddle with the end of her braid. Her hair was like velvet against his fingers. He wanted to undo her braid and tangle his fingers in it.

"You're larger than I expected," she said.

He blinked at the reminder that she still thought him his brother. He leaned down. "I am the best prince," he said again. "I'll prove it."

"I'm counting on that," she said. She was focused on his neck for some reason, so he traced her lips with his fingertip. That brought her gaze where he wanted it. On his own mouth.

He leaned down the rest of the way.

And tasted heaven.

Olerra knew she should get Andrastus out of here as quickly as possible, but he seduced her oh so prettily, and she wasn't prepared for the feeling of his mouth on hers.

She'd been kissed before, of course. But those were boys in her earlier years, before she decided that in order to keep her secret she needed to distance herself from the opposite sex.

She'd never been kissed by a man.

His lips didn't kiss her so much as devour her. He moaned as he took her bottom lip between his own, letting his tongue dart across her skin. His teeth closed over the same spot and pulled gently. It felt as though he pulled on something deep within her, a tether that reached between her legs and was her undoing.

She shoved him against the closed door to the room and kissed him in earnest, loving this intensity that was so new to her. Andrastus made a sound of surprise deep in his throat but didn't stop. His hands found her braid again. When her hair fell loose, she realized he'd undone the band. And then his fingers were tracing up and down her scalp, cupping the back of her head to keep their mouths fused together.

Oh, but she liked that.

He ran light fingers down her neck, over the top of her cloak, and finally reached her breasts, where he took the biggest handfuls he could get and squeezed gently.

He groaned.

"I need your skin against mine," he said, just before he put his tongue in her mouth.

The tongue was distracting. It spread fire throughout her limbs, making her ache. It was a stark contrast to his words, which reminded her she had a task to perform.

She wasn't here for sex. She was here for a husband.

She opened her eyes during the open-mouthed kisses, finding that the way his lashes lay against his cheeks was utterly beautiful.

Focus!

She flipped open the hinge on the ring she wore, revealing the barb underneath.

He was ready to help her remove her cloak when he felt something sharp pierce his neck.

Sanos thought to ignore it and continue, but his body didn't seem to be working properly. Instead of reaching up to unveil what he wanted, he was falling. The woman bent before he could connect with the floor, catching his waist on her shoulder. Then she stood, grunting under his weight.

It was odd that she should be the one to carry him to the bed, but he wasn't nearly as concerned with that as he was by the fact that he couldn't seem to work his hands or his mouth to ask what was happening. He was staring at her backside. In fact, his nose kept bumping into it with the strides she was taking.

"There you go, Andrastus," she said.

Then he was falling.

He landed on his back, the impact jarring his bones. He felt something soft beneath him, though not soft enough for the fall to be painless. After another *thud*, the woman landed beside him on what he suspected was a pile of blankets.

"We've got him, Ydra. Let's go," she said before meticulously covering him with blankets.

As Sanos stared up at the star-covered night, he managed to put a few things together.

She'd stuck him with some kind of paralytic.

She'd dumped him out a window.

He'd landed on the bed of a cart.

Horses were moving, taking him someplace.

As the mystery woman placed a final blanket over the top of him, this time covering his head, he suspected that she wasn't working for his brothers.

She was no whore, and this was no game.

By the time the cart stopped hours later, he could move the first and second joints of his fingers, but no more. He was also fully aroused.

Painfully so.

What the hell was in that toxin?

Was this some nasty test of his father's to prove himself a man yet again? Had he set up some elaborate ruse to see how Sanos would handle himself under pressure? It was just the kind of thing the king would do. He was always fond of torturing his eldest son and claiming it was all to build his character.

Before he could move his fingers into a fist, the two women bound him with ropes, securing his arms and legs to the sides of the cart so he was spread-eagle. Now that it was starting to get light out, he could see more of the second woman.

She was smaller than the one who'd thrown him out the window. She was fair, with yellow locks that she also wore in one long braid down her back. Her eyes were gray, and she had a bow slung over one shoulder.

Finally, he found he could move his lips. "Did my father put you up to this?" he asked when the fairer one—Ydra—came into his line of sight.

She smiled at him but said nothing.

At least not to him.

"He's not what I expected," she said instead to her companion.

"Nor I," the other answered.

"Does he meet your approval?"

Olerra climbed into the cart with the man she intended to wed and gave Ydra's question due consideration.

Andrastus was a big man. Far heavier than she'd expected him to be. She reached out a hand to wrap it around a bicep and felt nothing but muscle. She hadn't really had the chance to touch him anywhere save his shoulders (to steady herself) and his neck (to apply the toxin). Physically, he was intimidating. She couldn't decide if she liked that or not.

Really, she shouldn't be surprised. Atalius was a massive man. Of course all his sons would be, too. Even the smallest of them.

The prince's hair was something else entirely. It was so blond as to almost be white, and it trailed down to his shoulders, thick yet straight as a board. His beard and eyebrows were darker, a light gold color. Olerra didn't know men could have hair of different colors on their chins. No men in Amarra wore beards. She wondered at the shape of his jaw.

His complexion was bone white, which she suspected was a result of his new circumstances. He would need special oils so as not to burn when they reached the heat of Amarra. She hadn't thought of that beforehand, but there was nothing to do about it now. They had a schedule to keep.

His eyes were black in this lighting, so she suspected they were a dark brown. And, oh, how they glared at her.

She finally let her gaze dip down to the bulge in his pants, a result of the vyra she'd injected him with. It both paralyzed men and made them hard. It was her cousin's favorite accessory for misbehaving bed partners. Olerra would never use it again on him now that she'd captured him.

But that didn't mean she wouldn't take advantage of its current effects.

Even with all his clothing on, she could tell his cock was proportionate to the rest of his body.

"I guess what they say is true. Brutus didn't bless his sons just with virility. He also gave them big cocks."

Ydra cackled. "Maybe I should kidnap a Brute."

Olerra watched the prince's eyes widen at the conversation. She made sure not to laugh at him. It would not be a great start to their relationship. She wanted to put him at ease, so she added, "The prince is a great kisser."

"Is that why you took so long nabbing him?"

Olerra grinned. "I might have gotten a little carried away." She rubbed her cheeks. "His beard is scratchy, though. I can't wait to kiss him again once we get all that wretched hair shaved off his face."

Andrastus narrowed his eyes, finally finding his voice. "You will not come near my beard," he said with the authority afforded only to a prince.

Olerra leaned down until she was only inches from his face. "I am Olerra Corasene, queen potential of Amarra. You will soon have the honor of being my husband. Your life is about to finally mean something. Your seed will create queens and conquerors, and you will be rewarded handsomely should you please me. Now get some sleep, Prince Andrastus. We've a bit of a journey ahead of us."

"There is no fucking wa—"

She gagged him.

5

At first, Sanos dismissed the words Olerra had shared, still convinced his father was behind this elaborate scheme. Then the flickering of a memory came to him. Hadn't he read somewhere that Amarran nobility sometimes stole husbands for themselves?

Besides, his father would never send *women* to mess with him.

Olerra had lifted him so effortlessly . . .

Because she had the power of her goddess and could overpower him.

That thought was unsettling. He'd only ever had to worry about his father hurting him. He knew exactly what cruelties to expect from him. But Princess Olerra? He knew nothing about her, save that she wanted his brother for her husband, and by his own damned idiocy, Sanos had managed to take his place.

What would she do if she learned he wasn't Andrastus? Kill him? Or did he risk revealing his identity and hope she would ransom him? Sanos dismissed the thought immediately. Either she would trade him for Andrastus—something Sanos would never allow to happen to his gentler brother—or try to ransom him to his father.

Then Atalius would kill him.

Allowing himself to be kidnapped by Amarrans? Shaming the Brutes? Embarrassing his father? The king would torture him until Sanos's heart failed.

And then he would turn his attention to Andrastus and train him as the new heir.

Neither option was acceptable.

Sanos would just have to endure until an opportunity for escape presented itself. He would return home, and his father would be none the wiser to his previous whereabouts. He'd pass off his absence to extended birthday celebrations and then his father would beat him thoroughly for it.

But that was better than being dead and turning this fate over to his brother.

The two women pulled the cart far from the road and unhitched the horses, allowing them to graze. Ydra set about gathering wood for a fire while Olerra came to stand before him.

She'd changed out of her hooded cloak and pants. Now she wore leather-studded armor over her torso. It was sleeveless, exposing most of her arms, though she wore bracers at her wrists. Her feet were covered by sturdy sandals. A short, pleated skirt hung around her thighs, and a cape trailed to her lower back. Now knowing she was a princess, he was shocked she showed off so much of her skin. And gods, but there was just so much of her. She was a big woman with an imposing presence.

It made him bring out the hardened man his father had forged from steel and a smoothed cane. "You will return me at once," he said the moment she removed his gag.

She smiled, as though she found him amusing. "Your voice is so deep. I rather like it."

Sanos blinked. *Was she complimenting him?*

"Your clothes are impractical," he spat back.

"Is your chin pointed or square-shaped?"

"Don't touch me!" he said as she reached out a hand.

"It's a bit late for that, don't you think?" she asked, but she crossed her arms and stared. Her eyes were wide as she drank him in. Were this any other situation, Sanos would have found the heated gaze extremely flattering.

"Stop looking at me," he demanded, even as he felt his whole body warm at the attention.

"You wanted me just a few hours ago. Has something changed?"

He glared in return, not dignifying that with a response.

"I'm afraid I cannot stop looking at you, Prince. I would have an awfully hard time feeding you if I had to close my eyes."

Feeding him? Surely she couldn't mean to keep him restrained?

The Amarrans boiled oats and added some spices. The two sat and ate before the fire. The conversation was too quiet for him to catch, but they'd occasionally look in his direction.

He hated that.

Once done eating, Olerra brought another steaming bowl to his side. She blew on a spoonful of food before raising it to his lips.

"Untie me. I am no child."

"I'm well aware. Twenty-four, aren't you? Three years my senior. Now, let's not behave as one, hmm?" She extended the spoon, and he wondered how she knew so much about Andrastus. How long had she studied his brother before intending to take him? Yet she had clearly never seen his brother before, for the two of them couldn't be more unalike in appearance. Andrastus always wore his hair long—well down his back. His features were more angular. He didn't wear a beard, and his muscles were less defined. The only thing the Ladicus brothers shared was that white-blond hair coloring, which came from their mother.

Sanos's stomach grumbled, yet his pride was too much. He inclined his head, but instead of wrapping his lips around the spoon, he sank his teeth into her fingers.

Her response was immediate. She dropped the hot food onto the cart, narrowly missing his crotch. One hand snaked forward to grab him by the hair. She jerked his head to the side, leaned down, and—

And bit him on the neck.

It was a territorial move, painful and somehow also arousing.

He could do no more than stare at her as she retreated, taking the cookware with her.

She'd branded him with her teeth. There was no doubt in his mind that if he looked in a mirror he would see the indents left behind. The bruising that would show soon.

Just who the fuck did she think she was?

He was a prince of Brutus. A warrior and a conqueror set to rule an entire kingdom one day.

And she'd just stolen him.

Like it was the easiest thing in the world.

They were back on the road shortly afterward. Olerra drove the horses while Ydra napped in the bed of the cart. Sanos was tied off to one side to make room for another person. He cold barely wiggle his fingers with how much rope they'd used on him.

He was hungry. He was angry.

And no one was coming for him.

No one would even think to check on him until afternoon the next day.

But what then?

Once he didn't return to the palace, his father would send men to find him. They'd scour the city and patrol the roads.

But they certainly wouldn't come this way.

Atalius would never suspect the Amarrans of stealing from him. Why would they? They'd already delivered a crushing defeat on the battlefield. They'd had his father in their clutches and could have demanded anything.

Hell, they probably wouldn't even pass a soul on the road. Because of the current contentions between the two countries, no one made the crossing from Amarra to Brutus.

Atalius would be enraged once he realized Sanos was missing. The king needed to control his sons. He especially needed his heir under his thumb.

But he wouldn't look in the right place.

Sanos was on his own, and he needed to get home. Who was to protect his mother and sister if not him? Who would look after Andrastus when Atalius turned his attention to his second-born son? Would Canus be sent to the front lines to deal with the Ephennans in Sanos's stead? What if the king thought Sanos had run away? What punishments would he dole out in his fury to find him?

Sanos would escape once the opportunity presented itself, and he would kill the two women who dared to take him.

After a few hours, the women swapped places. Ydra drove the horses while Olerra climbed into the cart. She offered him some water. This time, he was too thirsty to try anything.

After he drained half the skin, Olerra wiped an errant drop from his face with her thumb.

Before he could chastise her for it, he watched as she brought it to her lips.

He wasn't sure if he glared because he thought it was what he should do, or if it was meant to hide his other physical reactions to her. The way his heart pounded faster. The hitch in his breath. She was brazen and forward. He'd been surprised enough back at the brothel when she'd pushed him against the nearest hard surface, taking charge in their kissing. He'd liked it at the time. Now he realized it must be some Amarran thing.

When she brought her own lips to the waterskin, where his were just seconds earlier, he shivered.

He pulled at his restraints, but they were as tight as before.

Olerra reclined upon the blankets at his feet and slept. She was turned toward him so he could see the smooth features of her face. Those large lips. Long feminine lashes. A light dusting of freckles on her sun-kissed cheeks. She made a face in her sleep, and a dimple appeared on one side.

He made himself stop looking at her, but he couldn't deny that he was curious.

These women kidnapped husbands, but *then* what did they do with them? Would he be caged like a dog in her home? Would she give him that horrid toxin and then take him at night while he was drugged beneath her? Would he be gagged at all hours of the night and day except for meals?

His mind continued to spin out of control with possibilities, making sleep impossible. He tried to work at the ropes securing him, but they would not loosen.

The three of them spent all the next day on the road. When Sanos was permitted to relieve himself, the one called Ydra would walk him off to the side of the road and keep a hand on his shoulder while his wrists were still bound. He endured the humiliation of pissing while she was standing at his back. If he tried to shrug out of her grip, she tightened her fingers. Gods, she was strong. It was unnatural. He had no hope of getting away from her like this.

When it was night again, they erected a tent around a nearby tree and tied him to the trunk. They left the gag in while sleeping.

It was only on the second full day of travel, when the two women were well rested, that Olerra bothered to speak to him again, joining him in the back of the cart.

"I have much to teach you and so little time to do it in. What do you know of my people?"

Sanos stared at her. Did she actually expect him to cooperate?

"I know your goddess has made you unnaturally strong and ugly," he said.

She snorted. "Is that why your breath hitches when I draw closer to you?"

His glare returned. He should know better than to call her unattractive. Not only was it entirely untrue, he'd proven just how attractive he found her when they first met.

I need your skin against mine.

He would not live those words down.

"This will be easier for us both if you make the most of our time together on the road before we reach my country."

"Things will be easier for *you* if you release me now, before my father knows where I've gone."

She laughed. "I have met your father four times on the battlefield now. I'm not worried."

Sanos's eyes widened. "*You're* the Amarran general?" The one who had shamed his father? The one who had stoked his ire and drove him to beat Sanos and Canus relentlessly?

"Yes."

She came closer, and he flinched backward. The move made her narrow her eyes. "I will not harm you, Andrastus. I don't know what you've heard about me or my people, but I am not cruel. I do not use my strength to harm others. I have taken you because I must in order to win my throne, but this is an arrangement that can be mutually beneficial. You are a second-born prince, set to inherit nothing. Now you will be a husband and sire. You have risen in station. You needn't work or want for anything. I will care for you.

"I hear you like literature. I have recently restocked our library with books by Brutish writers and poets. There's a theater in Zinaeya where you can attend plays, operas, and more. I would see you happy and thriving."

If only Sanos liked any of those things. Sanos preferred hunting and movement. He liked parties and drinking. He read for enlightenment, not for pleasure. And he detested poetry.

But he had to pretend to be Andrastus . . .

Fuck that. Anger seemed to be the best approach.

"You think you can bribe me into doing what you want?" he asked.

"It's not bribery. It's a mutually beneficial arrangement."

"And what would you be getting out of this arrangement?"

"Certainly not your pleasing personality."

"You kidnapped me."

She grinned. "I did, didn't I? Couldn't have planned the whole thing any better."

Amarra's tits, she thought he was complimenting her.

"You will have much to prove when we arrive in Amarra," she said. "Physically, I think we can say the court will be impressed by you, but your manners need some work."

Was she fucking serious?

"Men are to be seen but not heard unless expressly told otherwise," she continued. "You are free to speak to me whenever you wish when we are alone. However, in front of the courtiers, you need to behave."

"And just how are you going to make me do that?"

She leaned farther into the blankets on the cart, propping herself up on two elbows. The crisp breeze in the Brutish air blew the loose strands of hair back from her face. "Women in my kingdom have been kidnapping and breaking men for nearly five hundred years. It is an art form that is taught to the nobility. While I don't particularly care for most of the methods, I will do what I must to ingrain some manners in you."

"Breaking men?" he questioned. He wasn't overly concerned.

There was nothing this woman could do to him that hadn't already been done. Except, he remembered, any nighttime plans she might have.

He refused to think about it.

"Housebreaking," she clarified. "Teaching you to be Amarran."

Housebreaking?

Every word out of her mouth was more ridiculous than the last.

"And what methods do you intend to use on me?" he asked.

"The most common practice is the denying of sexual favors."

He blinked once. Twice. "You're going to withhold sex from me?" He laughed. "That only works if I want sex from you, which I can assure you, I no longer do."

"Your words would have greater weight if you hadn't been pawing at me just two nights ago." When he tried to argue, she added, "Let's not bicker now, as delightful as it is to go head-to-head with you. Let's become better acquainted. The only things I know about you are what my spies have told me. Tell me something real."

The question startled him. No one had asked to know anything about him before. How could they when he kept everyone at arm's length?

"I—" he started, and cut himself off.

After a beat, she said, "Would it be easier if I went first? You already know I'm a soldier and a general. A princess. I also like to sing. I enjoy games of strategy. And . . . I'm afraid of bees."

He wanted to make a harsh comment so she would feel its bite, but he couldn't. He processed the words slowly. Felt how real they were, and something ever so small shifted within him.

"Bees," he deadpanned.

"Yes, they're loud. They sting. And they stand between me and the smell of a full blossom. There. Now you tell me something."

He ought to snap. To yell at her some more and tell her he wasn't going to play along.

Instead, he found himself saying, "I've always wanted to see the ocean."

Her eyes met his, and her smile was open. "I'll take you."

She smiled so damned much. Why did she have so much to smile about?

"I need to shit," he told her, stopping any further conversation.

She showed no reaction to his crass language. She had her friend stall the cart, then Olerra untied him from the railings at the side. She retied his bindings so his ankles and wrists remained close together. He had to shuffle off the road, her hand on his arm the whole way.

When they reached a tree, he turned to her. "Are you going to watch?"

"Of course not. I won't be far, though."

"Naturally."

He really did need to relieve himself, so he took care of business the moment he heard her footsteps recede. After he tucked himself back inside his pants, he looked about for a sharp stick or rock. Anything to cut his bonds.

There was nothing in the near vicinity, so he started to creep farther from the road. He couldn't see her when he looked over his shoulder, so he picked up speed.

"Are you finished?" she called out to him.

"Not yet," he said, raising his voice so she would think him closer.

Finally he found a rock. He crouched beside some bushes and began to saw the ropes binding his hands.

It was taking too long.

She'd come for him soon. He looked around desperately for somewhere to hide.

There were some brambles not far off. He lay flat on his back and rolled, careful to hold on to the rock. The thorns bit into his skin, but at least he was out of sight now. No sooner had he resumed his sawing did he hear their voices.

"Told you he'd run off the first time you left him alone." Ydra.

"You did."

"It wasn't your lack of charm. He's a Brute. They're taught to hate us. You picked the most difficult man for housebreaking."

"To impress the court!" Olerra defended.

"I know. I'm just saying, don't expect to work miracles after your first conversation with him."

They were getting closer, and he made his fingers work faster. Until he saw a pair of sandals right next to his head. He paused. Held his breath.

"Where do you think he went?" Ydra asked.

"He couldn't have climbed with his feet bound. He's either behind a tree trunk or tucked under some shrubs. Can I borrow your bow?"

"Sure."

They walked on. Sanos finally made it through the last of the fibers. His hands were free, but he couldn't reach his feet in this position. He counted to thirty, then rolled back out of the brambles, earning himself some more scratches.

Olerra was there. She'd moved out of his direct line of sight but no farther. She'd known exactly where he was.

Shit.

Sanos ran as fast as the ropes would let him, which wasn't much better than a walk. If he could just get to the horses. Behind a tree. Something!

As he hobbled, he didn't hear any sounds of pursuit, so he turned his head.

She took aim with the arrow and loosed.

He braced himself for pain—and then tripped.

His hands took the brunt of the fall, and when he tried to rise, he found he couldn't get his feet under him.

Because he hadn't tripped at all.

She'd shot the ropes between his ankles, pinning him to the ground. He couldn't even roll onto his back until she retrieved the arrow. When she did, he planted his ass on the ground and stared up at her.

Olerra spun the arrow over her fingers in such a way that suggested she was very familiar with the weapon, as though the shot hadn't already proven that.

"Let's get something clear, Prince. I have claimed you. That means you belong to me now. We can do this the easy way or the hard way. But make no mistake, our fates are bound together from now on. You can fight all you like, but you're not going home. And by the time I'm done with you?"

She crouched next to him, gave him a heated perusal.

"You won't want to."

Olerra pulled the cart to the side of the road even though there was still more sunlight illuminating the path ahead. She was restless, and sitting for hours at a time was not natural for her. She needed to move before she went mad.

Ydra didn't ask questions, no doubt sensing what she needed already, as she often did. Her friend started to make camp while Olerra dealt with her new man.

Andrastus snored lightly from the bed of the cart. She was relieved to see him finally sleeping. He'd done very little so far, and she knew that would only make him more difficult to work with. Being as silent as possible, she climbed into the cart and checked the bandages she'd placed on him earlier for the cuts sustained from the thorny bush he'd hidden under. One of them had been fairly deep, and she'd had to dig the barb from his skin. She changed the bandage and wondered if her betrothed was always a deep sleeper or if he was simply too tired to rouse now.

That done, she unhitched the horses so they could roam on leads near the stream. Ydra had finished erecting the tent, so the two gathered firewood. It felt good to move, but Olerra needed more. She wondered if she dared leave Ydra and the prince to go for a run . . .

"Come here."

Olerra turned to find Ydra standing in a clearing just a short ways from camp. She had her feet spread apart and arms held aloft in the first stance of luet, the Amarran wrestling technique.

Thank the gods.

Olerra removed her weapons and set them outside their makeshift ring. She moved her head from side to side, stretching her neck and swinging her arms to loosen the muscles.

When she was ready, she matched Ydra's stance and swung a fist.

She met air. Ydra was quick, but not nearly so quick as Olerra. Olerra had spent her entire life training to be the very best. She did not have the magic, so it was the only way she could protect herself. Every day she worked her muscles until they wouldn't move anymore. She lifted weights or ran until she couldn't breathe. She sparred with Ydra or anyone else willing to take her on.

Few dared.

In another twenty seconds, Olerra had Ydra flat on her back.

The second woman coughed. "How do you do that? Every damned time."

Olerra could handle all manner of weaponry, like all women from Amarra, but hand-to-hand combat was her favorite.

"Just lucky, I guess."

"Yeah, lucky to have been born with bones harder than rock."

Olerra was proud of her shape. She was a large woman. Taller than most, with wide thighs and a stomach that rounded outward almost as far as her breasts, she was physically more intimidating than many women. Still, there were several who outweighed her. She liked fighting against those the most.

"Don't forget I have a face to make men and sirems swoon."

Ydra rolled her eyes. "You're just lucky I can't use the Gift against you. Then you'd be in trouble."

It was true. No woman could use the magic against another woman. Nor could it be used against madorns—individuals born into masculine bodies who identified as female, or madereo—individuals who were neither male nor female or fluctuated between the two.

It was a discerning magic, one that saw true genders, and yet, it had rejected Olerra.

For the longest time, she thought perhaps she was madae—individuals born into female bodies who identified as male. But she knew in her mind and heart she was female. Maybe there was something about her that was broken.

Or maybe the goddess saw shame in the union of a sire who would kill his wife, and Olerra bore the punishment as a result. They say there was a storm unlike any Amarra had ever seen on the day of Olerra's birth. Perhaps her very existence displeased the goddess.

"Whatever you're thinking, stop it," Ydra said as the two took up starting positions again.

Olerra looked over her shoulder to ensure the prince was still sleeping. Ydra used the opportunity to hook a foot around one of her ankles. Olerra rolled the moment she hit the ground and came back up on her feet.

"I just . . . I want him to like me."

"He will," Ydra said. "But first he'll hate you. He has to for the sake of his pride. Besides, you should be more worried about whether you'll like him. What if he's awful?"

"Then he's a means to an end. I'll bed him, wed him, and—"

"Behead him?"

"Very funny. I was going to say I'll let him go once he's served his purpose."

Ydra slapped Olerra's hands away when she tried to grab her. "Do you want to like him?"

She was torn. She wanted a partner. She wanted someone to love and be loved by. But she also couldn't risk him learning her secret. It would certainly be easier if he was unlikable. He could be a pretty face in her court, help her win her throne, and then he could live the rest of his days wherever he wanted doing whatever he wanted.

"I don't know," Olerra said honestly. "Either way, I will attempt to win him over."

Then she charged her friend, slamming her into the ground. Ydra threw an elbow down onto her shoulder blade, so Olerra moved her arm to cover her friend's throat.

Ydra glared at her as she slapped her arm twice.

Olerra rose and held down a hand to help her up.

When she looked over Ydra's shoulder, she saw Andrastus watching the two of them. They were too far for him to hear their words, but she wondered if he'd meant what he'd said earlier. Could he turn off his attraction so easily? Did he truly no longer want her?

And if so, what could she do to change that?

6

Time seemed to slow for Olerra as Andrastus fought her every step of the journey. When she tried to give him a history lesson, he talked over her, and so she gagged him. He would look anywhere but at her. To show that he wasn't paying attention.

She tried to explain what their day-to-day lives would be like.

"In the mornings, we will dine together with the nobles. Afterward, I will resume my work with the queen's armies, while you're free to go to the gymnasium, where most of the husbands and harems spend their free time. You are welcome to pursue any activities you wish. In the evenings, we will dine together and enjoy the city together. We will retire together." Here she paused, gauging his reaction. "After our nightly routine, we will separate until the next morning. You will have your own room. Most of your time will be your own, but I do need you to make appearances to impress everyone."

"Fuck off!" he'd shout whenever she tried to remove his gag.

He was loud and obnoxious when he wanted to be, and she feared that he would be unsuitable for company when they reached Amarra.

For days Olerra tried to give him the information he would need. He ate from her hands. He gave her scathing looks. Nothing was changing.

She hadn't expected immediate results, of course. But she'd hoped for *something*.

The night before they reached their destination, Ydra said, "We've tried your way, Olerra. It's not working. Gentle coaxing isn't something the Brutes understand. You need to show him the alternative. How he will be treated if he doesn't behave. Treat him as most of the court treats their men. You can be gentle as a reward. For now, it's time to show strength. It may be the only thing he responds to."

Andrastus overheard their exchange, as was Ydra's intent.

Olerra pulled her friend aside, this time out of earshot. "What do you propose?"

"Make a mockery of him when we arrive at the palace. He doesn't want to act like a prince? Don't treat him like one. Make him a plaything as the other courtiers do of their common men. Not in private. Just in public."

Olerra looked over her shoulder to where he was still strapped to the cart. "I didn't want it to be like that between us."

"I know, but it's not forever. Just until he comes around. You cannot deny that our ancestors perfected these methods. They're used for a reason."

Olerra took a deep breath. He would hate her even more for this.

But as long as that hate turned into want, it would be worth it.

The next morning, they removed Sanos's shirt. It felt nice in the overheated Amarran air, but then he had to guess *why* they were removing his shirt.

"What happened to your chest?" Olerra said, outraged.

Sanos looked down his torso, where patches of hair were missing from the birthday party traditions.

"My brothers," he explained.

Olerra looked to Ydra.

"No one will notice from a distance," her friend assured her.

Next they removed his shoes, then hoisted him up like a flag and tied his bound hands to the back of their seat so he would be forced to stand.

Only then did they ride through the city gates.

Trumpets sounded, heralding the return of the queen potential, and Sanos bore the scrutiny of the masses as they clopped through the city. He felt his skin burning from the direct contact with the sun. Palm trees swayed in the breeze, and he could taste the salt in the air from the nearby ocean.

Women pointed and commented on his physique. Men stood by their sides, holding groceries or other wares for their wives or mothers. Those whose genders he couldn't discern were in the mix, too. Some appeared male but wore dresses. Some appeared female yet drew beards on their faces with makeup. There were also unusual pairings in the streets. Men holding the hands of other men. Women with women.

It wasn't done in his country. Same-sex pairings were illegal, yet here they were in the open. Here they seemed to flourish.

The men paired with women wore peculiar armbands around their left biceps. Some were made with thin wires or twine. Some had rocks or seashells beaded through. Must have been some Amarran fashion.

He thought it peculiar that the men wore more jewelry than the women, but Sanos had more pressing concerns.

Despite his best attempts on the road, he was now in Zinaeya, the Amarran capital. Escape would be much harder now, but he was determined to find a way out of this. He would never stop fighting. He would not leave his family to their fate. He would not allow this woman to make a mockery of him. He would not wed her. He would not bed her. In fact, he would slit her fucking throat the second he had the chance.

They pulled up to what must be the palace. Scarlet banners hung from the windows, the icon of a pointed helmet with long hair trailing down the back painted on each one. A retinue was waiting for them when the cart finally came to a stop. There was cheering and much more gawking directed at them.

Olerra and Ydra didn't give him a look as they jumped to the ground.

"I'm to report to my aunt," Olerra said. "See that the prince is bathed and readied for tonight."

Those words sent a burst of anger through his limbs, but he forced himself to remain still as the servants came forward to untie him from the cart.

The second he was free, he tried to bolt. One of the men caught him around the waist and another slung a fist into his stomach. Even as the breath whooshed out of him, he still tried to fight. While they outnumbered him, it was clear that the men were not trained fighters.

Sanos struggled until his breath finally returned to him, then he struck out with his bare foot, sweeping the legs out from under one of the men.

"Ydra," Olerra said lazily. "Put a stop to that, will you? He's going to hurt the eunuchs."

The what?

Sanos barely had a chance to look in Olerra's direction before Ydra launched herself at him. He prepared to snap her neck, but he'd barely made contact with her skin before Ydra threw him to the ground as though he weighed nothing. She pinned him effortlessly, even though her body weight shouldn't have been able to manage it. Then she pulled back his arms and secured him with rope before *lifting* him off the ground and onto his knees without so much as a grunt.

A horrible sinking sensation took root in his body as Ydra turned him to face Olerra. He hated kneeling before her.

The princess *tsk*ed at him, as though he were no more bothersome than a fly. "I understand that in Brutus, you men are taught to behave like animals, but we do not tolerate that kind of behavior in Amarra. Since you are still learning our ways, I will only deny you your dinner's rations as punishment. But should you fight like this again, especially publicly, you will be denied much greater necessities than food. Get him out of my sight until tonight."

Sanos spat at her feet and muttered, "I will see you dead," before he was gagged again.

Everyone laughed, but not because he was insulting the princess.

They laughed *at him*.

As though he were some great entertainment brought all this way for their enjoyment.

The princess leaned down to be at his eye level. She pressed her lips to his ear. "Are we making promises to each other? Unlike yours, I will actually keep mine. Soon, I will have you begging to be inside me. You will worship my curves, and you will love me."

That was the last thing she said to him before they dragged him away. Everything was a blur after that. He couldn't take in any of his surroundings through the fury and hatred that clouded his vision. He nearly fell down the stairs amid his distraction. A heated sheen of air brushed against his skin. He was in some sort of bathing chamber down low, low in the palace.

They cut his clothes away with shears. The men. The eunuchs. He knew exactly what that word meant the moment they undressed to properly bathe him.

They were missing their manhood. Had the Amarrans *done* that to them?

He could do no more than stare as Olerra's words from before took real meaning in his mind. He would be denied much greater necessities than food. Gods, was his manhood what she'd meant?

They cleaned every inch of him, including his ass and foreskin, and

Sanos was horrified to have another man's hands in so many places. The eunuchs said not a word to him, nor did they look him in the eye, as if they knew what they would find there and would rather not have to blatantly ignore it.

Once they dried him with fresh, warm towels, he thought that would be the worst of it, but a man wearing nothing but a scarlet skirt came into the room to examine him.

"What in the gods' names happened to your chest?"

Sanos looked down and saw the blank patches of chest hair. Since he was still gagged, it was clear that the man didn't expect an actual answer.

"Bring me the shears and the wax."

Sanos startled at that word. She'd threatened to take his beard. But surely they couldn't mean to—

They tied him to a slab of rock, arms outstretched, as some too-hot, thick substance was rubbed onto his chest. The man laid a cloth atop it.

"Brace yourself, Andrastus. This will hurt." Then the new man caught the cloth between his fingers and pulled.

Agony ripped through him.

The man in the skirt grabbed another section and pulled. Sanos was suddenly grateful for the gag; otherwise he'd likely bite off his own tongue.

Gods, but it hurt. Way worse than his birthday hair-ripping. This was fire. He'd swear it hurt worse than the time a sword tore through him during his first training practice with sharpened blades.

Uncontrollable tears ran down his cheeks, and it was only when they removed the gag that he realized what was next.

"If you put that gods-awful wax on my face, I swear I will gut you," Sanos said.

"The wax, My Prince, is only used on the chest. It doesn't grow back as quickly that way, you see. We will use a razor on your chin and testicles."

"My—"

The outrage was silenced as a thin blade was brought close to his throat. "If you don't wish to be cut, I suggest you hold very still."

He endured it. The cutting of his beard. The trimming of his intimate parts. What the hell was wrong with these women that they wanted their men naked as wee babes?

They threw more water over him to rinse off the trimmings, and he almost choked on it. Almost yelped as cold water was flung onto his cock and balls.

They dressed him in very little. Some sort of cloth that wrapped around his waist and tied at the side. A skirt. It was flimsy. White. Too exposing.

He hated everything about it.

The gag was replaced as he was escorted through hallways and stairways that he now managed to observe with a careful eye. Escape was his foremost concern, and he would memorize every passage they took him through, though the trip didn't take long.

They stopped at a bedroom.

Her bedroom, no doubt.

There was a grand bed more than big enough for two. An unlit hearth took up one wall, while a thick white rug was laid out before it. The room was strangely bare other than that, as though it had been recently gutted. Because of his arrival?

They didn't take him to the bed. No, they opened one of the many adjoining doors and brought him into a smaller room with an equally grand bed.

That was where they tied him, spread-eagle. Arms and legs secured to the posts with knots he didn't know how to form. He thought he might know what came next. That dreadful toxin that would render him paralyzed and harden his cock, but the eunuchs left him without so much as a word of farewell.

Sanos couldn't say how long he waited strapped to that bed. It was at least an hour. Perhaps two, and there was a horrid itch on his left foot that he couldn't reach.

When the door opened and *she* walked in, he ceased moving.

She was . . . different.

She'd bathed from their time on the road. Her hair was pulled half back, smoothed into some intricacy, and the rest fell around her shoulders in dark luscious waves. There was black ink around her eyes. Red paint on her lips. A hint of her breasts was exposed despite the robe she wore. The rest of her was a silhouette through the fine silk.

For some reason, his mouth watered, though he could barely swallow around the gag.

She approached slowly and touched his gag. "I'm going to remove this now, and you're not going to make any awful sounds. If you do, I will administer the vyra again. Do you understand?"

He nodded, and his body rose in temperature from the fervor of his hatred for this woman.

Olerra removed his gag and set it on the bedside table. She seated herself on the bed, and it dipped under her weight. She offered him a glass of water, tilting it to his mouth, and he was too thirsty to refuse it. When done, she drew her legs up onto the bed beside her, lounging like a queen as she settled herself back and observed him.

The look-over she gave him heated his blood, but he kept his anger to the forefront.

"If you can overpower me, then why am I tied to this bed?" he asked. If he could trick her into untying him, then he could attempt escaping. He was fast. Surely faster than her.

"Being unchained is a right you have not yet earned. As I said before. Good behavior is rewarded. Poor behavior is punished."

He swallowed. "The eunuchs? Is that what you do to men who misbehave?"

"Gods, no," she said, looking baffled by the question. "No, the men *choose* it. It is an honor to serve in the palace, one of the highest positions a common man can attain in Amarra. Many apply for the chance but few are chosen."

"They *apply* to lose their manhood?" He could not believe any man would choose that.

"Yes, it is a simple procedure, done under anesthetic. They don't feel a thing. They forsake sex for honor and wealth and high standing."

"This place is horrific."

She ran one hand over the soft cotton sheets, and Sanos wondered if she was still listening to the conversation at hand. Then she said, "I can see why you would think so, but I promise it's not. All will be well, Prince. You needn't fear." She lowered her eyes to his chest, taking in all his exposed skin.

His voice rang out like thunder. "Whatever you think is going to happen tonight, forget it. You will not touch me."

He ignored the excitement that mingled with his fury. That couldn't be helped and had *nothing* to do with her. He was used to going a year without sex. But tied up as he'd been for the past week, without the relief of his own hand?

He'd never gone more than a night or two without that.

And she was wearing transparent silk, for gods' sakes.

"Unlike the men in your country," she said, "I do not force myself upon those who do not wish it. You needn't fear that kind of violation from me, Andrastus."

"Then why are you dressed like that?"

She looked down at herself and even took a moment to admire the silk.

When she returned her gaze to his, he wasn't sure what look was there.

His breath stuttered out of him as she left the room, and he thought perhaps that was it.

But she returned a moment later, some sort of box in her hands.

"What is that?" he asked.

"So many questions . . . We could have covered all of this on the road had you not been so difficult. Do they not teach anything of the laws and customs of Amarra to you Brutish royals?"

They did. The Amarrans kidnapped men and made mockeries of them. Forced men to lie with them. And apparently cut parts of them off. What more could she possibly be referring to?

She took his silence as answer. "In Amarra, it is an offense punishable by death for a man to cause a woman to bleed. There are exceptions, of course. Accidents are often overlooked. Men in the army are given a pass during training. Injuries taken during battle don't count. The queen wouldn't have time for anything else if she had to track down every man who'd ever killed one of her soldiers."

"Death?" he echoed, catching on the most important word.

"Yes. You can see how the First Night must be treaded carefully."

"First Night?"

She rolled her eyes. "I had hoped you at least had some idea of what would happen between us tonight. No matter. I'll explain it as we do to our children once they start to mature. Do you know what happens to some women the first time they have sex?"

"They bleed," Sanos answered, not liking her tone. He wasn't stupid. Or inexperienced.

"You seemed to frequent brothels. I thought perhaps you'd never taken a virgin."

"I haven't. That doesn't mean I don't know about *sex*."

"It is hard to tell where the gaps in your knowledge lie."

"I know women."

"Just not our women, it would seem." Her eyes promised that would change.

It took him a moment before he finally put her words together. "You kill the men who bed virgins for making them bleed?"

"Yes," she said simply.

His eyes widened.

"If a man is patient and slow, he can perform the First Night without blood. But since most men are eager fools too intent on their own pleasure, we've found a way not to lose any more of the male population."

Then she opened the box and presented it to him. Sanos could not say what he expected to be contained within, but it certainly wasn't a dozen phalluses.

"What are those for?" he asked.

"Before a woman beds her first man, she can purchase such a kit to get the nasty business of widening her opening over with. Then she need not experience any pain nor bleed."

"Why would— You're a virgin?"

Her face didn't change. She said, "Obviously. Have you listened to nothing I've said?"

She set down the kit, walked forward until she was level with his waist, then drew off the skirt covering his nakedness with one swift tug.

He felt a twinge go through him at the stirring of cloth over sensitive flesh. Then he could do no more than stare at her staring at him. She didn't seem . . . surprised by the look of him. Or . . . impressed, as she'd been when examining his bulge on the road. Not that he wanted her to be impressed. He was large for a Brutish man—or so the women at the brothel had told him frequently. Wait, were they paid to say that?

"Why am I naked?" he asked.

"I need to gauge your size so that I might know the correct phallus to work myself up to."

Blood thundered in his ears, but he managed, "You said you wouldn't force me."

"And I won't. But it won't be long before you're ready. I had best be prepared for that eventuality."

"Cocksure, are you?"

"I don't have a cock, but I told you that it is only a matter of time before you want me, before you ache for me. That is a promise I intend to fulfill."

He hated the way she seemed so sure of the future. Like he was predictable. Sanos promised himself right then that no matter how long he was stuck on Amarran soil, he would not ask her. Even if he couldn't see to his own needs with his hand.

"I hate to break it to you, Princess, but my cock is much bigger when it's aroused."

"I know."

He wanted to know how she knew how cocks worked if she'd never bedded a man, but that wasn't foremost on his mind. No, it was her *plans* for the evening that most concerned him.

"Obviously," she said simply, "I need to see you aroused. Then I can select the correct phallus, and we'll be done for the evening, Prince."

They both looked down at the cock that was perfectly flaccid, and he laughed. "Good luck with that. I'm hungry, angry, and in pain from the tortures your men put me through." His chest still had a light pink tint to it. Then he stilled. "Don't give me that foul toxin again. I don't—"

"Shhh," she said gently.

Then she drew open her robe.

7

Andrastus cleaned up beautifully.

His hair-free chest was gorgeous: smooth and ridged and taut. Olerra wanted to splay her hands across it, but she refrained, knowing that kind of touch would be unwelcome.

She could see now why everyone called him pretty. The beard had hidden his perfectly sharp jaw. His chin jutted out slightly and had the tiniest divot in the center. She wanted to run her tongue over it.

Now clean-shaven, his eyes stood out more, those deep brown depths framed by dark blond lashes and thick brows. Before, he'd looked so stern. Now he appeared softer. Undeniably masculine, but beautiful, too.

She couldn't wait to kiss him again. This time without the beard.

Olerra stopped her thoughts before they got more out of control and focused on the task at hand. She wore an outfit that Ydra had picked out for her from the Pleasure Market. It hugged her curves and pulled up her breasts. Her legs were completely bare, as were her arms. She felt beautiful in it. She felt powerful as she watched Andrastus's eyes slide over every inch of her. But his cock did not so much as twitch.

She knew he would be tricky, but she'd been trained well. Learning to control a man was just as important for her tutors to teach her as arithmetic was.

She started by raising one arm slowly and letting down the rest of her hair. It pooled to her waist, still damp in some places from the bath she'd taken earlier. She ran her fingers along her scalp, then through her hair. She threw it over her shoulders so he could see her figure clearly.

Olerra slid one strap over her shoulder. Then did the same to the other. Keeping her eyes on his, she drew a finger down her own breast over the top of her clothing, drawing a circle over where her nipple rested.

"That'll only get you aroused, not me," Andrastus said, though his voice wasn't as harsh as it had been during the rest of the evening.

She said, in the most seductive voice she could manage, "I'm imagining it's you touching me."

There. That interested his cock.

She palmed herself. Both breasts at the same time. She went slowly, touching herself the way she'd always dreamed a man would someday. The way this man would someday. It felt delicious, and she let a little pant escape her mouth.

His cock twitched again, and Olerra began to undo the laces at her front, exposing more of her breasts and her belly to him. She stopped just shy of her hips.

She pulled out her right breast, showed him how hard the nipple was and watched in satisfaction as he gritted his teeth. What was once flaccid was less and less so by the second.

Andrastus slammed his eyes closed, as if that would stop what was happening to him. Clearly he didn't like that she could get to him like this, and she loved that she could.

"Did you know, my breasts are so large that I can lick the nipples with my own tongue?"

He gasped as his eyes wrenched open.

"Show me," he demanded.

She raised her breast with her hand, bringing it to her mouth and flicking out her tongue.

That's when he lost the fight. When he must have decided that losing was winning. For his cock jutted upward, coming to full attention.

But she wasn't done. For while she'd never had a man before, she knew how to please herself just fine. She shirked out of the straps completely and let the garment pool at her hips.

"The rest of it," he barked. "Take the rest of it off now."

She cocked her head to the side. "Do you want me to take you now? Are you ready to beg so soon?"

He closed his eyes again, clearly trying to gain some modicum of control when he had already lost. Let him do what he liked. She was taunting him, of course. She wouldn't follow through with it no matter what he said. She wasn't ready for him yet. That was the whole purpose of tonight.

Olerra gauged the appropriate phallus size and marked it with her eye.

Now she wanted to come.

Olerra slid her hand under the remaining fabric and stroked her seam. She was wetter than usual. Something about the sight of him wanting her made her even more excited. Her clit throbbed, and she wasted no more time before letting her fingers drift where she wanted them.

She gasped, eyes on his manhood, and Andrastus lost the battle and opened his again.

"Fuck," he said at what he saw. He could not see her sex, as it was still covered by the lingerie, but there could be little doubt as to what her hand was doing.

Her eyes rose to his as she found a rhythm that pleased her. She angled her hips so she could move with her fingers. Every brush of her clit was like fire through her body, and she could feel the end coming sooner than usual.

"Slow down," he demanded of her. "It'll be over too—"

She whimpered as release coursed through her. It was brief, but it cleared her head and reminded her of who was in charge here.

Olerra picked up the correct phallus and showed it to him. "A fine likeness, don't you think?"

He glared at her. Just glared at her.

"Have a good night," she said to him, turning.

"You're not leaving me here like this?"

"Like what?" she asked, stopping by the door. "Aroused? Strapped to the bed? Yes, I am. You don't get to come unless it is by my hands, Andrastus. You will not touch yourself, unless it is by my instruction. Only when you're a good boy will you get what you yearn for. Sleep well."

And she left him just as he was. Hard and unsatiated.

Back in her own room, Olerra stared at the phallus. It was large. Not the largest in the kit, but certainly not the smallest. She was going to have to fit this inside her if she wanted to fully claim her man.

And, oh, how she wanted that. When she'd first captured him, she'd thought the breadth of his body too big, the planes of him too hard. But seeing him naked and aroused had changed something. She saw how things could be between them in the bedroom. And she wanted that future.

Someday she wanted to procreate with him, too. Their babies would be so strong and solid. Absolutely beautiful.

She just had to get him to consent to letting her bed him. It was only a matter of time. She would have him eating out of the palm of her hand soon enough.

Olerra used her nondominant hand to reach for her opening, measuring the distance with her fingers before comparing it to the phallus before her.

It definitely wasn't going to fit yet.

Still, she was determined to try. She lay on her back atop her bed. She was still wet from the previous orgasm, so that would help. It also helped knowing that Andrastus was just one door away, aroused and likely still thinking about her.

She put the head to her opening and had to bite her lip as she applied pressure.

Fuck, it hurt, and if she pushed any harder, she would likely tear her skin. She drew the phallus away. Then massaged her aching flesh.

Olerra pitied the women born in Brutus. The way her teachers taught it, men shoved their members into unready openings on women's First Nights. They didn't wait for them to be wet. Nor did they take the time to help them stretch over weeks to prepare. Women's openings came in all different sizes, and it was foolish of men to think that just because something felt good to them that it felt good to the woman. How many women bled for men who didn't do them the courtesy of adhering to women's pain over their own pleasure? It made her angry. It reminded her that the Brutes didn't deserve courtesy or kindness. She hoped Andrastus would be different.

It was also unfair. Men got to have sex all the livelong day without experiencing any pain, but women had to first endure this.

Olerra returned to the box, picked a much smaller phallus, and tried again. This one stretched her as she applied pressure, and it hurt, but it wasn't so bad that she couldn't stand it. She did as her tutors suggested, counting to ten and then pulling the phallus out to relax her flesh for another ten. Then applying the phallus once more.

She kept at this for perhaps five minutes. Then she washed both phalluses before returning them to her kit. She used the chamber pot despite not feeling as though she had to urinate—she was taught to always relieve herself after a phallus or cock was inside her to stave off unwanted infections.

The eunuchs had drawn her a bath with boiling water while she was in Andrastus's room, and the water was now cooled down enough to soak. She lowered herself and felt her body relax. She needed it. She still had a lot of work ahead of her.

Olerra had to woo her soon-to-be husband. But first, she had to teach him some manners. He hadn't responded well to her teachings on the road, so now they were going to try things the hard way.

Olerra woke as the sun did. Since she wasn't going to be training with her soldiers today, she opted for a cream-colored tunic that hung to mid-thigh and a pair of tight shorts underneath in the same color, to avoid the chafing from her thighs rubbing together. A belt cinched around her waist, from which her weapons hung. She was one of the few in the country who had mastered the complicated whipblade, which had a sharp blade attached to the end of a long rope. She also wore a sword on her other side for close-quarters combat. She didn't bother with her helmet. Only when she took a shift on guard duty or went into battle did she wear one. Even when she knew her cousin was resorting to sending assassins after her.

She hadn't any proof that the past two attempts on her life were ordered by her cousin, so there was no point in bringing it up with her aunt. And given the fact that Olerra was the best fighter in her kingdom, she wasn't going to lose sleep over it.

She'd tell Andrastus about it if it ever became necessary. He was already overburdened with the newness of this place. She didn't think his mind could withstand much more stress.

Servants prepared Andrastus for her. He was wearing his new palace clothes, which she could tell he hated the moment she laid eyes on him.

The shirt was white and lightweight with a long sleeve on the right and no sleeve on the left, as all his clothing was designed to show his left bicep. The top of the exposed shoulder was a little red from riding shirtless through the city yesterday. The eunuchs would have already treated it, though. The neckline of Andrastus's shirt went clear down to his navel, showing off hints of his pectorals and the ripples of muscle going down his abdomen. The redness from the waxing was gone, but she assumed the skin would still be tender. She had a hard time feeling any sympathy for him, considering the pain she'd had to endure last night.

Besides, too much hair on a man was unhygienic.

The leather shorts were tight from the ass to mid-thigh. They accentuated the curves of his muscles and the bulge in the front. The sandals went clear up to his knees, framing his strong calves.

He looked Amarran now, and she loved that. There was only one thing missing.

Olerra retrieved a box from her bedside table. Inside rested the armband she'd had made for him. It was forged of pure silver, the ends twisting into a swirling design at the top and bottom. A single teardrop onyx hung down in the center.

His eyes locked with hers as she approached. For some reason, he didn't resist as she slipped the armband onto his left hand, sliding it upward until it fit snug just above his bicep.

She loved the way it looked on him, almost as much as the way it marked him as hers.

"It looks perfect on you," she said.

"What is it?" he asked.

"Protection. As long as you wear this, no one in Amarra will dare to touch you or hurt you."

"But what is it?"

"It is an armband; husbands and harem members wear them."

"I'm not marrying you," he said, defiance creeping into his voice once more. He tried to reach for the armband, but the eunuchs leaped forward to stop him. One brought a pair of padded manacles for him to wear. Another had a similar set, slightly bigger. The first was meant for his wrists while the other went around his ankles. Andrastus tried to fight them off.

"You will let them put on the manacles or you will go without breakfast, too."

That didn't seem to motivate him to stop wriggling out of their grasp like a beached fish. Olerra began to worry. She *could not* take him to breakfast if he behaved like this. She tried instead, "Let them put on the manacles, and I will forgo the gag today."

That got through to him. His body stilled as he looked to her over all the eunuchs attempting to restrain him.

"They should be much more comfortable than what you had to wear on our trip to Amarra. These were designed for comfortable bedroom play. Not pain. They are merely a precaution."

"I am a prince, yet you would parade me about in chains?"

"You're not cooperating, Andrastus, which means you will be treated like a prisoner instead of a guest. Leave us," she said to the eunuchs once he was properly secured.

When it was just the two of them, she forced her posture to remain calm. He didn't know she wasn't stronger than he was. He knew she was a trained general. She could very likely take him even if it came to a fight. The only risk was him learning her secret.

Your way isn't working, Ydra had said.

Her sister-chosen was right. Olerra needed to try another approach to taming Andrastus. Some misbehavior was expected of husbands who were taken from their homes. Olerra's strength would come through as she showed the court how she could handle him. However, if he behaved as poorly as he had on the road, she would have to discipline him severely and publicly or risk appearing weak. She didn't want to hurt him. She couldn't risk him stepping too far out of line. It would ruin their relationship before it could even begin. Worse yet, it could reveal her secret if he overpowered her.

She used the voice she used with her troops. "I'm going to be honest with you, Andrastus. I only took you because I need a husband if I'm to rule Amarra one day. While I have the queen's favor, my cousin is adored by many of the nobles, since she spends all her time kissing their asses. It is a majority vote of the nobles that determines the next queen, so let me put this simply. If I'm not made crown princess, I have no use for you. If you don't behave, you will die."

His face went slack, but she pressed on.

"Good, I see I have your attention. When I am named crown princess, we don't have to live like this." She gestured to the door adjoining their rooms. "You won't have to be so close to me or such a reminder to the people of my dominance. You can go about your own life as you see fit. Perhaps even return to Brutus if that is your desire. But I need to win the favor of the nobility, and I need you to do it."

He didn't speak for a moment. Then, "Why do you need me?"

"We Amarrans value strength. Dominance. Fighting ability. By taking you, I proved myself. The hardest part is yet ahead of me, though. I have to show the court that I can manage you, exert my dominance. Our relationship doesn't really need to be that way. I just need for it to appear as though we are that way. Do you understand?"

He drew his eyes together. "You need me to pretend that I'm docile and subservient to you so that you can become queen?"

"That's right."

"Then what the hell was last night about?"

Olerra delighted in the way his cheeks reddened as he spoke. "I'm still holding out hope that things can be . . . amicable between us. I want to be ready for when they are. Besides, we're going to be married. It isn't legitimate unless it's consummated." Of course, she wouldn't take him if he really didn't want it, but she hoped to get him thinking about the idea.

"There will be *nothing* between us," he spat. "And I don't care about your politics or future."

"You don't need to care about that, but I'm counting on you caring enough to save your own skin. Your life is on the line, Andrastus, so make me proud." She paused. "Do you care for your people? The common Brutes?"

"Of course I do. It is my job as a royal to care for them and see to their well-being."

"Then you understand that I must be harsh with you for the sake of mine. My cousin is not a good person. She will run the common people of Amarra into the ground to pamper the royals and nobility. She is cruel and self-serving. I would see my kingdom happy and thriving, from the poorest pauper to the richest courtier. Male and female and everyone in between and outside of the binary. I am the only option that does that. Therefore, I must become queen."

She didn't bother to tell him the other part. The more important part. That she *needed* to be queen. Olerra had to prove her worth when the goddess didn't think her worthy of her Gift. To prove she was the best.

Also, she deserved it. She'd worked her ass off to be Amarra's best fighter while hiding her secret.

"I do not care for Amarra's people," Andrastus said, "but I will not give you cause to execute me."

"Good. Then you behave, and we will both be just fine. Now," she continued, "we went over this on the road, so this should only be a refresher. This is how today is going to be. You go where I go. You will follow a step behind me at all times. If, for any reason, I should touch you in an amorous way in public, you are to return the sentiment. With enthusiasm. Look at me as though you dote on me. Do not speak unless spoken to or unless you are directing a question to me. Look like you're happy to be here. Look honored to have been chosen by me. You should be, you know. I am the most eligible and soon-to-be powerful woman in the world. Mothers have been trying to wed their sons to me since I was fifteen."

"Then why am I here?" he asked. "Why not settle on some gentle, pretty boy from Amarra?"

"For starters, I was led to believe you were far prettier and gentler than you are, but I suppose that the men of your kingdom are so terrible that you are what passes for both. Don't give me that look, Andrastus. I do find you pleasing. Furthermore, I need a nobleman to help strengthen my own line. There are many ways to gain favor in the eyes of the nobility and the people. The potential for noble heirs is one. Making myself a strong political candidate is another. And the final is to show how my men respect and obey me."

"Men?" he hedged, catching on the plural.

"I only have one for now," she said.

"What do you mean *for now?*" he asked, but she'd grown tired of the conversation and began to move.

Olerra was relieved to hear him following her from the room. The chains clinked faintly as he walked. She kept her pace slow so he could follow even with the shackles.

"These clothes are ridiculous," he said from behind her.

"They match your protests, don't you think?"

"I think you're a fool for taking me. My father—"

"Has too many sons. Think of all the good you'll do uniting our kingdoms. Even you can see the benefits of ceasing the fighting between our people. Since you're so badly losing. Now, stand up straight. Flex whenever you notice a woman looking at you. Always smile."

"Flex and smile," he deadpanned.

"That's right." Gods, he really wasn't listening on the road.

The prince went quiet, and Olerra assumed he was taking in the palace. Escape must be foremost on his mind. He would be memorizing routes to and from every location they traversed and looking for doors that led outside. Olerra said nothing, instead looking at her favorite portraits. One depicted the first queen of Amarra as she held up her hands to the heavens, asking the goddess to end her suffering. The story was five hundred years old, and while it had been told throughout the ages, the queen's name was lost to time. She was instead referred to as Amarra's Chosen.

A tapestry detailed the first battle with the Brutes, taking place along the Fren River. Horses carried their riders through the water, and as the cavalry struck the enemy foot soldiers, the current swept them away.

Weapons throughout the ages hung from hooks on the walls. Special pieces from real battles were encased in glass. The Amarrans loved art, and war was the form they were the best at.

As they walked, Olerra listened for any telling movements from

Andrastus. She knew the thought of getting the better of her from behind had to have crossed his mind. He could take a step, throw those manacled arms over her head and be at her throat.

But there were guards spaced evenly along the corridor. If he attempted to kill her, it would mean a swift death for him. He must have been self-serving enough not to attempt it.

What a relief.

8

A servant greeted them as Olerra strode into the breakfast room. Usually, she preferred to eat with her soldiers, but for the foreseeable future she needed to be seen by important people in court. More important, her prince needed to be shown off.

Olerra prayed he would behave as she looked over her shoulder to see if Andrastus was keeping apace with her. His eyes were as round as eggs as he took in the room.

Finely dressed women were seated all around the table, their men standing behind them or curled up at their feet. The men all had their armbands on full display, the design meant to show which woman had claimed each. Most men wore matching jewelry in other places. Earrings, necklaces, nipple clamps, other piercings. They were done up in various amounts of makeup, from kohl-rimmed eyes to glitter in their hair.

Olerra hadn't bothered with makeup for Andrastus yet. Mostly because she was too worried he'd smudge it on purpose. Baby steps.

"Behave," she whispered to him, "and I won't ever have to put another gag on you. It would be a shame anyway. That mouth is too pretty not to have out on full display."

He seemed startled by her flirtatious words, but she didn't retract them. His lips were the perfect color of pink. They looked darker when compared to his ivory skin and near-white hair.

Focus, she told herself.

Ydra intercepted them. Olerra was relieved to see that she'd shown up. Unlike the rest of the noblewomen, she didn't bring boys from her harem to court. In fact, Ydra's harem was the least traditional of the bunch.

Andrastus had a scowl for Olerra's second-in-command, but once Olerra touched his arm, he turned the scowl on her.

"Remember," she said. "Smiles and flexing. Your life is on the line. Make me proud today."

Andrastus had a pained grin for Ydra, and Ydra rolled her lips under her teeth, trying not to laugh at him.

"Well met, Prince," she said. "I didn't know you knew how to smile."

"I'm still not certain he does," Olerra said.

Andrastus's jaw clenched.

"I do not envy the work ahead of you," Ydra said to Olerra. "Oh, and before I forget, remember the matter you wanted me to look into?"

Olerra was staring at Andrastus's left bicep. She wanted to run her finger over the armband but knew that she was already walking a fine line with him after last night. And her instructions for today.

"Hmm?" she responded. Gods, it was so hard to focus with him dressed like this. She wasn't prepared for this level of attraction to her soon-to-be husband. She would just need to stop looking at him.

Olerra turned her attention to Ydra.

"Daneryn has returned from his travels. He's here."

"What?" she exclaimed. "Why? When?"

"It would seem—"

Ydra was cut off by the appearance of none other than Daneryn himself. He was alone, though his mother must be in the room somewhere if he was permitted at the queen's breakfast table. He was taller and broader than when last she'd seen him a couple of years ago. He had light brown skin, just a shade lighter than his mother's. His head was covered in brushed-out black curls, each one perfectly shaped. His eyes were bright green.

And they were looking at Olerra with such hurt that she almost looked away.

Daneryn spoke first, a bold move that was outside the bounds of propriety. She allowed it this once.

"Princess," he said. "I heard of your latest skirmish with the Brutes. Congratulations on another victory."

"Thank you, Daneryn."

"I am relieved to see you unharmed."

Olerra tried not to roll her eyes. The only reason Daneryn wanted her unharmed was because he'd wanted her for himself for years.

The son of a countess, Daneryn was twenty-two years old. He was also the *only* nobleman of Amarra over the age of twenty. During the coup led by Glen's father, the queen's own brother, Daneryn was fortunate to have been studying abroad with his sister, a rare opportunity afforded to a man. As he was absent from the court and none of his direct relatives had been involved in the revolt, he was innocent of having any hand in it.

But the son of a countess held no interest for Olerra, not when she could have a prince. Besides, she always knew she would need to kidnap a husband, like her mother before her. Daneryn was the easier route and would not show her strength to the nobles.

When he'd returned from his studies a couple of years ago, Daneryn had immediately set his sights on Olerra for two simple reasons. She was the highest-ranking woman in his kingdom he could marry, and she wasn't so cruel as her cousin.

Olerra had liked the attention, but she hadn't been ready to get close to anyone and risk her secret. So Daneryn had left for more studies and sightseeing.

Until now, it would seem.

When Daneryn looked at Andrastus, his eyes nearly watered, and Olerra wondered if she'd misunderstood how genuine his affections truly were. Either that or he was an excellent actor. She really should find out more about those studies he'd had abroad.

"You said you weren't ready to marry when last we spoke," he said, lowering his voice.

"I wasn't."

"But now you are? You've taken a *Brute*? One of the very men you've been fighting against for so much of your time as general?"

Andrastus seemed interested in the conversation, and she didn't like that one bit. Olerra decided being nice wasn't getting the job done. She hardened her voice. "I am a princess, and I will choose whomever I see fit."

"It's not too late. You haven't wed him yet. Wed *me*, Olerra. I would be better to you than this ill-tempered man. Keep him for your harem if you must, but I am the best choice for husband, and everyone knows it. Look at how he's fidgeting with those manacles. Olerra, I would be *honored* to wear your chains. I've ached for your onyx on my arm since the day I could perform."

As declarations of love went, it wasn't bad. However, Daneryn was beginning to draw the attention of more people around the table.

"If I ever decide I want to have this conversation with you, Daneryn, it will be in private. Not near a breakfast table where all can hear. Do not accost me like this again or I won't be so lenient. Do you understand?"

His head fell. "Yes, Princess. My humblest apologies. Is there any way I might serve you today?"

Andrastus looked sickened now. Daneryn's submissiveness was truly abhorrent to him.

It would have pleased any other woman, but Olerra knew Daneryn was a social climber. The second he found out about her lack of goddess-given power, he would tell the highest bidder. Andrastus might do the same thing, except she held his freedom over him like a knife. He was the better choice.

"No, Daneryn. You are dismissed. Do not seek me out again."

The man walked off, his shoulders drooping with disappointment.

"What the hell was that?" Andrastus asked.

"Nothing," Olerra said. Then she hooked her arm around one of his and began to lead him in a slow walk around the grand table. Olerra didn't stop until they came upon four older women, conveniently seated together.

While the entirety of the nobility held Olerra's future in their hands, it was really only four individuals whose favor she had to garner, as they held the most sway over the rest. The first was a lost cause, being that she was Glenaerys's mother. Shaelwyn obviously wanted her daughter to be queen. As the richest woman in Amarra, she had huge sway over the nobility and their votes.

The second was Enadra, who was the former general over Amarra's armies. Being older than many of the other nobles, she garnered respect from the masses. She'd trained and fought with Olerra her whole life, and so Olerra already had her vote.

Then there were the two wild cards. Cyssia, who was childhood best friends with the three royal siblings: the queen, Olerra's mother, and Glen's father. Having an attachment to all of them meant that she wasn't swayed to either cousin's side yet.

Finally there was Usstra, who had her hand in a lot of pockets. There wasn't a soul in Amarra she didn't know. Aside from being well-connected, she was also a great source of information to the spy networks. How Usstra knew what she did, no one knew. Nor did anyone know which of the cousins she was favoring.

Olerra tried to gauge their reactions to Andrastus. Shaelwyn's sneer was to be expected. The others were considering. Good. There was still time to win more of them over.

She winked at Shaelwyn, because she knew it would irritate her. To the others, she said, "I'll catch you for breakfast another time. For today, the queen has first rights to meet him."

And they continued on.

Sanos knew he was being shown off. There was no other reason to circle the room. Olerra wasn't taking him anywhere. No, she paused when women oohed at him and adjusted him as she liked. Moving his arms to flex his muscles. Changing the angle of his neck. Giving everyone in the room a spectacle. No one halted their conversation, but they were all riveted.

When they stopped at the head of the table, before the woman who must be the queen, Olerra took his chin in one hand and tipped it up.

He couldn't take it anymore. Sanos jerked from her grip and tried to step back.

Olerra responded by pinching his nipple. Hard.

He felt that pressure travel all the way down his body. It made him both shiver and frown at her. He *hated* the way this woman affected him.

"Soften your brow." She placed a finger over the V between his eyes.

"Stop fucking touching me."

"We're almost done. *Behave.*"

Oh, but he *loathed* the way she barked orders at him. He felt his temper sweep over him and push aside all sense of self-preservation. Sanos took a swing at her, trying to connect the hard metal at his wrist with her jaw.

She ducked so quickly that he lost sight of her. And then pain shot through his groin; it was so acute that it drove him to the floor.

As he struggled to breathe, Sanos realized that *she'd punched him*. There!

Women giggled as she dragged him by the chains around his ankles, but Sanos could barely register that, as the pain was all-consuming. When water stopped forming at his eyes, he saw her wave away a handful of eunuchs who tried to step forward to help.

She let go of the shackles and bent to be at his level. "Are you done?"

"I will never stop fighting you," he barked.

She reached behind herself, grabbed a knife from the breakfast table, and leveled it at his neck.

Now the room was quiet. Everyone strained to overhear their conversation.

"Perhaps you thought my earlier words were an exaggeration. You have a choice to make, Prince. I can spill all your blood on this floor or you can mind your manners and enjoy breakfast with me. Choose."

With all the Amarran nobility watching, Sanos could only surmise that she was telling the truth. She would really kill him if he didn't go along with her plans. It wasn't necessarily that he'd doubted her words earlier, but he hadn't thought her capable of disciplining him here, in front of everyone. All the beatings from his father were dealt in private. The king didn't want anyone to know what a hateful bastard he was.

But Olerra was different. She had felled him with a single blow for all to see, and now she held a knife to his throat.

Sanos wanted to demand death. He wanted to fight her until one of them succumbed to the other, but then he thought of his mother and sister. Of his brothers. So many needed him to return home.

He needed to live.

Sanos raised his hands in surrender, but his lip curled in disgust. Olerra stepped back and gestured at an empty chair with the knife.

He peeled himself off the floor and sat. Olerra drew a key from her pocket, undid his manacles, and reattached them behind the back of the chair.

He wasn't going anywhere now.

When Olerra righted herself, she looked about the room. "They say the most dangerous stallions are the best to ride once they're broken."

The room erupted into laughter. Sanos did not care for the comparison.

"And since I know you're all dying to ask me, I'll tell you now." She looked at Sanos beneath her lashes. "The rumors about Brutish men are true."

The Amarrans whistled and clapped. Sanos had no clue what rumors they spoke of, and by the reaction of the crowd, he wasn't sure he wanted to know. He looked around at the other men in the room, searching for a sympathetic face.

He found none.

They looked at their women adoringly. One was petting the armband above his left bicep.

Sanos realized that all the men in the room wore armbands. The ornamentation consisted of all manner of stones cut into different shapes. Different metals twining around arms, each bent into unique designs.

The man from earlier, Daneryn, had said something about wanting to wear Olerra's onyx. As Sanos looked through the masses, he didn't see any other men with onyx on their arms.

It was a mark that made him hers, he realized.

Olerra caught the look of approval her aunt shot her way. Olerra was also proud of herself. Not only had she managed to fight Andrastus without anyone suspecting her secret, she'd played off the altercation to her favor.

She'd thought that if Andrastus resisted her, it would make her look weak. Instead, it allowed her to show her strength in taming him. It would take time, but she actually might pull this off. She could do this.

She just wished the words she'd had to say to the crowd hadn't been at her betrothed's expense. He wasn't a stallion. He was a man, and she knew that. His gender as a whole might be full of disappointments, especially outside of Amarra, but Andrastus deserved better treatment. Not for the first time, Olerra hated the part she had to play in rallying the nobles to her side. She knew why. Men had to be controlled or else they would seek to control women. Little girls were told horror stories of the way their ancestors had lived under the rule of men.

But there had to be a better way. One she could explore once she was finally queen.

Until then, she had a part to play while convincing Andrastus to like her. If she even could. Right now, he was so irate that he wouldn't look at her.

That changed the moment she lowered herself into his lap.

Olerra felt his whole body stiffen, but at least his tautness meant he was flexing. As she looked to the curve of a bicep, she realized it was enormous compared to that of other men at the table. She'd thought the measurements impressive when she'd given them to the smithy last night. The blacksmith had stayed up all night to make this armband in time. Olerra hadn't realized the size difference until Sanos was here for her to compare to the other men.

Just what kind of training had Andrastus done to get this kind of form? And what did his other brothers look like? Especially the eldest? The warrior?

"I would ask how you two are getting along, but I think I already know," the queen said.

Olerra looked up at her man and ran a hand down his hard jaw, trying to soften the expression there. "We're working on it."

"How was your first night together?"

Andrastus's face didn't move as she said, "Delicious."

That fair skin of his couldn't hide the red tint that entered his cheeks. She'd never seen another man blush before. Were they so prudish in Brutus? She rather liked seeing how she affected him.

"Excellent. I think you'll find that your decision is well supported among your allies in the palace. Even your cousin seemed upset by the whole thing."

"Good."

As though their talking summoned the woman, Glenaerys appeared, one man on each arm. She stared at the noblewoman seated across from Olerra until the duchess took the hint and vacated it. Olerra's cousin had one man sit at her feet while the other stood behind her, massaging her shoulders. They were both lean and handsome, but they blended in with all the other men in the room. Perfectly housebroken. Almost too pretty to look at. Too smooth for Olerra's tastes. She liked that her prince had calluses and scars and a bit more roughness to him. It made him stand out. It made women turn their heads.

"How was your trip to *Brutus*, cousin?" Glenaerys asked. "So strange, I could have sworn you'd told me you were going to Kalundir."

"Did I? I must have misspoken."

Glen looked furious. Olerra tried not to look smug.

Glenaerys glanced over Olerra's shoulder. "Do you find him more pleasing when he's all bound up, or have you not managed to convince him he wants to be here?"

Without missing a beat, Olerra said, "I didn't pay money for him. I took him. Which means breaking him will actually be a challenge. I like challenges."

Glenaerys's perfect nose scrunched at the implied insult.

"Speaking of which," the queen said, "when can we expect you to make designs on a husband of your own, Glenaerys?"

"When one is needed. Honestly, with all my nighttime activities, you'd think I'd be with child by now."

The man sitting in between her legs looked up at her with a grin.

"Really, I've far more chances of getting pregnant than Olerra does with only one man seeing to her."

Andrastus froze underneath her yet again. She felt him pull at the manacles behind his chair.

Olerra lowered her hand to his thigh, hoping it was a reassuring touch. He didn't jerk away, so she left it there.

The queen said, "At least Olerra will soon have a husband to oversee any children such a union will produce. Who will raise your common-born children, Glenaerys? Your whores?"

"Why not? They're naturally loving."

The man behind her applied more pressure to a knot in her back. The one at her feet stroked up and down her calf.

"They're uneducated," Queen Lemya said.

"Good thing I can afford tutors, then. And nursemaids and playmates and anything else my daughters may need. Now, why is the conversation all about me? I personally want to hear more about Olerra's soon-to-be husband. What does an uncivilized Brute think of the Amarran palace?"

Olerra had to nudge Andrastus before he realized her cousin was addressing him.

"It's different than I'm used to."

"Grander, you mean?"

His jaw clenched. "Different."

"He's not very talkative, is he? What do they teach the men over in Brutus?"

The question was clearly rhetorical, yet Andrastus said, "How to be warriors." He looked at the two docile men seeing to Glenaerys with disdain.

"Oh, is *that* where your true skills lie? Not in pleasing your mistress but in fighting? What a useless skill since Olerra would offer you more protection than you ever could her."

He didn't respond, so Olerra said, "I like that he's a warrior. He has more stamina than the average man from Amarra." That earned her a few claps of approval down the table, as well as another blush from Andrastus.

Glenaerys's face took on a wicked gleam. "Let's put that warrior claim to the test. Why not have a bout between your new man and one of mine?"

9

The room went quiet as Olerra considered the question. For some reason, she didn't seem to like the idea, which baffled Sanos. He was an excellent fighter. Not that he had any desire to show her. To have her *approve* of him. He was still of half a mind to strangle her with these manacles, the guards and witnesses be damned.

But then he remembered that she thought him his younger, poetry-loving brother. She'd meant to take fucking Andrastus, who was likely shitting himself trying to figure out how to take on the temporary role of heir while Sanos was missing.

If Sanos was going to get out of this horrid mess, he first had to get out of these damned manacles. That meant pleasing Olerra. Surely winning this proposed fight was a good step in the right direction.

He leaned his lips down to her ear.

"I'll do it," he whispered. "I'll win for you."

She met his gaze, before her eyes roved over the muscles that could be seen through his outfit. He didn't know why she deliberated so carefully, but in the end she said, "Done. Andrastus will face any man from your harem you choose."

"Excellent," Glenaerys replied. "I shall have it all set up by this afternoon. The whole court should witness the display."

Sanos didn't understand Olerra's hatred of her cousin. As far as he could tell, she was a beauty who thought highly of herself. Not someone so dangerous or troublesome as Olerra had made her out to be.

Glenaerys went rigid, yelled, "Ouch," then turned and struck the man massaging her across the face. He fell down to his knees, but it was hard to tell what was from the force of the blow versus the natural reaction of the whore to go to his knees before her.

"Forgive me, mistress."

"I shall," she said, not missing a beat. "Tonight after the lash."

"Yes, mistress. Thank you, mistress."

Had he just thanked her for being sentenced to a lashing?

"You," Glenaerys said, pointing to the one on the floor. "Finish my massage."

The men immediately swapped places, and Olerra's cousin took to running her fingers through the hair of the man who had worked at a knot in her back in a way she didn't like. It was not difficult to see that she occasionally pulled his hair. Hard. Just because she could.

Sanos didn't want to imagine the kind of tortures she made the men withstand in her bedroom.

When Sanos had agreed to fight for Olerra, he hadn't realized the scale of what her cousin had planned. They were outdoors, the sun shining down on the faces of countless women packed into an amphitheater that had to house around a thousand. There were clearly more than just the nobility who'd come out to watch. How could the people in the farthest stands even see him? Why would they want to see him? And how had Glenaerys gotten word out so fast?

Olerra waved at a gathering of women dressed in armor with strange helmets and red-tipped spears. Women she fought with? Was the entire blasted army here to witness him fight off some pretty bedroom boy?

He knew this wouldn't be the most elegant thing he'd ever done. Battling a whore for sport.

Then he reminded himself that this was what other people thought he was to Olerra. They thought she was bedding him and would continue to do so up until their wedding day, which he'd overheard would be some three months from now.

That was how long he had until escape became vital.

"Be careful," Olerra said to him from where they stood on the outskirts of some sort of fighting ring at the center of the audience. "It was trouble enough taking you. I'd hate to find myself a new husband."

She said it with a smile, as though she were joking or he were a joke to her.

"Afraid I'll mar my pretty face?" he asked. "Be unsuitable for your bedroom activities?"

She stepped up to him, looked him carefully in the eye. "Our bedroom activities have yet to begin. Would you like to change that?"

"Apparently," he said carefully, "there is someone else who would like to participate in your bedroom activities."

She cocked her head to the side. "Are you jealous?"

He did not dignify that with a response.

"I'll admit there were times when I was flattered by Daneryn's attention, but I've put a stop to it. He won't approach me like that again. He is a power-climber, and I will not be his ladder."

"You'd rather step on me instead," Sanos said.

"I would not step on you. I would have you rise with me until we are both gloriously untouchable."

He looked pointedly at his chains.

"Right," she said. "Best take these off for now. Though it would be humorous to watch you try to fight with them." She was clearly ignoring his intended meaning on purpose, but Sanos didn't press for now. Not when she removed the key from some hidden pocket of her tunic and undid first the lock of the shackles at his feet. Then the manacles at his wrists.

He was unbound for the first time since arriving in this horrible kingdom.

And he could do nothing. Not with nearly a thousand spectators watching. With hundreds of guards surrounding this place in case . . . what? The spectators got out of hand? Were all the women so bloodthirsty?

"Undress," Olerra said.

"What?" he asked, certain he'd misheard her.

"Disrobe," she said, as though perhaps he was too stupid to understand what the first word meant.

And then with horror he noted the naked man standing in the fighting ring, waiting for him.

"I'm to battle *naked*?" he asked.

"Of course. That is the way of wrestling, is it not?"

"In front of other men. Not *women*."

"Well, the only people of importance here are women. Now strip, Andrastus, before you forfeit the match."

He must have been taking too long, because Glenaerys showed up. "What's the matter, Olerra? Having second thoughts once you noted my pick?"

Olerra turned toward the man standing in the ring, and all the color left her cheeks. Sanos focused on Glenaerys's pick for the fight, wondering if he'd missed something during his first perusal. The man was massive. Much bigger than Sanos, though nowhere near his father's proportions. Glen's man was covered in scars, as though fighting were something he did for a living. Sanos wasn't scared, though. He regularly bested men bigger than he was.

Except for his father.

"What is Athon doing here?" Olerra asked.

"You haven't heard?" Glenaerys asked. "We've been courting."

"Since when?"

"About a day after you left to kidnap the Brute."

Sanos may not have been an expert in Amarran customs, but he knew politics. Whatever the reason for Glen courting Athon, it was strategic. Olerra's face showed it. She was visibly upset.

Why?

Olerra glared at her cousin. "Always games with you."

"I'm just too good at winning them. Now hurry it up. The prince still has to get oiled."

"*Oiled?*" Sanos caught on that word with horror.

Glenaerys raised one perfect blond brow. "Shall we call it off?"

"No," Olerra barked. Then she reached over and literally ripped the shirt from Sanos's shoulders. He was disgusted by the look Glenaerys gave him. The way she bit her lip as she admired the sight of his bare torso. He realized the tight shorts were doing him fewer favors on than they would off.

So he slipped out of them until he was standing in nothing, save the armband.

The crowd *roared*.

Sanos nearly jolted. He'd almost forgotten the crowd while observing the exchange between the two royal cousins.

But the masses had taken notice of his state of undress immediately, even though he wasn't on the stage yet. They applauded. They screamed. They shouted praises at him.

He was the heir of Brutus, and he stood in an amphitheater bursting at the seams with women—without a stitch of clothing on.

It should have been mortifying, but Sanos couldn't manage the proper emotion with the way everyone was cheering for him. Rooting for him.

He was the obvious favorite of the crowd, who hadn't applauded for Glen's man.

It didn't go unnoticed by Glen. She took in the crowd with distaste before stalking off.

Olerra was grinning at Sanos when he turned back to her.

"Can you blame them?" she asked. "You're magnificent."

He didn't know what to feel in that moment. Pride tried to claim every corner of his brain, but he felt as though he ought to press harder for outrage. However, his sense of modesty was nowhere to be found. The whistles and screams felt good. They made him feel wanted. Chosen. Accepted.

He couldn't accept the attention of women back home, lest his father hurt them. But here—here he could embrace it.

After sweeping the crowd, his eyes landed on Olerra.

He could embrace *this* woman without fear of harm to her. In fact, he might *welcome* harm to her as he remembered his sore nether region.

He was ashamed the thought even entered his mind, but it did enter. How could it not with all the looks she'd been shooting his way? Her suggestive comments? That searing kiss they'd shared at the brothel?

His body wanted her even if his mind didn't. In fact, his mind still wanted to murder her.

It was a heady combination.

Sanos stood there, basking in the attention of the crowd, wrestling with his thoughts, as Olerra poured a decent amount of oil into her hands before rubbing her fingers up and down his chest.

Sanos meant to step away from that touch, but when she uttered, "I'm sorry," he found himself rooted to the spot. "I expected you to be fighting a soft bedroom boy." Olerra was looking at Athon on the stage.

"I didn't even consider that she would—but of course she would. That is her way. Cheat when she can. Sabotage when she can't."

He tried to ignore the feel of her fingers on his skin, which was far more pleasant than it should have been.

"Why does her courting that man upset you?" he asked. Was he a former paramour of Olerra's? Was there any man in this country who didn't fancy her?

"He is—was—one of my soldiers."

"I'm not following."

"He was the first man we allowed to join our ranks. He worked so hard to be competitive with the women. Put on an enormous amount of muscle so he'd stand a chance. And now he's given it all up for some affection and her money."

"Why do you care?"

"First, because you're going to take harder hits than I anticipated. And second, when you beat him, Andrastus—and you *are* going to beat him—Glenaerys will punish him in ways I cannot save him from."

He knew that feeling all too well. How many times had the king hurt his mother or siblings with Sanos helpless but to watch?

He mentally shook himself. He wasn't going to find kinship with this woman. They were not the same.

"I still don't understand why you're worried for a man."

Amarran women treated men as their playthings. Why should she be so concerned?

"Because I'm responsible for my soldiers. And just because some in my kingdom are demeaning and degrading toward men, do not think for a moment I am one of them."

Sanos looked pointedly at his swollen wrists.

"You are the exception, as you continue to be difficult." She bent to oil up his legs next. "I thought Athon a friend, but Glen has turned him against me, just as she's done with everything else. I suspect it won't be long before she tries to come for you, too. But she can't have you. You're mine."

The hands on his skin suddenly felt different. *Hotter*, most prominently. That heat started to travel upward.

No.

He was naked, and he *refused* to become aroused for this entire crowd to see.

"Can't I oil myself up?"

"With this many people looking? Not a chance. We have a show to put on. We're supposed to be already fucking."

She really should not say that word while she had her hands on him *and he was naked.*

Desperate now, Sanos tried to find some sort of topic change.

"You said I would beat him. I didn't realize you had such faith in me."

She stood and walked behind him to tend to his back. "You said you were a fighter, and I can't afford to lose in front of the entire country. So, yes, you're going to win, because there is no other option. I have the popularity vote of the people. Glenaerys knows it. This was a desperate play to garner more of their favor." She paused. "How much training, exactly, have you had?"

"Swordplay and wrestling every day of my life for as long as I can remember."

"How often do you win?"

"There is only one man who has beaten me in recent years."

"Your father or your brother Sanos?"

The pause perhaps lasted longer than he should have let it. He'd slipped up. He was rumored to be one of the best fighters in his kingdom. Being better than Sanos would be an outrageous claim for Andrastus.

"My father," he said carefully. "I let Sanos win because to not do so would have drastic results."

"I see. Men and their fragile egos. The crown prince cannot have his younger brother besting him. What will the world think?"

"Precisely."

A pause. "I may hate the man entirely, but Atalius is a masterful fighter. If he's taught you half of what he knows, I'm eager to see you fight."

He hated the praise heaped upon his father, even though she gave it begrudgingly. Almost as much as he hated making himself seem like a spoiled brat.

And then she said, "You may yet redeem yourself for allowing me to walk off with you out of your own kingdom."

He scowled even though she couldn't see it from behind him. "In the past, I've never had cause to worry for my life at brothels."

She said nothing in response, so he continued. "You shouldn't have taken me from there, you know. The whores will likely be put to death for aiding you. There's no way you managed to pull that off without the assistance of the madam."

Olerra moved her fingers up to his neck. "Then I suppose it's a good thing I paid them each a small fortune and moved the lot of them to Amarra."

He rounded on her. "What?"

She grabbed his forearm before continuing her ministrations. "They were a few hours behind us on the road. I gave Madam Blanchette enough vyra to poison every man in the brothel. Then she and the girls were escorted by palace staff all the way here to start new lives."

He didn't know whether to be impressed or livid.

"You uprooted the best brothel in Brutus? Just picked it up and moved it here?"

"I doubt Madam Blanchette still runs the brothel. The women now have other options, and the business wouldn't be nearly as lucrative here."

"Why?" he demanded, his incredulity rising with every new revelation.

"Because most of the clientele are differre women. Amarran brothels are mostly full of male prostitutes and the occasional madae and madereo."

He went quiet. Even if he escaped and made it home, Blanchette's was gone forever. His brothers would murder him for this. He would murder her for this—if her other crimes against him hadn't been enough cause for it, this one surely was.

She stepped close, and he had to force himself to remain still under the threat of her proximity. "Remember your fear when you thought I might give you that toxin and take you against your will?"

He blinked.

"Imagine allowing others to touch you being the only way to scrape out a living. You men in Brutus are pigs, denying women their own land. Their own money most of the time. Women who have no men to look after them must sell their bodies to them instead. Is that the way you would have it?"

"They like being whores!" he protested.

"They're paid to act like they like it. Would you have such a fun time sticking your cock inside them if they looked miserable the whole time?"

"You act all high and mighty, when your men are forced into that life here. It is the same."

She said, so quietly he almost missed it, "Perhaps it shouldn't be." But then she said, in her usual tone, "We didn't choose this. Your sex did. My society is a result of the crimes of men."

"What does that mean?"

Her eyes narrowed. "I tried to give you history lessons on the road. You refused to listen. Now enough talk."

Sanos leaped forward when he felt her hands on his ass.

"I suppose next you'll need to sluice up my cock?" he asked bitterly.

"Only if you think your competitor will try to grab you by it?"

"What the hell kind of wrestling is this?"

"The kind meant for female enjoyment. Now, get out there and don't get yourself hurt."

She slapped his ass before he could walk toward the center stage, and the crowd went wild again. Sanos wanted to turn and glare at her, but he realized a moment later that she was putting on a show. They needed to appear to be fucking for her sake. He needed to be housebroken to secure her throne. So he could eventually be allowed to go home.

And apparently the first real course of action he was to take toward that goal was to wrestle another man almost twice his size, while naked.

There were stones laid into the shape of a circle at the bottom of the amphitheater. Soft mats spread over the center. At least if he fell, he wouldn't break something. No, any breaking would come from the large man opposite him.

"Are you ready, Athon?" the eunuch overseer asked. Sanos recognized him from the palace.

"Yeah," the man barked in return.

"Prince Andrastus, are you ready?"

Up close, Sanos registered that Athon was a foot taller, a truly impressive feat considering he himself was over six feet. His competitor's muscles were godly, almost unsightly with the way they bulged off his skin. He was covered in scars, earned from sword nicks and battle wounds.

Still, he said, "I'm ready," to the overseer.

"No biting or going for the groin," the eunuch announced. "Anything else is fair game." He held both hands high in the air before dropping them.

Athon lunged.

10

Olerra forced herself not to wince as Athon launched himself toward Andrastus. The prince managed to sidestep the swinging arms directed toward his stomach. He pivoted on one foot and drove a fist into the larger man's exposed back.

The crowd shouted, and Olerra relaxed her posture. She, Ydra, and her cousin were seated in cushioned chairs beneath a canopy just out of range of the circling fighters.

"Very nice," Ydra said.

"Don't get too excited," Glenaerys said from her other side. "My man's just getting warmed up."

Indeed, Athon shook himself off before throwing a kick and catching Andrastus around the ankle, sweeping his legs out from under him. Athon threw himself on top of Andrastus.

Olerra could see the panic on Andrastus's face from here. Perhaps if the two men hadn't been oiled up, it would have been over, but Athon slid as he went to his knees astride Andrastus. The smaller man managed to roll over the bigger one.

Then they were both standing once more.

"How will you reward him when he wins?" Ydra asked, and Olerra knew it was a barely hidden goad with Glenaerys present to hear.

"I haven't decided yet."

"You could have Stryan tend to him."

Stryan was a eunuch trained in full-body massage. Talented though he may be, Olerra didn't think for a second that Andrastus would appreciate such a thing.

Still, she said, "I'll take it under consideration."

"When Athon wins," Glen cut in, "I'm going to ride him so hard, he will be unable to think of anything except being inside me."

Ydra could not mask her disgust. "He won't think of anything else until you inevitably break something of his. An arm or a leg. You are not known for showing the restraint you should in the bedroom."

"My men are not being paid for me to be gentle with them. They're paid so that I might have my way."

Olerra scoffed. "I thought you said you were courting Athon. Wouldn't that imply you were wooing him rather than paying him?"

"There's no difference. I can pay him with money, or I can pay him with my attention and goodwill. Either way, men only care that they're being compensated."

Ydra shook her head. "Is there any problem you don't throw money at?"

"I haven't hired someone to take care of you yet." And then Glenaerys's gaze shot to Olerra for the briefest moment.

Olerra knew that Glenaerys was coming for her, but she hadn't dreamed that she might come for Ydra, too. Olerra's lip curled as she leaned toward her cousin. "This fight for power is between you and me. If you come for Ydra, I may just have to start hiring assassins of my own. And I have better contacts in that regard, you will recall."

Glenaerys rolled her eyes, but Olerra could tell the movement was forced. A brief moment of fear had shown through her cousin's stoicism. "I will concede that Ydra is off-limits as long as you don't come after my harem."

"Agreed."

They returned their attention to the fight. Andrastus had managed to get Athon into a choke hold. Each time the bigger man tried to grip the arm around his neck, his hands slipped. However, Andrastus didn't exactly have the best hold. He was trying to keep Athon as far from his body as possible, as though he detested their naked skin coming into contact.

"That man's prudish ways might get him killed," Glenaerys said gleefully, as Athon finally dug an elbow into Andrastus's stomach. "Athon shouldn't have had enough leeway to swing that hard. Tut, tut."

Olerra massaged her temples as she watched Andrastus fall to the mat yet again with the bigger man on top of him. She'd wanted to let Andrastus fight this one on his own. To show that she believed in him and to give him some confidence in this country where he'd been taken prisoner. But it would seem she'd let this continue for too long. She'd given Andrastus his chance. Now she needed to intervene.

Olerra wanted to call for a respite, but she couldn't do so while Glenaerys's man had the upper hand. Olerra waited and sent a prayer up to Goddess Amarra that her chosen would gain a modicum of intelligence within the next five seconds.

Losing this fight meant looking weak in front of the nobles, the very people she was supposed to be winning over by wedding Andrastus. Olerra vowed to take greater caution where her cousin was concerned.

Andrastus managed to wiggle enough to get a leg between himself and the bigger man. He kicked, sending Athon backward. Andrastus stood, gaining the upper hand for a moment.

Olerra took the chance, standing and shouting, "I call for a respite."

The eunuch jumped between the two men before Andrastus could descend on the fallen man. Glenaerys called to her, "What's this about?"

"See to your man, and I will see to mine" was all Olerra said in return. She hurried to the mat, for she would only get a minute before the fight was resumed.

"What did you do that for?" Andrastus asked between heaving pants as she pulled him off to the side. "I had him."

"You might as well be dancing with him for all the damage you're doing," she said. "Or playing keep-away. You've barely landed a blow!"

"If you hadn't slicked me up in this horrid concoction, the fight would already be over."

"Yes, but not with you the victor."

He glared at her, as though she wounded him with the comment.

"We don't have much time," she continued. "You gave it your best shot. Now let me help you."

"What, you want to take my place on the mat?"

"No, I'm not permitted. It's a bout between you and Athon. But I can give you an edge."

"How's that?"

"My cousin thought to one-up me by courting the strongest man in Amarra. She knew I was taking a husband, and she wanted to stay evenly matched without having to leave Amarran soil. But she's overlooked one very important thing."

Andrastus looked over her head to glimpse her cousin. "What's that?"

"Athon is *my* soldier, and I know how he fights. So here's what you're going to do . . ."

Sanos turned back to the ring. Sweat mingled with the oil on his skin, both his and Athon's. It was gross, yet he knew he needed to take Olerra's words to heart if he was going to win this.

Quit distancing yourself from your opponent. I don't care if you have an aversion to naked males. You beat him, and you beat him good like you promised. I don't care if your prick ends up in his face.

Such an eloquent speaker, as always, this princess of Amarra.

Her words were ringing in his head. He hated them because he needed them. He was disappointed in himself for not being able to handle this challenge on his own.

In all fairness, he was naked in front of thousands of women who were whistling at him, and he was covered in enough oil that the entire crowd could lap it up with bread. The weather was warmer than he'd ever experienced. The heat blared on his still-burned shoulders.

Given time, he would adjust to this style of fighting and work his way to the top, as he'd done with every other physical test that came his way.

Not that I'll be around long enough for that.

Sanos pushed all of it aside. He ignored the sounds of the crowd, the smell of his sweating opponent, and the feel of the too-hot sun on his skin. It was just him and Athon and Olerra's words in his mind.

"Fight!" the eunuch called, stepping away to give the mat to the two competitors.

Athon will always attack first. He's spent his whole life trying to outplay the women he's pitted against. His chances are greater if he attacks first and doesn't waste any time defending himself. You must be faster. Strike first.

Athon was a big man, so Sanos struck low, getting inside the other man's guard and kicking at his knee with the ball of his foot.

Athon was sent off-balance.

Get him on the ground as quickly as you can.

Sanos shoved him the rest of the way. Athon went down to the mat.

Once he's down, you subdue him. Your arms aren't big enough to do the trick against a man like that. Use your legs, and let go of your sense of modesty, for gods' sakes.

Sanos looked up for only a split second. He shot Olerra a foul look before he joined the other man on the floor.

Olerra was riveted as she watched Andrastus wrap his thighs around Athon's throat. He held the position, no matter how Athon tried to slap at him.

She also knew with absolute certainty that her prince was imagining it was her throat that he was squeezing and squeezing. The way his eyes never left hers the whole while was proof of it. His unfaltering gaze warmed her skin, no matter what emotions were behind it. She had his full attention, and there was something undeniably alluring about that.

She watched him watching her, and she made herself relax, leaning back in her seat, laying an arm against the back of it.

The seconds dragged out as Athon continued to try to fight him off. Until finally, the larger man pounded his hand on the mat twice, and the eunuch called the match.

"Princess Olerra's champion wins!"

The crowd was wild on their feet. They chanted her name, breaking it into three lovely syllables. O-LER-RA. Some of the noblewomen in the front rows were clapping and chanting along. Others sent her nods of goodwill. Others were studiously avoiding her gaze, desperate not to get on Glenaerys's bad side.

As she stood, Ydra moved between the cousins and threw one arm over each of their shoulders. "Well, Glen, it may have been a wasted courtship, but at least you made Olerra look good."

If Olerra hadn't just bargained for her best friend's life, she might have worried for it with the look Glenaerys shot her.

"Next time, perhaps find a man whose fighting style I'm not already familiar with," Olerra said, trying to take Glen's attention off her friend.

"Sleep with one eye open," Glen shot her way before stalking off.

"Did you just threaten the princess? With a witness present?" Ydra demanded.

"Let her go," Olerra insisted. "She has wounds to lick. Also, see if you can get Athon out of here before she—"

Too late.

Glenaerys picked Athon off the mat by his hair, lifting him effortlessly to his feet with the Goddess's Gift. She hooked her arm around his. She used her free hand to dig her nails into the skin of his bicep. The moment she tried to walk off with him—

Andrastus blocked her path.

Shit.

"What's this?" Glen asked, turning that dangerous gaze on Andrastus. Olerra was already running, placing herself beside her man.

"You're hurting him," Andrastus said, eyeing the blood that was coating Glen's nails.

Glen cocked her head to one side. "Does that bother you? Me hurting another man? Do you wish it was you I was hurting?"

The look of disgust Andrastus gave her was telling enough.

"No?" she asked. "Then you worry for him? You worry over a sore head and a little blood?"

"Andrastus, let's go," Olerra said. She looked around, relieved to find that the other nobles were too far away to overhear the exchange. She wasn't nearly so worried for her standing as she was for her prince's safety, however.

Odd.

"Wait," Glen said. "Andrastus is concerned, Olerra. We must put it to rights. Athon, tell the prince you're fine."

"I'm fine," Athon said, not a hitch in his breath.

"Tell him you like it when I hurt you."

"I like it when she hurts me. Anything that brings my mistress pleasure brings me pleasure."

Olerra tried to touch Andrastus's arm, but he pulled away easily with the oil still coating his skin.

"He doesn't seem convinced, Athon," Glen said. "You must try harder." Then Olerra's cousin reached between Athon's legs to grab his testicles. She pulled.

Athon grunted in pain. "Thank you, Princess."

Olerra could see the tension in Andrastus. She knew he would spring soon. Just like he'd done at the breakfast table that morning.

Olerra physically put herself between Andrastus and Glen. She took his face in her hands. "You give her power by reacting," she said quietly. "She will continue to use this against you. If we leave now, she won't have anyone to put on a show for. There's nothing you can do for him."

Her prince was still poised for a fight.

It was Ydra who finally defused the situation.

"Olerra, you and Andrastus have many admirers who wish to greet you. Come." She took Andrastus's other arm, and together they forced him away from Glen.

"Don't look back," Olerra cautioned.

Andrastus closed his eyes, blessedly listening. Forcing himself to breathe deeply. "How can you all just stand by? He did nothing but lose."

"He embarrassed her."

"And that means he should suffer her torments?"

"No, but he did this to himself. Athon was a soldier under my protection. He chose to leave and side with Glen. Against me. There is nothing I can do for him, and I wouldn't even if I could. He betrayed me. He sided with her after everything I've done for him. Glen got her claws into him in only two weeks. And now that she knows you hate it when she disciplines her men, she will do it around you whenever she can."

"So it's my fault that men are to be punished?"

"No. It is only she who is at fault. What you can do is help me gain the throne so we can put a stop to her."

Andrastus nodded once.

"Now, I need you to smile and put on a show for some courtiers," she said.

Ydra escorted him to a small crowd that had gathered, all waiting to chat with Olerra's chosen. Olerra risked turning around, but Glenaerys and Athon were already gone. Olerra took a steadying breath. She needed a moment to get ahold of herself. She couldn't recall being so afraid for another person as when Glen had turned her full attention on Andrastus. They had to be more careful.

After a few deep breaths, Olerra turned back around.

Andrastus was composed, though he certainly didn't look pleased by his current predicament.

"You fight with such skill, Prince Andrastus," Countess Ingras preened. "You and the princess are a match made by the gods."

Daneryn, who sat beside his mother, shot her the most affronted look. As though his own mother had betrayed him with the compliment.

"Oh, I don't know about that," Andrastus said uncertainly.

"What did she say to aid you in victory during the respite?" a duchess wanted to know.

Olerra caught the prince's gaze, raising one brow.

"She told me she believed in me."

"Ah," the duchess said. "The princess knows how to motivate a man. She will likewise prove worthy in ruling our people."

It was a bold statement, but Olerra took the compliment. The duchess of Wenda had professed her loyalties long ago and voiced them loudly whenever possible. If only it would sway more.

There were too many who preferred Glenaerys's "firm hand" over men to Olerra's battle prowess.

Andrastus shot Olerra a look that suggested he very much wanted to leave the amphitheater, but she ignored it. All the attention was just what they needed. Andrastus was doing his job without even realizing it. To the nobility, his discomfort must have come off as modesty, for they praised his humility. He handled the compliments just as poorly as he did the attention. The nobility found it adorable, but Olerra was bewildered. Did he not receive attention and compliments back home? He was a prince. Surely his tutors and favor-climbing nobility did what they could to endear him to them, even as a second son. He was handsome. Women must have heaped praise upon him.

When Olerra earned his trust, they would talk about it. She wanted to understand him. She wanted to know more about his life back home. Until then, he deserved a reward. Today's victory over her cousin felt sweeter than any chocolate, and Olerra would remove his chains as a thank-you.

She let him do whatever he wished for the rest of the day. Sanos bathed. He wasn't alone, but the eunuchs didn't touch him, allowing him to wash the oil and stink from the other man away on his own. He was permitted to walk through the hallways of the palace with an escort. He familiarized himself with the front door, the quickest path to it from her rooms.

He learned where the stables were so he might steal a horse. He observed the guard changes at high-traffic areas—all under the guise of familiarizing himself with his new home.

As if. The treatment of Athon by Glenaerys was only further proof that he needed to leave this place. These women were all barbaric. His very life was on the line.

Olerra left him alone until the evening, when she bid him good night. There was no outrageous night ritual this time. No more strange Amarran customs for her to spring upon him.

He heard the lock slide into place after she shut the door separating his room from hers. His hands and feet were still free of shackles, a reward for winning the fight, and he intended to use the opportunity to flee.

His first order of business was removing the blasted armband. He tossed it aside, heard it land on some thick carpet. Then he climbed into bed, though he had no intention of staying there. Sanos wanted to keep up appearances in case she thought to check on him within the next couple of hours. But as he lay there, staring up at the ceiling, the door didn't creak open once. The hours passed painfully, slowly, and when he was sure she must be asleep and the palace must all be resting for the night save the guard, he rolled from his mattress silently.

She may have locked the door between the two of them, but there was another door in the room, and he went to it, ensuring his steps were silent. It was blessedly unlocked, and as he eased it open, he was surprised to find another bedroom. It was identical to his, save a bit smaller. No one resided within.

There was another door on the opposite wall, so Sanos went to it.

He opened it to find yet another bedroom. Another door. Another made bed and warm rug before the hearth. Bedroom after bedroom after bedroom. After the tenth one, he finally realized what this was.

It was for her harem.

Sanos wasn't sure if he was horrified or pleased that she'd been telling the truth about him being the only man in her life. He kept going, wondering just how many rooms there could possibly be. How many men did a woman of her status really need?

Fifty, it would seem.

He counted fifty rooms before the final door let him out into a hallway he did not recognize. Better yet, there didn't seem to be any guards in sight.

Goodbye, Princess.

Sanos traversed the hallway slowly, listening for any telltale sounds of approaching feet. He didn't like that he was in unfamiliar territory, but right now the most important thing was to get away from her. With her ridiculous notions and her box of phalluses and the way she gasped when she came. He wanted none of it.

He would go home, think of some lie that was less humiliating than the truth to tell his family, and get on with his life.

Without Blanchette's, he thought with despair.

The hallway let out into yet a bigger one with long columns holding up the ceiling. Torches flickered in their sconces, and Sanos hid behind one when he heard the chinking of armor. Women in red bearing spears marched by, and he waited long after they were gone before carrying on.

At the next curve in the hall, he saw a woman standing guard, her back to him. Clearly the Amarran guards were more concerned with people entering, rather than leaving, this place. He snuck up behind her, ready to clobber her on the back of the head with his elbow, before he remembered one of the first things he'd been taught about this place.

To make a woman bleed was a death sentence.

At the last moment, he switched tactics, instead wrapping one arm around her throat, the other covering her mouth and nose. From this angle, she couldn't dislodge him, and she eventually passed out from the lack of oxygen.

He let her slump to the floor and stared at her spear for a moment before deciding to leave it behind. The weapon was too large. It would make him easier to spot.

As he rounded the next corner, he was brought up short.

She was there.

Olerra.

Fully dressed, arms crossed, weapons sheathed at her side, a pleasant smile on her face.

"I expected you over an hour ago," she said.

11

"What took you so long?" she asked.

"I didn't realize I was expected."

"I took off your manacles for the first time, and you didn't think I would test you? Just what kind of wife do you think I am?"

He gritted his teeth. "We are not married."

"Yet."

Sanos looked around the hallway, his eyes catching on a door off to the side. Olerra blocked the path ahead, but this door was equidistant to the two of them, on the right side of the hall. He could probably beat her to it, but what if the path was a dead end? She would give chase, and he had no idea what she'd do if she caught him.

"No entourage?" he asked, gesturing around her. "Last time you had a herd of eunuchs carting me about the place."

"I don't need them to keep you in line. Would you rather deal with them than me?"

He didn't like the question. Mostly because he didn't know the answer.

There was tension in the empty space between them. Sanos could not move without breaking it. Without her springing into action—he was certain of this. Backing up would cause her to step forward. Moving forward would cause her to hold her ground, bringing him closer to the woman determined to claim him for her own. The single door was looking more and more appealing by the second. Perhaps it locked from the inside, giving him time to find another exit. He'd take a window, despite them being on the third floor.

"You're not answering any of my questions," Olerra said. "What took you so long? Shall I summon the eunuchs? And while we're at it, what did you do to poor Aevia?"

Keeping her talking seemed the safest course of action at the moment.

"I waited for you to fall into what I thought was a deep sleep. Then I had to go through fifty bedrooms before finding an exit. Why do all the bedrooms connect to one another?"

"It keeps men in line." At his arched brow, she added, "When members of the harem watch me cross through their bedroom to reach another man's, it's an incentive to behave. To try harder for my affections."

Just when Sanos thought he couldn't be more horrified by this kingdom . . .

He shook himself. "Don't summon the eunuchs. They make me uncomfortable."

"Because their manhood is gone?"

"Because I don't like to be touched by other men."

"You only like to be touched by women?"

"I only like to be touched when that touch is wanted."

She snorted.

"What?" he asked.

"Oh, just the hypocrisy is all."

He continued to stare at her.

"I'm told that in Brutus, you men force women into all kinds of unwanted marriage situations. Often the moment they begin bleeding. Do you not barter and trade your women like cattle, regardless of their desires?"

"How is that any different from what you're doing to men here?" he demanded.

"The difference, Prince, is that the women of Amarra became this way to counter the way men were treating them. Your sex started this. The current point, however, is that it's ridiculous for you to be offended by the way you're being treated when your own people practice it. It's just always been in your favor until now."

Her words struck him deeper than he liked.

"You're in Amarra, not Brutus," she continued. "You will adjust to our ways, and if you start behaving, I won't have to have you handled by the men in the castle's employ. Now, what of Aevia?"

Sanos itched to have a sword in his hand. He was certain it would make him feel more confident in this situation. "I choked her. She'll come to eventually."

"Bloodless," she said with a smile. "I'm impressed. It's a relief that you're not to face execution. I'd hate to have to find a new husband after all the trouble you've caused me."

"You're not concerned for the girl?"

"She's new. This was as much a test for her as it was you. She failed. She needs more training before she's ready to be a palace guard." She shrugged.

He didn't want to ask, but he needed to. Not knowing was killing him. "What happens now?"

Olerra reached behind her and pulled out his padded manacles. She tossed them to him. "First, you're going to put those back on, because you're clearly not ready to have them off. Then I will escort you back to your room and lock you in for the night."

"And tomorrow?"

"Tomorrow, you'll wish you'd stayed in your room instead of trying to escape."

Sanos burned with hatred as he stared at the manacles he held loosely in one hand. "And if I refuse to put these on?"

"You will be punished."

"No breakfast tomorrow?"

"Food doesn't seem to motivate you, so I'll have to resort to other means."

"Such as?"

"Only one way to find out," she said.

The exit was *right there*. Just over her shoulder. If he could only get to it.

Fighting her would be absolute lunacy. If he made her bleed, she could have him killed. But if he did not fight, if he didn't try, there was no guarantee that he would have another chance like this any time soon.

He could choke her like he did the other guard . . .

He looked her up and down. They weren't oiled or naked. He wasn't furious past the point of reason. This would be a *good* fight.

Sanos deliberately tossed the manacles off to the side.

Olerra grinned, as though he hadn't disappointed her in the least. In fact, he felt like he'd fallen into her plans once again.

———◆———

This was exactly what Olerra needed. A chance to pit herself against her would-be husband to see who would come out on top. Could she win as she was? Unblessed by her goddess. With Ydra hiding behind the door in the hall, there was no way this could end terribly for her. She had planned this encounter carefully. She'd wanted to confront him, and she'd wanted an excuse to fight him.

Andrastus had fallen into her plans beautifully.

Olerra undid her sword belt and tossed it behind her so it wouldn't get in the way. She was going to discipline this man, who had a good fifty pounds on her. She took a step forward.

The prince held his ground.

Smiling, she took another step.

Andrastus shifted backward ever so slightly. Then, realizing that's what he was doing, he made himself hold.

But a third step in his direction proved to be too much for the prince. He dove toward her, taking her advice from earlier to heart. *Attack first.*

She sidestepped him easily and drove an elbow into his back. He was slow. Perhaps not to most, but everyone was slow to her. He barely avoided losing his feet, and he grunted. Andrastus blinked as he turned around, finding her in his original position.

Then he tried to run.

Olerra caught him after three steps. She tripped him, hooking an ankle under one of his feet. This time he went down. There were no mats in this fight. The fall had to be bruising.

Olerra didn't want to hurt him. She reminded herself this was a fair fight. In fact, it was a fight in his favor, as he was likely stronger. He just didn't know the fight was in his favor. And she had to keep him from leaving. She had to put on a display. This was a punishment.

When he rose next, he turned toward her, realizing he had to dispatch her if he wanted to carry on with his plans for escape.

At least he's not stupid. It was a point in his favor, despite the ill-conceived escape attempt. She had a running mental list of his flaws and attributes. He was a good fighter who took orders well. He had a nasty temper, but the way he looked at her with a heated gaze at times . . .

Oh, she wanted to see that temper come out in the bedroom. She wanted to match it. Dominate it.

She flashed him a smile as he sized her up, searching her from head to toe for a weakness. *Perhaps he's a fast learner*, she thought. That would be another point in his favor.

He rushed her again, but it was only a feint. She could tell he anticipated her to dodge right again, so she went left. When she spun around, she pressed her toe against his ass, shoving him to the floor. He did not like that. His scowl was evidence enough. She wondered if he'd fare any better if he had a sword. As it was, his attempts were half-hearted at best. Then a thought struck her.

"Are you—" She paused. "You're trying not to hurt me." It was a statement rather than a question.

"I don't have a death wish," he said.

"No, you don't, but surely you've guessed by now that I would pardon you if you made me bleed while we fought. Something else is holding you back. Tell me what it is. You've had opportunities to strike me, yet you're only going for a grapple."

There was a pause in which she didn't expect him to answer. Then he said, "A man does not strike a woman."

Olerra cocked her head to the side. "Did Atalius teach you that?"

"My mother."

That brought Olerra up short. She couldn't imagine the dynamic between the Brutish king and his queen. They must not get on well at all.

"You tried to strike me at breakfast," she said.

"You deserved it then."

"And now I don't?"

"You do."

"Then why?"

He was such a puzzle, and she was so excited that he was finally speaking to her.

"I will beat you as the man I made myself, not the monster my father created."

What had Atalius done to him? Why did the Brute hold himself in check?

What did he think would happen if he let himself face her with his full strength?

Andrastus neared slowly, trying to back her into a corner and increase his chances of getting ahold of her. She didn't let that happen. Quick as a flash, she jolted forward, grabbed him around the knees, and tossed him over her head.

It wasn't easy. He was heavier than anyone she had ever fought before. But she could do it. Her strength was enough.

Years and years of tension seemed to melt off her. She'd worried about anyone learning her secret, but her natural strength was enough. She likely wouldn't win against him in an arm wrestling match. But like this? Weighing their skills against each other? She could do this.

That confidence bolstered her as she threw him onto the floor.

The breath rushed out of him, giving her time to spin around, straddle him, pin down his arms, and lower her face until they were only half a foot apart.

She was high on her victory, on the knowledge of her own strength. She forgot that this was meant to be disciplining him.

"I'm sorry things had to go this way," she said to him. "Would you like to hear what I had planned if you passed my test?"

He still couldn't draw in air, so she continued. "If you didn't try to escape tonight, I was going to let you service me. Doesn't that sound much more fun than this?"

Andrastus processed the words slowly, as though he didn't grasp their meaning at first. When he finally did, his nostrils flared, and the breath finally rushed back into him. He wiggled an arm free, grabbed her hip, and spun them, pinning her between him and the floor.

It was not, necessarily, a bad place to be in. When Olerra imagined herself having sex, she always pictured herself on top, but snug against Andrastus's sculpted frame from beneath had a certain appeal, too, she could see.

"Stop that," he said.

"Stop what?"

"You're ogling."

She met his eyes. "I can't help it. You're a very attractive man. You make me wish I was naked right now."

The whites of his eyes were more visible than ever before. "You keep saying wildly ridiculous things."

"Is it ridiculous to yearn for the man I've chosen to be my husband? Would you rather I didn't desire you?"

She shifted her hips ever so slightly from underneath him, and Andrastus let out a breath of air that caused a shiver to race down her spine. He adjusted his stance, letting one of his knees slide up between her legs to press against her sex.

Gods, yes. That was where she wanted him. But more important—

She reached up with her legs to wrap them around his waist, and then she sent him sailing toward the floor. In another heartbeat, she had her arms around his neck, cutting off his air supply. It was just as her instructors had said. You could always distract a man with sex to win.

His face started to turn red, but still she held on. Until he went limp.

"He's out," Olerra said.

Ydra entered from the door in the hallway. They both stared down at the unconscious Brute.

"Well done," Ydra said.

"I'm relieved."

"You should be proud. You really are the best fighter among us."

"Do you think I hurt him too much?"

Ydra looked heavenward. "You barely hurt him at all by the looks of it. He deserved worse for trying to escape. A lashing at best."

"Both he and his pride are bruised. That is enough."

"You're lucky no one else saw him, otherwise you would have been forced to do much worse."

"I know. That's why I removed all the guards between here and my rooms, save one."

Ydra picked up Andrastus. She didn't grunt as Olerra would have under his weight. She walked effortlessly, without so much as a stumble. Olerra felt the usual envy wash through her system. She reminded herself that she'd beaten him. It was enough.

It had to be enough.

When Sanos woke hours later, he was chained to his bed. Alone. It took a while for the night to come back to him.

She'd choked him, just as he'd done to her guard.

His body was sore. His back throbbed from the elbow she'd thrown. And he'd fallen hard to the stone floor at least twice. Thrice? He couldn't quite remember. He had been so desperate to escape. So angry with her for taking him in the first place.

He turned his head slightly and saw that the armband was returned to him. She'd taken the time to replace it before chaining him back up. That made him unspeakably angry.

And then he remembered the disarming things she'd said!

You make me wish I was naked.

You're a very attractive man.

I was going to let you service me.

It was impossible not to picture it once she'd suggested it. Him on his knees. Her legs parted above him.

He'd never done that before.

Not because he hadn't wanted to, but because his only sexual encounters were with prostitutes who could be carrying any manner of diseases. He was always sheathed when he bedded them. But he couldn't protect his mouth.

But Olerra was a virgin . . .

He stopped that line of thinking immediately.

He was manacled to one of her beds. And he would not think of her.

As long as it took him to fall back asleep, he failed.

12

Olerra slept fitfully that night. Yesterday had been a victory in some ways. Putting Glen in her place was fantastic, but Andrastus's escape attempt was disappointing. She'd expected it, of course. She knew, logically, she couldn't expect her man to want to please her from the start. He wasn't born or raised in Amarra. He needed their ways drilled into him until it was second nature.

Today wouldn't bring them closer together, that was for sure. No, today was punishment for his antics yesterday.

"What the fuck is that?" she heard shouted from the next room.

She allowed herself a grin before hiding it as she entered Andrastus's room.

"Problem?" she asked innocently.

"No problem, Princess," Vernys said as the eunuch redid Andrastus's manacles to settle behind his back instead of in front of him.

Only then did they manage to attach the nipple clamps.

They were made of pure silver, with small onyx stones interspersed along the chain connecting them. A solid silver collar went around Andrastus's neck, and Olerra was handed the end of the attached leash.

"He's ready, Princess, unless you would like him to wear the harness, too."

Olerra raised a brow in Andrastus's direction, and the prince wisely shut his mouth. "I don't think that will be necessary today. Remove his sandals, though. I think he'll be better off barefoot."

He glared at her as two men stooped over to remove his shoes. Andrastus wore very little. A short black skirt that reached down to his mid-thigh. It made his ivory skin even paler. Other than the chains and ornamentation and armband, he was bare.

"Hmm," she said. "I think he's missing something. Ring for the palace piercer. He needs a jewel in his ear. Maybe two. I haven't decided yet. We'll see her tonight. We've a busy day today."

The men all nodded before leaving them alone. The leather-wrapped handle in Olerra's hand made a noise as she tightened her fist around it. She gave an experimental tug, and Andrastus was forced forward by the neck.

"If you think I'm leaving this room dressed like—"

She didn't let him finish. "I'm really not in the mood for your temper today. You made me proud yesterday at the match against my cousin's man, but you lost any favor gained when you tried to escape."

"As if I fucking care about your favor."

"You ought to. Because if I don't care, no one else will. Everyone thinks you soiled by me. No other woman would look twice at you. The brothels might take you in, but you are essentially a broken man in a kingdom where no one gives a fuck who your father is. Today is a disciplinary day. I have a full schedule planned for us. It will be unpleasant but necessary. After that, we continue with our courtship as usual."

He scoffed.

Olerra yanked on the cord, drawing Andrastus forward until they were nose-to-nose. "I chose you, Prince, to be mine. You haven't let me woo you properly yet. And your antics yesterday have set us back. But we'll get there. Today, I'm going to show you who I am and who my people are. Tomorrow, I will begin to show you what you are to me. Now, behave like a good little boy." She finished her spiel by biting his neck. Not hard enough to break skin. Just enough for him to know whom he belonged to.

Olerra propped the leash over her shoulder. If she felt too much tension in the cord, she was sure to slow her pace. While causing him discomfort was her foremost concern today, hurting him never was. She would not be abusive. She was not her cousin.

Heads turned as they entered the breakfast hall. The conversations around the room abruptly changed, as the women ogled her betrothed. She liked knowing that others found him pleasing. She liked others seeing that he was hers.

Yesterday she'd introduced Andrastus to her aunt. Today it was time for Cyssia and Usstra to properly meet him.

Ydra, ever on her side, was sitting across from the two women in question with an empty seat beside her, clearly meant for Olerra. Ydra was a blessing from the goddess, through and through. Olerra knew that once she became queen, Ydra would become the next general, raising her own station. But that wasn't why Ydra did what she did. It was the sisterhood they shared.

"Cyssia, Usstra," Olerra said as she approached the table, "would you like to meet Andrastus?"

Cyssia looked him up and down. "After that fight yesterday? Absolutely. Sit with us."

Cyssia's man sat at her feet, massaging them. Usstra had no man to see to her, as she was amise. She preferred to surround herself with friends.

Olerra held up a finger for a servant. "A pillow, please," she said once the serving girl appeared.

The requested item was placed on the floor beside Olerra's chair. Olerra looked Andrastus in the eye.

"Kneel," she said.

The muscles in Andrastus's neck went taut. There was a moment of challenge, where she thought he might be throwing his noble ideas of not striking women right out the window. Again. She leaned into his ear.

"You will kneel on your own or I will make you kneel," she whispered, tightening her grip on the leash.

Slowly, Andrastus went to his knees on the cushion. Feeling somewhat guilty, Olerra lowered herself into the chair.

It's only because he tried to escape. Today has to be punishment. Tomorrow you can woo him.

"Say hello, Andrastus," Olerra said without looking at him.

It took a moment, as though he didn't realize at first that she was talking to him. "Greetings," he said stiffly.

"I see he still has much learning to do," Usstra said as she sipped from her goblet.

"It's been some time since anyone has taken a husband from our neighbors, has it not?" Ydra chimed in. "It's easy to forget how hostile they are in the beginning."

"It definitely speaks to your character that you performed such a feat," Cyssia said. "And to choose one so large and Brutish!"

Olerra selected a slice of apple from the tray before her and bit it in half. She offered the other half to Andrastus, who looked at the proffered food as though it were poisonous. She raised a single eyebrow at him, waiting.

Andrastus looked around to all the women watching him, then back to Olerra. She could see the moment he realized that this was the only way he would get breakfast, with his hands still captured behind his back. Finally, murder in his eyes, he lowered his head to eat the fruit from her fingers.

"He may be large and somewhat uncivilized for now, but those lips make my heart race," Olerra said.

Cyssia made a sound of agreement. "This is a good show of your power, Olerra. I am pleased to see you take this step to secure your line. It's a wonder your cousin hasn't settled down by selecting a man of her own."

"She's a bit wild," Usstra agreed, "running around with all those men of common blood."

Someone cleared their throat over Ydra's shoulder, and the four women turned to see Glenaerys standing there. She wasn't alone.

Athon was there, too. He was done up even more than Andrastus was. His armband was made of rose gold, and it had three opals inlaid in the center. His skirt was shorter. Chains had been wrapped around his waist and dangled in between his legs. A harness went around his entire head so the man couldn't eat, and he walked with a limp.

One that Andrastus definitely hadn't given him during the fight.

She felt the prince stiffen beside her.

"It's to be expected," Olerra offered. "Glen's no fighter. She hires people to do her dirty work for her. Kidnapping a husband is no easy feat. She's just not cut out for it."

"That's a real shame," Cyssia said. "I can't see any differre woman as a ruler if she can't capture a noble-born husband. The children will be common, otherwise. Unless you have plans to wed Daneryn, of course?"

Glen's face was a mask, despite the insults thrown her way. "Rumors suggest that Olerra has already had him. What use is a dull sword?"

At this, Andrastus twitched slightly.

"The rumors are untrue," Olerra said, for her prince's sake, not Glen's. She suspected Daneryn had started the rumors himself to try to guilt her into marrying him.

Glenaerys ignored her. "I will take a husband when I can, Cyssia. I do have my hands full with collecting intel and managing much of the finances of our country. Not all of us have the free time to spend a couple of weeks in another country."

"That's why delegating was invented," Olerra said, now offering a cube of cheese to Andrastus. He bit into it, his teeth gently skimming her finger. She tossed the remainder into her own mouth, savoring both the richness of the food and the knowledge that his lips touched what she now consumed.

"Unlike the ability to wave a sword through the air, my job cannot be performed by just anyone," Glenaerys said. "I'm sure Usstra understands the care with which I must handle our nation's secrets."

"I also understand an excuse when I see one," Usstra responded.

Olerra took great care to keep her face straight. Ydra didn't quite succeed.

Glenaerys met Olerra's eye. Something dangerous lurked within. Something Olerra had learned to recognize even when they were young girls. Glenaerys didn't get wild or out of control when she was angry. No, she grew calm and calculating. She didn't do rage. She did revenge.

And Olerra knew that whatever she was planning, it wouldn't be good.

"There don't seem to be any more available chairs at the table," Glen said. Then she turned to Athon. "On your hands and knees."

The former soldier obeyed, wincing slightly with his bad leg. All the while, Glen made eye contact with Andrastus.

"A bit lower, Athon. I'm not so tall."

Athon awkwardly lowered himself further, and then Glen sat, using his back as a bench.

Andrastus's breathing picked up, and Olerra weighed her options.

She could leave, allowing Glen more time alone with the two women who now held the most sway over their futures.

Or she could remain to try to garner more favor, yet risk Andrastus saying something stupid. Thankfully, no one was speaking to him directly, and Olerra was sure he wouldn't just voice—

"Something to say?" Glenaerys asked of the prince.

Olerra held in a groan.

Sanos *hated* this woman, perhaps even more than he hated Olerra.

He took longer to answer than was probably acceptable, but the time was necessary to think of an adequate response. He remembered that he and Olerra were supposed to act like they were fucking, and he knew that anything to do with Olerra angered Glenaerys.

He said, "I was just thinking that when I'm underneath Olerra, she ensures the experience is pleasurable for the two of us. I'm lucky to have been chosen by her and not you."

It appeared to be exactly the thing to say.

Cyssia laughed and clapped. "He has a wicked tongue."

Olerra picked up her goblet. "In more ways than one."

Usstra, however, remained unreadable. She eyed Sanos. "You dislike Glenaerys's firm hand?"

"I dislike bullies."

Usstra nodded. "Me too."

Sanos couldn't help but smile as he turned back to Glen. She had her arms crossed, her mind working. Sanos instead turned to Olerra, who looked so proud she might be ready to kiss him. He really hoped she wouldn't. He wanted to hurt her cousin. Never mind that it helped Olerra simultaneously.

"Bully?" Glen questioned. "Athon was a nobody before I graced him with my favor. Are you displeased with my attentions, Athon?"

Then, remembering the harness, Glenaerys undid the straps at the back of his head. A glob of saliva slid from his mouth as the contraption was removed.

He swallowed and breathed deeply before answering. "No, mistress."

"Do you miss your soldier life?"

"No, mistress."

"Are you happier now?"

"Yes, mistress."

"A man who cannot answer truthfully without fear of reprisal is going to say what you wish to hear," Sanos said.

"And what is that supposed to mean?"

Olerra looked worried. She put her hand on Sanos's hip, but he ignored it. "You can beat him all day long without fear of consequence. If he makes you bleed, his life is forfeit."

Glen snorted. "I heard in your country that women who are unfaithful to their husbands are executed. Even a rumor of infidelity will ruin their entire lives. But there is no such punishment for men who fuck women who aren't their wives. Is this true?"

Sanos was so sick of women turning Brutish ways against him. "It is."

"This is why I would never stoop so low as to wed a Brute," Glen said emphatically. "Their habits are foul. Olerra dishonors herself by bedding one."

Cyssia looked at Sanos with a considering gaze.

How had Glen turned the conversation so quickly? She was a master with her words. Sanos should avoid going head-to-head with her.

Glen lowered a hand to Athon's throat. She stroked it. Squeezed it. Dug in her fingers. Athon would wheeze for air, and then she'd let him be. Soothing the attack with slow circles of the pads of her fingers.

Sanos pulled at the manacles behind his back.

He shouldn't care. These men were Amarran. Athon chose this.

But the whole thing reminded him too much of his father, who would harm his sons whenever fancy struck him. Sanos couldn't do anything about it. He couldn't move. Couldn't attack. He could tell that's exactly what Glen wanted him to do. This was all a display meant for him.

He hated it. But he was no young lad easily egged into violence. He could behave no matter how much he wished otherwise. He endured the rest of breakfast and didn't look across the table at Olerra's cousin again.

When Olerra rose to leave the breakfast table, Ydra asked, "Do you need help with anything today?"

"If you could continue to fill in for me while I show Andrastus around, I would appreciate it," Olerra said.

"Of course. Where are you off to today?"

"The market and then the pit."

Ydra turned her gaze to Andrastus before looking at Olerra once more. "You sure he's up for that?"

"Of course he is," Cyssia responded for her. "It's healthy for a man to remember that actions have consequences. They're so terribly behaved outside of our borders. The pit builds character."

"Let's go," Olerra said to him.

When Andrastus didn't rise right away, she hooked a finger in the chain connecting the nipple clamps and gently pulled upward. The breath rushed out of Andrastus as he rose, his eyes darkening.

"See you all later."

13

Once Sanos didn't have to spend all his willpower ignoring Glenaerys, he had the energy to again be upset about his current predicament.

I am a prince. The crown prince of Brutus, and I'm wearing a godsdamned nipple chain.

It wasn't uncomfortable. His nipples weren't particularly sensitive. It was just humiliating to have so much jewelry hanging off him.

Olerra made him follow her outside. The stones were warm beneath his bare feet, and he had to take more care to ensure he didn't step on loose rocks or other sharp objects. His soles would be filthy once they finished running her errands, whatever they may be.

Olerra took one look at his bare skin before calling for some kind of oil. She rubbed it all over him, assuring him it would prevent him from burning. Then she led him into a carriage, sitting close enough to him that their thighs brushed.

"That was well done back there," she said when the carriage took off. "You have a level of intelligence that I find admirable."

"Great, I can die happy now," he deadpanned.

"Your sense of humor is somewhat lacking, but I will take it given the current circumstances." She laid an arm along the back of the carriage seat and used it to run her fingers up and down the side of his neck.

His skin burned at that touch. Realizing that he was enjoying it all too much, he pivoted to sit on the opposite bench of the carriage. "Keep your hands to yourself," he said to her.

"Is that what you prefer?" she asked. "Would you rather watch while I touch myself again?"

"No," he said, if a bit too loudly.

"Shame," she said. "It was better when you were watching me. I've never come so quickly in my life."

Sanos closed his eyes against the memory that presented itself in his mind. "Must you speak?"

"Must you continue to pretend you don't want me?"

"I pretend nothing. I've told you my desires from the start. I want out of these chains. I want to go home."

She leaned back in her seat. "And what is so great about home? What would you be doing if you were in Brutus?"

With his birthday over, he'd be on his way back to the border to fight the Ephennans. He'd be alone on the road, with his mind free to wander. He'd worry about his family.

Gods, his family.

Sanos turned to Olerra.

His heart pounded as urgency surged through him, but there was nothing he could do to be free. He would be stuck here until an opportunity for escape presented itself. There was only one thing he could do.

"I would ask something of you," he said.

He could tell she was surprised by the topic change. "Today is meant to be disciplinary, yet you would ask for a favor?"

He pressed on. "I have come to realize that I will be in your country for quite some time, despite my best efforts. I know that you cannot tell my family where I am, but could you deliver a message to my mother, telling her I am well? I don't want her to worry any more than she needs to."

His request was met with a beat of silence.

"Why would she worry?" Olerra said at last. "Are you not prone to leaving the palace from time to time?"

He reminded himself she thought him his younger brother. Andrastus was more free to go where he wished.

"Hardly ever," he said. "Only on brief outings with my brothers. She will think the worst has happened. This is not some ploy to get a secret message to her. Anyone can write it. I just want her to know that I'm alive and I'm all right."

Olerra sat back in her seat, keeping her eyes on him. "And what will you give me in return if I do this for you?"

He swallowed his pride, though it nearly killed him. "I will behave. No more fighting you in public."

The princess thought it over carefully. "All right, Prince. I will send word to your mother the moment we return."

"Thank you."

It felt wrong to thank her after everything she'd done, but she needed to know he was sincere in his request and promise.

The city swept past them slowly. The traffic was horrible, causing the carriage to jolt to a stop many times. Sanos looked out the window, taking in businesses and neighborhoods. The common people of Amarra seemed happy enough. Sanos didn't see any homeless or destitute among them.

He must have voiced that aloud, for Olerra said proudly, "We have programs in place to care for the mentally ill and those who need help finding their way." Her voice lowered. "Despite Glenaerys's best efforts."

He brought his head back inside the carriage. "What do you mean?"

"She wants to cut off the money for such programs. They're funded by the richest among us. She would give that money back to the nobles. Just another reason why she's so popular among them."

He returned his attention outside. Compared to the palace, the common people looked so normal. The men didn't wear makeup or obscene amounts of jewelry. They wore simple armbands out of common materials. They weren't paraded about. They were doing chores like everyone else. It would seem that only the nobility made spectacles of their men, showing them off like trophies.

He watched a father bend down to pick up his daughter and hoist her high on his shoulders. She wrapped her thin arms around his head and laughed. Another man leaned down and kissed his wife on the cheek before resting his head on her shoulder as she bargained for something at one of the vendors.

He'd never seen peasants looking so pleased with their lot. In Brutus, there were homeless on every street. In Ephenna, he saw urchins fleeing in droves away from his soldiers as they marched on each city.

The Amarrans may have had a fucked-up society, but they were doing something right with their common people, at least.

Sanos scowled as he realized he'd thought something complimentary about this place. He turned away from the streets again.

Olerra was watching him. "What are you thinking?"

"Nothing."

She smiled as though she'd guessed his thoughts. "You never answered my question from earlier. What would you be doing if you were back in Brutus right now?"

He felt petulant. "It doesn't matter what I'd be doing. Only that I'd have freedom once again."

"Freedom? You mean drinking and whoring? Is that what you miss? Is it the thought of being tied down to one woman that scares you so much?"

"If that's what you think of me, then why in the world did you take me?"

"Because I have hope for what comes after."

"After what?"

"After you accept what has happened." She was silent for a moment. "There are two ways I see this playing out. Either you accept that this is your life, give us a chance, and we have a shot at happily ever after . . ."

"Or?" he asked, knowing that option was never going to be his future.

"Or you help me win my throne and we go our separate ways. Either way, we both win, don't you think?"

"What about the option where you let me go and we pretend this never happened?"

"I will not entertain any ideas that don't result in me ruling this kingdom." Her tone had the ring of finality about it.

When they reached their destination, Olerra exited the carriage first. She reached out a hand to help him down the steps, but he ignored it. His hands may have been bound behind his back, but he didn't need help walking. They moved slowly to accommodate his bindings, but he also suspected it was because she wanted him to study his surroundings.

They were in some kind of market, that was clear. Hot foods could be purchased, the smells filling the streets to cover up the less pleasant stenches of filth and sex. Olerra's knuckles tightened on the leash, though she didn't tug him with any force.

There was a ring where men fought, the onlookers placing bets. One woman collected money, while another was conversing with a group of nearby women.

"Who wants a night with the winner?"

The onlookers started bidding, the amounts raising to sums that made no sense to Sanos. Their money was different from his. But from the amount of gold that was exchanged, he couldn't imagine the sums being small.

In another area, there was an upraised bed on a dais. A woman sat on the edge, a man kneeling at her feet. "This is Barov. He's got a tongue like a serpent, and the bidding starts at two ederos. Who would like to see him perform?"

A cheer went up from the watching crowd. At a nod from the woman, Barov leaned forward, pulling down the woman's pants before burying his head between her thighs for all to see. Her moans were covered by the cheers of the crowd.

"A sex market?" Sanos barked. "That's what you brought me to see? You want me to mind myself so you don't decide to sell me off here, is that it?"

Olerra didn't answer, just dragged him farther down the street, passing by more vendors with less obscene wares.

They neared a merchant with all kinds of trinkets that Sanos didn't recognize, until his eye caught on the various phallus boxes for sale like the one Olerra had used.

A woman perusing the stall picked up some kind of metal device and held it up to the vendor. It consisted of wires that were shaped like a flaccid cock and had a lock on one end.

"Will it rust if it gets wet?" the woman asked the vendor.

"No, it's perfectly suited for bath play."

Sanos realized a moment later that it was a device meant to keep a man's member from hardening. "Fuck," he whispered, the horrors of Amarra drawing the swear from him. This place was a nightmare, one he hadn't even known he should be afraid of. Everywhere, women shuffled men about, their superior strength allowing them to control them. Men were little better than slaves here, and while they put on brave faces before the crowds, he could see others behind the stalls, waiting their turns. Some smoked to take the edge off. Others had faces downcast and souls broken.

How could Olerra stand it?

When he turned to her, he saw that she wasn't taking it all in like he was. No, she watched him carefully.

She tugged on his chain, and he jostled forward by the neck. "What you are witnessing right now is not how most in my country behave. It is a select few—the most extreme. Do you fear for these men? Does it hurt you to see their pain?"

"You know it does."

Olerra nodded. "I want to tell you a story. It is about Amarra's Chosen, the first queen of this country. Will you hear it?"

He'd take anything to distract himself from what was happening on the streets. He nodded.

So she began:

Once upon a time, there was a queen who wept.

She had four daughters and no sons, and her husband beat her for it daily. One day, he beat her until she blacked out and then fucked her unconscious body. When she came to, in her pain-filled delirium, she called out to her goddess.

Please, she said, let me suffer no more.

She wanted to die.

For there was nothing she could do. She could not smuggle her daughters away from the castle. The law gave her husband full control. She was nothing without him. Could not have a title or property or money or anything else. That was the way of the world. Men were leaders. Women were followers.

If they tried to be anything more, they were punished.

For nothing brought out a man's anger quite so much as his authority being threatened.

Goddess Amarra heard the cries of her daughter, and she granted her a gift. The next time the king tried to beat her, the queen fended off his blows, and she struck back.

He could no longer overpower her. She was now the superior in strength. And the queen wasn't the only one.

All the women in Amarra awoke with a new power. They broke free from the chains of men. And they rewrote the rules. They exerted power over their former oppressors.

From now on it would be a woman's job to rule. It was a man's job to endure.

The queen looked upon her transformed kingdom with pleasure.

See how they like it.

"That story," Olerra said, "happened five hundred years ago, but we remember. The women of my country were once treated the way the women in your country are. Until our goddess took pity on us. She blessed us to overcome our male oppressors."

"Instead of making the world a better place, your ancestor flipped it," Sanos said.

"Yes, for that is what fury brings."

There was silence. Only the sounds of the busy market buzzed about them.

"Imagine that you had an abuser," Olerra said. "What would you do if they suddenly had no power over you?"

It was a hypothetical question. Olerra obviously had no idea how his father treated him. Sanos wanted to say he'd be noble. That he'd seek justice.

"I'd want revenge," he said. He'd give his father everything he deserved and more.

"So would I."

"What will you do?" Sanos asked. "If you are made queen, will you keep things as they are? How long must innocent men suffer for the sins of their fathers?"

"What will you do?" she said, turning the question back on him. "Let's say I return you to Brutus. When your brother becomes king, will you bother asking him to change laws that have always benefited your sex? Would you have even given a second thought to the way women are treated if you hadn't been brought here?"

He wanted to argue. To claim he'd be noble, but the truth was he wouldn't have.

He saw how helpless his mother and sister were against his father, but it never would have occurred to him to change the laws. He would have thought it enough that he could be good to them. Once his father was gone, he would protect them.

But what about other women? Women who didn't have kind men to look out for them? Was it really right to trust their well-being to imperfect men? Why not allow them the means to leave bad situations?

"You didn't answer my question," Sanos said. "Will you change things?"

"The first thing I will do," Olerra said, "is dismantle the evil in this market and free the men in Glen's harem." She tugged gently on his chain.

After fifteen minutes of walking, Sanos's bare feet were beginning to feel sore. He'd stepped on a dozen rocks and at least two bugs. Sweat ran down his chest and back from the sun, but his skin didn't burn. His arms ached from holding them so tightly behind his back. The bindings were uncomfortable. And every new horror the street revealed caused him to tense.

Finally she led him into a building. An arena, of sorts, with a sunken pit in the middle of the room.

People recognized her. Friends waved her over, and the two of them were led to seats near the front.

Sanos smelled the blood before he saw it.

More fighting? he wondered.

He couldn't make sense of what was before him. Blood congealed on the floor, covering rocks and dirt and every other surface. Sharp devices he didn't have names for littered the space. A woman hauled a man in chains behind her.

"Did you know that other kingdoms sometimes send their criminals here?" Olerra asked him, leaning forward to speak directly into his ear. Even then, he only just caught the words. The crowd started to get louder as the chained man was brought forward.

"No," he responded.

"We believe that the punishment should fit the crime. Unjust murderers are murdered. Thieves have time stolen from them in the prisons. And here"—she gestured to the arena—"here is where we deal with rapists."

Rapists.

The word was foreign to him, but it didn't sound good, the phonetics rough against his ears. He deliberated whether to ask what it meant. He didn't want to seem foolish, not with his ignorance of all other things Amarran, but by the look of horror on the man awaiting his punishment, he dared not remain in ignorance.

"I don't know what that means," he admitted to her.

Her face looked disappointed at the admission. "I forget," she said. "It is not even a crime in Brutus. How could you have a word for it?" She shook herself. "It is when a person forces sex upon someone who does not want it."

Sanos's eyes went wide, and suddenly it seemed strange that his country didn't have a word for such a thing. It was what his father did to his mother in the marriage bed. He'd heard soldiers brag about conquests when they'd find lone women in the streets . . . It never sat comfortably with him, but he took comfort in knowing that he was not like that. His brothers weren't like that. Despite everything, the Ladicus brothers were nothing like their cruel father.

But then Sanos wondered, had he ever paid an unwilling woman? Someone who was so desperate for money to buy herself food and clothes and a roof overhead that she couldn't say no despite wanting to?

Sanos felt sick. Worse than sick.

He hated that he'd never given it a second thought until this woman entered his life.

"What did he do?" Olerra asked the woman next to her, gesturing to the man awaiting punishment.

"He was the family friend of some nobility in Ephenna. He was caught in the bedroom of the nobleman's ten-year-old daughter. The nurse thought to check on her and caught him. He was sent here for punishment."

A child.

Sanos couldn't help it. The smell of blood was so rich in the air, he leaned over the stands and vomited into the pit below.

Olerra rubbed his back soothingly. She used a handkerchief to wipe his face before he returned to his seat. She offered him her waterskin to wash down the taste of bile.

And then it was starting.

The sentenced man was dragged toward a large structure in the middle of the room. It was shaped like an X, two large wood beams making the shape. He was chained to each end, hands on the top, feet on the bottom. Then a contraption was rolled over to him.

The device was also made out of wood. It consisted of a single small hole like one would see in a stocks for hands and a head, but smaller. The device also had a metal blade.

A guard produced a knife, cutting off the man's pants so they fell around his ankles. He spat in her face as she worked, but she ignored it, clearly long used to the treatment.

Then a voice echoed through the room, and Sanos spotted another woman on the other side of the pit, speaking through a voice-magnifying trumpet.

"Revlin Darigan, for the crime of misusing your member, you have been sentenced to lose it." The announcer nodded to the guard in the pit, who still had the man's spit shining on her face.

The guard rolled the device until it trapped the man between the cross and it. She yanked on the pulley, which raised the wooden block with the sharp blade attached.

It looked like—

A guillotine.

For a man's cock.

The sentenced man started to thrash as the woman used a rod to lift his member and place it in the designated indentation. The crowd started to chant, but Sanos couldn't quite make out the words. Sweat ran down the man's face, and he was spewing venom from his mouth, too far for Sanos to hear. It was probably for the best.

And then, all at once, the blade was released. It plummeted toward the ground and the man's member.

Sanos shut his eyes at the last moment, unable to watch. It heightened his hearing, allowing him to finally discern the chant.

"Cut! Cut! Cut!"

The scream made the hair at the back of his neck stand on end. The crowd silenced as though to hear it better. When Sanos opened his eyes, he couldn't bear to stare at the scene in front of him, so he looked to Olerra instead.

That was a mistake.

"Look," she demanded, nodding toward the pit.

He shook his head.

She wrenched on the leash, forcing him forward. His eyes focused without him giving them the command to do so.

Another woman had entered the arena. She wore gloves and a medical coat. She also held some sort of thin tubing in her hands. There was a second scream as she hunched over the bound man, doing something that couldn't be seen with her blocking his lower half with her own body.

When she stepped aside, the tubing hung from where his cock once was.

So he could still urinate.

Finally they brought what appeared to be a hot poker, to cauterize—

Sanos nearly passed out as the man screamed a third time.

14

Andrastus dragged his feet as they returned to the carriage. Olerra bought him lunch, though he didn't eat it. She wasn't surprised that he'd lost his appetite after their last stop. She enjoyed the chicken skewers on her own, handing out the extras to anyone on the street who looked hungry. The prince was quiet, which she knew by now was not his natural state. She worried for him but left him to his thoughts.

He didn't speak until the carriage was halfway back to the palace.

"Why did you show me that? So I would know what awaits me should I misbehave again?"

She turned to him in alarm. "Andrastus, no. *No.* I told you. We believe the punishment should fit the crime. The point was to show you the ugliest side of both your gender and mine. To punish you by making you watch, yes. But you would never be sentenced to such a thing unless you first committed the crime."

He didn't seem convinced.

"Let me remind you that you lost your breakfast when you learned of the man's crimes. Not when you saw what happened to him. Did you think the punishment unfitting?"

"That man is permanently scarred," Andrastus said.

"And you think the children he hurt aren't? Their scars might be internal, but they are still there and just as lasting."

Silence spread between them, but Olerra broke it once more. "One thing I wish I could make men understand," she said, "is empathy. Most men will never understand the horrors of rape. It happens, but not nearly so often to them. So most never even think of it. You do not realize the pain and shame and *fear* that women in the world carry with them."

"But in Amarra, surely that doesn't happen often," he said.

"No, not often. But it was only five hundred years ago that our goddess blessed her daughters with her strength. It was not so long ago that we don't remember the way things were, especially when we can still see it in our neighbors. So many women flee to our borders to escape their lives. We make room for them. Because this is a place where all women should feel safe and cared for. And not just them, but all the minorities: amise, madae, madereo, madorn, siro, turé, and even sirem, who are not revered as they are in our country."

The prince said, "Everyone except men with a preference for women."

"You're learning."

"So I'm to be hated and treated like trash because of my preference for women?"

Olerra leaned forward until their knees were touching. She was pleased that he didn't move away from her. "No. If you let me, Andrastus, I would be *so* good to you. I only wanted to help you understand. To punish you, yes, but, more importantly, to help you compare your country to mine and see the world through our eyes. I'm not saying it's right. Just that there is a *reason* for it. Most in my country believe that if we don't dominate men, then they will go right back to oppressing us. We must behave this way to protect ourselves."

Quieter, she asked, "What reason is there for the way the men of your country treat women?"

He didn't answer.

When they returned to the palace, Sanos was relieved, thinking that would be that, but no, she had one more torture for him to endure that evening.

"Who the fuck is that?" he demanded.

A woman was waiting in his room. On his bedside table, she unrolled a leather case containing all manner of needles. There was also a bucket of ice, a burning candle, and vials of ointments.

"Sit," Olerra instructed. When he resisted, she motioned for the eunuchs to strap him to his bed. He fought, but as usual, it did no good when he was so outnumbered.

"I'm honored that you sent for me," the new woman said. She looked to be in her mid-thirties and was riddled with tattoos on her throat and arms.

"Thank you for coming, Ersha. We're going to do a single piercing on the right lobe, I think."

Piercing. Only now Sanos recalled her saying that word earlier. He hadn't associated it with this, because why in the world would it mean *this*?

His protests went ignored.

"And for the earring?" Ersha asked.

"Let's do an onyx stud, please."

"To match the armband. How perfect."

Sanos watched her bring a hollow needle into his line of sight. She held it over the candle flame first. Then she put some sort of ointment on it. She cleaned his ear with the same ointment, using a warm rag.

"Ready?" the piercer asked him.

"Fuck off."

"Breathe in," she instructed. "And breathe out."

"Fuck!"

"Just a moment more," Ersha said.

He felt a lesser pinch, which must have been the earring going in. Then came the ice, which soothed his heated skin.

"Keep it clean. Use these vials twice a day. You know the routine," the piercer said.

Olerra leaned over him to inspect his ear. Ersha removed the ice for her.

"Oh, it's beautiful."

Beautiful.

That was not a word one should use to describe a man.

Certainly not the crown prince of Brutus.

"I love it, Ersha. Thank you!" Olerra said.

She hugged the woman. Hugged her.

Then they both left.

Sanos fumed in the empty room. He stared at the ceiling, and he was surprised that his thoughts quickly drifted from his mutilated ear. It didn't hurt at all anymore. Not even when he tilted his head to lay his right ear on the pillow.

Which meant he was left to think on other things. If the story Olerra shared with him was true, then the women of Amarra had made themselves cruel and heartless to retaliate against the abuses of men. Sounded like an excuse to be cruel and heartless. To justify doing bad things.

But the question she'd asked earlier rang in his mind.

What reason is there for the way the men of your country treat women?

Because they could.

Because no one had the power to stop them.

So how could he blame the Amarrans for what they'd done to protect themselves? What he'd seen today was no worse than what he'd witnessed in his own country. The only difference was that the victims were men. It hit harder because it was his own sex being hurt.

Olerra was forcing him to question so much.

Gods, he needed to get out of this place.

Olerra didn't come for him in the morning. The eunuchs dressed him as usual, thankfully in more clothing now that he wasn't being punished, and then they took him to what one of them called the gymnasium, which he vaguely remembered Olerra mentioning on their travels to Amarra.

It was entirely bizarre.

Sanos hadn't thought about what the husbands and consorts did all day while the women went about their work. He never would have pictured this, though.

It was a series of massive rooms with vaulted ceilings. In one, a track went along the outskirts of the room, and men were jogging it. In the center, weight lifting equipment of all kinds was spaced evenly apart. Mirrors covered most of the walls, and Sanos drew closer to one so he could inspect his ear.

He blinked. It didn't . . . look terrible. The onyx was small, and he thought it gave him a slight roguish appearance. Gods, but his father would hate it, and that thought made Sanos like it more.

He shouldn't like it at all, but he reasoned that if he ripped it out, Olerra would only have someone put it back in. He would leave it untouched.

For now.

Continuing his exploration, Sanos found padded chairs and tables in another room. Some of the men played cards or dice. Others simply lounged, talking with one another, drinks or food in hand.

As he traversed deeper, he found a room with easels and paint. Needles and thread. Another with gardening supplies and a glass ceiling. A library with settees and thousands upon thousands of books. Everywhere he went were all manner of arts and crafts to entertain.

His personal escort followed him at a distance, relaxing against the walls of whatever room he chose to occupy. They weren't the only eunuchs in attendance. Many oversaw the activities taking place. Sanos picked them out because they were the only men who didn't wear armbands. There were also female guards, relaxed yet holding spears. He had a feeling it wasn't because anyone tried to escape. No, they were there to break up fights.

Sanos had no intention of causing trouble, and he wasn't there to make friends. He was biding his time until he could make his escape. Keeping his body fit seemed to be the best course of action. He headed for the weights first. The week in the cart and nights spent practically immovable had taken their toll.

He started with his arms, lifting heavy weights until they were too sore to move. Then he did the muscles of his legs, lying back on a machine and pressing up weights with his feet. He paused to stretch and get some water before deciding a jog might be nice. He didn't know what the Amarrans did to keep the interior of the gymnasium so much cooler than outside, but it felt nice.

After his first loop, another man joined him on the track.

He didn't have to turn his head. Sanos could see the bulk of him out of the corner of his eye.

Athon.

Sanos welcomed his appearance, especially since the man's limp was gone. He thought they might run in silence together. Or that Athon might wish to thank him for the things he'd said. Perhaps he might find a soul who hated this place as much as he did.

"Could you stop being such a prick?" were the first words out of Athon's mouth.

Sanos almost tripped over his own feet. "Excuse me?"

"You think yourself better than me."

"No—"

"Save it," Athon snarled. "Glenaerys chose me. I am honored to be hers. I don't need you speaking like you know anything about us."

"I wasn't."

"You think you're special because you have Olerra? Because she's nice? Glen is going to be queen one day. I will be the envy of every man."

"Except the thirty others who are also sharing her bed."

He regretted the words as soon as he said them. He didn't know why Athon was egging him on so.

"Exactly. Thirty out of hundreds of thousands of men. Glenaerys honors us."

"Fine."

Sanos sped up a little, hoping Athon would take the hint.

The bigger man matched his speed.

"I want a rematch," Athon said. "I will prove myself to Glen. Next time, I can beat you."

There was a nasty taste in the prince's mouth. "Is your entire existence centered on that woman? Didn't you only start courting a couple of weeks ago?"

"I was nobody. Now I'm everything. Quit changing the subject."

Sanos started to get pissed. This man was utterly stupid. Sanos had been doing his utmost to help him, but he didn't see it that way. Athon genuinely liked where he was. He only didn't like that he'd lost.

"We're done," Sanos said with finality.

"I say we're not." And Athon shoved him.

He hadn't been expecting it, and Sanos quickly lost his footing. He landed with skinned knees and smarting palms. Before he could get up, Athon threw a kick under his stomach, sending the breath out of him.

But Sanos had been made to fight his whole life while injured. It didn't matter that his lungs couldn't draw in air. He spun and flung a fist at Athon. The bigger man hadn't been expecting him to recover so quickly. His face flew to the side and blood dripped from his mouth.

Then they threw themselves at each other.

Sanos maintained that he was defending himself. But this was so much more than that. He was being attacked by someone with whom he could finally fight back. Athon was no king. No woman. He was a soldier. He was a bed slave. He was a pain in the ass.

So Sanos took blows and landed blows. Though certain he'd win, it didn't go on for too long before someone tried to break up the fight. A strong hand landed on Sanos's bicep to pull him back. He shoved at the figure so he could continue laying into the man in front of him.

But the gym went silent. Even Athon froze, and Sanos wasn't about to fight a man who wouldn't fight him back.

So Sanos turned to see what everyone was looking at.

On the floor was none other than Glenaerys. She'd been the one who'd tried to pull Sanos off her man. He'd shoved her. She'd landed on the track, scraping her elbow on the floor.

And it was bleeding.

The guards were on him faster than he could blink. Two held each of his arms in check. Another wrapped an elbow around his neck from behind.

Glenaerys rose and surveyed the entire gymnasium, which had witnessed the encounter. She looked at Sanos with a sneer.

She said, "I want his head."

They dragged him from the room.

Sanos fought. He tried his hardest to break the holds on him, but the women were too strong. He knew with certainty that he was about to be put to death. He had committed one of the gravest of crimes in Amarra.

They'd nearly gotten him to the exit when he managed a last look back. He saw Glen cupping the face of Athon, whispering something in his ear. He looked smugly back at Sanos.

He had fallen right into Glen's trap.

Sanos thought he might be taken to a dungeon to await a trial, but that didn't happen at all. No, he was dragged through the palace to a chamber he'd never visited. They put chains around his neck, wrists, and ankles. Weighted balls kept him from moving. He was a prisoner in a crowded room.

The faces all blurred together. Some might have been in the gymnasium earlier, but he wasn't certain. The room heated quickly from all the bodies, and Sanos sweated through his clothing. Movement up ahead caught his eye, and he watched Glen seat herself on a cushioned chair, Athon at her side. Courtiers surrounded her.

Sanos could barely breathe, and it had nothing to do with the fight from earlier. His chest heaved; he couldn't think with all the noise in the room. Noblewomen shouted obscenities at him. Men in the room gave testimony. All those who had witnessed the altercation.

It was happening too fast.

He could do nothing to stop it. Couldn't move more than a few feet in either direction with the heavy weights.

And then a device was rolled into the room.

It was much like the one at the pit, but larger. This guillotine was designed for a head, not a cock.

He was going to die. Without a chance to explain himself. To say it had been Glen's plan all along. She wanted revenge for what he'd said in front of those older noblewomen at breakfast. She wanted to weaken Olerra. He'd been tricked. It was all a setup. He tried to talk over the voices around him, but no one would hear any of it.

The guillotine came closer and closer. They pushed him to his knees and locked a slab of wood around his neck. His hands were useless at his sides. His nails chipped as he tried to claw at the contraption. When the blade at the top began to wobble from his efforts, he went still.

The room quieted.

"What is going on?"

Glenaerys turned toward the voice, one Sanos never thought he'd be glad to hear. "Ah, Olerra, you're just in time. Andrastus has struck me. I've demanded his head."

The general stepped in front of Sanos. Her back was to him as she faced down her cousin.

"That is my man, and you may do no such thing without speaking to *me* first. Else I have the right to make *you* bleed."

Glen didn't seem the least bit worried. "What is there to tell you? You cannot waive his punishment. As the afflicted party, it is my right to demand it."

"And as the woman this man belongs to, it is my right to demand substitution."

The room went *silent*.

So silent one would have thought it had suddenly emptied.

"Substitution?" Glen said, outraged. "No one has asked for such a thing in—"

"A hundred years," another voice said, and suddenly everyone in the room went down on their knees.

The queen has arrived.

Olerra and Glen rose after a brief bow.

"I will take the punishment," Olerra said.

"Female royalty cannot be killed!" Glenaerys shot back. She turned to the queen. "Olerra knows this. She's trying to take advantage of a loophole in the law. Your Majesty, you cannot allow this crime to go unpunished. I was harmed by that man"—she pointed to Sanos—"while trying to stop him from hurting Athon. He's a violent Brute and should live on our soil no longer!"

Queen Lemya was taller than Sanos had first thought, having only seen her seated at her breakfast table. She walked around where Sanos was strapped to the guillotine, her long legs taking their time as she made slow circles. He kept his head bowed, trying to look contrite.

"Glenaerys, do not presume to tell me what to do," the queen said. "Do you not think I know how to dole out justice, even where my own family is concerned?"

Glen trembled with anger. "Forgive me, My Queen." The words sounded sincere enough, but she looked far from sorry.

The queen stopped right in front of Sanos, and he dared to look up. Eyes on him, she said, "The law is the law. Olerra has the right to demand substitution, but she cannot be killed. Therefore, Olerra can either live out her life in exile or take a beating so that her betrothed might live." The queen turned to Olerra. "Is that a choice you really want to make, niece?"

Olerra turned around, and Sanos saw her face for the first time that day. She might as well have worn a mask over her features for all the emotion she showed. Was she feeling sympathetic? Was she furious with him? Was she ready to let him die for this? He didn't know what she was doing or why. But she must have seen his terror. Bewilderment. And now a spark of hope.

Olerra nodded once. "I will take the beating. Release him."

Sanos was let out of the stocks, but they kept him bound in the chains.

"As the afflicted party," Glenaerys said, recovering quickly from the disruption, "I demand to choose the one who will dole out the punishment."

The queen said, "Very well, Glenaerys, but it must be a willing person you select and not a man, for obvious reasons."

"Oh, I assure you I'm willing. Now, restrain her."

At first, no one moved. The queen's guard didn't take orders from Glenaerys, and it seemed that any common soldiers from the gymnasium were loyal to Olerra. It was only as Glen cast angry glances to her personal guard that the order was finally followed.

They tied Olerra's hands together so she could not fight back. Sanos felt sick. He felt grateful. He was confused. Why would she do this? How could the queen let this happen?

Hadn't Olerra said that Glen wasn't a trained fighter? Surely this couldn't be too bad.

It was, in fact, worse than he could have imagined.

Olerra couldn't remember the last time she'd been so afraid.

Andrastus was her responsibility. When a loyal servant had brought her the news that her prince was to be beheaded, she'd run faster than ever.

She couldn't explain why she felt an attachment to this man, but if he'd broken the laws in some way, then she clearly hadn't done a good job training him. It was her job to provide food and shelter and safety. She'd even given him space after the trauma of what she'd made him witness yesterday.

She had no choice but to demand substitution. It was the only way to save him. To continue to be a provider and a protector for him. It was a matter of honor.

Even if it meant submitting herself to her cousin.

Glenaerys donned a pair of brass knuckles, padded where they wrapped around her fingers. Did she keep those on her at all times?

Despicable. Glen couldn't even throw a proper punch without risking breaking her hand. She'd use a foul instrument to make it hurt harder and protect her delicate bones.

The audience of nobility was, at least, not blood hungry like they'd been the other day for Andrastus's wrestling match. The women in the room were silent. Anticipatory, yes, but it was unclear how much of the anticipation was horror versus eagerness. Who in the room was on Glenaerys's side and who was on Olerra's?

The first punch slammed into Olerra's left cheek. She felt the metal connect with bone, tasted blood in her mouth, and heard Glen's exhale.

Olerra was proud that she kept her feet.

The second hit, however, caused her to lose her balance. She landed on the floor but quickly righted herself.

Glenaerys hit her again. She struck Olerra in the stomach this time, catching a rib on her brass knuckles. Olerra grunted out in pain, doubling over.

She would not look at her aunt. She didn't need saving. Didn't need anything. She would accept this. She'd suffered far worse on the battlefield. There was nothing Glen could do to her that was worse than what a Brutish soldier had doled out.

Glenaerys got more creative as she went on. Throwing kicks. Experimenting with Olerra's shoulders and hips and other places. Learning where would do the most damage. Learning what would send her toppling to the ground.

Everything hurt now. Olerra was bleeding in too many places to count, the knuckles splitting skin and fracturing bones.

Glenaerys's breathing became labored. The room was still silent enough for all to hear it.

Olerra made the mistake of looking at her.

The unmasked hatred on her cousin's face was another blow. Olerra was certain she wasn't deserving of that ire. It was that of someone ripe with jealousy, and now Glen had an outlet for that feeling as she struck Olerra again and again.

Glen resented Olerra for being a general. For being strong. For being the one to stand between her and a throne. In their youth, they'd been the best of friends, but that was a different lifetime.

Another hit sent Olerra to the ground. It took her longer to regain her feet. The room spun.

"That's enough," Ydra said, stepping out from the crowd. When had she arrived?

Glen shot a look to Ydra as though she'd forgotten an audience was even there. Glen didn't respond to her, instead turning toward the queen. "Your Majesty, it is a life sentence that Olerra is the substitute for. The beating must be of equal value."

The queen nodded gravely. Olerra blinked when her aunt's figure started to double.

When next she landed on the floor, Olerra could not get up again. Glen sent her foot into Olerra's stomach again and again. When a kick struck her face, the world went dark.

15

Sanos felt every blow as if it landed on his own skin.

He was used to beatings. Used to watching as his brothers received theirs. But he'd never been forced to endure this.

He watched as this impossible woman took his punishment. No one had ever done such a thing before. And she barely knew him. She had no cause to do this. Surely the effort of taking herself a new husband was more appealing than this. So then why? Why subject herself to such pain and humiliation in front of a room of people who decided whether she would be the next ruler of her country?

What hidden motive did she have?

She took the beating silently. She took it admirably, rising each time she was struck to the floor. Until she no longer had the strength to stand. Until she could no longer keep her eyes open.

All for him.

The relief he felt when the queen's guard finally dragged Glenaerys away from Olerra could not be described with words.

The princess was a mottled mess of blood and broken skin, but she was breathing.

Ydra was already approaching her with physicians in tow. They loaded her onto a mat that they hoisted up into the air. To his eunuch guards, Ydra said, "Bring him."

Ydra bowed before the queen. "I will take her to my estate to recover safely."

The queen nodded. Whether words failed her or she was a woman of very few, Sanos didn't know. They removed his chains and made him follow.

For once, Sanos didn't fight.

Ydra's estate was quite large. Sanos admired the marble columns and beautiful exterior gardens for all of a second before he was ushered inside and locked within a bedroom.

He was not bound, for which he was grateful. He was, however, left with nothing but his thoughts.

It didn't matter that Olerra was a general and a warrior. He *hated* seeing her hurt, and he hated that he hated it. He didn't want to feel like he owed her. It was her fault that he was in this mess in the first place. He should not have had to deal with any of this, and yet, there he was.

He paced the room.

Why had she done it?

In his country, if a man saved another's life, he was owed a life debt. The debt could only be repaid in one way. The one who had been saved spent their life in servitude to the one who had spared them until such a day came that the spared was able to save their savior's life in return. These rules did not, exactly, extend to the royal family—because royals could not be expected to serve in such a capacity. But still, Sanos felt honor bound to this woman.

He growled aloud. She'd taken his life away first! She'd stolen him. And now she'd saved him. If anything, they were even. Except that he was still trapped and forced to do her bidding.

Sanos continued pacing until his last image of her sprang to mind. She had lain so still on the floor, her blood pooling onto the red obsidian tiles.

Damn her!

He would still escape at the first opportunity. He would be rid of her and this place, but his conscience needled at him, and he hated her for it.

When the door opened, Ydra was there alone.

"You fucking idiot," she seethed.

"How is she?" he asked, meeting her gaze.

"Four fractured ribs. A broken nose. Bruises on every inch of skin. She'll be recovering for weeks. Maybe longer."

"I didn't ask her to do that," he said, getting defensive at her tone.

"Of course she did it!" Ydra was shouting at him now. "She is an honorable woman, the best I've ever known. You are hers, and that means she will always protect you. No matter what that entails. How could you be so stupid as to strike Glenaerys?!"

"It was an accident. She set me up."

"Obviously, but you played right into her plans! She wanted you dead to weaken Olerra's claim to the throne, but now she's gotten something even better. She made Olerra look weak when she stepped in to save *you*. You've set us back."

"Her generosity made her look weak?"

"*Saving you made her look weak.* You're a man. And not even an Amarran. The nobles whose favor we did garner might be lost after this. And it doesn't help that Glen got to show strength by beating the shit out of her." Ydra rubbed her temples. Her tone was absolutely livid as she said, "She is a better woman than you deserve."

"I never asked to be here!" he thundered.

"Well, you're here now! So get your shit together, Brute. Screw up this badly again, and I will kill you myself! I'd do it now except that would render her sacrifice useless, and I love her too much for that. There are guards everywhere in the house in case Glen tries anything while Olerra is weakened. So don't *you* try anything. Now stay out of trouble for one godsdamned moment."

She slammed the door behind her.

It did not, however, lock this time.

He was free to roam her home, it would seem, which was why she'd bothered to mention the guards.

The first night, shame and anger kept him in the room.

The next day, he decided to explore to keep his thoughts off Olerra.

Ydra's home was rather large. There were many wings to the manor and so much staff. Ydra must be wealthy. Since he knew she worked in the army, like Olerra, he assumed the wealth was inherited. He suspected, then, that her parents were no longer around.

He found the library quickly and located many books on Amarran history and politics. He pulled them from the shelves to make a stack to read later, since he didn't know how long he would be there.

The floors were decorated with exotic fur pelts. Some wildcat and bear varieties. He wondered if Ydra was the huntress or if it had been someone else in her family.

Sanos continued his perusal. As he reached higher levels of the manor, he heard noises. There were soldiers along the hallway, but they didn't prevent him from entering the room where the most sound emanated.

Inside he found five boys talking animatedly over some kind of game board.

"It's my move. Give me the dice!" The first boy rolled, and everyone cackled at whatever number he received. "No," he groaned.

There was a guard in the room, who eyed Sanos carefully.

Then the boys noticed his appearance.

"Who are you?" one boy asked. Then, seeing his armband, he said, "You're Olerra's!"

"We love Olerra," another boy said. "She plays games with us."

They were all in their younger teen years. So young, yet far too old to be Ydra's children.

"Are you . . . Ydra's cousins?" Sanos guessed.

The first boy scoffed. He pointed to the armband that Sanos had initially overlooked.

It was made of pure gold and had a rectangular emerald within.

"I don't understand," Sanos said.

"We're part of Ydra's harem," another boy said, this one even more youthful-looking than the last.

"She—you—" Sanos felt as though he wanted to throw up.

The final boy, seeing his struggle, rolled his eyes. "It's not like that. She took us off the streets. She takes care of us so no one else takes advantage of us. She has tutors for us so we can join the workforce when we're ready. I'm training to be a cloth merchant."

One of the other boys elbowed him. "We're not supposed to tell anyone that we're not *really* part of Ydra's harem."

"But he's Olerra's. Olerra knows, so why shouldn't he?"

Ydra . . . was helping them. She didn't bed them. She kept them safe.

Just as Olerra had done with him.

He wasn't sure if he liked this new information. He wanted no reasons not to murder Ydra along with Olerra when he got the chance. Gods, he hated this place.

Sanos cleared his throat. "What game are you playing?"

"Corgo. You want to join us?"

It took him a week to get up the courage to ask to speak to Olerra. And at first, he was denied.

"She's not fit for visitors," Ydra insisted.

"She doesn't have to do or say anything. I just want to see her."

"No."

He asked again the next day.

"No."

And the next.

"Absolutely not."

It was another week before he insisted, "Will you just ask her? *Tell* her at least that I want to speak to her. Surely she wants to make her own decisions about such things."

It worked. The next day, Ydra led him up the stairs. She did not look happy about it. Sanos was wise enough not to say anything to her, and he kept his smugness to himself.

Ydra entered the room first, Sanos trailing behind. Olerra was sitting up in bed at least. Her face was mottled with yellowing bruises. Her nose was still lightly swollen, and bandages were tightly wrapped around her upper waist. He could see the gauze poking out through the sleeveless nightdress she wore.

Sanos tried to approach the bed, but Ydra halted him. "That's close enough."

He glared at her. "Are you going to stand there the whole time?"

"You're damned right I am. I don't trust you."

"Ydra," Olerra admonished.

"I'm not going anywhere. This is my home, and if you want to see him, you can do it with me standing here or not at all."

Olerra rolled her eyes but didn't protest further. She adjusted a pillow behind her back and set aside a book she had been reading. She looked at him expectantly.

Right, he'd called this meeting. He should say something.

"You look to be healing well," he started.

"I am. The doctors say I can start walking again soon, but we will remain here until I am back to full strength."

"Because your cousin might try something?"

"Among other people," Ydra said under her breath. With the way she was looking at him, he realized she meant *him*. As if he would hurt Olerra after what she'd done for him.

Well, he might. He still wasn't sure about that. It depended on his mood. Right now, taking in her injuries and wrapped bandages, he couldn't muster the proper anger.

"Yes," Olerra answered.

There was an awkward silence. Sanos began to wonder why he'd thought this was a good idea. He'd just wanted to see her with his own eyes. Make sure she wasn't dying.

He should leave now. She was clearly healing.

Just turn around and leave.

"Thank you," he spat out instead.

It was unclear if he or Olerra were more surprised by the words.

She recovered first. "You're welcome."

Sanos tried to pretend Ydra wasn't there. "Why did you do it? Why not let me die? And don't tell me taking a new husband wouldn't have been easier."

"It would have been much easier," Olerra said, and she stifled a groan as she moved in a way that must have hurt her injuries.

"Then . . . ?"

Olerra looked him dead-on. "You are mine, *and no one takes what's mine*. Especially my fucking cousin."

Sanos accepted that answer.

Obviously it didn't have anything to do with her feelings about him or her character. It came down to one simple thing: her hatred of Glenaerys.

He let himself out.

Olerra stared at his retreating back. That was twice that he'd thanked her. First, for sending the letter to his mother. Then again for saving his life.

The Brute didn't want his mother to worry, and he was concerned for Olerra's health.

It was hidden, but Olerra felt like she'd finally found that gentler side to Andrastus that the rumors had hinted at. He must have buried it to protect himself upon being stolen away to Amarra.

She liked seeing that gentleness.

Olerra was glad she'd allowed the audience. At first, she hadn't wanted him to see her weak and beaten a second time. It was bad enough that the entire nobility had been present to witness Glen's victory. She didn't want the man who would be hers to ever have cause to think of her that way again.

"You lied to him," Ydra said when it was just the two of them. "I know you saved him because you feel honor bound to do so."

"He thinks me a villain. I gave him an answer he would believe."

"He is such a bastard. He's not good enough for you."

Olerra smiled at her friend's protectiveness. "You're just upset because I took a beating."

"A beating," Ydra repeated. "No, ten lashes is a beating. What you took was just short of a death sentence."

"It could be nothing less to save him."

"Nobody would have blinked if you'd let him die. Now the whole of Amarra knows you hold him in higher regard than your cousin."

Olerra agreed. "We will need to do something to fix this once I'm healed."

"I've been thinking about that. You could challenge your cousin. Give her a taste of her own medicine."

"She would refuse." Olerra would relish the opportunity for a fair fight between the two of them, but there was no such thing. Olerra was the more skilled fighter. She would always win. "And then she would turn it around somehow to make it seem as though I were the bully and she the harmless victim."

"She nearly killed you!"

"My aunt never would have allowed that."

Ydra stepped forward until she could sit on the edge of the bed. She took a deep breath to calm her anger. "Perhaps we could start by strengthening what we already have. Glen has the nobles, but you have the army and the people. When you're healed, you could take Andrastus on a ride through the city. Show him off. Show your strength. Let the people cheer. Later, you can bring him to meet the troops."

"That's a great idea, but what of the nobles? They will not be so easily swayed after I risked myself for him."

"*I'm* angry that you risked yourself for him."

"As if you wouldn't for any one of your boys."

"They're innocents! That prince is anything but. He doesn't deserve your kindness."

Olerra adjusted the blankets around her. "You hate him for being born a Brute, but it is because of his noble blood that I need him."

"You could have chosen literally any other kingdom."

"I needed to send a message to Atalius."

"He doesn't even know you took his son!"

"But he will. And that will make it all worth it."

Ydra took her hand. "You cannot afford to be gentle with him any longer. Not in public. You must show your dominance now more than ever. You must get him to submit. He feels indebted to you now. Use that to make him behave."

"I will do what I can. He's so unpredictable."

"You could start beating him."

Olerra laughed. "You don't mean that. You must get over what happened."

"Fine, but it will take time. Sister, I *hated* seeing you like that. I would have taken your place if I could."

Olerra knew it. Once substitution had been granted, however, no one else could claim it.

"We will come back from this," Olerra said.

"We will," Ydra agreed. "We will get you that throne no matter what."

It was another couple of weeks before Olerra felt fully healed. She took walks around Ydra's manor and estate but never left the grounds. Glen's spies and assassins could take any opportunity to try something. They were likely watching the manor.

She used the time to get her strength back. She ran and put herself through her exercises, slowly at first, until her body was well on its way back to full speed.

Only then did she allow herself to be alone with Andrastus.

"We have a lot of work ahead of us," Olerra said to him on the ride back to the palace. "I cannot afford to seem weak after . . . what happened. The nobles must see me having a firmer hand with you. They must think me in love to have risked so much for you. We must sell it."

"Well, which is it?" he asked with irritation. "Are you going to be more cruel to me or act in love with me?"

"Not cruel. Firmer. It means when you misstep, I will need a firmer hand in reprimanding you. If you help me sell the ruse, if you do not misstep, there will be no need for any of it. If we can sell a true romance, give the nobles something to root for, then neither of us should have to deal with any unpleasantness."

"That makes absolutely no sense."

"To you. To an Amarran, it makes perfect sense. Can I count on you?"

He looked away from her. Something outside the window suddenly held his complete attention.

She continued with "Just remember, Prince, this arrangement can have an end date. I promise that if you cooperate, I will give you back your life when this is all said and done."

He said nothing, and Olerra thought that would be the end of it. Then: "Do you swear it?"

He wouldn't look at her, but the words felt vulnerable. As though he were used to people disappointing him every day.

"I swear it, Andrastus."

"Swear on something that matters."

It was a bit pushy, but when Olerra held most of the power, she could allow him this. She said, "I swear on the ashes of my mother. I will ensure your safe travel home as soon as I am declared crown princess."

The tightness about his shoulders lessened. "I'm not saying that I won't try to escape if the opportunity presents itself, but I will not make a mistake like the one I did with your cousin. I will not make you look bad again."

Olerra believed him. Andrastus would give Glenaerys and her harem a wide berth after this.

And she would never expect him to stay if he thought he could get away.

They had an understanding, and that was enough for Olerra.

For now.

Olerra took Ydra's advice.

The day after their arrival at the palace, Olerra ordered her carriage readied. Unlike the practical one she'd taken to show Andrastus the Pleasure Market and the pit, this one was more elaborate. This was to be their first official outing for the people, and Olerra wanted to do it in style. The people loved a good show.

The wide carriage was raised high off the ground on massive wheels and painted scarlet after the red obsidian the court was known for. There was a canopied top to shade them, held up by four thick poles, one in each corner. Instead of windows, the top half of the carriage was open to the outdoors. Andrastus needed to be as visible as possible, and it allowed for a nice breeze.

Her prince was done up much as he'd been all those weeks ago. Short skirt. Barefoot and bare-chested. Hands manacled behind his back. Nipple clamps in place. His hair was styled to perfection. At his temples were twin braids plaited against the scalp, keeping the hair away from his face. The rest of his hair was slicked back with cream. It shimmered golden in the sunlight. He was freshly shaven, and her onyx gleamed on his upper arm.

Gods, but he was a sight.

Andrastus was clearly displeased with his attire and the situation at large. He had to be prodded up the steps of the carriage. When he sat, he moved as far from her as possible.

She sighed but let him have his space.

A handful of soldiers rode on horseback, both in front of and behind the carriage. Olerra never experienced any trouble in the streets, but it was good to have more women she trusted on hand, just in case.

A herald rode at the head of the party, calling out every few blocks, "Her Royal Highness, Princess Olerra Corasene, and her intended, Prince Andrastus Ladicus of Brutus."

People stopped in the streets. They waved, and Olerra tossed coins occasionally to the onlookers, who cheered and stooped to fill their pockets. Some women tossed flowers into the carriage. Others walked up to hand Olerra baked sweets and bread. She accepted the gifts with heartfelt thanks.

Meanwhile, Andrastus looked ill at ease.

"What's the matter?" Olerra asked. "Is the heat getting to you?" His skin had healed from the initial burns of his arrival. He had a new dusting of freckles on his shoulders. They were adorable, not that she'd tell him.

"It's not that," he said irritably. "I don't love having my hands tied behind my back."

"Sorry, Prince, but I can't risk you trying anything while we're away from the security of the palace. Besides, it's not like you'd rather be waving at them. Or accepting flowers and sweets. Doesn't that go against some unspoken code of manliness for you Brutes?"

"There is no manliness code."

"Isn't there? No crying. No showing emotion. And any qualities that could be considered even slightly feminine ought to be stomped out."

He looked away from her. Olerra sat back in her seat and sampled some freshly baked bread. "Would you like some?" she asked.

"I would prefer not to eat from your fingers in front of the masses."

"Even if it would help my ruling?"

"You're being needlessly annoying."

Olerra unwrapped a bag of candied nuts, looked curiously at Andrastus, then tossed one high into the air in his direction.

On instinct, the prince opened his mouth and caught it on his tongue.

Olerra smiled, and the watching commoners clapped.

He glared at her. "I'm not a dog you can get to do tricks."

"You said you wouldn't eat from my fingers. What else was I supposed to do?"

"Stop trying to feed me."

"Why? Food makes everything better."

"Not everything," he said pointedly before looking away.

"Everything," she insisted. "Name one thing it doesn't."

He thought for a moment. "Bathing."

"You've never had a slice of cake while taking a bath? Definitely better. What else?"

"How about a beating?"

"You don't think chocolate makes injuries feel better? Next."

"This is ridiculous. I'm not playing these absurd games with you."

"Because you know I'm right." She tossed another nut to him. He let this one hit the top of his head before it fell to the floor.

"Spoilsport," she said.

16

They rode for hours through what felt like every street in the city. The herald even had to be switched out so her voice wouldn't go dry.

Olerra tried to engage Andrastus, but he wasn't having any of it. The man was so stubborn he put his father to shame. He was a true Brute indeed.

"Do you know how to have fun?" she asked him, utterly exasperated a couple of hours later.

They were along the outskirts of the city now. Soon they would cross the bridge over the Fren River before taking a road south back to the palace. There were hardly any homes around anymore, but Olerra loved the scenery. All the palm trees and flowering shrubs were a picturesque backdrop. Perfect for romancing her prince.

"Fun," he repeated.

"Yes, a good time? Surely you've had one before?"

He said nothing.

"You won't eat. You barely talk. You only tolerate the masses. What do you usually do as a prince in Brutus?"

"I didn't realize having fun was a goal you had for me," he said dryly.

"Of course it is. We're to be married. You think I want our time together to be miserable? Surely there's something fun we can decide on?"

There was a sound outside, a rumble that had the horses halting and whinnying. Up ahead, Olerra saw the bridge over the river collapsing, with her forward guard still upon it. They fell into the churning current below, which carried them and their horses away.

Before Olerra could so much as move, she heard the distinct *shink* that could only be that of an arrow.

"Get down!" Olerra shouted, throwing Andrastus to the floor and covering him with her body. A volley shot toward them. She heard the rear guard grunting in pain and falling off their horses. Arrows imbedding into the carriage door. The driver falling from her perch.

When all was still, Olerra rolled off the prince and dared a glance over the lip of the carriage. There were eight of them, all on horses and with crossbows. They reloaded now.

"Shit," she said.

"What is it?"

"Another of my cousin's assassination attempts."

"*What?*"

"Stay out of sight."

Olerra dug the key to his bindings out of her pocket and pressed it to his fingers.

Then she exited out the door opposite of the attackers.

She wouldn't let them get anywhere near Andrastus.

———※———

Sanos fumbled with the key, nearly dropping it in his disbelief and excitement. She was just *giving* it to him? Why? So he could help her fight off the attackers?

He heard more arrows loose and did drop the key this time.

Stupid.

He made himself take a deep breath. Yes, he was manacled and half naked. Yes, Olerra was outside, armed with a sword against projectiles. And he'd dropped the damned key.

Panic would only lead to death. He rolled around on his back, crushing his hands as they blindly sought out the key. Someone outside screamed, and he didn't know if it was Olerra, her guards, or someone else.

Not that I care.

His fingers throbbed as he finally brushed against the small metal key. He angled himself as best he could, leaning back on his ass and attempting to grip the stupid thing.

There!

His right hand had the key, and his left valiantly searched for the keyhole to his cuffs. This would be so much easier if he could just see.

There was a metallic sound outside. Possibly that of a bolt striking a sword. Was she *deflecting arrows*?

He finally found the keyhole, but his fingers were twisted the wrong way. He wiggled it, willing the key to go where he needed it.

The manacles slid loose, and he didn't waste a moment before taking the key to those restricting his ankles. Then the clamp at his neck. That damn collar.

Lastly, he removed the nipple clamps. He thought to throw them far away, but upon seeing the jewels spaced along the chain, he figured he could sell it for food during the journey home. He wrapped it around one of his wrists.

Then he got onto his knees to peer over the carriage as she had earlier.

What he saw was incredible.

Three attackers were already down, either dead or wounded by her sword. He couldn't see Olerra at first, but then he saw her hiding behind one of the horses of the fallen guards. She had one foot in the stirrup, one hand on the horn as she held herself parallel with the ground, using the horse's body to completely hide herself from view. The attackers must have lost sight of her as they were reloading for the next volley.

And they didn't suspect a lone horse for a second.

He looked behind the carriage. Olerra's guard had all been slaughtered by the arrow volleys. The ambush had done what it was meant to, rendering the princess entirely alone.

Olerra somehow directed the horse with nudges of her knee to its side, the mare turning away from the contact, until it pulled up beside one of the other riders.

She reached up and tugged the other woman off the horse.

He watched as Olerra released herself from her own horse, landing atop the woman on the ground. Olerra found a loose rock and clipped her in the head with it.

Gods, she was ruthless. She was something else to behold as she fought.

An arrow loosed, striking the horse that she hid behind and sending it bolting. Olerra didn't hesitate before leaning over to pick up the unconscious guard she'd just dispatched and use her like a meat shield. Two more bolts landed, hitting their accomplice instead of the queen potential of Amarra.

He was so caught up that he forgot escape should have been foremost on his mind. Shaking himself for his distraction, he exited the opposite door of the carriage as she had, closing it quietly behind him. Not that Olerra was likely to do anything if she heard it.

Sanos took in the scenery before him. A copse of trees waited a hundred yards off. If he could reach it, he would have cover as he made his escape.

But for some reason, he peered around the carriage. Just to get one more look at her.

Another assassin was down, and Olerra had discarded her meat shield. She'd gotten another rider off her horse, and the two battled with swords. As they spun, Olerra looked in his direction and spotted him.

"Run for the cover of the trees," she told him, returning her eyes to her opponent immediately. "Keep yourself safe. I'll find you when I'm done."

What the fuck?

She wanted him to run. She'd given him the key so he could be safe from the fighting. She knew he would go to the trees. She intended to come after him.

He ducked back around the carriage to look ahead of and behind the direction they'd been traveling. Was there somewhere else he could go? Somewhere she wouldn't expect him to travel to? Someplace he could finally be free of this woman?

Out of his periphery, he spotted a new assassin entering the fight. Someone who hadn't originally attacked them. Someone who had hung back, obviously intent on catching Olerra unawares. Sanos looked around the carriage again, just to ensure she saw the newcomer. Then he'd see about freeing one of the horses from the carriage and galloping away.

She battled all three of the previously saddle-ridden assassins. They were on their feet, all holding melee weapons of one kind or another. The newcomer approached, a long spear in hand.

Olerra didn't notice.

She'd be skewered.

Good, a voice muttered in his head.

The other part of him didn't speak. It simply remembered her being beaten to a bloody pulp for him.

She'd shown him her city, the good and the bad. She'd told him her hopes for changing things for the better. Her hopes for how things could be between them.

He couldn't leave her to die.

Sanos snarled in frustration.

He unwound the nipple chain from his wrist and gripped either end tightly in both fists. Silently, he overtook the new woman and garroted her. She dropped her spear, scratching at the chain that dug into her neck. Sanos only pulled harder, despite the pain it caused in his own palms. The assassin reached her dominant hand over her shoulder, trying to get a grip on him, but it was no use.

When Olerra finally killed the last of the assassins circling her, she turned to find Sanos dropping the woman to the ground.

Her eyes did a quick count of the fallen guards. He could see her take in the spear and his makeshift weapon. Then her gaze turned to the guard in front of Sanos. He had to sidestep the body before he could see what she was looking at.

A drop of blood welling from the wound he'd made.

"I take it you'll pardon that?" His voice came out harsh. He was angry with himself for not being on the road to Brutus.

"This was an attempt on my life. You're permitted to defend me. You will get to regale everyone with the tale of how you strangled a woman with your nipple chain."

She cracked a smile, but he found none of this funny. Gods, why wasn't he turning away and running now?

She'd only catch me. She's faster, and I'm barefoot.

"You helped me," she said, as though it didn't quite make sense.

He scoffed. "You mean *saved* you."

"I took out eight, Prince. You felled one."

"One that you never saw coming. She would have killed you."

"Maybe. I suppose we'll never know."

Olerra searched each fallen assassin. At first Sanos thought she was looting the bodies, but then he realized she must be looking for orders. Some hint of who hired them. Olerra had told him it was Glen, so she must be searching for proof. When she came up empty-handed, she surveyed her fallen soldiers. Sanos wondered how many of them she knew personally. Placing a hand on her heart, Olerra looked as though she might be saying a silent prayer.

"Come," she said, her voice hard, though not for his sake. "It isn't safe. More could come. We will hurry to the palace and send riders for the fallen and the injured horses."

Olerra sat in the driver's perch and held a hand down to Sanos.

He took it, and together they rode for the palace side by side.

Olerra would have kept one of the assassins alive if she didn't also have Andrastus to worry about. It hardly mattered, though. None of the ones she'd caught before had given Glen up.

Olerra was certain her cousin was behind the attack but once again had no means of proving it. She must retaliate in some way. Glenaerys had cost her a dozen good soldiers. A dozen friends. And she'd put her *betrothed* in danger twice now. Olerra would not allow a third, but she didn't see a path forward. She couldn't punish her cousin. She couldn't outmaneuver her. Olerra had played the only card she'd had: taking Andrastus. She'd bet everything she'd had on him.

And today, he'd saved her.

For some strange reason, the man hadn't tried to escape again.

She'd thought for sure when she'd handed him the key that she would find the carriage empty and tracks leading into the trees nearby. Instead, she'd found him watching her, as though he cared whether she survived. She'd told him to run, and he'd ignored her. He'd killed for her.

And that deserved to be rewarded. She wanted to show him how grateful she was.

With the reins in one hand, Olerra reached over with the other to pat his knee where it was exposed to the air because of the outfit she'd made him wear. He didn't flinch from the contact, so she left her hand there, squeezing gently.

"I won't forget this," she told him. "You showed me kindness today, and I will repay it. As soon as you're ready."

His gaze cut to her. "You'll free me?"

A sad smile stole over her lips. "I'm afraid I can't do that, Andrastus. I need you to help me secure my throne. Remember, you will be freed as soon as I have it. You have my word on that." She paused. "But I can give you pleasure. Let me show you what your kindness meant to me. Tonight or any night you choose."

He tensed up.

"I won't take you," she hurried to add. "I promised I wouldn't until you asked for it. But perhaps you'd settle for something else? Let me please you." She brazenly slid her hand up his leg a little higher.

He looked away from her and scooted his leg to his side of the carriage, letting her hand fall.

The rejection stung, and she clenched her teeth against the irritation that rose from it. Really, now, did he find her so displeasing that just her touching him was unwanted? She tried to remind herself of their first night. He'd been eager. He'd loved watching her please herself, so why—

"No transactions," he said finally. The words were almost too soft for her to hear.

"What?" she asked.

"I don't want a transaction. I don't want you to pleasure me because you think I've earned it. I want you to do it because you want it."

"Why can't it be both?"

"I've already told you I am not a dog that you give treats to."

That was harsh but fair, she supposed. Still, she fired back with "And the whores you paid for at the brothel I stole you from? You only want to make transactions with them? You seemed pleased enough by me when you thought I worked at Blanchette's."

His breathing picked up, but he didn't respond. Because he recognized his hypocrisy? Or was it more complicated than that?

"I don't want any more transactions where sex is concerned," he explained. "Never again."

"Something changed you?"

"You, you baffling woman. You've ruined me entirely."

She looked away so he wouldn't see her grin.

"Andrastus, I don't know how many times I need to say this, but I find you extremely attractive. The more I learn about you, the more that attraction grows. We're to be wedded, and I am eager to bed you. If anything, I'm the one trying to trick you into a sexual encounter by disguising it as a reward.

"Now, may I please pleasure you tonight?" She tried to keep the exasperation out of her voice, but it still crept in.

He was silent so long that Olerra was certain he meant to ignore her.

But then she caught it.

His nod.

17

Sanos's mind was running wild with possibilities.

Would she use her hands or her mouth? Would she do it on the bed or on her knees? Would she be clothed or naked?

The moment they reached the palace, she separated from him, likely to fill in the queen on the events of the day or perhaps to confront her cousin. He didn't know, and he had a hard time thinking too much about it with Olerra's plans for the evening.

He didn't even protest as the eunuchs led him to the bathing chamber this time around. He daydreamed as they washed him, even as they cleaned his foreskin and his ass. Although, he flinched when someone came up behind him and spread his cheeks wide, holding some small contraption in his hands. A moment later, he felt warm water shoot up his ass.

"What the fuck?"

"The princess requested a more thorough cleaning for tonight," the man behind him said. "Just a few times more." The water came again. It wasn't unpleasant. He just didn't like that these men were seeing every intimate part of him laid bare.

He needed to bargain with Olerra for private baths. She'd probably insist that he couldn't be as thorough as the eunuchs, and she'd be right. No man washed himself this completely. Why the hell would he need to?

They took extra care with his feet, which were scraped and raw from the day's activities. They washed them gently before covering them in ointment and soft cloths.

The same man from his first evening in the palace showed up. The one who'd stripped the hair from his chest. Sanos winced at the sight of him.

"Well met, Prince."

He started to forget what the night promised, his mood turning sour as the eunuchs tied him down so he couldn't fight. The waxing burned, as usual. Though he wasn't quite as sore afterward, as if his body remembered this pain and accepted it.

They shaved the hair from his face that had already grown back since the morning, before rubbing some sort of soothing cream into his skin. It felt nice and smelled nicer. Was it a scent Olerra liked? Or something they used on everyone?

Why do I care?

Gods, but this place was getting to him.

What would another month do?

What about after the marriage?

He couldn't think like that. Sanos would get Olerra her throne or find a different opportunity to escape.

After Olerra pleasured him.

He would take what he could from her. He was *owed* for all the inconveniences of being here. And then he would get out.

They put him in another short skirt that tied at the side before leading him back to Olerra's wing of the palace. When they entered her bedroom, she wasn't there. They bypassed her bed and went into his room. He thought perhaps they'd tie him to the bed once more. Instead, he found something new inside. There was a chain hanging from the ceiling. One of the eunuchs brought forth a hook and attached it to the chain. Another lowered the pulley so the hook rested between Sanos's manacled hands.

He should have guessed what came next. They hoisted him until his wrists were high in the air and he stood on his toes.

Then the men left without a word, and he was staring at the bare wall in front of him.

Every minute of waiting seemed like a lifetime. There was nothing to do, nothing to see. He could only feel the strain in his muscles and feet, which were already sore from the barefoot excursions of the day, though the ointment was doing wonders for him.

When the door opened, his muscles went taut, and his cock started to move. Gods, he couldn't even see her yet. How was she doing this?

"Good evening, Prince," she said from behind him.

Her voice sent a shiver through him, and he was already half-hard. He absolutely shouldn't be. Not trussed up like a pig hung to dry.

"Why am I chained to the ceiling?" he asked, silently applauding himself for his calm tone. She couldn't see his cock yet. Had no idea the effect she had on him.

"It'll be better this way."

"For you, you mean?"

"For us both."

"I think the bed would be much more comfortable for a cocksucking."

"Who said anything about a cocksucking?"

So she would use her hands. The knowledge heated his skin. Yes, he wanted her hands on him. Wanted it right now.

There was a scraping against the floor as she moved something. Furniture? He managed to turn enough to see a small table. There was a pot on top, a lid hiding its contents.

"What is that?"

"Again with the questions. You still have so much for me to teach you, Prince."

That drew a laugh from him. "Of the two of us, only I have had sexual relations. I should think you would have questions for me."

"I would wager that I know how your body works far better than you do."

"Unlikely," he breathed back in response.

"We teach our people anatomy and physiology from the time they are children. My understanding is that all sexual experiences in your kingdom are only experienced firsthand, which I imagine leads to many disappointing encounters."

"And how are these things taught?" he asked.

"During the teen years, with books, both fiction and nonfiction. With diagrams and detailed descriptions in the classroom. And women are allowed to observe at the brothels should they choose."

His breath hiked up. "You're voyeurs," he said, though the thought of her watching others in the act also excited him. The fact that she knew what to do pleased him. He wouldn't have to talk her through how to touch him.

"Call it what you like, Prince, but some people like to be watched. Now, before I begin, I need your consent. Do I have it?"

He let his head drift forward.

"I'm afraid I'm going to need verbal assent, Andrastus."

He clenched his teeth. "Prince."

"What?"

"While we do this. Call me Prince, rather than by my name." It shouldn't have mattered. He'd listened to her call him Andrastus dozens of times by now.

But right now, he didn't want to hear his brother's name.

There was a silence. "As you like, but I'm going to insist that you call me by my name. You've never said it when talking to me. Not once. Now tell me that you want this and use my name."

His next breath released on a shudder. "I want this, Olerra."

She hummed from behind him, much closer now. "I like the way that sounds on your lips. Will you scream it when I make you come?"

He couldn't answer her. No, instead his hips jerked forward, seeking friction without his say-so.

A laugh rumbled out of her. "Let's see if I can get it out of you. Now, I will check in with you as we go, but if at any time you wish me to stop, simply say so. You say the word *stop*, and I stop. Understood?"

"Yes," he said.

"Yes, what?"

He closed his eyes. "Yes, Olerra."

"Good boy."

He heard the lid to the pot removed, and a pleasant smell wafted into the room. Something earthy with just the lightest fragrance of roses.

"What is that?"

"Oil, Prince. Special oil for bedtime activities."

He swallowed.

"May I touch you?"

"Yes, Olerra."

She drew away the only piece of cloth covering him. He felt overheated, despite the lack of clothing.

A single finger touched the back of his neck and trailed down his spine. It was so light he almost couldn't feel it, and goose bumps erupted on his naked flesh. She stopped at his lower back.

Then he could feel her hot breath on his upper back as she traced the same path with her lips. She couldn't reach his neck from this position, which was a shame, but he reveled in the feel of her skin tracing his. She didn't kiss him, just let her lips skim the path. Her tongue darted out once when she reached his lower back this time, and he jerked forward again. Seeking contact that wasn't there with her behind him.

Her breath teased his shoulders once more, and he braced himself for whatever torture she had in store next.

It was her teeth that trailed his spine next. They skimmed his skin, nipping occasionally. He was breathing faster once she finished.

Her hands touched his shoulders, and in the next moment, she was massaging him. Working the knots from his tense muscles. He leaned back into that touch, the padded manacles keeping him aloft. His tense muscles relaxed, but his hard cock sure didn't.

No one had . . . ever touched him this way before. When he paid for companionship, the deed was usually over pretty quickly . . .

Because the women at the brothels wanted it over as soon as possible, he now realized.

Olerra worked her way down his back, scoring her thumbs into his muscles. Her hands went lower and lower, and he wondered when exactly she would stop.

She didn't; she kept up her ministrations when she reached his ass, kneading, in his opinion, expertly.

"What about this?" he asked on a pant. "Have you done this to anyone else before?" He wasn't sure why he bothered to voice the question. Maybe it felt strange to simply hang there without touching. Without looking.

"Just you, My Prince." She made that delicious humming noise again. "Your muscles are so large everywhere. Even here." She cupped his cheeks, one hand on either side, and he relished in the sensation. He wished he could touch her right now.

Her hands left him, and he felt empty immediately. Tension built as he waited to feel what she would do next. He waited for her to appear in front of him.

He heard her messing with the pot, the sluicing sound of her wetting her hands. The slickness would give him the perfect slide when she finally got her fingers around him.

Instead, he felt a finger in a place he never had before.

She circled his entrance, and he lunged forward with his hips once more.

He heard the smile. "Was that a good or bad retreat?"

His lips parted to tell her bad. He meant to ask her what the fuck she was doing. He wanted to know why she wasn't on her knees yet. Why the hell—

She traced a finger up the seam of him, and the word he exhaled was "Good."

Because it did feel good. It felt like nothing he'd ever felt before.

"Good," she echoed.

And then her finger dipped inside. He exhaled so sharply. Not because it hurt. She couldn't have been deeper than a single knuckle, but his surprise was impossible to mask.

"What are you doing?" he asked.

"I thought you knew your body better than I did." Her tone was self-important. He didn't care for it.

"I think—"

Her finger slid in a little deeper, meeting the resistance of his internal muscles, but with the slick oil on her hand, she barely had to apply more pressure to break past it. The sensation was . . . not exactly comfortable.

He said in as calm a tone as possible, "Why is your finger in my ass?"

"You're about to answer that question yourself."

Just as he meant to demand she leave his ass alone, she curled her finger.

A burst of pleasure spread through him, cracking like a lightning bolt through his body. The sound he made was unintelligible, even to his own ears.

"There you go," she said, and she made the motion again.

Gods, what was that? What sorcery was she performing back there? Was it magic oil? She placed her free hand on his hip to hold him steady, and then she found a slow rhythm.

"Fucking hell," he panted, rocking backward on his toes to meet the thrusting of that finger.

"Are you enjoying yourself, Prince?" she asked him.

"Yes," he mewled.

Her finger stopped.

"Yes, Olerra," he corrected, and she continued once more.

He closed his eyes, and there was something about not seeing, only feeling, that made everything so much more erotic.

She kissed his back, nipping and licking where she could reach, never letting up with her finger. She was so careful with him. She would hit that spot that made stars dance across his vision, and then she would retreat, hitting another area inside him. She knew exactly what she was doing, and he did, too.

She was getting him as close to the edge as possible without letting him tip over.

"Please," he said. "Olerra," he tacked on belatedly.

"Would you like another finger?" she asked.

He swallowed, sweat trickling down his chest. He barely had to think over the question. "Yes, Olerra."

Another finger joined the first, and the sensation was uncomfortable at first, until the doubled pressure hit that fucking spot again.

"Look at you," she said. "All these beautiful muscles and pearly white skin. Oh, I wish you could see. I'm going to order a mirror brought into this room so the next time you're a good boy you can see yourself riding my fingers."

Gods but her words were filthy. They excited him to no end. The thought of *next time* was a sweet promise he intended to hold her to.

The pressure built and built, his cock beading with moisture. Just when he was close to something, she shifted her fingers.

"For gods' sakes, Olerra!" he cried.

Her chuckle was sinful. "All right. I've had my fun. Let it out, Prince. Crane your neck toward me. I want to watch your face as you come."

Her movements doubled, and every time her fingers slid inside, they brushed that spot that made him wild. It felt like dying until it felt like being born again. Getting a deep breath of air after spending an eternity of drowning.

His eyes met hers, his neck craned as far as it would go. He didn't mean to, but it was her name he cried when he came, spilling his seed on the floor in front of him.

She leaned her forehead against his back, and the two of them stood still. He was catching his breath, and he suspected she was calming herself.

Olerra stepped away, and he felt the loss of her touch more strongly than he expected. When she returned, she stood before him holding a wet rag.

She cleaned her fingers and his cock before taking a separate rag to the floor. Then she leaned against the wall opposite him, drinking in the sight of him hanging, sweat-soaked and satisfied.

She cocked her head to the side. "Does the prince of Brutus like to be fucked in the ass by his woman?"

He didn't know what she saw in his eyes. Was it hatred? Was it pleasure? The two were so tied together he didn't know anymore.

He looked at the discarded rag, the evidence of his pleasure

"I want to hear you say it," she insisted.

"Why? So you can say I told you so?"

"No, Prince. It will only make me burn hotter for you. As soon as I leave you, I will take my satisfaction in my own room. I will think about the noises you just made while I touch myself. Would you like to hear me? I can be extra loud so you know exactly what's happening."

Impossibly, his cock twitched.

She grinned.

"What was in that oil?" he asked.

She rolled her eyes. "That's what you think brought you pleasure?" She stepped forward. "No, Prince. That was my fingers, touching the part inside you that brings immense pleasure. Make me proud, and I'll do it again for you."

Gods, but he wanted that. He shouldn't want that. He should want to kill her. Instead, he found himself fantasizing about what she looked like naked and spread before him.

She pulled the lever that summoned the servants before leaving him chained up. When the eunuchs let him down, they attached him to the bed for the night.

Now that he had some distance from her, he could think clearly again. As he remembered the feel of her inside him, he knew that he couldn't let that happen again. *He didn't need it again.* He'd used her for pleasure, though it felt like she had used him. Still, he should be done now. Ready to move on.

But with his body still vibrating from the best orgasm he had ever experienced, he could only imagine what it would be like between them if he were the one inside her.

He needed to get out before she could ensorcell him again.

18

Andrastus was such a sight when he lost control. He was so incredibly strong, even while chained up. She'd feared for a moment that he'd knock her over with the way he was thrusting back into her.

Olerra had wondered why he'd asked her not to call him by his name, though not enough to question it. Perhaps his family called him by a nickname that he wasn't ready to share with her. Maybe he hated his given name. She didn't linger on the oddity of it long.

She was so wet she could feel it as she walked to her room. The thought of touching herself while he watched again had crossed her mind, but she wanted to leave him wanting more. She wanted to let his imagination run wild while she was in the next room.

Olerra selected a phallus, one slightly bigger than she'd used last time—before she'd been beaten by her cousin. It fit, though not without some strain. Olerra worked her clit while she left the instrument inside her, pretending it belonged to her prince. She screamed nice and loud when she came and could have sworn she heard a muttered curse from his room.

The next morning, she knew she couldn't put off her duties any longer to spend time with her betrothed. Becoming incapacitated had really thrown off her plans. She'd intended to spend several weeks alone with him, but that time was all gone. As a general, Olerra needed to see to her troops.

Ydra was at the training field when she arrived, overseeing the morning exercises being performed by a squadron. The sight of women in armor, performing their drills in perfect synchronization was one that brought Olerra calm.

As much as she itched to move, she went to her office just off the yard. There were reports that needed reading. Supplies that needed to be allocated. The quarterly budget needed reviewing. Olerra was good with numbers, doing sums in her head that others often required quill and parchment for.

Yet, as she stared at the documents before her, the figures swam in and out of place.

Her brain much preferred dwelling on the timbre of Andrastus's voice as her name fell from his lips over and over again.

Yes, Olerra. Please, Olerra. I want this, Olerra.

She crossed her legs as her whole body warmed and heat pooled in her core.

She wanted his fingers on her. Not her own. She hated that things had to be this way.

Fine, she'd get to the reports in a moment. Movement seemed to be a better idea first. She returned outside, stepping up beside Ydra and crossing her arms.

"Report," she said, the word coming out harsher than she'd intended.

"And a good morning to you, too, General. Has a certain prince gotten under our skin today?" Ydra asked cheekily.

Olerra closed her eyes and rubbed her brow.

"Or perhaps we wish he were under our pants?" she added.

"Stop talking in the plural about my betrothed," Olerra snapped.

Ydra chuckled. "I'm supposed to be the one pissed at him. What did he do?"

"Nothing."

"Fine." Ydra matched her stance to Olerra's, crossing her arms over her chest and observing the training ahead with a cold gaze.

No one else in all of Amarra could get away with mocking the general.

Olerra sighed. "We had a sexual encounter last night."

"And it was disappointing?"

"No, it was perfect."

"So what's the problem?"

Olerra cracked her knuckles. "I chained him to the ceiling and took him from behind."

"Very exciting."

"And then I went to bed."

Ydra placed her body directly in front of her. "Why would you do that?"

"Because I can't exactly let him reciprocate, can I?"

Ydra gave her a sad smile. "Is this about what happened to your mother?"

"Of course it is. Everything comes back to that. I can't trust him. What if he uses pleasure time to try to hurt me? To try to escape? I can't exactly have people listening in to intervene! Word would spread, and I want that man all to myself. No onlookers."

"So we're feeling sexually frustrated because we can't allow the man to pleasure us back."

Olerra shot her a warning look.

"Okay, here's what I think *you* should do."

Yes, practical advice! This is exactly what Olerra needed.

"Stop worrying about it."

Olerra glared at her. "He's not harmless. You remember how he took out Aevia. And that assassin. And you know that I don't—" Their conversation may have been private, but even Olerra couldn't risk saying her deepest secret aloud.

"You need a bout," Ydra said.

"You're offering to fight me?" Olerra asked.

"Until you can trust him. Until you get to know him better, you need to work out that energy in other ways. You've been following him around and then recovering. You haven't gotten your usual workouts in. Let's go a round, and then you can pick on some of the captains."

"I knew there was a reason I loved you."

"You love me because I'm right about everything. Now, let's do this before I change my mind."

Sanos was back in the gymnasium, only this time it wasn't a group of eunuchs who followed him around. It was some of Olerra's troops.

The women didn't speak to him, much like their general, whom he suspected was hiding from him. The last time she'd done this was after that horrible ride to the pit. Then, she'd been giving him space and distance.

This time? He didn't know.

Was she embarrassed after what had happened between them?

Because he fucking was. Did anyone know what he'd let her do to him? He tried to guess as he trailed along the large room full of husbands and consorts. But no one gave him any particular attention, just like the last time he entered, save when Athon created his disturbance.

Sanos's guards followed at a distance, and they didn't let any men approach him. Clearly Olerra wasn't taking any chances with him or Glenaerys this time. He was almost grateful for the guard. Much as he might hate her, Glen also made him uneasy. In one simple act, she'd had him on his knees, ready to lose his head.

He suppressed a shiver.

Sanos worked his body again today. He ran laps around the track and lifted weights. When that was done, he sat himself in the solarium to take in all the beautiful flora growing indoors. He managed to find a quiet spot separate from the men working the soil, giving him the illusion of privacy, even though he knew the guards were right behind him.

There was a commotion. A woman was calling a name as she walked into the rooms. Distantly he heard his brother's name on her lips.

"Andrastus?"

One of his guards located the woman and brought her to his destination.

She carried a giant vase of flowers and set the enormous arrangement on the floor before extending a letter out to him. He took it, glancing around to see if the exchange was catching any sort of attention. If the other husbands and consorts in the solarium thought the display strange, they didn't show it.

Sanos opened the note.

My Prince,
Here is one petal for every time I've thought about you today.
My warmest regards,
Olerra

Sanos swallowed. Then he read the words again just to be certain his mind wasn't playing tricks on him. She'd . . . sent him flowers and a . . . love letter. It was brief and direct, just as she always was, but how could it be called anything else?

Sanos still wasn't used to how forward Amarran women could be, and he had a feeling his princess was leagues above the rest in that regard. There must have been two dozen flowers in the bundle. Blossoms he didn't know the names of. Hundreds and hundreds of petals.

He felt his cheeks warm as he looked up, ensuring that still no one watched him.

An attendant stepped forward. "Shall I have these taken to your room, Prince?"

"Yes." It was odd, giving the order. Sanos had done nothing except receive instructions since arriving. It never occurred to him that he'd have any sort of power as a future husband to the princess.

He kept hold of the note, tracing the curves of her handwriting with his eyes. He already had it memorized, but there was something about looking at it that made his chest warm.

"May I approach?"

An older man stood some paces away, addressing his guard. His hair was fully silver, lines creased at the corners of his eyes and along his neck. He must have been older than even Sanos's father.

"Prince, Obar is deemed safe by the queen potential. Would you like to speak to him, or shall we have him move along?" The head of his guard was speaking to him.

Twice in quick succession, he was being asked a question. Given power to answer.

"I'll speak with him."

"You may," the guard told Obar.

The older man walked easily and lowered himself onto the bench beside Sanos. His armband was made out of a black metal, and the stone appeared to be topaz.

"Obar," Sanos said. "That doesn't sound like an Amarran name."

"It isn't. I'm from Dyphankar. Like you, I was kidnapped and brought here to wed."

Sanos was surprised by this. Surprised, and horrified. Here was a man who was still fit and energetic yet hadn't managed to escape?

"How long have you been here?" Sanos asked. "Who is your wife?"

"Over forty years. My wife is Enadra, the former general, and Olerra's mentor."

Forty years.

Sanos had so many questions, but he started with "Why do you wish to speak to me?"

"Because I was once like you."

"Are you here to tell me to give up hope now? Accept my lot?"

Obar crossed his legs at the ankles. "I'm not here to tell you what to do. I'm sure your betrothed is doing that plenty." His eyes shimmered with humor. "I just thought you might like to talk to someone who understands, even if you might not like my thoughts on the matter."

"Do you care for the woman who took you?"

"I love Enadra more than my own life."

Oh gods. This man had been brainwashed by the Amarrans. Sanos wished he'd never let him approach.

"I know what you're thinking," Obar said. "You think me mad. Swept up by this place. But let me tell you something. I was the second-born son of a nobleman in Dyphankar. I had no purpose. No trade. No land or money to inherit. When Enadra took me, I was furious. It took years before I realized that I went from having nothing to everything.

"She gave me a purpose. I wasn't just a second-born son with nothing to do. I became a husband, a father, a friend to many here in the gymnasium. More important, though, she gave me love. It was a shock to come here. To learn the customs and accept them. But once I did, I was happier than I'd ever been."

Sanos narrowed his eyes. "Did Olerra put you up to this?"

Obar laughed. "You're much like I was, though I was no prince, so I won't presume to know what you might be giving up to be here. I lost nothing, save my pride, and gained everything." The older man stood. "I came on no one's orders, Prince. Just know that I am here, if you seek a friend. Most of the men here will be too afraid to approach you, because no one wants Glen's ire. She wouldn't dare cross Enadra, however, when my wife is one of the four who holds the princess's future in her hands. Good day."

He left Sanos sitting there with more concerns than assurances. The prince pocketed his love letter and stood, suddenly needing movement. He walked aimlessly through the different rooms of the gymnasium.

But no matter where he went, the sweet scent of flowers permeated the air.

The guards left his side once the eunuchs were escorting him from the gymnasium. Without the threat of Glen's consorts nearby, there was clearly no need of them.

Sanos was excited to go back to his rooms, and when he realized it was because he had those flowers waiting for him, he instantly became irritated. So engrossed was he that he didn't notice right away when the eunuchs veered off course. He was in a section of the palace he didn't recognize. When a door was opened and Sanos was shoved inside alone, he didn't know what to make of it.

"Leave us," a voice said, and the door behind him shut, taking all light with it.

Sanos turned every which way, looking for the source. He thought he might recognize the tone, but he couldn't be sure.

A candle lit, revealing the face of Olerra's cousin.

They were alone in a simple room. There was no window, only two chairs and a small table. They were in little more than a closet.

"Andrastus," Glenaerys said. "It's time you and I became better acquainted."

He kept his face a mask, meeting her gaze, despite the way her men always went submissive when she turned that cold stare on them.

He was in danger but couldn't show it, somehow knowing that would only make her more feral.

"And what does that entail?" he asked.

She laughed. "Is that anger I hear in your voice? You're not still upset over the whole beheading thing, are you? That was . . . almost a month ago. Besides, you gave me the greatest gift imaginable when Olerra took your place. I've wanted to put my cousin in her place for years. Let us forget it and be friends instead."

Sanos wanted to tell her she could take her offer and shove it up her ass, so he remained silent.

"You're smart to be wary of me," she said. "I'm far more dangerous than Olerra; that's for sure. Olerra could make you withstand all kinds of tortures, but I could bury you in such a way that you'd never be found again. You would simply disappear."

He held steady, waiting for her to get to the point.

"Nothing to say? No more questions?" she asked.

"I'm sure you'll tell me when and if you want to."

"I want my cousin dead."

Well, that was forthright. "Yes, you attempted that yesterday."

Glenaerys gritted her teeth. "I lost a lot of loyal women."

"Aren't you worried that by telling me this I'll tell Olerra?"

"As if Olerra doesn't already know. Besides, who else would believe you over me? Your whole purpose in existing is to please Olerra. You would say or do anything for her."

Now it was his turn to bare his teeth. "I would not do anything for her. You forget I am not some simple Amarran man."

Glenaerys smiled, and it was somehow more frightening. "That's exactly what I was hoping to hear, Prince, which is why I have a proposition for you."

"My body is off the table," he said immediately.

She laughed again. "Olerra has had you. I don't want spoiled goods."

Sanos didn't correct her.

"No, Prince, what I want is for you to kill her for me."

Glenaerys pulled a knife from seemingly nowhere and set it on the table between them. It was nothing special. No gems or other adornments. Simple steel sharpened to a point.

He realized that if he didn't tell her what she wanted to hear or make a convincing argument, this conversation would end with that knife embedded in his heart. His pulse raced.

"She chains me up at night. There's no way to get free."

Glenaerys tilted her head. "Why would she do that?"

He didn't understand why this interested her. "It makes our nighttime activities easier for her, I suppose."

Glen's gaze turned inward. She was silent for a full minute as she thought something through. Finally, she shook her head. "Then you had better earn her trust. In the meantime, you hold on to that." She nodded at the weapon.

"What if she searches my room?"

"Find a good hiding place. Let's get something straight, Andrastus. I couldn't care less if you died. In fact, your death would make Olerra weaker, but I want her dead even more than that, and I play the long game. Make no mistake, you are just one tool I'm utilizing. I have dozens of other plans in place if you fail."

"And why would I be motivated to do this for you," he asked, "after everything?"

"Because if you succeed, I will have you returned to your father. It is the only way you will ever see your home again."

She didn't know of his deal with Olerra. He was already bound for home, unless the queen potential had lied on her mother's ashes.

Still, he played along. "So you assume none of the risk but receive all the rewards, just like with your other assassins."

"I am a strategist. This is what I do. It's how I will protect and serve this country."

No, it was why she was the poorer choice, Sanos knew. She didn't care to suffer for her people. In fact, she hurt them regularly, starting with her own harem.

"Can't you procure the keys to my cuffs?" Sanos asked, thinking to use her to aid in his plans of escape. "Might speed up this plan of yours."

"I could," she said. "But then Olerra might be warier around you if you strike too soon. You're more likely to succeed if she trusts you first. Besides, she is a skilled warrior. She could fight you off easily. No, it has to be when you've gained her trust."

Sanos took the knife and tucked it into his waistband.

"Excellent," Glenaerys said.

Sanos knew full well that Glenaerys had no intention of helping him, whether he did this for her or not. She was self-serving, and he couldn't imagine anything other than a lie dripping from her lips. She thought him too stupid and inconsequential to see through it.

Still, he felt much better knowing he had a weapon. Whether he'd use it was up to him. These days, he didn't know if he wanted to stab Olerra or fuck her.

"The eunuchs are waiting for you outside. Don't disappoint me."

He felt her watch his ass as he walked away.

His entourage kept straight faces, as though they hadn't just betrayed Olerra by bringing Sanos to her cousin. They carried on as they always did. Silently. He wondered how Glenaerys had bribed them to do her bidding. Just how deep were her pockets?

They returned him to his room, and Sanos immediately spotted the new vase of flowers.

One petal for every time I've thought about you today.

He shook his head and looked around, waiting for the eunuchs to chain him to something. They didn't move. No, they watched him expectantly, and he realized they were waiting for him to hide the knife.

Sanos swept his gaze over the room, and he immediately noticed the new addition. A massive mirror hung from floor to ceiling along the wall where Olerra had had him hung before fucking him senseless.

His blood heated at the memory, but he quickly looked away before the eunuchs noticed the change in him.

Where to hide his new weapon?

The fireplace was his first thought, but none of the bricks were loose. Then he thought of the mattress or the floorboards. He knew his initial thoughts were likely where she would search first.

And then his eyes fell on the door, the one intended for the next member of Olerra's harem once she chose one. He let himself inside. She would have no reason to search this room while it was unoccupied. No one would come to light fires or turn down the bed. He buried the knife under ashes in the hearth. Then he washed his hands in the adjoining washing chamber to his room.

As soon as it was done, the eunuchs trussed him up and went on their way. Sanos's gaze immediately went back to the mirror. He could see himself reflected in it from the bed. Not only could she watch him, he could watch her as he fuck—

The door opened, and he quickly looked anywhere else, lest she guess the direction of his thoughts.

"Good evening, Prince. Did you like my gift?" Her voice was warm and sultry.

He took too long to answer, wondering if she meant the mirror or the flowers.

"They're . . . unnecessary."

"You don't like flowers?" She seemed genuinely disappointed by that.

"I didn't say that. Only that I don't need flowers."

"Nobody needs flowers. Do you enjoy them?"

He finally looked at her, really looked at her, and did a double take. "What happened to you?"

She cracked her neck from side to side. "I had a few bouts with some of my soldiers. Don't worry. I won them all."

She was covered in scratches and a few bruises, though these weren't nearly so bad as when she'd taken a beating from Glenaerys. She looked more lively today, not less so. Still, he didn't like the sight of her injuries. How they looked painful. How could she be in such good spirits?

"Fear not, Prince, you should see my captains. This is what women do. We challenge and test ourselves."

Only the wild women here. He'd never seen women fight before he came to this backward country.

Olerra strode closer to the bed, and he found himself holding his breath for some reason. As she peered down at him, he willed his cock not to react.

"That doesn't look terribly comfortable," she said.

"Forced to sleep in one position all night long? It isn't."

"Let's see what I can do about that." She unlatched his wrists from each bedpost and brought his hands together above his head, where she reattached each separate manacle to a chain on the wall. Then she undid his ankles from the bedposts, discarded one of the shackles, and chained his feet together instead. "How is that?"

Sanos tried rolling over and found that the chain in the wall rotated in place. He could easily get to his stomach or side to change positions in the night.

"Much better. Thank you," he said.

"Tomorrow I was thinking we could spend some time getting to know each other better. I've spent all this time trying to show you my country and my people, but I realize that I haven't told you nearly enough about me. What do you think?"

He was surprised to find she was asking him his opinion. He could answer any way he liked, and he knew she would respect the decision. Something was . . . different between them. He shouldn't like that difference, whatever it was.

"That sounds nice," he said.

There was a pause, as though she waited for him to say something more. When he didn't, she said, "Excellent. I'll see you then. Good night, Prince."

She left without a backward glance, and he found disappointment taking him over. What had he wanted? For her to touch him? With him chained up and hardly able to move? He shouldn't be so titillated by the thought.

But he was.

Instead, he was forced to listen through the wall while she used her kit. Gods above.

His cock rose, and there was absolutely nothing he could do about it. He lay there and listened as her routine met its inevitable conclusion. This time, she screamed his brother's name when she came.

"Andrastus!"

Nothing could have made his cock soften faster.

19

Sanos had trained his whole life to be a master of the sword, but he'd had to be careful. He could run drills with other men. Lead men. He could not befriend them. He had a reputation for being standoffish, even if he was well-liked.

Olerra was clearly friends with a great deal of her soldiers. She greeted them by name. Asked about their families. They, in turn, asked how things were going with, well, him.

The princess smiled and turned to him. "How are things going?" she asked, forcing him to answer.

He narrowed his eyes, wondering if she dared him to speak truthfully or come up with some great lie.

"Well enough," he said finally.

The women giggled.

Olerra trained alongside her soldiers, running, fighting, sweating. These days, Sanos had to leave most of the training to other men, as he was in the war tent planning their next move. But Amarra wasn't at war, which meant Olerra was free to spend her time as she saw fit.

He envied that. Sanos was so sick of war. At least this detour to Amarra had spared him from the gore of the front lines. He'd also had more full nights of sleep than he could ever recall in his life.

When Olerra saw him watching her troops at their drills, she asked, "Would you like to join us?"

He must have nodded, because his chains were removed. He was handed a wooden training sword.

He learned quickly, watching the women around him and learning how to move as they did. Kick. Thrust. Slash. Pivot. Block.

The drills were different from the Brutish stances of combat, but he liked the idea of knowing how the Amarrans fought. It would only serve him well the next time he had to fight one.

Olerra moved from the front to stand beside him, letting Ydra lead. She didn't say a word to him, just continued the drills at his side. Right swing. Left swing. Spin. Jump. Duck.

They were dancing, and Olerra was the most captivating of all of them. She moved with a grace that he couldn't take his eyes off of. Her limbs were fluid, her sword steady. He wondered if she could beat his father in a bout.

Sanos tired faster than the others, unused to the hours of training with his new palace life, so he excused himself from the rest of them to stretch. A eunuch offered him water.

He wasn't required to wear the chains for the rest of the day. At night, however, eunuchs returned them to him. He was strapped to his bed yet again, though in the more comfortable way, where he could roll over in his sleep if needed.

Olerra let herself into his room. She wore a loose nightdress made of a very thin material. He could see her nipples through the fabric.

Gods.

She didn't make any move to approach him.

"You seemed happy today," she said.

"I enjoyed myself," he corrected.

"I'm glad. Would you like to come train with us tomorrow as well?"

"Yes."

There was another pause. Just as there was last night. As though she waited for him to say something. He didn't know what she wanted from him.

"Good night, Prince."

She left as quickly as she'd come.

Olerra felt like an idiot. She wanted to instigate more intimacy between them but knew that ultimately it needed to be his choice. By his request. So when he said nothing—requested nothing of her—she'd left. But not before ensuring she'd see him again tomorrow on the training yard. She liked seeing him at peace. She *loved* seeing him out of the chains and with a weapon in hand, even if it was a harmless one. Her troops didn't speak to him, but they accepted him, because he was hers.

Maybe things could begin to be friendly between them. Andrastus liked her. He didn't like that he liked her. She knew that. She knew he had so much to figure out for himself. There was nothing to do but give it time.

In the meantime, she continued to stretch herself with the next biggest phallus in the kit. She would have thought this was a pain her body would get used to, but it didn't. So she made her mind think of other things. She thought of how she and Andrastus had bolstered the people with his presence, handing out coins and letting everyone see him. Her troops would grow to like him as he garnered their respect while training with them. It was an unforeseen result that she was quite happy with.

All that was left was winning over the nobility after the . . . setback.

Andrastus was well-behaved at breakfast each day, but the damage had been done. Apparently it was so obvious that her aunt eventually summoned her.

Queen Lemya was scratching her quill against parchment when Olerra was admitted to her rooms. Toria read a book on the settee, lounging with her long legs in front of her.

"Auntie," Olerra said, giving a short bow, even though the queen wasn't looking.

"You've lost Cyssia and Usstra."

"I know."

"Only a quarter of the nobility—at best—are in your corner, and it has just been decided that the heir will be named at the anniversary of the Goddess's Gift."

Olerra's heart sank. "So soon?" Barely over a month from now.

"Shaelwyn has been pushing for it to happen sooner rather than later, what with Glen having the most support currently. It seems most everyone is in agreement."

Olerra looked down. She felt shame. Not because of what she'd done for her prince but because she was losing a campaign she *had* to win.

"I had to save him, Auntie. It was the honorable thing to do. My recovery took longer than expected. I knew Glen would take advantage of me being gone. I don't know how to fix this. I don't know how to win them back."

"You should have let him die. You like him perhaps too much. But what's done is done. So here is what is going to happen. Glen has just announced she will be hosting a party to celebrate her relationship with that new soldier boy. You and that man of yours need to steal the spotlight. The whole of Amarra depends on it."

"When is the party?"

"One week's time."

"We'll be ready."

"I expect nothing less."

Toria offered a sympathetic wave as Olerra left, and Olerra returned it. She didn't know how she was going to do this. She enjoyed parties, but only when she was free to spend them with the people she liked. Competing with Glen didn't sound like a good time. And Andrastus? What would she have to do to get him to cooperate? Should she prepare him for the party or spring it on him?

She kept it to herself for now.

She needed time to think.

For four days now, Sanos had joined Olerra at work, training and getting to know some of her troops. Olerra's captains had especially taken to him. Among them were Meyla and Riakah, who were together. Sirem, they called it. When women liked women. And then there was Lumen, whom Sanos learned was not a he or a she but a them. The Amarran term was madereo. He liked talking with Lumen best because they always had new things to teach him.

"You're strong for a man," Meyla said to him.

"Is that a compliment?" Sanos asked.

"Obviously."

"Then thank you."

"It's too bad you're to be a husband," Riakah said. "You would be a boon to the army."

"Husbands can't be soldiers?" Sanos asked.

The two women shared a look.

"Technically, there's nothing in the rules that says you can't," Lumen explained, joining the conversation. "It would just be . . . highly unusual."

"Why?"

"Well, most palace husbands prefer a life of luxury. Everything you need is already provided for you, and in your case, you're not even Amarran. Why should you wish to fight for our country?"

Sanos said, "For purpose. Shouldn't all lives have meaning?"

The two women laughed at him, but Lumen leaned forward.

"Spoken like someone who has never had to work a day in their life just for food and shelter."

He fired back with "Some people need to have their basic needs met so they can rule and make changes for all the others."

Riakah scoffed. "What changes have you made for the poor Brutes?"

Well, none, yet. But when he was back home, that would change.

"That's what I thought," Riakah said.

"What's going on here?"

The three soldiers stood on their feet and placed a fist over their hearts. "Commander," they said in unison as Ydra approached.

"Not causing trouble, are you?" Ydra asked Sanos, who was still seated around the campfire they'd been using to cook their food.

"No," he responded.

"On your feet."

Sanos obeyed.

"If you're going to train with us, then you'd best learn to behave like us. When a superior officer approaches, you show respect."

Sanos nodded, mimicking the motion the others had made. He didn't know why it was easier to take orders from Ydra than it was Olerra. Perhaps it was because Ydra wasn't trying to bed him.

"I'd like a word with the prince, please," Ydra said, and the rest of them scampered off.

He wasn't sure what to expect when they were alone. Sanos knew Ydra hated him after what had happened with Glenaerys. He knew she was loyal to Olerra, so he wasn't in physical danger when near her. Perhaps she wanted to shout at him some more.

"Why do you hold yourself back from her?" she demanded.

"Excuse me?"

Ydra eyed him from head to toe. "Olerra says you can perform. Admirably, even. So why do you keep yourself distant? Do you not think my sister beautiful? Do you dislike her character? Why haven't you asked her to be physical with you again?"

First, Sanos felt his cheeks flame. Olerra had told Ydra what had happened between them. That was mortifying. Second, outrage took over. How dare Ydra come to him like this and question him about personal matters? Finally, a horrible realization set in. Is that what Olerra had been waiting for each night before she left him? She'd wanted him to invite her to . . . what? Not sex. She was still *preparing*, but other things. Things that potentially involved the giant mirror she'd had hung in his room.

Olerra wanted an invitation. Amarra's tits, she'd been giving him space, yet opportunity . . .

And he'd been none the wiser.

How the fuck was he supposed to know that? He wasn't a bloody mind reader.

Instead of telling Ydra all that, he got defensive. "That is none of your business."

"Wrong. Olerra is the best person I know, and I make it my business to help her achieve happiness. You are keeping yourself from her. You're making her work harder than she should have to in order to secure the throne. Why?"

"I am *stolen*," he reminded her.

"Would you get over that already? It may have been the start of your relationship, but it doesn't have to be the end. You need to treat her better. You have no idea the honor she has bestowed upon you."

"Why? Because I'm her first husband? Lucky me. I think I'll feel less special once she fills all those bedrooms with more conquests."

Ydra took a step closer. "You stupid boy."

"I'm fairly confident that I'm older than you."

"Yet you behave like a child. Olerra isn't taking a harem like me. Just this week she has declared you her seul. It is an honor usually only bestowed to a sirem, who takes only one woman as her wife, such as the queen has done."

"I don't understand."

"She's not taking any men for a harem. Only you for some unfathomable reason, you complete twat."

Before Sanos could even think of a response to that, Olerra showed up. She smiled at them. "Are you two getting better acquainted?"

"Yes, Andrastus is a delight," Ydra said so convincingly that Sanos almost believed it.

"I'm so glad you think so." Olerra ran a finger over the armband Sanos wore on his left bicep as Ydra left them. "And what do you think of my sister-chosen?"

"She's— What's a seul?"

Olerra snapped her gaze to Ydra's retreating back so quickly he was surprised it didn't hurt her neck. "Where did you learn that?"

"Ydra might have mentioned something."

Olerra rolled her eyes. "It's when a woman chooses only one partner to share her life with. Only one to bed."

"And you've chosen me?" he asked in a voice almost too quiet to hear.

She nodded once.

And then he had to know: "Did you decide this before or after you'd taken me?"

Was this for Andrastus or him?

"After."

The word shattered him. It made no sense. She hardly knew him, yet she all but announced that he was special to her.

"You didn't want me to know?" he asked.

"You seem to pull away from me the more affectionate I become."

It was true. Even now he felt the immense desire to flee. He couldn't handle the emotions she wrought in him or how these last few days with her soldiers had been some of the best of his life.

Gods, if his father found out . . .

Perhaps she could see him spiraling because she quickly added, "It's because my cousin is winning, and I needed to do something drastic to win over the nobility."

"How does this win them over?"

"I told you. If they think I'm madly in love with you, they will not think me so weak for taking that beating for you. It is a ruse, Andrastus. You and I are the only ones who know how things really are between us."

Did they? Did he?

She'd given up sex with another man for him.

No, not *him*, for a throne. Sanos would do that and more if it would make him the Brutish king.

Then why did Ydra seem to think there was so much more to it?

Sanos wanted to ask but didn't want to admit he was thinking so hard about it.

"There's more," Olerra said, interrupting his thoughts. "I need to ask something of you, and I need you to take it seriously."

"What?"

"My cousin is throwing a party. We have to be seen together. We have to seem in love, and I need you to show up the men in her harem."

"What?" he repeated.

"At parties, the men will often show off their talents. They perform the entertainments for the night. It's the perfect opportunity for you to prove yourself better than any man from Glen's harem. Perhaps you could recite some poetry you're fond of? Do something in front of everyone to make them like you?"

"Recite poetry," he repeated.

"Yes, I've heard you do recitations that bring crowds to tears."

Fuck.

He tried to think quickly. "Not large crowds. Private audiences. I don't—"

"Please, Andrastus. I need this. My people need this."

For the first time since meeting her, he wanted to do what she asked. He knew better the stakes—what would happen if Glenaerys were made queen instead of Olerra. And some part of him deep down wanted to do this for her just because she'd asked. He told himself it was because once he was king of Brutus, he'd rather deal with Olerra than Glen as queen of Amarra.

If he could make that happen before he escaped, then why wouldn't he?

Sanos took a breath. "I will need some books from the library."

"Yes, of course. Whatever you need! I will tell your escorts, and I shan't bother you."

Whatever face he bore, she seemed to think he needed encouragement. "I believe in you," she told him. "I know you can do this."

He gritted his teeth. "You will owe me for this."

"Gladly."

Though there was a library in the gymnasium, Sanos was allowed access to the royal library as Olerra's soon-to-be husband. She'd claimed there were Brutish texts within, and he might find some "favorites" there. He really hoped he could find something familiar, at the very least.

Poetry.

Fucking poetry.

Sanos could recount the great wars of his people. He could list important dates and figures, recite the winning maneuvers in important battles.

But poetry?

That hadn't been part of his required reading growing up, and he didn't gravitate toward it naturally. Now he had to memorize something. And deliver it with finesse.

This wasn't going to work. He wished he could ask Andrastus for help. He missed his brothers something fierce, even Canus.

Were they getting on well without him? Was his father terrorizing Andrastus? Were his brothers blamed for his disappearance? Was his father keeping it quiet, or did he have the entire country searching for him? Gods, he wished he could have some news from home. Anything.

He wished he could move his mother and siblings here into Amarra with him.

The thought startled him.

It was the first time he'd thought about bringing his family here rather than going home.

An accident, surely.

He was a literal prisoner.

But he hadn't been beaten once. He'd participated in fights, but nothing like on the battlefront. The Amarrans, his so-called enemies, treated him better than his own father did.

Olerra protected him from the threat of her cousin. By taking him, he realized she was protecting him from his father without even knowing it.

But there's no one to protect my family now.

And this place was horrible. Sanos made himself remember the market and the pit. Then again, Olerra had plans to dismantle the evil of that place and make things better for Amarra's people.

But only if she was made crown princess, and for that to happen, she needed him.

He was stuck here, but he could help Olerra win her throne.

With poetry.

He found a stack of titles and started to read.

Olerra invited herself over to Ydra's for dinner. She hadn't gotten to spend nearly enough time of late with her friend, and since Andrastus seemed to like it whenever they left the palace, she took him with her.

Besides, she had something to discuss with her sister-chosen.

The dinner table was heavy-laden with stuffed birds, herb-covered breads, and roasted vegetables dripping with gravy. Ydra's large dining room could have seated almost the entire court, but they took up only part of one end. Aside from Olerra, Ydra, and Andrastus, five of Ydra's harem were present. These were the older boys who could be trusted not to reveal the true purpose of Ydra's harem, though Olerra suspected Andrastus had already guessed what really went on in the house.

Ydra didn't have nearly the sway that Shaelwyn, Enadra, Cyssia, or Usstra did, but as Olerra's biggest supporter, she needed to maintain a certain reputation: that of the dominant Amarran woman. The gods only knew what Glenaerys would do if she learned that Ydra's harem was just for show. That Ydra "lowered" herself by caring for and protecting these boys from those who would misuse them at their tender ages.

"Did you have to meddle?" Olerra whispered to Ydra, who sat right beside her at the table.

Ydra turned a falsely innocent face to her. "Hmm?"

"He doesn't like special treatment. He doesn't like being wooed.

Why did you have to tell him he was my seul? That was for the rest of the nobility to know. Not him. He's . . . delicate."

"I was trying to speed things along. Help you to be less mopey so you can turn your mind to other things."

"All you've done is make things more awkward."

They both turned toward the empty seat beside Olerra. Andrastus had elected to sit next to one of the boys rather than her. The prince was chatting with Jurn, who laughed at whatever he had to say.

Ydra's face fell. "I'm sorry. I thought I was helping."

"Just talk to me first the next time you want to help."

Ydra pushed her food aside and pouted spectacularly.

The next course was brought in, and everyone's mouths had to be watering at the smell of roasted venison.

"You know, Olerra," Ydra said loudly as she cut into her meat, "you've inspired me. I'm thinking perhaps it's time I planned out my own husband heist."

The room went silent. Andrastus paused with a forkful halfway to his mouth.

"What are you doing?" Olerra quietly asked.

Ydra ignored her and turned to Andrastus. "Are you lonely, Prince? Would you like it if I brought one of your brothers into Amarra?"

Andrastus froze. "Absolutely not."

"No, you're not lonely, or no, you don't want me to take one of your brothers for my own?"

Andrastus looked down, methodically cutting his food into small bites with the knife. Perhaps they shouldn't have allowed him one, but Olerra was confident she and Ydra could wrest it from him before he did any damage should it come to that.

"You wouldn't want them," he said.

"And why's that?" Ydra asked.

"Too old for you."

Ydra didn't take offense. "Really? Just how old is the youngest?"

"Eighteen."

"Hmm," she said. "For the sake of argument, let's say I am willing to finally take a *man* into my bed. Which brother would you recommend?"

"You're not touching my brothers, Ydra."

"I thought you would be happier to have family close by."

"They can visit," he insisted.

Ydra shot Olerra an *Isn't he impossible?* look.

"Stop helping," Olerra whisper-shouted to her friend.

"Fine," Ydra said back.

The only sounds were that of the young boys' chewing and utensils clacking on plates.

Olerra chose to break it. "Will you tell me about your brothers?"

Andrastus considered the question before looking at Ydra with concern.

Olerra assured him, "She's not really going to take one. Ydra's not ready for a husband. Isn't that right?"

"I suppose," Ydra said before taking a sip of wine.

Andrastus said, "Canus is third-born. He is . . . difficult at times. Definitely the hardest for me to get along with. Father won't allow him to join the fighting against the Ephennans, so he's been known to visit the smithies to learn more about weaponry. He trains quite a bit with the guards stationed in the barracks. He's desperate to prove himself."

"Maybe I'd like him if you don't get along with him," Ydra pointed out.

Olerra shot her a warning look.

"Trantos is fourth-born," Andrastus went on, ignoring Ydra's comment, "and he's a bit wild. Always missing. Always late for everything. I genuinely don't know what he gets up to, but he's a peacemaker at heart. Not that he hasn't been trained like the rest of us; he just would prefer not to fight.

"Ikanos is the youngest, and he recites the most gods-awful poetry when he's drunk. He still works with tutors and doesn't know what he wants to do with his life yet. Not that any of us have much say in the matter. Father lets us know exactly what is expected of us."

Andrastus took another bite of food.

"What of the crown prince?" Olerra asked. "You said nothing of Sanos."

Andrastus met her eyes and said, "You wouldn't like Sanos."

The words didn't match his tone. "Why is that?"

"He's contentious. Calculating. A fighter."

"I actually like the sound of that," Ydra said. "Too bad taking the crown prince would start a war."

"He wouldn't like you," Andrastus said with certainty.

"Guess we won't know until he comes to visit," Ydra replied.

The prince glared at Olerra's friend.

"There," Ydra whispered to Olerra as she dabbed her face with a napkin. "Now he's angry with me and not you. You're welcome. Get him ready for the party."

20

The night before the party, Andrastus approached Olerra. He'd been silent during drills and the breaks in between them. If she didn't know any better, she'd say he was nervous.

"Be honest, how many other men are likely to perform recitations?" he asked.

It took her a moment to realize what he was talking about. "At the party you mean? A few. Why?"

"It doesn't seem likely that I will gain you much favor by performing a feat several others are already doing. It doesn't attract attention, and it doesn't elevate you in any way."

"We must work with what we have."

He ran his fingers through his white-blond hair. "I have an idea. It's . . . a bit reckless and involves you allowing me to have sharp objects."

She narrowed her eyes. "What did you have in mind?"

What he said was ridiculous, but if he could actually do it, she couldn't imagine anyone not being impressed.

"Can I trust you?" she asked.

"In this? Yes."

"Swear on something that matters."

"I swear on the life of my little sister. There is no trick here."

Olerra blinked. "You have a sister?"

"Yes, Emorra is the youngest. My brothers and I work very hard to ensure our father's attention doesn't stray to her. She doesn't get brought up often, and we keep her out of the public eye."

"What do you mean?"

They were talking more, so much more that Sanos hadn't realized when he'd slipped just now. It wasn't that he was keeping things from her, aside from his identity. It was that he didn't like to address the violence in his life.

He must have been silent for a while, because Olerra reached out to touch his arm. "You don't have to tell me," she said. "But if you want to, I will listen."

He kept his voice neutral. "My father is a violent man. He has creative ways to keep us in line."

"He beats you?" she asked.

"Regularly and under the guise of torture training."

"Where?" She was looking him all over, as though remembering what he looked like naked. The lack of repeated scars. Just those of typical training.

"Our backs mostly. He has a cane he likes to use. It doesn't break the skin." Gods, he felt so exposed. So ashamed by this secret.

"And he does this to your sister?"

"Not in many years. We . . . make sure to keep his attention."

Olerra said nothing. She was staring off in the distance. Did she believe him? That was perhaps his worst fear. That she would dismiss his words.

"Do any of your brothers take after him?" she finally asked.

Why did she want to know? "No. We all detest him. We do not prey on others for sport."

She bit her full lower lip in thought. "Let's head home for the day. You are distracted and should go to bed early. You will need to practice your routine before the party."

He nodded.

She was silent on the trek back to the palace from the training grounds. The eunuchs followed at a distance. Sanos left her to her thoughts.

They had a quiet dinner together, and then the evening routine was the same. Sanos was chained to the bed, just as he always was, and she walked in wearing skimpy nightclothes to bid him good night.

She strode forward until she was nearly touching the bed. Her eyes met his. "I want you to know that your father will never lay a hand on you again. Not while I have air to breathe. I swear it on my mother's ashes."

His heart hurt. There was something about the way she was looking at him, not with pity, but with protectiveness.

He swallowed. "I believe you."

She nodded once, and then that usual silence filled the room. Ydra had told him that she was waiting for him to instigate something. He grew excited by the thought, but he'd been thinking about this for days. About what he wanted.

He said, "I will not ask for intimacy from you until I am allowed to do so without chains. I loved it when you touched me, but I want to touch you, too."

Her mouth rounded into the smallest O. He'd surprised her.

She stood still for so long he thought perhaps she might step forward to unchain him. His breath hitched as he waited for it.

She said, "You need your rest, Prince."

And left.

Olerra locked the door between their rooms and pressed her hand to her chest. Her heart felt as though it might try to beat its way free. She wanted so desperately to take him up on his offer of intimacy. She wanted him to touch her. She wanted it more than anything except the throne.

But her mother's death loomed between them. The threat of what he could do to her, what he could find out about her, was too much. She'd fled before doing something stupid, like releasing him from his chains.

Olerra stared at the box of phalluses and had the overwhelming urge to fling it across the room. What was it all for? What was the point? Did she really think he would be content strapped down for every sexual encounter they had? That it would be enough for him? That it would be enough for *her*? She was a fool. A fool for taking him. A fool for thinking this would work.

Grief swung out of nowhere, and Olerra was struck with the pain of missing her mother stronger than she'd felt it in years.

She barely remembered the woman, but she wanted her advice. Would she have been able to tell Olerra why she didn't have the Goddess's Gift? Did she know? Would she have protected her?

Olerra opened the kit. She was one phallus away from the one she needed to fit inside her. After tonight, she could be ready for him. But would she ever be able to have him?

She used oil to get the phallus inside her and went to bed without coming.

———◆———

The next night, the last thing Olerra wanted to do was be in a room with her cousin.

Over a dozen guards followed Olerra and Andrastus to Glenaerys's wing of the palace. They were dressed in beautiful dresses or decorative pants, their hair done up in elaborate twisting braids. But each woman wore a sword at her side. They had all been invited to the party, and Olerra had personally requested that they escort her and her betrothed. She needed women she could trust surrounding them at all times.

Though Glen had thrown many parties for the sake of having a party, Olerra knew this one had some other purpose. She knew to suspect *something* from Glen. She just didn't know how deadly those plans would be.

But, gods, Olerra hoped Glen gave her a reason to smack her. Without legal repercussions.

Olerra's guards entered the party in twos and threes ahead of them, in order to look less conspicuous. They had strict orders to always keep one eye on her and Andrastus.

The prince had been quiet this evening, not even complaining about the clothes she'd picked out for him. He wore a white shirt that sparkled in the light, faceted beads sewn throughout in a swirling design. His left arm was uncovered by the garment, as always, to show off the silver-and-onyx armband. The right side of his hair was braided away from his face so the matching onyx earring could be seen. His pants only reached down to his mid-calf to show off the anklet made of black diamonds. Sturdy sandals encased his feet.

She had a hard time keeping her eyes off him, but when they walked through the doors, into Glen's domain, Olerra was instantly on alert.

"Damn," Sanos said.

"Yes, Glen is known for sparing no expense."

That was an understatement. The room resembled the inside of a jewelry box. One might think it would be the women who sparkled like gems, but it was the men, and none were so elegant as Glen's harem. They wore headdresses dripping with opals. White diamonds pierced their nipples and ears. And in one man's case, his tongue. Sanos saw it as he threw his head back to laugh. So much skin was on display, and tight clothing highlighted muscles and asses and front bulges. Sanos almost felt out of place in his simpler attire.

"Can I get you something to drink?" Olerra asked.

"Gods, yes."

She returned with a sweet-smelling drink. It was crisp and tasted of apples and cherries. It burned slightly as it went down his throat. He noticed that her glass had a different-colored liquid within.

"What are you drinking?" he asked her.

She took a sip. "I prefer a strong ale to the sweeter mead. I thought you'd like the better-tasting of the two."

Sanos downed his cup. "That was delicious, but I'll take an ale, please."

She grinned as she left to fetch him one.

The air filled with drums and stringed instruments. The room was split into two tiers. Women lounged on the bottom floor, sprawled on pillows, resting their drinks on low tables. The men, meanwhile, were mostly on the upper tier. There was a raised dais, and the men danced provocatively, thrusting hips and showing off their flexibility. It was hard for Sanos to watch them for too long, yet it was strangely informative.

When Olerra returned with his second drink, he pointed to the dancers. "Is that where I'm meant to be?"

"No, you're to stay by my side the entire evening."

He supposed there were a few men on the main floor. They had their heads in the laps of their women or could be found offering massages.

They weren't talking. They were silently performing, just like the men dancing.

Olerra and Sanos were meant to be selling a romance, yet she hadn't asked anything of him. Aside from the chaste arm-holding when they walked places, they always stood apart.

He looked at her now, wondering where he might touch her to put on a show. She wore her hair down for once. Thick braids pulled the strands away from her scalp, but the majority of it trailed down her back. It was beautiful and thick, and he wanted to put his hands through it.

So he did.

He threaded his fingers at the back of her scalp, where the braids ended, and massaged lightly as he swallowed more ale.

Olerra startled at the contact. She looked at him out of the corner of her eye, then leaned into him. "How is your drink?"

"Good. It would seem the Amarrans are vastly superior to the Brutes in fermentation. It's the only superiority I will concede to."

"Really, now? The only one?"

He grinned against his cup as he took another sip.

And that's when Daneryn showed up.

Olerra barely managed not to groan aloud. She and her prince were enjoying themselves, talking, *touching*, and then Daneryn just had to appear. She thought to ignore him. Daneryn wouldn't dare speak to her first a second time, but Andrastus had other plans.

"I don't think we were properly introduced last time. I'm Andrastus." He tilted his drink toward Daneryn in acknowledgment.

Daneryn swayed lightly on his feet to the music, and he had a dreamy smile for Olerra. He took Olerra's other side, daring to stand close, as though he had a right to be there. Andrastus's fingers felt lovely as they massaged her scalp. She curled her fingers against his hip, showing him that his company was the one she preferred.

"I'm Daneryn, but you already knew that."

Olerra wanted to chastise him for being rude, but the moment she said a word to him, she was giving him leave to speak to her. She didn't know what ridiculous things he'd utter this time, but she knew it would ruin the moment she and her prince were having.

"I did," Andrastus said. "I just wanted you to acknowledge that I was real."

Daneryn honed in on where Andrastus had his fingers in her hair. "I see you've changed your mind about my princess."

"Your princess? I don't recall her screaming your name at night."

Olerra kept her face carefully blank, but she wanted to squeal in delight at the way he was handling Daneryn.

The countess's son swayed in place again, and Olerra realized that it wasn't in tune to the music. He was drunk.

And that's when he put his hand on her.

It was a gentle touch to the side of her face, but Olerra smacked his hand away before Andrastus could even react. She said firmly, "I have declared Andrastus my seul. What are you doing?"

Daneryn pouted and blinked as though everything was out of focus. "Glen said you wanted to see me. She said I should go to you now."

Olerra did a sweep of the room, but she couldn't see her cousin anywhere. "Why would you listen to her? You *know* how she is."

"I don't feel so good." Daneryn put his hand on Olerra's hip to steady himself as he bent at the waist.

She knew he was about to vomit, so she carefully removed his hand and rotated behind him to offer support as his mead came up.

"I think he might be drugged," Andrastus said. "Especially if Glen sent him over here."

"I think you're right," Olerra said. "Don't drink anything unless I hand it to you."

Her prince nodded.

Daneryn suddenly was deadweight in Olerra's arms. She increased her grip, but thankfully Andrastus stepped forward to take the bulk of his weight before Olerra could learn whether she had the strength to hold him up at this angle.

A few servants finally noticed and sprang forward to help. They took Daneryn off their hands and cleaned the mess. Olerra and Andrastus found another corner of the room to occupy.

"What do you think that was about?" the prince asked.

"She could be trying to unsettle me or it could be part of something bigger. It's impossible to know with her. We just need to be careful tonight."

Andrastus nodded. "Would you like to dance?"

The musicians had started a slower song, and many of the men left the raised platform to find their mistresses. Women took to the dance floor, towing three or four men along after them. Sanos didn't know any Amarran dances, and he didn't know how to dance with more than one partner, but he rather liked the idea of having more excuses to touch Olerra.

"A Brute who dances?" Olerra asked.

"I'm instructed in over thirty different dances for four different kingdoms, but I don't know any Amarran ones."

"Then I'll teach you."

She led him to the raised platform. While all dances from different countries had different moves, they often started the same, with the hands clasped.

Not so in Amarra.

"On your knees," Olerra said.

He looked around, noting that the other men were sitting at their mistresses' feet. Perhaps this was a very bad idea.

Then Olerra started to move.

She circled him, letting her fingers trail over his shoulders, across his chest. The men around him did nothing. They watched their mistresses, so Sanos did the same. When she turned her eyes on him, he couldn't move if he'd wanted to.

It was like watching her fight, the way she moved. She held her arms above her head, then lowered to the floor. She rolled onto her back, came back up on her feet, flung her hair behind herself.

And then she came to him.

Olerra tugged him to his feet, pulled him in so close there was no space between them. She spun so her back was to his front and looped her arms around his neck. Without her eyes on him, he could take in the other dancers. Men were touching the women, swaying their hips together, each man taking turns to be the one at her back.

Olerra was all his.

Sanos put his hands on her hips. They moved as one, swaying side to side. Other couples were thrusting in the imitation of sex, and he wondered if they should, too . . .

Olerra moved away and spun to face him, and the opportunity was lost to him. The next part of the dance was more familiar. It appeared meant for women who had lots of partners, as each took turns holding her, spinning her. The women led in these dances, and he followed as Olerra moved herself in and out of his arms. He moved his limbs as he saw the other men do, and each time he touched Olerra, more and more of his surroundings were forgotten.

And then she drew her face toward his until their mouths were a hairbreadth apart.

Sanos closed his eyes, welcoming her kiss.

But then the music stopped.

It was over before it could begin, and Olerra pulled back, clapping for the artists who'd played their instruments so beautifully. Sanos wanted to glare at them for ending the song.

A voice rang out, and Sanos finally tore his eyes away from Olerra.

"Thank you all for coming. Tonight's entertainment is about to start. Take your seats and make sure you get a good view of the dais."

They finally had eyes on Glenaerys. She wore a golden dress and sandals. Her hair was braided so intricately that Sanos couldn't begin to guess how it was done. When she saw Olerra and Sanos, she offered them a warm smile.

"Come," Olerra said, taking his hand and leading him to where Ydra and some of Olerra's captains were already situated. They weren't far from where the queen and queen consort were seated, apart from everyone else on raised thrones, where they could observe without distractions. Attendants and guards were not far off. As though the queen couldn't trust her own niece not to try anything at her party.

The first member of Glen's harem took the stage with a lute in tow. He strummed the instrument and sang so beautifully that the whole crowd was mesmerized. His voice reached impossibly high for a man; he must practice every day to be able to accomplish it. Sanos had seen the music rooms in the gymnasium, but he'd never bothered to enter, because he had no inclination or talent in that regard.

Applause sounded, and the crowd refreshed their drinks and food. Olerra brought Sanos some snacks to try. Fruits and salted meats. Fresh breads and honey. It was all delicious, of course.

And then the next man took his turn on the dais.

"A poem dedicated to the Goddess's Gift," he declared, and then he proceeded to recite a story rapt with emotion and tension. He rhymed in places, raised and lowered his voice, spoke as though the telling of the story was just as important as the words themselves.

One thing was for certain. While Andrastus might have given him a run for his money, there was no way that Sanos could have even come close to so rich a delivery.

Olerra leaned forward. "He wrote that himself."

Sanos felt his stomach sink. The man didn't just read poetry, he *wrote* it? Sanos had never felt incompetent compared to Amarran men until this moment.

Another harem member performed a dance that was so erotic, many of the women in the room were fanning themselves. Sanos snuck a glance to Olerra, but she was engaged in conversation with Ydra, not watching.

For some reason that made him feel better.

Someone did acrobatics. Another man did ballet. It was quickly apparent that all of Glen's harem were trained in not only the bedroom but performing. He noticed, however, that Athon didn't take the stage. No, he had already played his hand in the fight with Sanos. It would seem he didn't have other talents.

To be fair, Sanos wasn't good for much. But he had four younger brothers, and they were all competitive, save Andrastus, which meant they got up to no good regularly. They liked to do dangerous things. Stupid things when their father wasn't looking. And sometimes, down at the training yard, things could get . . . interesting.

When another bout of applause echoed off the walls after a different man read yet more poetry, Glenaerys rose and spoke loudly enough for the crowd at large to hear, but her eyes were on Olerra.

"Cousin, would Andrastus care to grace us with a recitation? I've heard he's been practicing for tonight."

Olerra said, "I think we've heard enough poetry for one evening."

"That's a shame. I hoped the man might prove useful in some regard after all the trouble he has caused you."

Every noblewoman in the room looked at them. Many had open dislike for Sanos, disappointment for Olerra. They didn't bother to hide the expressions on their faces. He hadn't realized just how bad things had become for her. Everyone still spoke civilly to the two of them, but with Glenaerys putting them on the spot, it was a chance for others to show their support for either cousin.

"Actually," Olerra declared, "Andrastus has prepared something else for our entertainment tonight."

"Is that right? Let him take the stage without delay, then. I'm most eager to see this."

Olerra nodded at him, and Sanos rose.

Her prince certainly put on a brave face, but Olerra could tell he was nervous. Was it because he worried he couldn't do this? Or did he think he might fail her? Something had changed between them of late, and she felt him really trying his best to help. Like he wanted to get her the throne of Amarra.

Eunuchs brought forward the requested supplies. A target was laid out on the opposite end of the dais. It was a simple fold-out, with three rings. White, yellow, and, at the center, red. A tall candelabra was placed on one side of Andrastus. It was nearly as tall as he was, and three lit candles flickered at the top. A table was laid on his other side. Sanos set a fresh drink of ale atop it, and another servant set five daggers next to it.

Glenaerys took notice of the target. "Are you allowing him something sharp?" she called across the room.

"I thought you'd take pleasure in seeing how tame and loyal he's become."

A muscle ticked in Glen's jaw, but she did not try to stop the performance. Olerra approached the musicians and asked them to play a number she thought would enhance Andrastus's display.

Her prince selected a knife from the table, holding it by the blade. He extended his arm, taking aim, then pulled back his bicep and released. With the majority of the women behind Andrastus, they could all see that it hit the target dead center.

A few hesitant hands clapped, but most women didn't know what to make of the display.

Glen laughed. "Athon can do that. Can't you, Athon?"

"Yes, mistress."

Andrastus threw another knife. It landed right next to the first. After the third knife, Glenaerys struck up a conversation with nearby women, taking their attention off Andrastus entirely. It angered Olerra. *She* wanted to throw something.

Andrastus retrieved the daggers, and then he dunked one into his glass of ale before holding it up to the flame of the candelabra.

The blade caught fire, but just to be sure everyone was watching, he threw it high in the air and caught it without damaging himself.

The room went quiet as all eyes fixed on her prince. Holding the first knife in his left hand, Andrastus dunked a second in his ale before lighting it. Then he did the same with a third. He threw them all up in the air in a circle, catching them effortlessly. Then, rapidly, each dagger hit the target one after another.

Dead center.

The applause was riotous. Many women whistled, so impressed were they with the display. Olerra had no idea such a talent existed until Andrastus had described it to her. She wondered how many times her prince had cut or burned himself as a child while he practiced this.

Glenaerys said nothing now. She was studiously ignoring the stage, talking to those around her who would listen. She held a juicy red apple in one hand and brought it to her mouth to take a bite.

Olerra saw the thought enter Andrastus's mind, but before she could tell him to stop, he threw.

A fourth dagger sailed through the air, faster than Olerra could open her mouth.

It landed, blade first, into the apple, not even a full inch away from Glen's fingers. Her cousin dropped the fruit as though it'd burned her, rolling away with the knife hilt sticking from it. Her eyes were wide with outrage, but the crowd was screaming now. Praise was heaped upon Andrastus. The queen gave him a standing ovation, and everyone was delighted by the show of strength.

Olerra ran up to the dais and kissed the cheek of her prince.

"Well done," she said, her voice no louder than a whisper. "But next time, don't do anything so foolish! What if you had missed?"

"If I had missed, then I would have repaid what I owe her."

21

The queen invited Sanos and Olerra to sit with her. Pillows were placed beside the thrones, and Sanos sat with his spine straight atop one while women came up to congratulate him on the performance. He was once again uncomfortable with such attention, but he bore it with good humor this time. For her. He was proud to have garnered some more respect for Olerra as heir. It probably didn't fix everything, but it had to be a step in the right direction.

"Where did you learn to do that?" one noblewoman asked him.

"Playing dare with my brothers."

She laughed, proclaiming Brutish boys brave devils.

Another woman whose name he didn't know approached and said, "I saw you dancing and drinking with the princess. You've clearly warmed up to her. What changed in so short a time?"

He was, for the most part, truthful in his answer. "When she saved my life, I knew that I needed to do more for her. To be more for her. And when she proclaimed me her seul, I knew that was the end of it for me."

The surrounding women were delighted by his responses. They brought him drinks and food, as though he needed more after all he'd been consuming. He took it gratefully but didn't try anything that didn't come straight from Olerra. The crowd around them grew bigger and bigger until it was larger than Glen's.

He locked eyes with Olerra, who beamed at him. He felt his whole heart swell. He was done ignoring his attraction to her. Done pretending that helping her get the throne wasn't the right thing to do or even the most beneficial thing for him in the long run.

There was his family to consider, but having Olerra as a powerful ally could only help him in that regard, too, he realized.

Feeling a bit brazen and perhaps a little drunk, he reached over and pulled Olerra off her pillow and into his lap. He stroked her hair, let one hand drift to her hip. He found excuses to lean down over her, bringing his lips to her ear as he spoke.

"How many of the court do you think are too drunk to remember anything tomorrow?" he asked.

Olerra grinned up at him. "I think we're safe. We've won some back to our side. Thank you for selling this romance so admirably."

When he looked down at her lips, he saw her breath catch. Gods, he wanted to kiss her more than anything. But not here. Not in front of this crowd, where it would be a show. He wanted it to be just the two of them. When it meant something only for them.

Olerra couldn't get enough of the way he was looking at her.

The usually frowning, intimidating, handsome prince of Brutus was something else when there was heat in his eyes. His attention was arresting when he was angry. But when he wasn't? It was hard not to squirm on his lap.

But her chosen was so much more than just an attractive body. He was a brother who protected his little sister. A prince who sought out fairness. A man who had killed for her.

There was still so much more to learn about each other, but she knew that each new revelation would only draw them closer. She looked forward to the time ahead of them.

Olerra met Ydra's eyes across the room. Her friend held up her cup before taking a large drink, and Olerra could hear her words from before.

Stop worrying about it.

Ydra had no doubt meant the lack of sex. As though Olerra could just stop thinking about how much she wanted Andrastus. But what if she'd actually meant to stop worrying about the fact she didn't have the Gift?

Women in other countries had to put their faith in men. Just trust that they wouldn't be hurt by them or taken advantage of. Olerra didn't have the goddess's strength, and that meant she would have to do the same if she wanted to draw closer to her Brute.

And she *really* wanted that.

Olerra rose and held down her hand to Andrastus, who took it. She helped haul him to his feet, showing her strength to the whole room.

"I think we'll retire now," she said.

"Enjoy your evening," Toria said.

The queen simply nodded.

Olerra tugged her prince after her, eager to reach her rooms.

The hallway was quiet, and Andrastus kept apace with her easily. He seemed just as eager to reach her rooms, which only made her more excited. They walked hand in hand. She kept darting glances at her man, waiting for him to drop the act now that they were alone.

He didn't.

She was so caught up in the moment that she failed to notice when they were no longer alone.

Something barreled into her from behind, sending her off-balance, and Olerra cursed herself for not being more observant.

Andrastus caught her before she could stumble more than a step, and he spun her behind him before Olerra could see what the danger was.

"Watch where you're going," the newcomer said. Olerra peered around Andrastus's body to find the boy that Glenaerys had bought at auction all those weeks ago, before Olerra had set out to steal her prince. He now wore Glen's armband, and his face had a bit of fear mixed with anger as he moved along. Did he not realize whom he'd shoved? Or was he afraid because he was on Glen's orders to do something?

Andrastus raised a hand as though to stop the boy for his rudeness and demand an apology, but Olerra wrapped a hand around his bicep. "Don't. Let him go. He doesn't have an easy time of it. He's one of hers."

Andrastus relented. Once the boy rounded the corner, he turned to her. "Are you hurt?"

"No."

Olerra's guards spilled into the hallway, having caught up with their sudden disappearance. One of them gave her a disapproving look, as if to chastise her for not telling them she and her prince were leaving.

Olerra had been so caught up in the moment, she hadn't even paused to think about safety. How did this man make her lose all sense?

"Let's go," Olerra said.

The prince seemed only too happy to follow.

Sanos had drunk plenty, but he'd always been one to hold his drink well. He was perfectly coherent as Olerra led him down the halls of the Amarran palace. She locked the door when they reached her rooms.

They were alone.

And he was unchained.

He had exactly zero desire to leave.

Not with the way she was smiling at him or the way her hand felt so warm in his.

The stab of guilt that suddenly jolted through his body was both unwelcome and unexpected, but it must have shown.

"What is it?" she asked, making no move to pull away or draw closer.

If they were going to do this, and he desperately wanted to do this, he needed to be honest with her. At least about the things he could.

"I have to show you something."

He left her room, entering his own and crossing over into the next bedroom. He got down on his knees, feeling Olerra's presence over his shoulder. His hand went to the ashes in the hearth, where he quickly found the hidden knife.

Olerra leaped back when she saw what he held, but Sanos carefully stayed on his knees. He adjusted his grip, holding the weapon by the blade and turning. He held the hilt out to her.

"Glenaerys gave me this. She wanted me to kill you. I accepted it, but not with the intent to hurt you. I wanted to keep the knife just in case escape ever became possible. I wanted something for the journey home. Your cousin is using every tool at her disposal, but I am not one of them. Take it."

Olerra looked down at the ash-covered weapon before turning her eyes to his. "How did she manage to get you alone to give you this?"

"Your eunuchs are in her employ."

Olerra's jaw clenched. She left the room, leaving Sanos on his knees before the hearth. His head and hopes fell. He understood she might be angry that he didn't tell her about this right away, but surely she had to believe his sincerity. He really hadn't intended to use it on her. This was for him. He thought that maybe after everything that had happened—

Olerra suddenly burst back into the room. "All right. The eunuchs are being dealt with. Their keys to my rooms are being revoked, and they're being locked up in the dungeons for further interrogation.

Thank gods I can trust Ydra to get things done. Now, how long ago did Glen give you this knife?"

The reappearance was jarring, but he said, "Not long. A week, perhaps."

"And how did she intend for you to harm me with this?"

"She told me to wait until you trusted me. Until you let me be around you without chains. Only then was I to strike. When you least expected it. This is the first you've allowed us to be alone together in your rooms, unchained, and I want you to know that you can trust me. *That I trust you.* I don't need this. I'm going to stay and help you win your throne."

Gods, he had so much to figure out. His men fought the Ephennans without him, and his family was without his protection. He needed time to come up with solutions, but he meant the words he said to her.

Her face unreadable, Olerra finally reached for the blade and took it. "Why the change?" she asked.

He was still asking himself that question, but the answer turned out to be right in front of him. "You, of course."

She raised a brow.

"Your forwardness and kindness. Your fierceness and loyalty. Your plans for the future of Amarra. You're unlike anyone I have ever met, and I would see you be the next queen. I'm in."

What was she meant to do with this prince on his knees offering her a dagger and a kingdom?

Kissing him seemed like a good start.

Olerra took the dagger from him and tossed it over her shoulder, not bothering to see where it landed. Then she pulled him to his feet. She meant to say thank you, but he was already closing the distance between them.

He claimed her mouth with a savagery that might be more suitable to a thief than a prince. His lips were firm, they were demanding, and she loved it.

She was expected to be in control of so much all the time, and she loved that he was just fine taking control of this moment, when he'd had so little autonomy since arriving in Amarra.

He tasted like ale when she sucked on his tongue. He had one hand in her hair, palming her scalp, while the other sank low, gripping as much of her ass as he could in one hand and squeezing. She drew closer, nibbled on his lower lip, and let her fingers roam over the parts of him she'd been admiring all night. His chest. His arms. That near-white hair.

Olerra let her lips trail down to his left shoulder, while her hand worked to pull the right sleeve down, and then she explored that shoulder with her mouth, too.

Andrastus was riveted to the spot, clearly enjoying everything she was doing. The most delightful rumbles came from his throat, so she rose onto her toes to give his neck some attention, too. Kissing and sucking and marking him as hers.

He seemed . . . unused to the touch, throwing back his head and relishing in her hands on him.

She pulled back. "Did the Brutish whores not kiss you?"

"Not like this."

That pleased her. She liked being the only one who had done this for him. Gods, but she needed to touch more of him. She reached for his shirt, and Andrastus drew it off for her. She traced as much of his arms as she could, wrapping her hands around his wrists and trailing upward. A spark of pleasure went through her when she reached the armband.

And then there was his bare chest.

She loved touching it. The smooth white skin, the ridges of his muscles, the slight peak of a hardened nipple. She pulled away from his lips long enough to kiss straight down the middle of him, needing to taste his skin.

The threat of the danger was there; it hovered above her like the blade of a guillotine about to drop, but she willfully ignored it.

Andrastus was starting to come around. Maybe after the haze of their victory that evening settled he'd be back to his usual, distant self, but for right now, she was going to be present. She was going to remember every second of this to replay over and over again in her mind.

When she reached below his navel, she moved her hands to his back and stood slowly, tracing the muscles there. There was no part of him that wasn't smooth or hard. It was incredible how well those two went together.

When she was standing fully once more, he drew her lips back to his. To her surprise, they were gentler this time, slowing with each pull of his lips, each delving of his tongue into her mouth. He savored her, like she was his favorite meal.

When she felt his fingers on the laces at the back of her dress, loosening them, heat shot through her entire body. He pulled the fabric down her arms, and she helped it along, letting it pool at her waist, exposing her breasts.

Andrastus stepped back and dropped his gaze to what he'd just laid bare, and the hunger in his eyes was enough for Olerra's knees to go weak. She backed up to the nearest wall, and he followed, lowering his head as soon as he caught her.

He kissed the small space between her breasts. Then he palmed one in his right hand. "You're so beautiful. Gods, I can't even fit you in my hand."

He stopped speaking to kiss his way over to the breast he wasn't holding. When his mouth reached the center, he drew her nipple into his mouth and sucked.

"Shit," Olerra said, throwing her head back.

He flicked his tongue back and forth over the tip, while letting his thumb roll small circles over the other one. Olerra heard her exhalations grow higher in pitch as he worked her skin.

"Naked," she panted. "I want you naked now."

He rose to his full height and asked, "Are you ready for me?"

She nodded eagerly. "But are you ready for me?"

He lowered his mouth to her ear. "I've been aching for you for too long. I was just too stubborn to see it."

When he drew back, he was somehow already naked, having shirked his clothing with miraculous speed while speaking. A man motivated beyond reason. He reached forward to help her get the rest of her dress and shorts over her hips. Until he could see all of her.

Andrastus lowered his hand to palm her sex while leaning down to kiss her again. Olerra rolled her hips into that hand, letting a delicious friction send jolts up her body. Gods, but she was so close already, she felt like she might explode at any moment.

"Wait," Andrastus said, taking his hand away.

Olerra had to bite her lip to prevent crying out in frustration.

"Not like that."

And then he lowered to his knees.

Just the visual was enough to make her come. She clapped her hand across her mouth as she felt the small orgasm ripple through her body. What was this man doing to her? Making her come without even touching her. She hoped he hadn't noticed.

He was grinning up at her. "That was beautiful, but I'm sure we can do better."

Sanos's erection was barely on his mind as he took in Olerra fully naked for the first time. She was all thick curves and smooth skin. Beautifully full breasts. She widened her stance so there was room for his head between her thighs. When that wasn't quite right, he picked up her left knee and threw it over his shoulder.

He looked up at her.

Olerra's eyes were trusting. They were beautifully dark and low-lidded.

His mouth watered as he looked at what lay at his eye level.

She was beautiful. Pink as the lips on her face, her opening glistened with her arousal. He leaned forward and licked over the seam.

He heard her head strike the wall. When he looked up, her eyes were closed.

He kissed along her intimate lips, finding them impossibly soft, the smell incredibly erotic. Olerra whimpered above him as he took his time testing every area down there, figuring out what she liked best.

He let his tongue delve inside her. She liked that. He did it again, then retreated, going up higher and higher to explore the full length of her.

When he reached the edge of her sex, his lips rubbed against a place that made her cry out, and he paused, drew back to look at it. There was the smallest little circle of skin within the folds of her, near the very top. He leaned in experimentally and licked it.

She gasped.

Pleased that he'd found something she really liked, he blew across the spot, then went back down to play with her entrance some more.

Her body seemed to relax now that he wasn't at the place that gave her the most pleasure. He couldn't have that, so without warning, he returned to the nub, took it into his mouth, and sucked.

"Fuck," she said, her hands going to his hair, as though she intended to keep him there. Catching herself, she lowered those hands.

"It's okay," he said against her skin. "You can touch me." And then he found a rhythm stroking that part of her that made her lose control.

Her hands immediately went back to his hair. She thrust against his mouth and whimpered every time he sucked on her. It took some time, since she'd already come once, but Sanos was determined. He was happy to be as patient as she needed.

He felt so in control. The way he could bring these noises out of her. He was on his knees yet the one holding all the power, and he loved it.

"Fu . . ." She trailed off on a gasp as her orgasm spread through her. Sanos kept licking to help her through it. He didn't stop until her hips and hands stilled. Then he gently set her leg back on the floor and rose.

As Olerra slowly opened her eyes, he grinned.

"You swear when you come," he said. "I hadn't noticed until just now."

"So?"

"I love it."

"Good, because if you do that on a regular basis, you're going to hear more foul language."

He liked the sound of that.

"What is this?" he asked, letting a finger touch that small part of her that drove her wild.

"Don't touch it," she shrieked, stepping away. "It's too sensitive now."

He chuckled. "Sorry."

"That is my clitoris. It is the part of the woman responsible for bringing pleasure."

Sanos scrunched his face. "But I thought . . . inside . . ."

Olerra was breathing deeply, her eyes somewhat unfocused as she struggled to have the conversation. "No. Most women cannot come only from having a man inside them. Most need this spot touched to orgasm."

His eyes widened. "When we . . . how can I make sure that you . . ."

She smiled as she leaned forward and kissed him so sweetly his heart swelled.

"There are so many ways. We get to discover what works best for us."

"*Us.* I like that word."

She did, too. She loved the thought of *them*. And she loved the thought of what came next.

"Is there more you'd like to talk about or would you like to try it?" she asked.

He looked down. "Are you sure you can handle more? You said you were too sensitive."

"Sweet man, I only needed a moment. Besides, I'd feel incredible if you kissed me some more."

He did just that. Lavishing her with beautiful kisses. He gave particular attention to her neck, a body part she suspected he was quite fond of. That and her breasts. He couldn't seem to stop touching them. Kissing them. Licking and sucking. She knew men were fond of breasts; she just didn't realize the extent.

It was like there was a string connecting her nipples to her sex. Every time he touched her there, she could feel the heat down low. Impossibly, she felt ready for a third orgasm. Something she'd never managed on her own. Two? Yes. But three?

Gods, what was he doing to her?

His erection was so hard between them, digging into her stomach. She was so familiar by now with its size. Was so ready for it to be inside her. But the phallus she'd used wasn't quite the same. Andrastus had a different texture, one she was dying to experience with her hands.

She asked, "Can I touch you?"

"Anywhere you'd like," he immediately answered.

She wrapped her hand around him. Gently, like she liked to be touched between her legs.

And his breath caught.

She marveled at how warm he was, something the phallus definitely was not. It was also attached to a breathing person who *reacted* to her touch. Something that she didn't realize she was missing. That she needed.

Her tutors had taught that the head was the most sensitive, so she swirled her thumb around it as she gripped him.

Andrastus closed his eyes. "You and your Amarran education will destroy me."

She smiled, pressing her thumb lightly into the slit, and he hissed like a snake.

"Come here," he said, pulling her toward the bed.

She went eagerly. So ready for what was to come next. They'd played. They'd kissed. Now she wanted this man inside her.

Andrastus pushed her onto her back, then held himself atop her on his hands. Olerra had the thought to swap their places, but she didn't see any reason why he couldn't take the lead this once. If it started to hurt for any reason, she could always roll him over.

He kissed her, returned even more attention to her breasts. Then he let his knee sneak up between her legs to feel how wet she was.

"Are you ready?" he asked.

"Yes."

"Do you have a sheath?"

"I take a tea once a month that prevents pregnancy."

He shut his eyes, as though the thought of being inside her without any barriers was almost too much for him. After a beat, he fit himself between her legs, let his cock touch the sensitive folds of her sex. He rubbed it around her entrance, then slid higher, until he reached her clit.

"Andrastus!" she shrieked. "No more playing, please."

And then he pulled away.

Her prince leaped off the bed, his entire body looking tighter than a bowstring.

"What is it?" she asked, worried that she'd done something wrong.

"I—"

The silence was cold and horrible. He wouldn't meet her eyes. He was still aroused, yet he would not come closer to the bed.

Olerra took a steadying breath. "You're not ready, are you?"

"I—" he tried again, but that was as far as he got.

She couldn't help the disappointment that sprang up, but she quashed it. His comfort was far more important than what she'd hoped would come of this evening.

"It's okay. We don't need to rush. We have time."

Andrastus slammed his eyes and lips closed, as though he were in immense pain. He nodded slowly.

Olerra rose and grabbed her clothing off the floor. She needed to get away from him and calm down. He was too much of a delicious sight, naked and hard before her.

"Good night, Prince. I will see you tomorrow. There is nothing bad between us. Not on my end."

He still wouldn't look at her. Even as he nodded.

She let herself into her room and replayed every magical moment until she fell asleep.

22

Sanos felt like an idiot.

No, scratch that. He *was* an idiot.

Keeping his identity hidden had been crucial to his survival, but he didn't have an excuse now. He should tell her.

Sanos, he would say. *My name is Sanos.*

How did he think this would work? That he would simply continue to pretend as their romance progressed. It was him she wanted, not his damned brother. She just had the wrong name.

And when she'd called out his brother's name right before he was about to take her, it'd been more effective than a bucket of ice water. He could not, *would not*, bed her as she called out another man's name. He wanted her to say *his* name. He wanted to hear it fall from her lips more than he wanted anything else.

But what would happen once he revealed the truth?

She couldn't have him, a crown prince. He was too politically important to Brutus. And she couldn't come with him to Brutus. He would *never* let her live in the same castle as his father. Not that it mattered. Olerra needed to remain in Amarra to become queen.

And to do that, she needed a husband. Would she ransom him for his brother? His father would make the trade. Of course he would. Atalius wanted his heir, the one he'd groomed since childhood to be just like him. He would hand Andrastus over in a heartbeat.

What kind of brother would Sanos be if he allowed that to happen?

Who the fuck was he kidding? It had nothing to do with letting his brother take his place and everything to do with the thought of Olerra bedding his brother.

She can't. She's mine.

But she wasn't, and she could never be unless she knew who he was.

It was a problem with no solution. No matter what he did, he lost.

The only thing he could do, the only thing he would do, was help her win her throne. He'd tell her once she was named crown princess. Hopefully his father didn't find out where he was before then.

So he would wait. He would tell her before anything drastic happened. But the best thing for her right now would be to get that vote from the nobility. He wouldn't let anything stop her from getting what she wanted most.

When Olerra entered Andrastus's room the next morning, she was beaming. Her guards outside the harem rooms reported seeing nothing in the night.

"You didn't try to escape," she said.

"As if I would have made it farther than I had last time."

"You like it here, admit it."

"I like *you*," he corrected. "I tolerate everything else."

"We'll make changes," she promised him. "The moment I'm named heir, I will speak to my aunt about making things better for you. For the other men who wish it. Whatever you want, we can discuss it. Together, we can make this place good for everyone."

He looked at her so fondly. His hair was mussed from sleep, and she could smell the delicious scent that was just him coming from the bed.

"May I kiss you good morning?" she asked.

His face visibly relaxed, as though he might have been worried what the state of things between them would be. "Always."

She smiled, leaned down, and gave him a chaste peck on the lips. The moment she tried to pull away, his hands went to the back of her head, keeping her in place. He pulled her onto his lap, and she giggled as she fell into place.

His kiss was not heated as it had been last night. It was deep and sweet. It was careful, as though he were trying to communicate something to her. She thought she might know what it was.

We're okay. Nothing is wrong. I just need to slow down.

She was perfectly fine with that. She didn't want anything that he didn't.

Olerra put her hands on his chest, pushing him back a few inches. He went without resisting.

"I just want to understand," she said.

Her hands curled around his biceps. She really liked the feel of them. The way her fingers had no hope of touching. The way he couldn't help but flex underneath her. As though he wanted her to find him impressive.

"Is it . . . intercourse that is off the table but everything else is fair game?" she asked.

Andrastus looked down at his lap as though he were ashamed.

"We don't have to talk about it if you don't want to. I just thought it might help if I understood. Perhaps we could avoid any discomfort. I want to know what is and isn't okay."

He raised his head, frustration clear in his eyes. "I don't know."

"That's okay, too," she said.

"What I do know is that you are nothing like I thought I wanted. Yet, I want you. Make no mistake of that. I want you more than anything. Just not yet."

"Would it help if I promised not to initiate intimacy without asking? Let you decide what you want and when you want it?"

"And what if I do something you don't like?" he asked.

"I'll like it," she promised. "But if you're unsure, you could always ask."

He said nothing, as though her words made no sense. She decided to be a little wicked and help him along. "For example, you could ask, Olerra, can I kiss you? Just as I asked you this morning. That wasn't strange, was it?"

He shook his head.

"You could ask, Olerra, would you like to put your hands on my cock?"

Andrastus swallowed.

"You could say, Olerra, could I put my cock into your mouth?"

His eyes were blazing, but he didn't move, as though he wanted to torture himself longer by hearing all the filthy things she could come up with.

"You could say, Olerra, would you like to sit on my face? Or—"

He silenced her with another kiss, this one hot and primal. He pulled back just enough to say, "All of it. I want to do all of it."

Olerra adjusted her position until she was straddling him. By touch alone she found the strings keeping his tight shorts closed. When she freed him, she wrapped her hand around him, relishing in the heat of him.

"Gods, Andrastus, you feel so perfect."

And then his body went rigid beneath her.

She let go of him immediately, her confusion profound. Was it her talking that bothered him? She'd thought he liked it when she spoke like this, despite his protests in the beginning. Naughty talk was her favorite, and she didn't want to give that up to please him. But she would. If it was what he needed.

"Do you . . . need silence when we— Is that it?"

Andrastus groaned. "I'm sorry, but I think I need a moment alone before we head to breakfast. Would that be all right?"

"Of course. We could even eat with the troops this morning if you'd prefer?"

He nodded.

"Great, I'll return in a few minutes."

Olerra shut herself within her room and sat on the edge of her bed. She didn't know what to do. He'd told her what he wanted. But that still didn't work. She wasn't sure what she was doing wrong. He had no problem becoming aroused. The problem wasn't his body's enthusiasm, that was for sure. It must be something in the mind.

And then a horrible thought struck her.

Had someone hurt him?

Abused him sexually?

Fiery anger propelled her to her feet, and she began to pace. Of course. *Of course.* Andrastus wouldn't be able to help when he was triggered. And he wasn't ready to talk about it. He probably *couldn't* talk about it.

Olerra wanted a name. She wanted the person responsible taken to the pit. She would lower the guillotine herself. Better yet, she'd take a fucking ax to them. She wouldn't just take the cock. She'd take all of it. Balls and hands while she was at it. Let the coward responsible be a mewling mess.

When she finally calmed down, she put her focus back on the matter at hand. Andrastus needed to go slow. He needed her to be patient. He needed her to make him feel safe.

She would do all of that. She would do whatever he needed. No one would hurt him again.

She vowed it.

There was no word fouler than his brother's name, Sanos decided.

He spent the next week talking with Olerra as much as possible. If they were talking, then they weren't being physical. If they weren't being physical, then he wouldn't have to hear fucking Andrastus's name called out in ecstasy in place of his.

It was torture.

He enjoyed the time they spent together. He enjoyed hearing her stories and telling her his. He enjoyed hearing her opinions on the way the world worked and how she would change it once she was in a position to do so. She was an incredible conversationalist. He felt bland by comparison, yet she seemed enchanted by him.

Twice he caught her reaching out as if to touch him and then pulling back. He pretended not to notice.

And he suffered.

One evening, when it was just the two of them having a quiet dinner in the seating area of her rooms, he asked, "Have you ever tried to kill her? Glen?"

The question didn't seem to hold any judgment, only curiosity, which interested Olerra. "No. Not once."

"Why not?"

"One, because it's a poor queen who has to take out her only competition in order to win a throne. And two—"

She hesitated, wondering what he would make of the next part if she told him the truth.

"I still remember her as a child. We grew up together. As close as Ydra and I are now."

Andrastus took this all in with a patience she'd never seen from him before. "What changed? How did you go from sisters to rivals?"

She couldn't help but ask, "Do you really find this interesting?"

He nodded.

"My parents both died when I was four. Glen declared I was her sister now. She would be my family. Though her mother, my aunt by marriage, kept me at a distance, she permitted the closeness we came to share. Glen was kind. She genuinely loved me. Though even back then she had a manipulative personality. She would ask me to do things for her."

"What kinds of things?"

"Little things at first. I was stronger. So she'd ask me to open a jar or be the soldier in our games where she played the princess. As we got older, she became a little more brazen. Asking me to run errands for her or deal with noblewomen who displeased her."

"Deal with them how?"

"At first, she wanted me to scare them off. Then she requested I get physical. That's when the queen noticed what was happening and stepped in. I was ten, and Auntie said we should spend more time together. She gently showed me what my cousin was doing and taught me that family doesn't demand so much of us. When I confronted Glenaerys about it, she seemed horrified that I would think that her love only came if I was doing things for her."

"You grew distant after that?" he asked.

"No. We remained close until we were fifteen. It's the age women must reach before they are permitted entrance to the brothels. For her birthday, Glenaerys wanted to go, insisting she couldn't bear to arrive by herself. She wanted me there, too. Even though I was not quite fifteen. I gave in, thinking I was hardly about to become more mature in another three months. We went to an establishment specifically for female differres.

"Because we're part of the royal family, the proprietor didn't blink at my appearance when he saw us enter. In fact, he was flattered that we'd chosen his establishment for our First Nights. He said the evening was on him. We could go through as many of his studs as we wanted until the sun came up."

"But you didn't . . ." Andrastus felt the need to clarify.

"I'll tell you exactly what happened if you can stay quiet."

He snapped his mouth shut.

"At the brothel, the doors have small openings at eye level that latch open and shut so guests can peer inside. If someone doesn't want to be observed, they can lock the latch from the inside. Otherwise, the prostitutes who are unoccupied leave their latches unlocked so anyone can look inside and make their selections. Glen and I took our time, looking through every single opening to examine all the pretty men." Olerra still remembered when they'd stumbled across the unlocked window of a door that already had two occupants. Glen and Olerra had peered within, side by side, as they watched the woman riding the man. She'd thrown her head back and moaned as soon as she'd realized she was being watched. As though such a thing excited her even more.

Olerra didn't say that part aloud. "When Glen decided on a man, I waited in the hallway. Told her I wasn't ready. She didn't give me a hard time about it at all. She simply went into the chosen room and said I could go. I'm not sure why I stayed. There was something erotic about the hallway, listening to moans and cries of pleasure. I'd never witnessed anything like it. All my instructions up until that point had been done with books and mannequins—but then something new cut through the space. A cry that was different from the others. One of pain. I ran for the proprietor, but when we arrived, it was already over. Glen was exiting the room, and she left a barely breathing man back on the bed. Bruises were already forming around his neck, and his arm was bent at an odd angle."

Olerra paused, remembering her shock from all those years ago. "She'd hurt him. She'd realized early on that pain made her more aroused, and she relished in it. She was banned from the brothel, and she blamed me for tattling on her. But more than that, I finally realized who she really is at her core."

Olerra turned to Andrastus. "I'm not a perfect person, but I'm leagues above my cousin. I'm not going to gain more power by picking on those I know to be weaker than I am. I'm not going to kill my once sister for a throne. I'm going to win it from her and bask in her defeat."

She was honorable, and she was loyal, even when others weren't deserving. Sanos admired that about her.

"What of you?" she asked in return. "Have you ever considered taking out your brother to inherit the throne of Brutus?"

Gods, he hated lying to her. "I am not politically ambitious. I don't have any desire to rule." Well, he supposed that wasn't exactly a lie. The only reason he wanted his crown was because it meant his father was dead. Otherwise, he wanted nothing to do with a legacy that once belonged to his father. Atalius and his ancestors could shove it up their asses.

But Olerra had shown him the changes for the better he could make in his country. For women. For the poor. There was so much he could learn from her still.

Even if that all seemed empty if she couldn't be there by his side.

"What do you dream of, then?" she asked.

With her large eyes and dark hair and pink lips, he couldn't deny such a powerful truth. "Do you know what? I think I was dreaming of you all these years."

She gave him a look that suggested she did not believe him, so he was forced to continue.

"I haven't gotten close to many people. My father is a jealous man who likes complete control. I could do nothing but dream of connection. I dreamed of friendship. I dreamed of courtship, even. I knew I would be wedded off for political advancement." He reached out to take her hand in his. "I dreamed of physical touch. Of hands that didn't beat me but soothed me. Excited me.

"I didn't realize that being taken by you was the thing that I needed most."

Olerra brought their clasped hands to her lips and kissed the back of his hand.

"You need never be alone again," she said.

He knew she meant it.

Thunder rumbled through the room, which was strange considering there was no storm. A second later, the door was kicked off its hinges.

The first face Sanos saw was Athon's. He was quickly followed by Glenaerys, and then members of her personal guard filtered in behind the pair.

"What are you doing?" Olerra demanded. Her hand went to her hip, but she didn't have any weapons on her. She'd taken them off for the evening while the two enjoyed their alone time. Sanos swiveled his head around the room, trying to tell where she'd dropped them so he could get them for her. Or use them himself. Whichever seemed more prudent at the time.

"Cousin," Glenaerys said. Then she turned to Sanos. "Prince. Look at you out of your manacles. Alone with Olerra. Who is still breathing."

"Is she?" he said with exaggerated sarcasm. "I hadn't noticed."

Glen's eyes narrowed. "We'll get to you in a moment. First, I need to test Olerra on something. I have a hunch she's been keeping secrets."

Olerra was certain her heart had stopped beating at the words.

No.

She couldn't know. She *couldn't*.

"Restrain them," Glen said to her guards.

"Touch me, and I'll have you all executed," Olerra said to the women fast approaching. They didn't slow.

Andrastus stepped in front of her.

"Don't you dare," she said to him.

One of the guards laid a hand on her prince, and Olerra grabbed the woman's wrist in one hand and drove her elbow down against the bone with the other.

There was a crack.

"Quickly now," Glen said, unimpressed.

When three tried to step toward Olerra simultaneously, Andrastus threw a punch. And the fight was on.

Olerra grappled with anyone who came near her. They tried to herd her into a corner, but she kept on her toes, circling. Unfortunately, that meant she lost sight of Andrastus and didn't notice more women spilling into the room until it was too late.

Blades were raised, and one woman brought a knife to Andrastus's throat. Olerra raised her hands in defeat.

"What are you going to do?" Olerra asked. "Auntie will throttle you for this. You won't get the throne with foul play!"

"It's only foul play if I'm wrong. You see, the prince here mentioned that you kept him chained up at night, and I thought that very odd.

Even I don't need to chain up my less enthusiastic men for bed play. What purpose could my cousin possibly have for doing such a thing? And then I got to thinking. Over the years, I couldn't recall seeing you physically overpower a man. Not once."

Dread curdled in her stomach. Olerra's world was about to crumble around her.

"Of course, obtaining proof is extremely difficult," Glen continued. "I'd wanted to do it publicly. Drugging Daneryn was supposed to prove it without a doubt, but the prince was just too eager to step in and lend his muscles. Then I persuaded little Jaron to shove you in the hallway. I assured him you were too softhearted to see him punished for such a thing. But when I asked him if you'd had a chance to steady yourself before he laid hands on you, he said he couldn't be sure. He's useless.

"And then our dear aunt has been away from the palace with her wife these past two weeks, enjoying some quiet time. I couldn't very well risk a positive result and not have her here to witness immediately, but I've just learned she's returned. So here we are. Athon?"

The big man stepped forward. He clasped Olerra's raised hands within his own.

Olerra's eyes met Andrastus's. He looked afraid for her. Worried. But she was more concerned about what would happen to him when all was revealed.

"Shove him away," Glen said.

"Excuse me?" Olerra said.

"Show me your strength. Shove. Athon. Away."

He was so much bigger than she was, and while Olerra could lift Andrastus, she very much doubted that she could do the same to this man. Still, she heaved in a heavy breath, gritted her teeth, and shoved.

Athon didn't budge.

The blades weren't necessary because Olerra no longer needed to be restrained. She let herself drop to the floor, her eyes on the floor in shame. *She'd been found out.*

Soon everyone would know.

She'd been a fool for thinking she was strong enough. Strong enough to hide her secret. Strong enough to be queen when she didn't even have the Goddess's Gift.

"That's what I thought," Glen said gleefully. She turned to two guards standing behind her. "Send for the queen."

Olerra couldn't look up. She couldn't bear to meet her cousin's gaze or her prince's. She felt small, defeated. Unfit. She couldn't stand her cousin, but she couldn't even fault her. If Olerra had found a similar weakness in her cousin, she would have exposed it immediately.

The queen's guards came in first, easily identified by their pointed helmets. They took up position around the room. There seemed to be so many of them. Too many to witness her defeat.

This was where she lost everything.

She still couldn't look at Andrastus.

When the queen entered the room, she said, "Call off your hired hands, Glenaerys. Whatever this is, there's no need for such a show of force. You will send half of your guard away."

Glen was too thrilled by the situation; she didn't even seem put out by the order. With a couple of hand motions she shooed some of her women out the door. Athon remained, though he took a step back from Olerra, as though to give the queen a better look at her.

"Now what is it?" Lemya asked. "Why is Olerra on the floor?"

"Your Majesty, I've just proven that Olerra doesn't have the Goddess's Gift." Glen wasted no time at all to spill her greatest secret.

Olerra's chest felt too tight. Her breathing became strained. This must be what dying of humiliation felt like.

She couldn't bear not to look.

Olerra met her aunt's gaze.

"Is this true?" the queen asked her.

Olerra couldn't find her voice, so she nodded.

The queen did not react to the admission. Lemya stood tall, hands at her sides. Not a soul in the room moved.

Olerra waited for the verdict. Waited for anything at all to happen.

"So what?"

The words came not from the queen, but from Andrastus.

Olerra loved him for it.

"So what if she doesn't have the Gift ? She's earned her rank as general. She's won every battle she's overseen. She's strong and brilliant and will make a great queen. Who cares if she doesn't have a little bit of magic? She's already unstoppable. You all didn't even notice until now, so how necessary is it really?"

"You will remember your place," Glenaerys said to him. "Olerra may let you run your mouth whenever you like, but you will not do so in my presence."

"Don't talk to him. You are in my rooms, and he can do whatever he likes here!" Olerra snapped back.

"That's enough," the queen interjected, and everyone returned their attention to Amarra's monarch.

"You kept this from me," Lemya said. "Why?"

Olerra was still on the floor, and she hung her head. "I was ashamed. I didn't want to disappoint you."

"For something that was out of your control? *Why?*" she demanded again.

"Because if the goddess didn't even see fit to give me her power, then how could I expect the people of Amarra to choose me as queen?"

Gods, she felt broken. Torn inside out, her deepest fears and weaknesses laid bare for the woman whose opinion she cared for most, and the cousin who used every weakness to hurt her the worst. The guards around the room were unmoving, but they had ears. The news would spread faster than even the queen could contain it. Everyone in the whole kingdom would know in a matter of hours.

"There's more," Glenaerys said, clearly not a fan of the silence or lack of scolding directed at Olerra.

"More?" the queen and Olerra said simultaneously.

Glenaerys grinned as she turned to Andrastus. "Would you like to tell them or should I?"

23

Sanos was fucked.
   Well and truly fucked.
But he was so shocked and unprepared for Glenaerys's words that he could do no more than stare at her.

"One of my spies in Atalius's court just brought me the most interesting news about his missing son. It turns out—"

"Stop," Sanos said, cutting her off. Glen was too delighted to chastise him for it.

His heart hurt. Everything was ruined. Not only had Glen broken Olerra by somehow learning a terrible secret, but now Sanos had to deliver another crushing blow. Gods, why now? Why like this?

He came forward, clasped Olerra's hands within his own. Thankfully, no one tried to stop him. He swallowed.

"Please know that what I'm about to say changes nothing. Not a thing I've said to you or the way I feel about you. None of it."

"Okay," she said.

Olerra's big eyes looked up at him, so trusting. How was he going to get the words out?

"I have only lied to you in regards to one thing. Just one thing. Please keep that in mind."

She pulled back slightly but didn't release his hands. "What is it?"

He closed his eyes. Took a deep breath. Somehow formed the words.

"I'm not Andrastus."

There, the first part, the part that was of the most importance to her, and he couldn't take it back. He watched Olerra process the words slowly, as though trying to make them fit into everything she knew of him.

"What?" she said at last, her hands tensing within his own. "Of course you are. I took you from that brothel. The madam sent you to my room. You have the Brutish royal hair."

He refused to look away from her. "My brother was very drunk that night. He passed out in the hallway, and I decided I would take his place."

"Your brother." Now she snatched her hands away and took a step back. He hated that little bit of distance. "Who are you?"

"I'm . . . Sanos."

"The heir?" the queen said in the background.

The revelation was punctuated with a delighted snicker from Glenaerys, who was clearly enjoying everyone's discomfort. Sanos didn't take his attention off Olerra.

She looked *furious*.

"You—you're Sanos?"

"Yes," he breathed, elated to finally have his name back.

She took in his features anew. The muscles and the way he held himself. "The fighter. The oldest. Of course. I had met so few Brutes not clad in armor; I just assumed . . ."

"I wanted to tell you," he said. "So many times. In the beginning, I stayed silent because I thought you might kill me or ransom me to my father if you learned I wasn't who you wanted. I couldn't have either option. And later—"

"What?" She cut him off, her tone lethal. "What possible reason could you have for not telling me *later*?"

The queen interrupted the heated discussion. "Glenaerys, take your people and leave. You've had your fun."

"Yes, Your Majesty." Glen threw one more haughty look her cousin's way before exiting, all her women in tow.

"Wait outside," the queen said to her own guards, who left the room as quickly as they came. The queen didn't draw herself closer to the two. She observed from a distance. "Olerra, it is only a matter of time before Atalius learns where his heir is. He will come for him."

"I know."

"You need to push aside your feelings and think like a leader."

"A leader? It's a bit late for that, isn't it?"

Sanos's heart broke for the woman before him. He loved her, but he couldn't help her. This was the first time he felt truly powerless in Amarra.

She turned back to him. "You're going back home."

"Wait, please—" he said.

"I think you've said plenty. And you let me say plenty. All those times when we were drawing closer physically and you'd pull away? I thought you were traumatized in some fashion. That someone had hurt you! No, you were guilty. Guilty when I'd say your brother's name."

"I didn't want to ruin things for you. To take your mind off the succession."

"And yet, here we are, and I was blindsided. I take responsibility for my own secret, but you? You ruined *everything*." Olerra turned to the queen. "Auntie, please take him away. I don't want to look at him."

"Olerra, wait."

"No, Prince. You wait. You wait in some dark, dank place until I decide what to do with you."

The queen called for her guards. He didn't put up a fight as they took him away.

Sanos.

The man she thought she'd loved was Sanos.

And he was a liar and a schemer. A betrayer.

She kept trying to process it, and her aunt gave her the space to do so. Olerra remembered every interaction. Every moment that was just a bit off, now seen through a new context.

Are you the prince?

I'm the best prince.

Furious tears slid down her cheeks. She brushed them away immediately.

"Everyone will know soon," she said. She wanted her aunt to talk and fill the silence. Olerra didn't want to think anymore.

"Yes."

"They will know that I am Giftless. That I nabbed the wrong prince."

"Yes."

"How can you be so calm? Why aren't you yelling at me for my stupidity?"

The queen stepped farther into the room and took a seat on a nearby settee. "You are beating yourself up better than I ever could."

"Tell me something. Anything. I cannot bear your silence on this matter."

"To be honest, I'm still trying to figure out where I went wrong. What did I do to cause you to believe that you needed to keep such a secret from me?"

"I feared you'd stop thinking of me as your heir. I needed your support. I crave your love more than anything."

The queen stretched her long legs out in front of her. "You thought that Toria and I would love you less if we knew?"

"No, but—"

"But what? That boy, stupid though he is, was right. So what? Do you think I love you because of how strong you are?"

"No, but that is why I'm your general. That is why I lead your armies." After swallowing, she amended, "Why I did."

"I'm not in the market for a new general, nor a new heir."

"The nobles will never have me when they learn about this. I can't come back from this."

The queen nodded. "I'm not going to lie to you. Your odds are almost nonexistent. Glenaerys will make this ugly. She won't just call you weak and unchosen. She'll call you a liar. A traitor to the country. She will do everything she can to blow this out of proportion. I will control the damage where I can, but you must prepare to weather what comes ahead."

"And the prince?"

"You could send word to Atalius. Make it sound intentional that you've had fun with his heir all this time. Then ransom him for the spare. Get the real Andrastus and make him yours. We could tell the court that you took the heir on purpose to teach Atalius a lesson. You lied about his identity for his own protection. It was all part of the plan."

Olerra shouldn't hate that thought. She didn't want to give her prince back, but she also didn't want to go through the trouble of kidnapping a new one. As if there was any point. What good would it do if the nobility already hated her and thought of her as a traitor?

"Everyone who was in this room knows the truth. I did nothing to hide my reactions."

"They will believe the royal family over a handful of guards, whom I can pay off."

"What of Glen's? There's no paying them off."

"We will just have to hope that we can spread our truth faster than Glen can spread hers. She should have challenged you publicly on this."

"She tried. She was cautious, in case she was wrong."

"That's to our benefit, then."

Olerra hated all of this. She hated that she needed to take action. She wanted to be alone. To think without anyone watching her or expecting anything from her.

But queens did not have that luxury.

And though she would never become one now, she should still behave like one.

Her nose burned as she forced away more tears. "Do I have any other options, Auntie?"

"You mean other than giving him back? No, Olerra. Atalius will start a war over this if you don't."

"I don't want to keep him," she said forcefully.

Liar. Her emotions were a tangled mess, but it was still a lie. The queen, probably sensing this, didn't bother to respond.

Olerra said, "I will send word to the king. He can come pick up his heir at his earliest convenience and swap him out for the spare."

In the meantime, she didn't want to go anywhere near Brutus's lying crown prince.

Sanos expected a dark cell as Olerra had promised. Instead, he was carted off to Ydra's estate. He recognized it from the carriage window, just over the shoulder of the guard who sat at his side. There were six inside with him. They exited before letting him do so.

Ydra met them at the front door. "What is this about?" she asked when she saw him and the queen's guard.

"The queen asks that you keep a careful eye on Prince Sanos," one said.

"*Prince Sanos?*"

"He is a prisoner, yet he's to be treated well."

"Of course," Ydra said. "I'm happy to do the queen's will. Thank you for delivering him."

As soon as she shut them indoors, Sanos turned to her. "Ydra."

He didn't get more than her name out before she strong-armed him into the nearest deserted room, some sort of parlor. She practically threw him into the nearest chair.

"Talk. Now."

Olerra sequestered herself in her aunts' rooms while the door to her own was being fixed. She sat at the queen's desk with a quill in hand and stared at the empty sheet of parchment before her. She needed to write to the king of Brutus, but she couldn't let any of her feelings show. The calculating general needed to come through.

Olerra separated the thoughts in her head by their usefulness. Anything unhelpful would go into the wooden chest she'd conjured in her mind.

Insecurity? The chest.

Fear? The chest.

Anger? That could stay.

Hurt? The chest.

Spite? That could stay, too.

She locked the chest and threw away the mental key.

Then she wrote.

Atalius, dear!
I hear you've misplaced your heir. I might know where he is. I'm guessing my bedroom, but it's also possible he's visiting the baths. I'd have to check.

I found him wandering the streets of Medos and have taken the poor dear in. He's been my special guest for the past two months. Now that I've had my fun, I'm prepared to give him back. My generosity will cost you, though. I want Andrastus. I'll trade you a son for a son. Your heir for the spare. This one's a bit too rebellious for my tastes anyway.

Kindly collect your prince at your earliest convenience, but if you show up empty-handed, no deal.

          Sincerely,
          The better general, Olerra

Olerra gave the letter to a messenger with strict instructions to deliver it directly into the king's hand. By then, her rooms were ready, and Olerra shut herself within. She kept a guard outside this time, in case Glen tried to force her way inside again.

Ydra came to visit Olerra that night, but Olerra told her she wanted to be alone. It was enough knowing that Ydra was there for her if she needed it.

Olerra didn't know what she needed. She spent hours alone with her thoughts, but she was no closer to making anything feel better. How long would it be before the nobility sought her out to demand if it was true that she was Giftless?

Olerra sighed deeply and didn't fall asleep until many hours later.

The knock came in the middle of the night. At first, she thought it might be Andrastus. Then she remembered that Andrastus was Sanos, and he wasn't in the palace. He was being held by the queen somewhere. Her despair from earlier returned, but she tried to forget it as she threw on a robe. Olerra rubbed the sleep from her eyes before turning the handle.

"What is it?" she asked.

Vorika, charged with Olerra's personal spy network, stood before her. Olerra felt her stomach sink, fearing the news must be terrible if the woman risked waking her.

Olerra let her into the room before closing the door.

"It's Atalius," Vorika said. "You wished to be notified at once if there was any movement."

"Go on."

"He's coming here."

"To Zinaeya?"

"Yes. The king has rallied a force three times the size of what you faced at Shamire. Our spies say he's coming for his son."

Olerra woke all the way up at those words. Since she'd just delivered the note and it took a week to reach the Brutish capital, there was no possible chance this was a response to her words. And if her spy was already here, then that meant Atalius had decided to march days ago.

"How far behind you on the road is he?" Olerra asked.

"A couple of days at most, General."

Olerra let out a mirthless laugh. "So curious that I receive word of Atalius's march on the same day that my cousin learned my prince's true identity." There was only one reason for it. "My crafty cousin. She has some nerve starting a war to further keep me from the succession. As if disclosing everything else wasn't enough."

"General?" Vorika asked in confusion.

"It's simple, really. Glenaerys decided to hurry up the succession battle between us. She thought to inform Atalius that I'm the one who has his son to start a war. To keep me busy. Yet in doing so, she learned that I nabbed the wrong prince." Olerra blinked slowly. "That's why she decided to test if I had the Goddess's Gift today. She had a backup plan in place in case everything went horribly wrong."

Vorika took all the news in stride. Since the woman dealt in secrets, there was no need for Olerra to ask her to keep hers. She kept the woman well compensated.

"Are there any orders for me, General?"

"Keep watching. Have the spies send reports if anything changes. In the meantime, it seems I have work to do."

Olerra strode to her closet and changed into fresh clothes and her leather armor. Her aunt said that she wasn't in the market for a new general. Olerra would do her duty to the best of her ability until anything changed.

She had to get an early start on preparing the city for their guests.

Olerra woke her soldiers from their beds. Thick bells were struck, and the barracks emptied in under five minutes, as her women were trained to do.

Ydra was absent, as she was staying on her estate, but Olerra sent word to rouse her. She would arrive as soon as she could.

They were one thousand strong staying at the palace, training and preparing to be stationed throughout the kingdom. They all stood before her now, crammed into the training field, spears held upright, swords strapped to their sides, helmets donned. They awaited orders.

Olerra walked along the outside of their ranks as she spoke.

"Some news has started circulating about me. I don't know what you've heard already, but let me set the matter straight. I was born without the Goddess's Gift. My cousin recently deduced this and has started to spread the news like wildfire.

"So here is what you need to know. I am your general. The queen is not appointing anyone new. I have yet to be bested by any of you in combat. There is no man I've met on the battlefield who I have been unable to kill. And while this all means that I may have lost all rights to the throne, as the nobility would never vote for me when the goddess has overlooked me—this does not make me any less of a formidable opponent to our enemies.

"King Atalius marches on Zinaeya. He will be here in a matter of days. We have work to do, but if there is anyone who is unable to do their jobs, now knowing my true nature, leave now, for I don't have time to deal with dissent."

She paused here. Ten seconds. Thirty. A minute.

Not a single soldier moved.

Olerra hid her relief. She may not be enough for those in the palace, but she had earned her place here in the training fields, putting women in the dirt, showing off her skills with the sword and whipblade.

She nodded to the crowd. "Good. Listen carefully for your assignments."

They dug ditches outside the city walls, sharpened logs to points, and placed them carefully around the perimeter. The main gates were reinforced. They brought people from nearby cities within the walls so Atalius couldn't hurt them on his march.

Zinaeya was already strategically built with large walls and larger towers throughout. Olerra walked the entire perimeter, looking for any weaknesses to reinforce.

At some point, Ydra showed up.

For the first few minutes, she was silent at Olerra's side, looking over everything with a second pair of eyes. Around them, women were busy with shovels and axes, digging the trenches and sharpening stakes.

Ydra finally spoke. "He's at my home. The queen asked me to keep an eye on him. Not sure if she's more afraid of what you might do to him or what he might try."

Olerra kept her voice emotionless. "I trust he hasn't been too much trouble?"

"No. He's keeping the boys company. They love having him around for some reason."

Olerra kept a steady pace, not slowing or looking away from the walls. "It boggles the mind."

"Yes, indeed." Ydra stepped closer so their conversation was less likely to be overheard. "So would you like to discuss how we took the wrong prince or how to bury your cousin in one of these trenches so she'll never be found again?"

"Talking won't solve anything. Everything is shit."

"Yes, Sanos told me everything that happened. Good thing, too. I would have hated to resort to torture."

Olerra huffed a breath that might be mistaken for a brief laugh. "Torture? You? The gentle heart who saves little boys as a hobby?"

"The prince claims my presence is torture, so naturally I haven't allowed him a moment's peace without me there."

It hurt to talk about him, but it would hurt worse not to know. Ydra was safe and wouldn't judge, so Olerra dared to ask, "Has he said anything about me?"

"He talks of little else. He misses you. He wishes he could take it all back. He doesn't want to leave Amarra. He wants everything to continue as is."

"And is he hoping I will start a war simply to keep him? That I will ignore all sense and choose love?"

"I don't think he's thought that far ahead."

Olerra found a crumbling brick in the structure up ahead. She called a worker over to see it replaced. "I have a kingdom to think of. I cannot put everyone in danger for him."

"I know that. He knows that."

"Then what does he want from me?"

Ydra tapped a hand on the pommel of her sword. "Maybe you should go talk to him."

"I'm a bit busy."

"Being a coward."

No one else could get away with saying those words to her. Still, Olerra found her dominant hand tightening into a fist. "Careful," she warned.

"You are being a coward, though. He now knows your secret. Everyone knows it, but you're most concerned about him knowing it. Because that means you can't trust him to be around you. What if *now* he takes advantage of knowing he can overpower you if he tries? You're still letting what happened to your mother control you."

Olerra let the words strike her skin and fall to the ground. "I already beat him. I'm not scared of him."

"No? You're not scared that now he knows everything, he might not want you?"

"It doesn't matter, Ydra!" As some of the soldiers looked up from their work, Olerra lowered her voice. "He's going home. I'm trading him for the real Andrastus. We're stopping a war. That's all I can do for my people now that I cannot rule over them."

"There has to be another way. Something we haven't thought of yet."

"I never thought of you as a romantic."

"I don't think I was one until I watched you two."

24

Olerra's presence was required at a meeting the next day. She'd had exactly one fitful hour of sleep before Vorika woke her, and she'd spent the rest of the night preparing the city for the approaching army. Olerra could do no more than wash the sweat from her body with a rag in the water basin. She put a serum below her eyes to try to remove some of the hollowness.

Then she dressed and headed for the meeting room.

All the women looked up at her approach. She was the last to arrive, it seemed. Already, the queen rested at the head of the table. Glenaerys was on her immediate left with her mother, Shaelwyn, on her other side. Next to her was Enadra, the former general. On the opposite side of the table sat Cyssia and Usstra.

Olerra went to take her usual seat on the queen's right, but she was halted. "You will sit at the end of the table today," Shaelwyn declared. "We have to determine if you're even worthy to be sitting with us. So you will sit where we can pass judgment most easily."

Olerra turned to her aunt, since Shaelwyn could not make such a demand on her own. When the queen nodded, Olerra knew that a majority vote had already been taken on this matter.

Olerra was losing.

She sat opposite the queen, at least two chairs between her and everyone else at the table. This was apparently to be a trial of sorts.

Enadra spoke first. "Princess Olerra, some nasty allegations have been hurtled your way. We need to hear your side of things."

"Of course, General."

Enadra may no longer hold the position, but the honorific remained.

Glen started to open her mouth, and Olerra refused to be questioned by her cousin, so she spoke first.

"It is true that I don't possess the Goddess's Gift. It is true that I tried to hide that fact because I worried what everyone would think of me. It is also true that I earned my place as general by being the best of the best of the queen's soldiers. I have won battles and killed many Brutes. I may not have the gift of strength over men, but I have Goddess Amarra's favor all the same."

Olerra hoped if she said those words enough, she'd start to believe them. She *had* earned her place as general, but it was hard to believe that she had the goddess's favor. Did the goddess even know who she was if she hadn't seen fit to bless her with her Gift?

But now was not the time to show uncertainty. Olerra needed to be strong in front of the women who would decide her future.

Enadra smiled at the response. "I agree wholeheartedly. I have trained Olerra myself, and no one has fought harder for the safety and peace of Amarran citizens. She is a good general and will bring us much success in the years to come."

"Except," Shaelwyn cut in, "that she's brought war to our city. King Atalius will be here in two days' time. What does the princess have to say to that?"

"If you wish to know something, Aunt, then you will address the question to *me*," Olerra responded.

Shaelwyn met her eyes. "You carelessly took Atalius's heir, and now he's bringing us war. What do you intend to do about it?"

Olerra allowed a smile she didn't feel grace her lips. "I did nothing carelessly. I took Atalius's heir to teach him a lesson after needlessly fighting us for Shamire again. I kept the prince's identity a secret for his own safety. Now that someone has so kindly informed the king about my activities"—Olerra barely refrained from looking at Glenaerys—"I will, of course, trade him for the spare when Atalius arrives. It's already been arranged. There will be no war. There will be no fighting. There will only be an exchange of princes."

"Are you accusing someone of something?" Glenaerys asked.

"Of course not, cousin." Olerra had no proof. Raising claims would only look like Olerra was the kind of woman to point fingers instead of accept responsibility for her actions.

And she *had* messed up. She took the wrong man, and now had to lie about it.

Cyssia said, "You claim that you took the heir on purpose to teach Atalius a lesson?"

"That's right," Olerra said at the same time Glenaerys scoffed.

"That's beautiful," Cyssia said. "You really are a delight, Olerra. It's a shame that you haven't any power. I would have liked to see you rule as queen."

"A lack of power does not necessarily make her unfit for the throne," the queen said.

"Nor does it endorse her," Usstra said, speaking for the first time.

"There must be some punishment for lying to everyone," Shaelwyn said. "I demand she be removed from all consideration for the succession."

"I did not lie," Olerra said. "No one asked. You all assumed. I was never untruthful. And I've clearly done a fine job without it, as I've pointed out. Glenaerys is no fighter. Period. She only strikes when her opponents have their hands tied. Yet everyone thinks her fit to be queen."

The tension in the room grew. Olerra could feel it. Her cousin's outrage. Shaelwyn's eagerness to see Olerra stricken from the line of succession. The queen's fear.

Usstra spoke again. "I move that the voting will continue as planned on the anniversary of the Goddess's Gift. We should see how Olerra handles the upcoming ordeal with the king before we make any hasty decisions. This is history we're talking about."

"All those in favor?" the queen asked.

Everyone raised their hands except Shaelwyn.

"Then we will continue as planned."

"She didn't take the heir on purpose!" Glenaerys finally spat out. "I have witnesses who will attest to what happened when the truth came out."

The queen turned to her other niece. "And I have witnesses who will say otherwise, Glen. Are you really calling me a liar?"

Glen looked at the table. Shaelwyn stiffened at her side.

Sanos wanted to hit something.

Yes, he'd kept a secret, but so had Olerra! Yet he was the one sent away, locked up in Ydra's home yet again.

If he could just see Olerra, he was prepared to take the high road. He'd tell her that he understood why she'd kept her secret from him, but if he'd known, he could have helped. He would have helped her hide everything from her nasty cousin.

And then she could forgive him for not telling her who he really was. They would fix this.

But what if she didn't forgive him?

Then he'd make her see reason! She'd stolen him; he was under no obligation to disclose his identity. She never asked who he was.

Oh, yes. Arguing with her will definitely bring her over to your side.

Gods, if he could just talk to her!

"This time," Ydra said, "you really can't. She's trying to sort out the giant mess her cousin made. She's busy."

It was kind of her to say that Glenaerys was responsible for the mess, as though he hadn't done anything to add to it.

Sanos felt useless. Restless. Beyond agitated.

"Has she decided what to do with me?" he dared to ask.

"She's trading you for your brother, the real Andrastus."

He felt his stomach sink. He'd hoped that had been an empty threat. Something she'd said in the heat of the moment.

"I don't want to go," he admitted.

"Liars get what's coming to them," she said unhelpfully.

"She doesn't want Andrastus," Sanos said.

"Jealousy doesn't look good on you."

"I'm serious! Andrastus would be boring for someone like her. She needs someone who will put up a fight. Dare to tell her when she's wrong. She needs me."

"Get over yourself."

Sanos just barely stopped himself from punching the nearest wall. "Don't you pretend like you don't like me. Like you don't want to see her with me."

Ydra set down her quill. "What I want is to see her happy. What I want is to see her on the throne of Amarra. What I want is to not be stuck with you in my home any longer!"

He deserved that. All of it. Ydra had every right to be upset.

"You will do as you're told for once," Ydra said. "When your father arrives, you will be the only useful thing left to Olerra: a bargaining chip. Is that understood?"

He didn't have a retort. He was overwhelmed by how much he

wanted to set things right. To help. But the last thing he wanted was to be returned to his father. To go back to being nothing but the king's pawn.

A messenger knocked on the open door to Ydra's study. The newcomer strode up to Ydra and handed her a note.

Ydra read it quickly before widening her eyes. She turned to Sanos. "Stay here. Don't get up to any trouble."

"What's wrong?" he asked.

"Nothing that requires your temper."

When Vorika delivered the news that part of the king's approaching army had branched off from the rest, Olerra had sent for Ydra immediately. She ordered that the scout be brought before her because she wanted to hear everything firsthand. Within a couple of hours, the woman stood before them in Olerra's office off the training yard.

Olerra and Ydra leaned against her desk while Vorika stood beside the wall with her arms crossed. The scout sat in the proffered chair.

"It's a small force," the scout, Iseri, said. "Only fifty. They've gone around the city and wait to the south."

Olerra turned to Ydra. "Fifty is not enough to breach the gate."

"And Atalius would know that," Ydra agreed.

Vorika added, "Some of my women have gone missing, and I don't think the Brutes would have bothered to hide their bodies if they were behind it."

"Who else would be involved?" Ydra asked. "Atalius is at war with the Ephennans. Kalundir profits greatly from the trade agreements we've set them at Shamire. Dyphankar, then?"

The lack of sleep was making her slow, but Olerra promised herself a full night's rest tonight.

"No," Olerra said as realization finally set in. "Atalius isn't splitting because he expects reinforcements. Someone has promised to let the small band of Brutes into the city."

Ydra's blond braid slid off her shoulder from the sharp movement of her head. "A traitor?"

Olerra smiled. "We already knew Glen told Atalius I had his heir. What if that wasn't enough? What if she made *plans* in case things still didn't go her way? She's an over-preparer. Always has been. She would leave nothing to chance."

"You think she agreed to let Atalius through the gates? To what end?"

"If she let him humiliate me and win the battle, he would use his forces to put her on the throne."

"That would be treason, if we could prove it."

"Glen will need to make contact with them somehow to finalize plans." Olerra turned to the scout. "Return to the small force of Brutes. If anyone from Amarra approaches the camp, you're to tell me who."

"Yes, General."

Several hours later, Olerra stood before the queen. Lemya had been roused from sleep, but there were no obvious signs of it. She was always put together, her eyes alert.

"You're telling me," Lemya said, "that Glen has conspired with our enemies, and you've captured one of her scouts, who confirmed it?"

"Yes, but the spy refuses to speak against Glenaerys publicly. My plan is to have women waiting at the southern gate to catch her guard in the act of trying to let in our enemies."

"Glen could easily turn things around. Claim it was her guard who caught *yours* trying to let our enemies through the gates."

Her aunt was right. "What then? Do we tell the council?"

"We can't tell the council without risking Shaelwyn finding out and warning her daughter. We need something more."

They paced. They strategized. Idea after idea was shut down. Finally, Olerra said, "What if I could get Atalius to admit publicly he was collaborating with Glen?"

"How?"

"Let me negotiate when he reaches Zinaeya. I can get him to talk. I've done it before."

Lemya stepped forward and put her hands on Olerra's shoulders. "It's up to you, then. Do what you can, but do not risk a battle unfolding. If it doesn't work, I will ask for a trial, and we will bring all the evidence we can against Glen."

"I will not fail you."

Two nights later, Sanos was roused in the middle of the night. Ydra stood in his doorway.

"Put this on," she said, and threw a very small item of clothing his way.

"What's going on?" he asked.

"You're finally going home."

He held up the garment with both hands and clenched his jaw. It was a white skirt, thick enough not to be transparent, but it was covered in faceted beads. He would shimmer as he walked. At least it was dark outside.

"If I'm leaving, then why do I need to wear Amarran clothing?"

"Stop stalling. Start dressing."

"I want answers, Ydra."

"You can put it on yourself or I can put it on for you."

He growled as he turned his back to her. He made quick work of the skirt and didn't spend too much time looking down at it.

"Smart choice," she said. "You can come in now."

Eunuchs from the palace entered, and they got to work putting on his jewelry and, for the first time, makeup.

He coughed when a brush got too close to his nose. Prior to coming to Amarra, he thought makeup was only to be worn on the face, but the eunuchs trailed creams and powders over his chest, arms, and neck, too.

He caught his reflection in a nearby mirror. They'd painted silver swirls on his shoulders. His cheeks were dusted with silver sparkles. They'd outlined his eyes in some sort of thin black paint.

He looked like an Amarran husband through and through.

But why?

They didn't remove his armband, but they added a silver necklace and the anklet. Thankfully, he was allowed to wear sandals this time. And they didn't bind his hands or ankles.

One eunuch adjusted his armband, which must have turned in the night, so the hanging onyx was shown front and center. The mark of Olerra as his woman. Sanos hadn't removed it, even after she'd sent him away.

Olerra entered the room.

She was beautiful in her leather armor. She wore a weapon at each hip and carried a helmet under one arm. Her hair was braided back from her face. War paint was slashed under each eye. The eunuchs were dismissed.

Sanos opened his mouth to speak.

"You will say nothing," Ydra hissed.

"The fuck I won't. What is going on?"

Olerra nodded to Ydra, who left them alone.

"Atalius is here with an army at my gates."

Sanos felt his heart rate pick up. When Ydra said he was going home, he'd thought that meant they were taking him to Brutus, not that his father was here *to collect him.*

"I have a plan," she continued, "but it requires you to wear this and play along. If you do this, you will get what you've always wanted. To go home."

Her voice was so devoid of emotion, they could have been talking about the change of the seasons. She looked tired but strong. Ready for battle.

But he had no clue what she was feeling.

"What if I don't want to go home anymore?"

"You must. It is the only way to prevent war. Or would you see our people slaughtered here tonight? You're a general, Sanos. Think like one."

He held himself tall. "Send me over to the Brutes. Let me talk to my father. I will prevent—"

"No. Here is what I need from you. Swap places with your brother. Andrastus will come here. You will go home and return to your life in Brutus. This is the only way I have a chance of winning my throne."

"And I will do this for you just because you ask it?"

"If you do this for me, then I swear to you that I will get your mother and sister out of Brutus. They will come here and be my special guests until such a time as you take your throne, and Atalius will be none the wiser."

All the air left Sanos's lungs. She knew him. Knew what he cared most about. She knew that if she dangled this in front of him, he would agree to just about anything.

"We both win, Sanos. I get Amarra, and you get to protect the ones you care about most. And with your mother and sister safely here, perhaps you might get to finally challenge your father."

He wanted to argue. This didn't feel like winning. And *she* was now in the category of people he cared about most.

Sanos's whole life had been about sacrifice. He went without companionship, friendship, to keep others safe. He fought on the front lines of Ephenna to keep his family safe. And now he would do this so his mother and sister wouldn't have to live with violence hanging over their heads.

"Very well," he said, matching her lifeless tone. "What do I have to do?"

"Walk with me. We don't have much time."

As they wove through Ydra's estate, Olerra said, "You are dressed this way because I need to use you to make your father angry. I will say things and do things that will be unpleasant for you. You must bear it. Unchained. You must stand there and take it."

They entered a carriage that took them toward the main gates. The streets were busy despite the late hour. People rushed to and fro, carrying their belongings. Closing windows and shutters.

Preparing for war.

"I can do that," he said. He would withstand anything she threw at him.

"Good."

"Are we going to talk about what happened?"

"There is no point."

"Can I apologize at least?"

"I would rather remain angry at you. It will make all of this much easier, don't you think?"

A low rumble carried on the wind. It was nonsense at first, but the closer they got to their destination, the better he could hear the chanting.

Meet the might of Brutus.
Meet the might of Brutus.
Meet the might of Brutus.

It was a shout he knew well. His father's troops repeated the refrain. It was so loud, the company had to be at least two thousand strong.

This would not go over well. He was wearing a fucking skirt, and hundreds of his countrymen were about to see it. The embarrassment would push his father to do terrible things. Sanos's very life might be in danger.

But if it meant his sister and mother would finally be safe, then he would take whatever came his way.

It was time to finally embrace being Amarran on the last night he would be considered one.

25

Olerra was quite pleased with the way the battlements had turned out. There were archers at every section of the wall. Each gate had vats of pitch and rocks for throwing. Her soldiers had even gotten at least four hours of sleep before the king arrived. His own forces would be tired from marching.

Olerra took the stairs confidently with Sanos at her side.

She was still unused to attaching that name to him. It wasn't the name he'd worn when she'd fallen for him, but it was the name he now used when she had to give him back.

She was so angry at him. Yes, because he'd lied, but even more so because he wasn't his brother.

She couldn't keep him, and that made her furious.

When Olerra reached the top of the wall, she looked out at Atalius's troops. The king's forces were larger than what she'd managed to put together on such short notice. But the Amarrans were stronger, and they had the home advantage. A fight would likely go their way, but they would take heavy losses.

Glenaerys and her mother stood twenty feet away along the wall. They'd no doubt come to watch Olerra fail and to get as far away from the southern gate as possible to claim innocence should they be found out.

Queen Lemya stood in the dead center above the main gate, and

Olerra took her right side. Sanos, true to his word, kept pace with her. Ydra took his other side.

The army waiting beyond the gates carried torches. They flickered in the night, showing hints of Brutes in full body armor. At Olerra's appearance, King Atalius separated from the majority of his forces, riding forward on his horse with a large retinue of personal guards surrounding him, all bearing shields. As though she would resort to firing an arrow at him. Tempting though that would be, it would only lead to war. And there was no honor in killing a monarch before they'd had a chance to parley.

Olerra took her whipblade from her side and wound the rope up her arm until the blade was grasped firmly in her hand. She put her arm around Sanos's neck, letting the blade rest against his jugular.

"This is all a show for him. Play along, and we might pull this off." She leaned forward to kiss his cheek.

She could see Atalius's lip curl even from this distance. Olerra hid her smile.

It was impossible to forget the sheer size of the Brutish king, but Sanos had forgotten what the mere sight of his father did to him. A couple of months in Amarra without his father's wrath had done that to him.

Now, seeing Atalius ride forward on his horse, Sanos remembered what it was to be afraid.

If he thought his father wouldn't recognize him trussed up in Amarran clothes, beardless, and covered in makeup, he was very, very wrong.

The king's eye cut toward him like a knife. It pierced his skin with disapproval. With hatred, even. Sanos could tell his father was tracking his skin, mentally mapping out how he would beat him once he got him alone.

Or perhaps the king was plotting how he would make Sanos's death look like an accident.

With Andrastus handed over to the Amarrans, his father had to be considering if Canus would make an acceptable king.

"Well, you made the trip," Olerra called down to the king. "Hope the weather was good to you."

The blade wasn't exactly digging into Sanos's neck, but he brushed it whenever he swallowed. He may have been taller than Olerra, but she had no problem angling him into the deadly position. He knew the chaste kiss from earlier had been for his father's benefit, but his cheek still burned from the contact. He ached for her. Ached to make things right between them before he was handed off to his father. Almost as much as he wanted to throttle her for his current predicament.

"I've come for my son," his father said.

"I don't suppose my missive reached you on your travels here?" Olerra called down. Sanos was surprised that the queen did not speak. Why was Olerra handling negotiations? She may have been general, but Atalius was at the queen's gates.

Glenaerys also seemed surprised by this.

"I received no missive," Atalius said.

Olerra nodded as though expecting this. Sanos could feel the motion with how close she was. She was so careful, though, not to nick his skin.

"If you will recall," Olerra said, "I said a son was the price of your life back in Shamire."

Sanos didn't know what she was talking about.

"I never agreed to that trade," Atalius said.

"You also didn't take the alternative, which was begging for your life, so I made the deal on your behalf."

Olerra stroked a finger down Sanos's cheek. It was masterful the way she managed to hold the blade still in the rest of her fingers while she did it.

"I will decimate your city if he isn't returned in one piece," Atalius threatened.

"Will you? And tell me, do you think you can take the city faster than I can slit his throat?"

She was putting on a show for Atalius, but Olerra couldn't deny that touching Sanos was nice, too. She let her mouth hover above his ear. "Why do you have to smell so good when I'm so angry with you?" She leaned into his neck until her nose brushed his skin. No one else could hear the exchange with her low tone.

Just as she hoped, his skin flushed scarlet. Atalius had to be able to see it from where he stood, for his own skin turned purple. It was remarkable how light the Brutish skin was. It showed everything.

"You would start a war over this?" the king asked.

"Absolutely," Olerra said loudly. "Despite being raised by you, he's an excellent fuck."

Sanos stiffened in Olerra's arms, and the queen turned toward her. Olerra could read the look in her aunt's eyes. *Careful.* Olerra knew what she was doing, though. She was getting Atalius riled up. Pushing him as far as she could without inciting him to war.

Glen tried to step forward, as though hoping to intervene, but Lemya raised a hand, and Glen returned to her mother's side.

Meanwhile, the Brutish troops were sniggering. Atalius turned around, and they quickly silenced.

Now that the king was off-kilter, Olerra began her taunting in earnest.

"But let me tell you exactly what will happen should you strike. You will launch your attack from there, attempting to break through our gate. While my archers slowly pick you off, your forces hidden on the south side of the city will try to sneak in through the other gate, thinking it less guarded. It's not, by the way. It's just as fortified as this one."

You could hear a pin drop in the silence from the Brutish troops, their utter shock that she already knew their plans. Glen didn't move a muscle, keeping her face carefully blank.

Olerra continued, "You might eventually break through, but we'll have picked off a quarter of your numbers by then. Next you will be bottlenecked as you try to enter the city, where my soldiers will mow you down by twos and threes, throwing their spears before you get in range with your swords. Hot pitch will fall from the gate, burning those who attempt to enter. Depending on how many are left, I might choose to ignite it.

"And then, when your numbers are pitifully low, you will retreat to lick your wounds back in Brutus. Or perhaps you'll attempt the same thing you did last time, Atalius, and push ahead all alone to try to take on my army by yourself. You will recall that last maneuver left you captured and in this mess. We'd hate to bargain your life for a second son, now, wouldn't we?"

No response. The Brutes had all gone very still, Olerra's words invoking rich fear, as she detailed out all their fates.

"We could play out the fight," Olerra continued. "Or you could just leave. You're better off attempting to send spies into the palace to recover him. A full-scale army? Was your plan to intimidate me into returning him?"

Olerra could see the veins standing out in Atalius's neck from here. Not only had she'd outmaneuvered him again, she'd shamed him publicly.

A handful of men stepped out of the crowd, likely advisers to the king. They surrounded Atalius, all of them whispering in his ears, probably counseling him against attacking.

"You should listen to whatever they have to say," Olerra said, further goading the man. "If you lose all the forces you've brought with you here today, your country will be vulnerable enough for me to wage an attack of my own. I rather like the idea of becoming queen of both Amarra and Brutus."

The Amarran soldiers reacted to that. Some raised their spears, while others gave a low cheer. Glen didn't like that. The king liked it less.

Glenaerys tried to step forward to say something again to the queen but was held back by Shaelwyn.

The chatting between the king and his advisers went on for some time. She wanted Atalius to think that a trading of princes was his idea, since he hadn't received her letter. And if he didn't get there on his own, she would propose the solution. Then she'd get him to reveal Glen's treason.

When next Atalius looked up from his huddle, it wasn't Olerra he glared at but Glenaerys. He shot her a meaningful glance, as though he expected her to do something. He was getting desperate to save face, keep all his sons, prevent a war.

One of the advisers gestured toward the front lines, and Olerra spotted the remaining Ladicus brothers. She wondered if Atalius had made them all come because of how she'd taunted the king at their last meeting, claiming he didn't want them around to see his defeat.

They were easy to distinguish from the rest of the company with that near-white hair. The youngest, Olerra knew, was eighteen. He was shorter than the others, but only just—as though he had more growing to do. Ikanos.

The next had a well-trimmed beard perhaps a hand-length long. It had lines of brown mixed with the blond. His brow stood out further than the others, and he resembled the king the most with his facial features. Trantos.

Then there was Canus. He was bigger than the others, almost as massive as the king. He had a knowing gaze that seemed to see more than all the others around him.

And then there was the last. He was willowy and graceful. His hair was long, almost to his waist and straight as a stick. His beauty was leagues above the others, his skin unblemished. He didn't bother growing a beard, or perhaps he could not.

The real Andrastus.

That was the man she was supposed to take. He was beautiful. Clearly not a fighter like the others. She could imagine this man reading poetry and enjoying days spent indoors. It was laughable that she'd ever thought the man at her side was him. No, the man on the battlefield would never drink hard ale or throw flaming daggers. He wouldn't kill for her or kiss her senseless or bark orders.

But this was the safest path toward their goals. She would prove Glen's treachery, wed Andrastus, and become queen. Sanos would return home, challenge his father when his mother and sister were safe, and become king. Their countries would finally be at peace. It was a good outcome.

But it wasn't the only possible outcome.

No, a plan was forming in Olerra's mind. Something reckless. Something that had so much potential for going wrong.

But if it went right . . .

26

The blade at Sanos's throat was abruptly wrenched away, and Olerra spun him in place. She swept her eyes over him in a look that was so possessive it was making his blood heat.

"You listen to me, and you listen well," she said. "I don't give a fuck what your name is."

His eyes widened.

"You're mine," she continued. "I claim you, and I choose you. And while you're going to spend forever making this up to me, there is no way I'm giving you back over to that tyrant. I made you a promise. He would never hurt you again. I'm keeping it."

Hope rooted in his chest as she spun him back around. He had no idea how there could be a way through this, and she had already started speaking to his father again before he could ask.

"We both want to avoid war, Atalius, so I'll tell you what. You want your heir? I'll fight you for him. Single combat."

Sanos reached back for her, as though he could stop the words she'd already said. The queen was turning toward them, clearly surprised by this turn of events. *Good, maybe she can stop this madness.*

No one faced his father and lived.

The king's advisers swept forward, ready with more opinions on the matter. Atalius shooed them all away with a single flick of his wrist.

The grin he shot Sanos froze his blood.

"Deal."

Sanos spun around on his own this time, heedless of whatever act he was supposed to be putting on. "What are you doing?"

"I just said what I was doing."

"You can't fight him. Let *me* fight him."

Olerra smiled, clearly touched by his offer. "This is a fight over you, Prince. You can't fight it. Besides, you said you couldn't beat him. I can."

He took her hands in his. "It's not that I don't believe in you. It's him. He's too good. I will not have you die for me."

"Yes," the queen interjected. "I will not have you dying for him, either."

"I will not die," Olerra said. "Trust me. I can do this. It will solve *all* our problems."

Sanos didn't know what other meaning Olerra was hinting at, and he didn't care. He needed her safe. Sanos prayed to his god that the queen would put a stop to this. If Olerra wouldn't listen to him, surely she would listen to her aunt.

"I trust you," the queen said at last. "Do what needs to be done."

"No!" Sanos said.

Olerra removed her hands from his and gripped him by the upper arms. Her right hand covered the armband. "I know you want to kill him. I know he has been tormenting you for years. I don't know the extent of your suffering, but I know this: I will end it. If you were to kill him publicly like this, fighting *for* the Amarrans, you'd have no hope of becoming the next king. You've spent your whole life protecting others. Now let me protect you."

"How am I supposed to become king *and* be with you?"

"*Trust* me."

He didn't want to. He wanted to rage and tie her up and hide her somewhere his father would never find her again. Sanos was a warrior. He'd been trained all his life to fight, to withstand physical torture. To lead and strategize.

He didn't know how to let another fight his battles. He didn't know how to stand by and do nothing.

But he realized that if there was any hope for their future, he had to fight for them, too.

By doing nothing.

By supporting her, believing in her when he didn't even know the full extent of her plan.

It nearly killed him, but he said, "All right."

The gates were opened, and Sanos remained standing between the queen and Ydra as Olerra strode between the two armies alone.

He eyed her best friend, looking for some hint of concern or worry, but Ydra seemed perfectly relaxed. Did she know who the better fighter was? Had she seen his father in combat? Was she at any of those battles in Shamire? As Olerra's second-in-command, she might have been required to stay behind and lead the forces here.

An overseer announced that the king and Olerra could each bring in two weapons. Sanos knew that meant his father would bring the Kingsword, a weapon passed down from father to son for generations, and a dagger, sheathed at his side.

Olerra brought in what she always wore, a sword and the whipblade.

He was regretting giving her his support. Losing her would destroy him, and losing her to his father would end him entirely.

Atalius said loudly, "I would tell you to leave the goddess's power out of this fight, since you've already got two weapons at your side, but if the rumors are true, you don't have a lick of magic in those veins."

Olerra's comeback was immediate. "I've lost count of the number of Brutes I've killed just fine without it."

The retort was good, but Sanos could sense her fury from here. His father had struck precisely where it would do the most damage. How did he know already? If he'd had spies in the palace, then how did they not know he'd been taken sooner?

"To first blood?" the king asked.

"To the death," Olerra amended.

Sanos closed his eyes, keeping his emotions in check.

I will do nothing. I will stand here and show my support.

When he opened his eyes again, he made the mistake of looking at Glenaerys. She and her mother were both grinning from ear to ear, as though this turn of events was better than they could have planned.

Olerra's suggestion was met with a pause from the king, as though battling to the death hadn't occurred to him.

"Something wrong?" Olerra asked the king as she stretched her arms.

"I thought we were meant to be preventing war. Will your soldiers not attack the moment I kill you?"

"The Amarrans will honor the outcome of the fight. The winner gets Sanos. No matter what happens, the Brutes return home peacefully. Do you agree?"

"Yes," the king said, loud enough for his troops to hear. "To the death, then. Brutish laws of combat."

"You're still upset about that rock? Or was it what came afterward? I thought the nudity was a nice touch."

"Brutish laws of combat," he repeated more forcefully.

"Very well. I will only use the two weapons I have brought in with me. Nothing more and nothing less."

"And no biting or hair pulling. No groin shots," the king said, as though perhaps she was unfamiliar with the full laws of combat.

If Olerra was insulted, she didn't show it. "Anything else?"

"No breaks or reprieves. No one interferes."

"Done."

They both drew their swords, and Sanos crossed his arms in an attempt to still his nerves.

The king and Olerra stood in a makeshift ring lined with torches, somewhere just outside the walls, between the two armies. History was being made right there, no matter who won. The air was thick with it, so thick Sanos could hardly breathe.

His father struck first, launching forward and swinging with bone-crushing strength. Olerra raised her sword in plenty of time, taking the full force of the strike. Her arm trembled from the weight of it, but she held.

Sanos was mesmerized by her strength. He almost didn't believe it wasn't goddess-given. His woman was strong all on her own. She was large and powerful and beautiful.

Perfect. She was perfect.

And that's why he didn't want her to fucking die.

Olerra threw off the attack and made one of her own, slicing downward. The king jumped back, and Olerra stepped up for another sweeping attack.

The way she moved was incredible. Her steps were precise. Her movements were so fast, faster than his father's. Yet his strikes were more powerful; Sanos knew she felt the impact in her bones. But she didn't let up. She didn't show any weakness save for that slight trembling, the pushing of her muscles to the brink.

Most bouts with the sword were quick, ending in two minutes or fewer. But this one? With two rivals of such skill? It went on and on and on. Olerra started to expend more energy to dodge the king's strikes rather than catch them on her sword, avoiding the pain of that contact. It must have been weighing on her.

It meant she would tire out faster.

Yet the king was not as young as he used to be, and those powerful strikes were costing him.

Sanos could feel his heart in his throat. Sweat gathered on his skin, and it had nothing to do with the Amarran heat.

The misstep could have happened to anyone. It was not an official ring they fought within. Though the space had been cleared quickly, there were still rocks and debris on the well-traveled road to the main city gates.

Olerra stepped on uneven ground and swayed off-balance.

"Recover," Ydra whispered beside him, and Sanos could only watch helplessly as his father drew first blood.

The cut was shallow, thanks to the light armor she wore. The stripe across her stomach could barely be seen from this distance.

But the red along the Kingsword flashed in the torchlight.

Olerra didn't make a sound of pain, only looked down at the wound, as though surprised and unfamiliar with it.

"It's not too late," the king said. "I will let you renegotiate to the drawing of first blood and call this my win."

"Not a chance," Olerra said, slamming forward to knock the king off-kilter with the weight of her own body.

It was becoming harder and harder to think as Olerra's body began to tire. She'd taken only the one injury, but it slowed her further. There was also no denying the fact that the more she watched the king fight, the more she had to admit—

He was superior with the sword. He knew it. He was putting on a show for his troops more than anything else. Letting this fight carry on to be something that bards would sing about for years to come. And prolonging Olerra's defeat.

"I really don't see how it took four battles before we finally caught you," Olerra said. "You fight like an old man."

The taunt cost her.

This time the slice took her on the side of the arm and went deeper than the first. Olerra drew in a breath of air, adjusting to the fresh pain. It was her sword arm, and it flared whenever she moved her muscles.

"And you fight like a girl who's been playing pretend for years," he said.

"Tell me, how many years has it been since you won a battle, Atalius?"

She just barely managed to block his next strike, but gods, it hurt. Her wounds seeped and pulsed with pain. She went on the offensive, biting back the agony, keeping her focus on the gaps in the king's armor.

No matter how fast she moved, he was always there to block her. As though he could anticipate her moves. That's what the years of extra training did for him.

"What is the point of this?" he asked her. "You've lost your chance at a crown. Beating me won't change that. Is this your final play? To die fighting? We both know you cannot beat me."

Her sword glanced off his armor, her strikes losing their power. "I already won," she said. "I took your heir. I've made him Amarran. Did you know he likes being my whore better than being your son?"

The last line was only a whisper meant for his ears.

And it was the tipping point.

Atalius *hated* that she'd put his son in bedroom clothes and paint. He flew at her with renewed fury, and his sword managed to land on the inside of her lower thigh.

The slice nearly drove her to the ground.

"You talk too much," the king said. "Were you mine, I'd have beaten some manners into you."

"Were I yours, I would have killed you long ago. It's a wonder Brutus has tolerated your tyranny this long. I think it's time we changed that."

The punch came so quickly, she couldn't so much as turn her head.

She tasted blood in her mouth. Her skin felt tight. The world blurred for the beat of a second.

She needed to move faster!

And then Atalius's sword went deep into her side, and she lost her footing, falling to her knees.

Olerra grunted in pain as the king drew his weapon from her flesh. She placed the point of her own weapon on the ground to keep herself from toppling over. She hoped the blade hadn't nicked anything important. Not that it mattered. It hurt so bad she might as well be dying.

Atalius circled her, hands raised, letting the shouts of his troops cry up into the air. Building the anticipation even more. He knew he had her. He knew he'd won.

"Tell me," Olerra shouted to be heard over the noise. "Why did it take you two months to figure out where your heir had gone?" Each breath was fire. She used her free hand to staunch the bleeding at her side. She kept her eyes on the king as he circled like a rabid dog. "I told you exactly what I wanted. A son for your life. Yet still you didn't suspect me. Why?"

The king didn't answer. He twisted his head from one side to the next, as though looking for the perfect angle for the killing blow.

"Admit it," she said. "You know your sons hate you. Sanos running away seemed far more likely, didn't it?"

Still the king said nothing. He flicked her blood from his sword, preparing it for the final strike.

"That's why you had to wait until my cousin approached with the truth." Olerra made sure her voice was nice and loud so those up on the wall could hear. "What I couldn't figure out at first was what she was doing in your country in the first place. It was her idea to form an alliance, yes? You're too proud and stupid to come up with something like that on your own. What did she promise you? My life if you helped her take the throne? Did she say she would let your soldiers within the gates to fight against the women under my command? Is that why part of your forces are on the other side of the city? She promised there would be someone to let them in? She did try. My troops are just better. I got the truth of it. Admit it, Atalius, you can't do anything without a strong woman guiding you."

Atalius charged her. He used two hands to bring down his massive sword against where she was kneeling in the dirt. Olerra raised her own weapon at the last moment and pushed her muscles to the limit, catching the blow.

They were locked in a battle of strength. As the king pushed, the blades rested against her helmet. The force of Olerra's entire body kept her upright.

"I came up with the idea," Atalius spat at her. "She wanted an alliance, but I set forth the terms. Clearly you Amarrans are all the same. Incapable of doing the simplest of tasks. But I don't need your cousin or you to take this stupid country out from under you. And I certainly don't need anyone's help to kill *you*."

Atalius kicked her, and Olerra rolled and rolled away from the king and his sword.

With the distance, Olerra looked up at her queen.

Lemya's smile was large. She nodded. To her guard, she said, "Arrest Glenaerys for conspiring with our enemies."

Olerra watched with satisfaction as women in scarlet armor surrounded both Glen and her mother. Olerra had done it.

But, gods, she hurt. Fire ripped across her skin, and the deep wound in her side throbbed and seeped blood, but she wasn't done yet.

Olerra stood and tossed aside her sword.

"It's too late to yield," Atalius said as he approached.

"I yield nothing," she said.

And then she drew her whipblade.

27

Sanos was exhausted from the effort of holding still. He'd watched Olerra take injury after injury and borne it. Now that she'd revealed her cousin's treachery, she looked different. Radiant. Victorious. Even though the fight was ongoing.

"You've been an admirable opponent, Olerra of Amarra," his father said calmly. "But I shan't miss you."

"The feeling is mutual, Atalius, but I would hardly call you admirable."

Olerra unwound the rope coiled in her hands. She began to swing it over her head, like farmers might do to lasso livestock.

"Sanos, have you seen Olerra with the whipblade?" Ydra asked.

"No."

"It takes years and years to master," Ydra said. "Most never manage it. Most manage to kill themselves with it, so dangerous is the whipblade. But Olerra? She's a natural."

Before the king could get within sword range, Olerra snapped her wrist forward.

The blade hit the king on the side of the knee, sliding right through the gaps in the thick plating. It appeared to imbed an inch or two deep before Olerra drew it back to herself by yanking on the rope and swinging first to her left, then to her right, in alternating arcs. The blade moved so quickly, it was hard to follow, and those close enough were streaked with the king's blood.

"It's an old weapon," Ydra was telling him conversationally now. "There was only one person alive who knew how to use it, until Olerra begged her to train her. She mastered the basics at a young age and has been developing her skill over time, in private."

Olerra sent her arm out in an arc, and there was absolutely nothing the king could do to block a second attack from what was essentially a whip striking out with a dagger on the end.

This strike hit his arm, digging in at the elbow, hitting the gap in the armor once more. Olerra's aim was impeccable, and the king dropped his sword. He pulled his dagger from his side with his off hand. Atalius tried to leap forward with his knife, but Olerra struck out quicker, her reach longer with the rope. A streak of red appeared on the king's cheek, disappearing into his beard.

Amarra's tits.

Olerra had been fighting with the sword only to get the king to reveal Glenaerys's plans. Now the real fight was happening.

Olerra started weaving the rope over her arms and around her neck, spinning and turning impossibly fast.

She struck Atalius at the shoulder. Then again at the neck, too far off from his jugular for the strike to be deadly.

"Show-off," Ydra muttered.

Atalius tried to dodge her strikes, but it was impossible for him to know where the rope would land. He wasn't used to combating such a weapon. He couldn't defend against it.

Sanos put his hands atop the wall and leaned forward. Everyone realized the inevitable conclusion to the fight, even his father.

The king dropped his knife, raised his hands high, and said, "I yield."

"You cannot yield, Atalius," Olerra said. "The fight was to the death. You can die with your weapon or without it. The choice is yours."

The king craned his head over his neck, judging the distance to his waiting army.

He tried to run.

Olerra struck with the rope again. This time, it wound around his feet before the blade dug into his ankle, felling him in a tangle of rope. Olerra picked up the Kingsword, struck the tip into the dirt, and started to pull on the rope.

Tug.

The king inched closer to where she waited, armor rattling as he tried to find purchase in the dirt. Sanos didn't blink. He didn't want to miss a second of this.

Tug.

As she pulled, the rope coiled at her feet in a neat circle.

Tug.

Now the king was screaming. "Stop this!" he commanded of his troops.

"Brutish laws of combat," Olerra reminded him. "No one can interfere."

Tug.

When he was close enough, Olerra flipped the man over. This way he would have to look at her as he died.

She said, "You never should have touched them. Your children. Your wife. I avenge their pain with your death."

And then she raised the man's own sword high into the air with both hands and struck straight down, the point piercing through his neck.

Sanos could do nothing but stare. She could have used her own sword, but she hadn't. She'd used the Kingsword, now Sanos's sword, as if to give him more connection to this moment.

His massive, violent, horrible father was gone.

He raised his gaze and met Canus's. His brother was too far for him to see his expression, but he knew it. He knew the princes all shared the same profound relief. Freedom. Joy, even.

"Tell them to open the gate," Sanos said to Ydra. Then he ran down the steps of the wall. When the portcullis rose too slowly, he ducked under it, not stopping until he'd reached Olerra's side.

She was swaying on her feet, so he wrapped her in his arms.

"You did it," he said. The words may have been obvious, but his mind was still having a hard time processing the reality of Atalius's death. "He's gone."

"Look at him," Olerra said.

Sanos did.

His father's mouth hung open from the effort of his last scream. His eyes were wide. The features that Sanos had feared and hated for so long were now still. Blood seeped around the sword at the dead king's throat.

Sanos kept one arm around Olerra and drew the Kingsword from his father's body with a *squelch*.

He raised his eyes to the waiting Brutish troops. They were leaderless. They were uncertain as to what to do now.

"I'll be right back," Sanos said.

Olerra nodded, nothing but trust in her eyes. He made sure she could stay on her feet before running toward the Brutes.

The armor-clad arms of his brothers felt cold against his skin, but he welcomed the hug they swallowed him in.

"She killed him," Ikanos said.

"He's gone," Andrastus said.

"You're alive," Trantos said.

"You fucker," Canus said. "We thought the worst had happened, but you've been here in Amarra getting sexed up all this time? Do you have any idea how miserable it's been without you?"

"You don't get to complain," Andrastus said. "You're not the one who's been left alone with Father day in and day out."

Sanos was so relieved to see them all intact. "Mother and Emorra?"

"They're fine," Canus said. "Perfectly fine back at the palace."

To Canus, Sanos said, "I want you to ride home with all haste. Bring them here. Will you do that for me?"

"Yes, but why?"

"There's not much time. I need you to get them out before word of Father's death spreads."

"All right." Canus left without another word.

His father's advisers approached.

"Sire, we should attack now," one said. "She killed the king, and the gate is opened."

"No," Sanos said. "My father agreed to peace. Select a number of guards to accompany you within the gates. It's time to begin real negotiations."

"You want us to go inside their walls with naught but a handful of guards?"

"We're the ones who showed up with an army at their gates."

"To rescue you!"

"And I'm fine. Thank you. Now, am I the next king of Brutus or am I not?"

"You are," they agreed.

"Then do as I said. I can't linger." To the rest of his brothers, he said, "Return home with the troops, but I will see you all soon. Await my orders."

And then, without seeing if anyone was doing as they were told, he ran back to Olerra. She was still conscious. Still bleeding. He couldn't carry her and the Kingsword at the same time, so he dropped the weapon and scooped her up into his arms, smearing blood on his bare chest. He didn't care.

"We need to get you to a healer."

It was as if she'd had only enough strength to hold on until he'd come to her, for she passed out as he brought her back through the gate.

When Olerra came to, she was washed and dressed, and her wounds had been tended. Her aunt sat beside her bed, one of her hands clasped around one of hers.

"How do you feel?" the queen asked when she noticed she was awake.

"Like a pincushion."

Lemya nodded, as though she suspected nothing less. As a warrior in her younger days, she knew acutely the injuries caused by Brutish steel.

"At what point did you make your own plan to keep your prince and challenge the king?"

"About ten seconds before I suggested it."

"He almost killed you," the queen said, voice accusatory.

"I could have beaten him at any time by drawing the whipblade."

"But you didn't draw it until the very end. You were meant to trade one prince for another. Get Atalius to admit Glen's treachery while standing safely on the wall beside me. Instead, you risked yourself again for the sake of Atalius's heir."

Olerra tested her side, the deepest of her wounds. It was sore, and she couldn't possibly sit up with the state of it. She'd have to say the words lying on her back, then.

"I love him."

The queen raised a brow. She'd surprised her. "How can you trust him? After all that has happened?"

"One day at a time, I suppose. If he'll have me."

Her aunt crossed one leg over another. "Oh, he'll have you. I've been in negotiations with the new king of Brutus and his advisers, brokering for peace and new terms regarding Shamire."

Olerra was surprised by this.

The queen continued. "You accidentally stole the crown prince and made him fall in love with you. Now there's talk of combining Brutus and Amarra into one country. Olerra, you singlehandedly gave us Brutus, and it couldn't have worked better if we'd planned it in advance."

Olerra laughed, but it hurt. She moaned as she put her hands over her stomach.

Lemya stood and leaned over the bed to kiss her cheek. "Rest well. There is much work ahead of you. You have until the anniversary of the Goddess's Gift to be well. Then you need to be seen as the nobles officially declare you crown princess."

Olerra swallowed. "Do you really think they'll choose me?"

"After your cousin's betrayal and with you dangling Brutus over their heads? Do you really have to ask?"

Something had changed over the last few days. Olerra's soldiers had followed her without question, despite knowing she didn't have the Goddess's Gift. Olerra had defeated the most feared man in the world without it. She had prevented war and brought two countries together.

She knew she could do incredible things without magic.

She said, "I know my own worth, Auntie. I just don't know if others will see it."

"They do. You're about to have everything. You rest now, and let me handle Glenaerys and Shaelwyn."

Olerra shook her head. "I want to be at the trial."

"Very well. We'll have you brought in."

"Thank you, Auntie. Now may I see him?"

"Of course. He's outside. We fought over who would get to be here when you woke."

"You mean you told him you would see me first and made him wait."

"Yes, exactly."

When Sanos was finally admitted into the healing quarters, he didn't know what he would say to her. Gods, but he hated seeing her covered in gauze yet again.

He managed, "I really wish you would stop getting hurt for me."

She shrugged, then grimaced at the pain. "With Brutus and Amarra joined, there should be few occasions for it. But if you're asking me to stop fighting, the answer is no. I will always fight to protect those I care about."

"And I'm part of that list?" he asked. There could be no doubt as to her feelings after what she'd done for him, but he wanted to hear her answer.

"You're the first name on it."

Sanos felt so out of his element. He didn't know how to go about this. They were tiptoeing around the issue. Both of them speaking as though their marriage was a sure thing. Yet not asking the important questions.

He decided to be brave.

"You told me once that I should be honored to become your husband. You spoke with such confidence on the matter that I hated you instantly."

She grinned.

"I hated you, and yet, I was enamored with you. You're so fierce and protective. And then I came to learn about your softer side. The way you care for your people. Your fear at not being enough for Amarra. I love all the parts of you. I love how you've taken care of me. I want to take care of you, too. I want us to be equals."

She patted the bed beside her, and Sanos sat.

"Lie down," she said. "Hold me because I can't hold you yet."

He didn't hesitate, placing his hands carefully where there wasn't gauze and stroking her skin.

"We will be equals," she declared. "We'll find a way, even if we have to work at it every day. The moment I am recovered, I will show you how much you mean to me."

He shivered at the words. "I look forward to it."

The trial was held in the same room where Glen once tried to behead Olerra's chosen. It seemed a fitting turn of events that her cousin would be forced to stand where Sanos once stood, looking around for aid where there was none.

No, her only ally, her mother, was by her side, covered in chains just as she was.

Olerra was healing well. She could walk now but not run. She couldn't lift most things. Not even a shirt to pull over her head, but she wasn't going to miss this.

Numerous allies of Glen came forward to speak on her character and all the things she'd done for the country. The spymaster spoke of instances where valuable information gathered by Glenaerys stopped assassination attempts on the queen. The treasurer spoke of how she improved the kingdom's finances. But no matter how many people spoke well of her, the testimonies of those bringing the charges against her were damning.

They had found letters sent to the king of Brutus with Glen's signature, stolen by Olerra's spy. The king hadn't bothered to burn them, likely because he lost nothing if his connection to Glen were found out.

The soldiers Glen had instructed to let Atalius's troops into the city gave her up. It took hours of questioning, but it finally happened. And then came the testimonies of everyone on the battlements who had heard the king admit to Glen's treason.

Sanos was by Olerra's side as the nobility found Glenaerys guilty of all charges. However, because she was royalty, she could not be killed. Just like Olerra could not when she'd demanded substitution on behalf of Sanos.

"I sentence you to a life of house arrest," Queen Lemya declared. "If exiled, Glenaerys would only find supporters to help her steal the throne. She is to remain on Amarran soil, where I can keep an eye on her."

Glenaerys met Olerra's eye, and Olerra wanted to say something. Anything to her cousin, whom she still loved despite everything. But there were no words.

"You, however," the queen said, turning to Glen's mother, "are not royalty. You have aided your daughter every step of the way in her attempts to align with Brutus to secure the throne, and you have funded her treachery. I sentence you to death, Shaelwyn, and I am redistributing your wealth to the throne and its people. I'll not have Glenaerys bribing her way out of house arrest."

Shaelwyn, usually so beautiful and so put together, turned toward Olerra, her face a cruel sneer. "You have no right to sit on the Amarran throne. You are Giftless! Ordinary! In bed with Brutus!"

"Would you like to lose your tongue before you lose your head?" the queen asked.

"I have kept this country running," Shaelwyn said. "It is my wealth that has funded your reign as queen. You are nothing without me."

"I have brought peace to our people for many years, and my legacy will live on through Olerra, the only rightful choice as queen."

Now Shaelwyn turned her venomous gaze on Olerra. "I should have killed you when I had the chance! Back when I killed your parents."

Olerra and the queen both stilled.

"That's right," Shaelwyn said, smug now. "I killed your mother and blamed it on your father! Then I killed him before he could give testimony. I cleared the path for Glenaerys to take the throne."

Olerra couldn't move. She wanted to stop the words but knew she needed to hear the rest of it.

"You were four years old. Easy pickings. I only spared you for the love my daughter had for you. But I never should have been swayed by such a trifling thing. You are nothing!"

The warrior queen of Amarra drew her sword for the first time in years. The soldiers cleared her path as she approached a chained Shaelwyn.

"She was my sister!" Queen Lemya shouted, and then she swung.

Shaelwyn's head fell from her shoulders and landed at Glenaerys's feet.

Olerra nearly sank to the floor at what had been revealed. Sanos was there to hold her up. He put an arm around her and supported her weight. His lips went to her temple. "I love you. You're safe. I'm so sorry."

All this time, Olerra had felt that she had something to prove because her mother had died at the hands of her father. But it wasn't true. It was what Shaelwyn had wanted her to believe. For all Olerra knew, her sire was a kind man who'd loved her and her mother.

Vengeance was already had. The queen had exacted it, so now Olerra was left with only her complicated feelings to sort through.

Olerra pushed free of Sanos gently and approached Glenaerys, who hadn't moved, staring at her mother's head.

"Did you know?" Olerra demanded. "Did you know she'd killed them?"

For the first time in her life, Olerra witnessed her cousin cry. She stroked the hair trailing behind her mother's head. "I didn't know," Glen said, "but if I had, I wouldn't have told you."

Olerra slapped her cousin across the face.

Glenaerys looked horrified, having never had Olerra raise a single hand to her.

"You may be trapped within these walls," Olerra said, "but I will not be visiting. From this day forward, you are dead to me."

Olerra turned from her cousin as the guards hauled her away.

28

Olerra dressed in her finest armor and tunic. Glenaerys would have worn some fancy dress, but Olerra was a warrior first, and she would remind all the nobility of it. Her victory over Atalius happened only a few weeks ago, but her battle garb would be a perfect reminder of how she'd thwarted her cousin and their greatest enemy in a single night.

Ydra did her hair in battle braids. The strands were combed to impressive volume atop her head. Then every piece of hair was plaited down her back. The plaits were braided into one long thick braid that rested over one shoulder. She wondered if she resembled her mother at all.

All week the Amarrans had been celebrating. The five hundredth anniversary of the Goddess's Gift deserved no less. Olerra had spent the week with Sanos, enjoying the foods and drink and dancing. They were both free to be themselves around each other for the first time, and it was glorious.

Her wounds were healing nicely. Only the one in her side still troubled her some when she bent the wrong way. Otherwise, she was up and back to normal, with restrictions on her training with the troops.

Today, the nobility would vote on the next successor, and tomorrow, Olerra would be wedded. She was most looking forward to tonight, however.

She'd gotten approval from the healer to explore nightly activities, as long as she was careful and stopped should anything cause pain.

She would tell Sanos after the vote, which would happen in the throne room. Olerra's personal guard escorted her there now. Her prince was at her side, dressed in a fine shirt and pants. The deal was that he could wear Brutish clothing as long as his left bicep was always bare. Sanos was more than happy to oblige.

"Are you nervous?" he asked her.

"An Amarran general is never nervous," she said.

At the look he gave her, she admitted, "A little."

He reached over and took her hand. "No matter what happens, it will be all right. The vote is really only a formality at this point, isn't it?"

"Not necessarily."

"They'd really still allow your cousin to rule?"

"No, but they could vote on a distant relative of mine."

"Now you're just being ridiculous."

She cracked the knuckles of her free hand. "Spoken like someone who already has his throne secured. How would you feel if everyone took a vote and decided Canus got to rule?"

"Relieved, most likely."

She rolled her eyes. It wasn't that her man lacked ambition. More like he'd never had to fight for his role. It was simply given to him. It was a wonder he hadn't turned into some spoiled brat as a result.

The doors to the throne room opened wide, and Olerra and her entourage stepped through. Sanos kissed her hand before releasing her so she could walk to the dais. She winked at him before she went.

Her aunts sat on twin thrones. Surrounding them were the remaining council members: Enadra, Cyssia, and Usstra. Then there was Menina, a wealthy viscountess who had taken Shaelwyn's place.

Olerra strode up the steps before kneeling before the women surrounding her, submitting herself to their decision.

The room was fuller than usual. Nobility from all over Amarra had traveled to join in the celebrations for the Goddess's Gift. They were there to cast their votes, which they would have done before Olerra was admitted into the room. The decision was already made. She only had to wait to hear it.

The queen stood. "Olerra Corasene, we have taken our vote. We were all very impressed with your victory over the king of Brutus and the way you exposed your cousin's treasonous schemes." Lemya nodded to Usstra.

"However," Usstra said, "you are Giftless, a fact that you hid from all of us. For that, we considered several of your third cousins for the role of crown princess."

Olerra caught her gasp before it was audible. Her body went cold as she realized she was about to be embarrassed publicly. Some cousin was about to be invited to join her on the dais.

After everything, it still wasn't enough.

Sanos's face rose behind her closed eyes.

And she felt peace.

All would be well. Olerra didn't have to hide who she was anymore. She would marry the man she loved soon, and no matter what, she would rule Brutus at his side and make things better for the women living there. It was enough.

Enadra took up her part of the speech. "We posed every eligible woman to the nobility for a majority vote."

"It was nearly unanimous," Menina said.

Cyssia smiled. "We bestow the title of crown princess to you."

"Rise, Olerra," the queen said.

It was emotional whiplash. Olerra raised her head and blinked up at her aunt. Somehow she found the strength to make the muscles in her legs work. Behind her, the room was applauding.

Lemya held a hand out to her, and Olerra took it. The queen turned her to face the room. "Witness your next queen, Crown Princess Olerra Corasene!"

The cheering grew louder. Olerra felt her eyes watering, and she could do nothing to stop it. She laughed as tears fell down her face. Toria and Lemya embraced her. Then all the nobility in the room swarmed her.

It was hours of chatting and appeasing nobles. Everyone in the room seemed to want to talk to his betrothed, now that she was officially heir.

He was so proud of her. Proud of what they'd accomplished together.

When Olerra finally broke away from the crowd, she took his hand. "Let's go, please."

They couldn't make a clean getaway. A few more people stopped them, but when they finally reached the hallway, Olerra sighed.

"Let's get some food in you," Sanos suggested. When they reached her rooms, he sent a eunuch off for refreshments.

After the ale and bread arrived, the two of them sat on a comfy sofa by the window. Olerra took a long drink.

"I'm crown princess," she said.

"Yes," he agreed.

"You're the king of Brutus."

"Yes."

"We're getting married tomorrow."

"Yes."

She turned to him, her eyes finally focusing. "I thought saying it out loud might help to make it all feel more real."

"And does it?"

"A little. Not enough."

"What do you need?"

Olerra smiled, plucking the drink from his hand and putting it on the table next to her own. She took his hand and dragged him toward the bed.

"You," she said. "I need you. Right now."

Sanos felt his blood heat. He was hard in an instant, but he tried to make his brain work. "Your injuries."

"The healer said I could if I was careful."

He narrowed his eyes. "Are you being truthful?"

"Would I lie to you?"

"For sex?"

She laughed. "I promise."

And then she was kissing him.

All his noble intentions went out the window as he decided to believe her. Gods, but he loved this woman so much. It had been torture to wait for her to heal. To not touch her when she'd done so much for him. Killing his father. Offering him a kingdom. Making him her seul. The extent of his feelings was overwhelming.

And now she was kissing him. He tried to keep his lips gentle, but Olerra was ravaging his mouth with hers. She stood on her toes, got a fist in his hair, and worked her lips over his. She kissed like she wanted to claim him as her own. As if he could ever be anyone else's.

He was scared to touch her, so he went slow, letting his fingers go to the back of her neck, securing her lips to his. His left hand went to the indent of her waist so he could press their hips together.

She made a little noise in her throat that he was going to try to never forget.

Suddenly impatient, Sanos pressed his tongue against her lips, needing to be inside.

She opened. Their tongues danced, and he was swept away with how right this was. To kiss a woman who kissed him because she wanted him. Not because he paid her. She'd initiated this kiss, and the thought of that somehow made him harder.

Olerra drew his tongue into her mouth and sucked on it. It was a move so reminiscent of sex that he felt himself shaking with need. He did his best to ignore his own urges, letting her decide the pace. She was injured. He needed to be care—

She shoved him backward onto the bed. He scooted toward the middle, keeping his eyes on hers. He watched as she removed her armor, one piece at a time. Then she crawled up over him.

Shit.

He tugged off his shirt and kicked off his sandals. She helped him with his pants. Though she was still fully clothed in her tunic, he was entirely naked, and she took him in hand.

He grunted, tilting back his head against the mattress.

"Eyes on me," she instructed.

"Yes, Olerra," he said.

"Good boy." She bent down and licked him from shaft to tip.

"Fucking hell. If you do that again, I swear I won't last."

She harrumphed. "I thought you Brutes were supposed to be virile. Doesn't that mean you recover quickly?"

His eyes heated. "Yes, we recover quickly, but not so quickly as to—"

She sucked the head between her lips.

"Dammit, Olerra."

He could feel her smile around him, and he nearly came from that sensation and knowledge. The smugness emanating off her. His woman was sexy as hell.

She took him all the way to the back of her throat, without so much as gagging, and he wondered what manner of apparatus she'd practiced on to be able to do this effortlessly. Was it another phallus from her kit? Gods, she'd be the death of him.

She toyed with him, just like when she fucked him with her fingers. She'd take up a rhythm, then pause to suckle the head or explore the underside of his shaft. He was going mad with need, which he suspected was exactly where she wanted him.

It was so good, but there was something he wanted even more. He needed her mouth free so he could hear the one thing that had been missing from their time together.

"Please, Olerra," he begged. "Come up here."

She drew her mouth off him entirely, and he whimpered at its absence.

She crawled up him until she straddled him. Then, slowly, she sat, taking him inside her.

He watched her face carefully, looking for any sign of pain, whether from him or her wounds. He could see nothing but ecstasy.

"Just a moment," she said. He could feel her internal walls contracting around him, getting used to the feel of him. It was the most perfect fit. He couldn't remember it feeling better.

"Are you all right?" he asked.

"I'm perfect," she said.

"Then why—"

"Because I'm so close to coming, and I don't want this to be over before it really even starts, so let me breathe a moment."

That shut him up.

He looked down, registering that the first two fingers of her right hand were wet. She'd been touching herself while sucking on him. No wonder she was ready to come. How could she multitask so splendidly?

He reached out a hand to move her braid over her shoulder, then rose to kiss her neck.

"That's not helping," she said.

"What shall I do, then? Talk of mundane things?"

She laughed. "No. I don't think that will help."

He nuzzled her. "If you come early, I will only make you come twice. Now, please, for the love of all five gods, move, woman."

The look she gave him was a mixture of irritation and arousal, two things that always seemed to go hand in hand with them. He kissed the expression from her lips.

"Let's get one thing straight," she said. "In the bedroom, I'm in charge."

He arched a brow. "But you're in charge outside of the bedroom. Shouldn't I be permitted to be in charge here?"

She smiled slowly. "How about we take turns?"

"Agreed. Now fucking move your hips."

She did.

So slowly it was agonizing. He put his hands on her waist, careful of the gauze still covering the wound made by his father. He tried to make her move faster, but she resisted, laughing.

"If you weren't injured," he threatened, "I'd have you on your back before you could blink. Then we'd see who's laughing."

"Poor prince," she said. "Maybe you could think of something to do to entice me to go faster."

At first, he thought she wanted him to bargain here in the bedroom, but then he understood. He licked his thumb before placing it over her clit.

"Good boy," she said, and then she really moved.

Sanos tried to take it all in at once. The shaking of the bed. Her panting breaths. The sweat on her skin mixing with his. The feel of her sex against his finger. Being wrapped in her tight, wet folds. It was too much. It wasn't enough. It was everything he never knew he needed.

He leaned forward and nipped at her breasts, and that only made her go faster. He was more breathing against her than anything else. Holding on. Trying to last until—

"Sanos!"

That was what he wanted. To hear his name on her lips. Gods, he'd wanted it more than he'd wanted his next breath.

It was all he needed to join her.

— • EPILOGUE • —

Olerra didn't remember drifting off to sleep. One moment she was in the arms of her prince, her *king*, and the next, she was dreaming.

It was one of those dreams where she couldn't control it. If she could, she would have chosen a much better scenery. Currently, it was pitch-black, like she stared at the back of her eyelids.

Olerra.

A voice called out to her. It was feminine and beautiful, familiar, yet distant. At first, she wondered if it belonged to her mother.

Olerra.

No, not her mother, but someone important.

"Olerra."

The voice was right beside her then. It was Goddess Amarra. Olerra wasn't sure how she knew this. She still couldn't see a thing, but she knew all the same.

"I'm here," Olerra said.

"I came to tell you something."

Olerra knew without needing to be told. "The reason why I'm Giftless."

"Yes, but I sense I don't need to. Surely you've figured it out."

She thought for a moment. "I don't need it."

"No, you don't."

"I became more *because* I don't have it."

"Yes," Amarra said. "You became sympathetic to those less fortunate than you. The men of my kingdom. The commoners. Do I not love all my children?"

"You do."

The voice grew distant, as though it were fading away into nothing.

And you will be the queen they all need. My chosen.

Olerra opened her eyes to startling brightness. It was so drastic from the darkness of her dream that she covered her head with her blankets.

"Don't go back to sleep," Sanos rumbled. "We're getting married today."

She threw the covers off as both the dream and the previous night came back to her. She didn't know if the dream was just that, a figment of her imagination, or if it was really the goddess sending her a message. A special gift on the eve of her anniversary.

It didn't matter.

Olerra knew who she was. And she was enough.

"Do you know what?" she said. "I think today is going to be a perfect day."

"You say that only because you haven't met my brothers yet."

"They can't be worse than you."

Sanos rolled atop her, yet held his weight up on his hands so as not to disturb her injury. She couldn't wait until she was well enough to feel all of him atop her.

"Cheeky thing," he said, before his lips descended to her neck.

"You seem entirely cured of your aversion to physicality," Olerra remarked. They had lain together not once, but three times in quick succession. The Brutish virility really was something remarkable.

"You know very well the cause of my former aversion."

"And you had no one to blame but yourself for that. Will I meet the real Andrastus today?"

"Ugh. Please don't say his name in our bed."

She grinned. "Our bed?"

Sanos looked at the door to his room. "Would you rather I spent my nights in my own bed?"

"I'm teasing. You'll be lucky if I ever let you leave our bed."

The look he sent her was carnal. "As if I'd ever want to."

His head disappeared under the covers.

Sanos's cheeks hurt, and it took him a moment to realize that it was from all the smiling he'd done of late. He wasn't used to . . . being happy.

Or sex in the daytime.

It was fantastic. He thought he might like morning sex even better than evening sex. Waking up to find Olerra still there after he closed his eyes at night was something he knew he would never get used to.

"Here we are," Olerra said proudly. "These used to be Glen's rooms, but now that she's locked up underneath the palace, this wing is more than big enough for your family. They're welcome to visit or stay permanently. Don't worry, it's been cleared out of all her belongings and thoroughly cleaned."

They'd received word this morning that Sanos's family had arrived. Canus had gotten their mother and Emorra out of the castle, but they were followed on the road. His father didn't give empty threats, and even though Sanos hadn't been the one to end Atalius, there were still men who'd gone after his sister and mother.

They'd had to take a circuitous route to Amarra. Canus had sent word ahead, keeping Sanos apprised of their movements. Sanos would get the full story from his brother some other time. For now, he just wanted to see that everyone was all right.

He knocked.

There was a rustling on the other side of the door, but eventually, Trantos answered, peeking his head around the door, ready to slam it closed if he didn't like who was on the other side.

"May we come in?" Sanos said mockingly.

Trantos grinned and swung the door wide. "Oh, it's only you. I was worried there would be more of those overenthusiastic men. They asked if we wanted help bathing before the ceremony tonight."

Sanos laughed at the thought of his brothers being strong-armed to the baths by the palace eunuchs.

The main greeting chamber was filled with fresh flowers and comfortable chairs. Tea had been sent ahead of them, and two women were already enjoying it.

"Sanos!" Emorra jumped from the sofa and threw herself at him. Her hair was even paler than the brothers, truly white. Sanos ran his fingers through it the way he knew she liked. "I missed you," she said. "Don't ever leave again."

His throat felt heavy. They were here. They were safe.

He set Emorra back on her feet, and his mother took her place.

There were tears on her cheeks. Sanos felt them as she pressed her face against his. "I don't know how you managed everything, but I am so proud of you."

"I didn't do it alone." He stepped back and took Olerra's hand. "This is Olerra. She did most of the heavy lifting."

His mother bowed politely in the Brutish fashion when being introduced to someone new, but Olerra drew her into a warm embrace.

Sanos just barely caught Olerra's whisper. "Thank you for your son. You brought a beautiful man into the world."

His heart threatened to burst.

"Thank you," Ferida said. "For saving him."

Sanos thought he ought to step away, that perhaps their conversation wasn't meant for his ears. And then Canus barreled into him.

The breath whooshed out of him, and he felt himself hoisted into the air.

"Wed-ding day. Wed-ding day," Ikanos chanted from somewhere, drawing out the three syllables.

Trantos and Canus carried him on their shoulders and joined in the chant.

"Put me down, you fools," Sanos demanded.

They did no such thing.

"You should probably listen," Andrastus said as he entered the room. "He's a king now. He can have you beheaded."

Sanos pulled the hair attached to the heads of the two idiots carting him around. Trantos and Canus finally dropped him.

"Mind your manners," their mother said, "and come meet your sister-in-law."

"Not for four more hours," Emorra said unhelpfully.

Olerra smiled politely at all of them. She didn't seem uncomfortable, exactly, but like she wasn't sure what to do with herself. When she caught Sanos's gaze, she said, "Sorry. I'm not used to so much family in one room. It's exciting."

Ikanos slung an arm around Olerra. "It's really easy. Basically, we all pick on Sanos."

"Hey!" Sanos said.

"I think I can manage that," Olerra said. "Shall I tell you about the time he wrestled another man naked in front of a thousand women?"

"Olerra, dear," Andrastus said, patting the cushion beside him. "You must sit down and tell us everything."

"Yes, leave out no details," Canus agreed.

"Okay," Sanos said, striding over to her. "I think that's enough family time."

"I want to hear the story." Emorra pouted.

"Don't you have to get ready?" he asked Olerra.

"Not for another hour," she said sweetly. She sat beside Andrastus, and the rest huddled around on nearby seats. "I'll start from the beginning."

Sanos massaged his temples to put on a show, but the truth was, he couldn't even muster up any true outrage. He had everything he needed in this room.

And now the power to keep them all safe.

He sat down to hear her side of the story of how they first met and fell in love.

Olerra wanted a massive wedding, and Ydra had helped her make it happen. The entire Amarran court was present, and many foreign nobles had come to extend their well-wishes. Not a seat was empty as she stared down the rows and rows of bodies.

Olerra's dress was midnight black to match the onyx on Sanos's armband. It was trimmed in silver, and the hem brushed her knees. The sleeves hung off her shoulders, and a leather corset cinched around her waist.

Her sandals were black leather. Beads had been strung onto the strings climbing her calves. Her hair was arranged in the traditional wedding braid, a crown of plaited hair wrapping around her head, the rest of the strands cascading down her back. Simple braids were interspersed, more silver beads woven throughout.

She and Ydra stood alone on a raised platform outdoors, the attendees extending before them in large rows. Most were in conversation with their neighbors. Few were looking at the two women on the dais.

"There are so many people," Ydra said.

"Isn't it exciting?"

"Better you than me."

"Someday this will be you," Olerra said.

"No, thank you."

"What happened to thinking of stealing a husband for your own?"

"I was putting on a show for your prince, and you know it."

"Have you ever considered it, though?" Olerra asked. "Taking a husband? A real one, I mean?"

"I asked my favorite whore once if he'd like me to take him away. He said he liked bedding a different woman every night and nothing could persuade him otherwise."

Olerra smiled. "You and your desire to save everyone. Someday, I hope you'll learn to let someone take care of you."

Ydra snorted. "I think you've spent too much time around your Brute. We are Amarran. Our job is to care and provide for the weaker sex."

"But not to the point where we forget to live for ourselves, too."

"I am—"

Ydra cut herself off because the queen had arrived to officiate the wedding. Lemya came to stand just behind Ydra and Olerra, her hands clasping a folded length of silk, which she would use to bind Olerra's and Sanos's hands during the ceremony.

"Ready?" the queen asked.

"Yes," Olerra said, her stomach tightening with excitement.

At a cue from the queen, the musicians in the back changed the tune they were playing to a wedding march. Olerra looked down the aisle between the rows of chairs eagerly.

First, Ikanos appeared. He wore a Brutish set of fancy robes that must have been stifling in the Amarran heat. He grinned as he walked, tossing out white rose petals. When he got to the end, he bowed to Olerra, before taking position at the far end of the dais.

Next, Trantos appeared. He was perhaps getting a bit too into the music. His hips swayed dramatically, and he even twirled for the audience, who clapped. He winked at Olerra before taking his place next to his brother.

Ydra suddenly froze beside her. "Who is that?" she whispered.

Canus was coming up the aisle now. He walked purposefully, clad in a black tunic and pants. His clothing was molded to his big frame.

"Sanos's brother Canus." Olerra turned to Ydra curiously.

Her friend swallowed. "I've never seen a man that big."

"The late king was bigger."

"Was he? I hadn't noticed." Ydra's eyes tracked Canus all the way to the dais.

Olerra was getting so much entertainment out of Ydra's fascination that she didn't notice Andrastus had appeared until he was already at the dais.

Olerra quickly returned her gaze to the end of the aisle, just in time to see Sanos make his appearance. His mother and sister each held one of his arms, but Olerra barely gave the Brutish women a thought.

Her man was stunning.

He'd opted for Amarran clothing, which pleased her greatly. The skirt was magnificent, showing off his legs to their greatest effect. It was black to match her dress, more onyx beads trailing across the garment. His silk shirt was white and sleeveless, the armband glinting in the sun.

His white-blond hair was braided out of his face, and he wore minimal makeup. Some kohl about his eyes, and a little silver over his eyelids. His trek to the front seemed to take forever. Olerra was almost ready to run to him, but she managed to stay in place.

When they finally arrived, Emorra and Ferida took their places beside Ydra, while Sanos stepped up to Olerra.

"Hi," she whispered.

"Hi," he said back.

The queen was speaking now, but Olerra didn't hear a word of it. She was too mesmerized by the man before her.

She was vaguely aware of the way the queen wound the silk about their clasped hands or the words Olerra had muttered to love and care for her beloved throughout all time. She watched Sanos's lips move as he promised to cherish her and support her in all things.

And then it was done.

She threw her arms around his neck and kissed him.

She knew the Brutes didn't show affection in public, typically, but Sanos was more than happy to participate in the last rite of the Amarran wedding.

He pulled her just as close. Met her lips just as enthusiastically.

And Olerra was thrilled to have her equal at her side, now bound to her forever.

— ACKNOWLEDGMENTS —

It's scary to try new things, but I'm lucky to have so many amazing people in my corner.

To the team at Feiwel, thank you! I appreciate you coming along with me on this new journey. Special thanks to Holly for championing this book, Jean for believing in this book, Meg for her design expertise, Starr for her copyedits, Gaby for marketing machinations, and Sam and Morgan for publicity power!

Thank you to BookEnds for representing me, especially my agent, Rachel Brooks, for your feedback and expertise. I rest easier knowing you're always on my side!

Martina Fačková has my thanks for creating the cover of my dreams. Though we weren't able to use the original, I thank you so much for bringing Olerra to life. It's always been my dream to have a plus-size woman on a fantasy cover, and you really nailed it!

Thank you to my family for your support, especially Alisa and Johnny, who watch Rosy while I travel.

Caitlyn, thanks so much for doing a quick read of this one for me. Sanos is so much stronger for your insights! Mikki, thank you for the write nights to help me stay on track!

Thank you to my UK team over at Pushkin, especially Sarah and Rima and India for bringing my books to life across the pond.

Thank you to all my other foreign publishers for your enthusiasm and support.

To my readers, thank you so, so much! I'm incredibly proud of this book, and it means the world to me that you've joined me on this journey, whether you're coming from my YA backlist or this is your first book from me.

– ABOUT THE AUTHOR –

Tricia Levenseller is the #1 *New York Times* and *USA Today* bestselling author of *The Darkness Within Us* and several other YA romantasy novels, including *Daughter of the Pirate King*. Tricia grew up in Oregon, where she spent her childhood climbing trees and playing make-believe. She now lives in Utah with her bossy dog, Rosy, where she writes full-time. When she's not writing or reading, Tricia enjoys putting together jigsaw puzzles, playing video games, and finding tasty restaurants to frequent. *What Fury Brings* is her debut novel for adults.

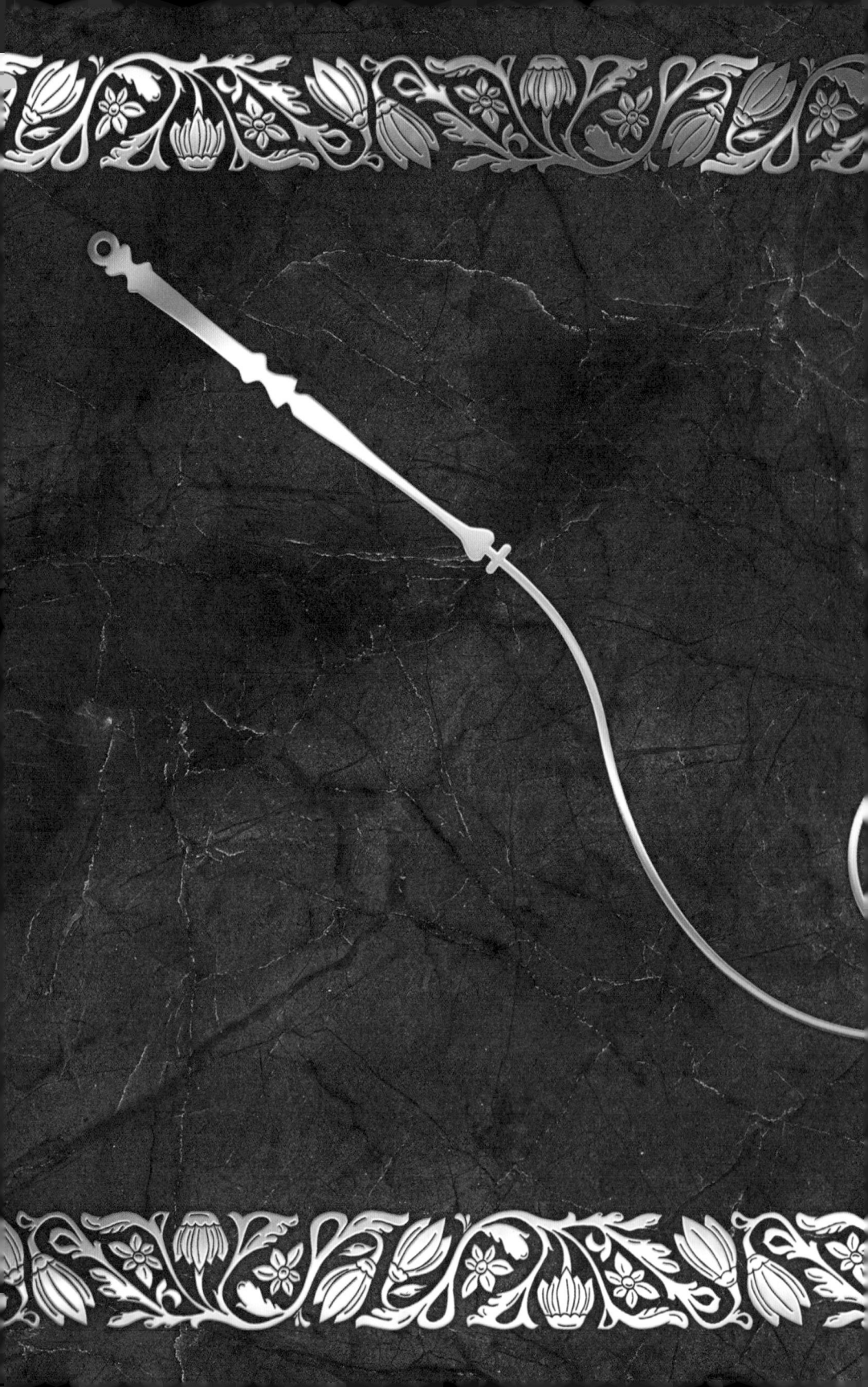